Olivia Ryan lives in Essex with her husband and three daughters. Before becoming a full-time mum, and now a novelist, she worked as a secretary, spending her lunch breaks writing stories and poetry.

Also by Olivia Ryan

Tales From a Hen Weekend

Tales From a Wedding Day

Olivia Ryan

PIATKUS

PIATKUS

First published in Great Britain as a paperback original in 2008
by Piatkus Books

A CIP catalogue record for this book
is available from the British Library.

ISBN 978-0-7499-3929-8

Typeset in Times by Action Publishing Technology Ltd
Printed and bound in Great Britain by
Clays Ltd, Bungay, Suffolk

Piatkus Books
An imprint of
Little, Brown Book Group
100 Victoria Embankment
London EC4Y 0DY

An Hachette Livre UK Company
www.hachettelivre.co.uk

www.littlebrown.co.uk

For Jenny and Pippa, this year's very special brides,
and Cheryl, their very special bridesmaid!

Four o'clock

Only four o'clock?

I think I've been awake all night. It's starting to get light now, and already there are some irritating birds awake at this ridiculous hour practising their trills and arpeggios ready for the full-blown chorus. My eyes are aching and stinging with tiredness. I can't believe it – tired already, with such an important, *stressful* day looming ahead of me! How unfair is this!

'Get off!' I mumble grumpily as Toffee gets up from his position on the end of the bed, stretches, turns round three times and tries to climb onto the mound of my legs. I shift my feet and the cat jumps, yowling in annoyance, onto the floor and trots over to the bedroom door. In the faint light from between the curtains, I can see his tail, upright and quivering with indignation, as he starts parading up and down at the door.

'Oh, I suppose you want to go out now!' Sighing, I roll out of bed and pad over to let the cat out of the room before he starts to really complain and wakes up the whole household. 'Didn't want you on my bed in the first place!'

The thing is, today is not about what I want. None

1

of this is about *me* at all – it's about Sam – Sam the bride, the queen for the day. Nobody else matters today – and especially not Toffee, who always wants to sleep on Sam's bed when she's staying here at her parents' house. We weren't going to let him do that last night, in case he kept her awake, so I got lumbered. Fair enough – all part of the bridesmaid's role, I suppose. Was I shown the job description for this post at any time?

I shoo Toffee out and pause for a minute in the open doorway. There's a light showing beneath the door of Sam's room. Is she awake too? We're both awake at four o'clock on the morning of her wedding? If neither of us can sleep, wouldn't it be nice to sit curled up together under her duvet and talk? We could have our very last, final, last ever, ever, ever, chat together as two single girls.

Holding my breath, I tiptoe across the landing, watching out for the squeaky floorboard I've known about since I was eleven years old and first came home from school to play with my new best friend.

'Sam?' I whisper outside the door.

I don't want to wake her up if she's just fallen asleep with the light on. Maybe I should just go downstairs and make myself a cup of hot chocolate instead? Turn on the bedside light and read a book? Count sheep? Count wedding guests?

No – Sam won't mind. She'll be glad. Aren't all brides supposed to be anxious and nervous on the morning of their wedding? She's probably lying there worrying about everything, and I'll be able to make her laugh and calm her down and get her back to sleep. That probably *is* part of the job description.

I turn the door handle quietly and peer into the

room. Sam's awake all right – she's sitting on the side of the bed, with her back to the door, facing the window. I'm just about to rush into the room and jump on the bed when I realise she's talking. To herself? Or saying a prayer for the wedding day? No – look, of course – she's got her phone in her hand. Probably an early morning call to Phil. Blimey – at four o'clock? One night apart and she misses him so much she has to call him at the crack of dawn? All right – to be honest, it feels strange to me, too, to be sleeping back here at Sam's parents' house – in her brother's old room instead of sharing with Sam like I used to when we had late nights out together when we were teenagers. But of course, I've got no boyfriend to miss. I'm used to sleeping alone.

I open the door and start to squeeze myself carefully through the doorway. What I'll do is I'll creep up behind her, make her jump and take the piss out of her about the phone call. She'll probably drop the phone and swear at me and we'll fall about laughing, and then she'll have to call Phil back and apologise for her crazy friend. But just as I'm about to make my move, I overhear a snatch of Sam's conversation, and the whole moment suddenly changes.

'*I know,*' she's saying softly, urgently, into the phone. '*But I had to say something. He needs to talk to her about it, Phil! Do you think I should have kept my mouth shut? Do you think she's going to hate me? Oh, God. I hope I haven't done the wrong thing. I couldn't bear it if anyone's upset. Not on our wedding day!*'

I step back and let the door close silently behind me, make my way back to my own room, climb under the duvet and turn to face the wall. What now? What upset, what incident, what terrible row's brewing *now* in this bloody family? I wish I'd never got up; I wish I'd never heard!

It was all very well Sam asking me to be her chief bridesmaid. That's what you do, isn't it, when you're best friends? You look after the bride on her special day. You're there to help and support her, straighten her dress, check her hair, calm her nerves. You're there to make sure everything goes smoothly, that there are no hitches, no disasters, nothing forgotten, no sour memories to spoil the sweet ones.

But how can I do all that when any disasters are likely to be caused by her own family? I've got no chance. It's all going to go horribly wrong – I just know it. And I won't be able to do a thing about it. What else could I expect from the Pattersons?

Half past six

Morning at last. I shrug off the duvet and lie on my back, watching the pattern of sunlight on the wall opposite the window. I think I've slept for an hour or so; I feel a bit better, anyway. It's a lovely day. Sam's wedding day! I can't believe it's finally arrived. All the time we've been busy with the preparations – the plans, the bookings, the endless, endless lists – I somehow never imagined that when it came to the crunch – when it came to the morning of the Actual Day – I was going to feel like this.

Like what?

Scared? Anxious? Worried that I'm not going to be able to make it perfect?

'It's not your responsibility,' said Sam when we were talking about this yesterday. 'Don't be ridiculous! I never asked you to take all this on your shoulders. You've done so much to help me, Abbie. Now just relax and let's enjoy the day.'

I'd like to. I really would like to be able to relax and enjoy it all. But how can I, when the bride comes from a family of total nutcases, any one of whom is likely to ruin her day with just a look, a frown in the wrong direction or a couple of ill-chosen words? And then she'll be upset and I'll feel like I've failed her. It's no good telling me it's not my responsibility! It is. She's my best friend.

The first time Sam brought me home to meet her family, I think I went into shock, and I haven't really recovered since. The thing is, you see, basically, we're so, so different. It's weird how we became friends, but we did: we liked each other straight away, from that very first day at James Radford High School. The teachers were cruel to their new intake of eleven-year-olds: they mixed up the year-group so that we weren't in the same classes as our friends from the various feeder primary schools. I remember sitting down in a free seat in our appointed homeroom and feeling so totally lost and alone without Carol, my only real friend from my junior school, that I wanted to cry. Or go home. The misery must have been clear on my face because I'd hardly sat down when the girl next to me nudged me, so hard that I flinched, and whispered: 'What's up?'

'Nothing.'

I wasn't going to admit to being scared and lonely. I'd been a target for teasing all my life, and I'd learned how best to avoid it. Keep quiet, don't show any weakness.

'Have you got any friends in here?' persisted my neighbour.

I shrugged.

'*I* haven't,' she went on. 'The bastards put my mates Jackie and Tina in 1G.'

I sniffed. I was *not* going to cry. And I was secretly shocked at her saying 'bastards' about the teachers. But she had a point.

6

'My friend Carol's in that class too,' I admitted.

'I'm Sam,' she said, giving me a grin that seemed to fill her whole face. 'Want to be my new friend?'

Even at that age, I think we knew that we complemented each other. Being with Sam gave me a new confidence; in her company life was brighter, more colourful, more fun. I forgot to worry about myself. I never quite understood what I gave her in return but it must have been enough, because we quickly became inseparable.

I never stopped being surprised by her house. It's a big old four-bedroomed semi with an extra room added on over the garage for Sam's granddad. My own dad was the vicar of a run-down, under-funded, unpopular church on the edge of our estate. The house that went with the job was a basic two-up, two-down, with a 'kitchenette', an unheated bathroom and tiny garden. There were only three of us in the family and I spent most of my time in my bedroom, reading – or sitting on the wooden bench in the garden, reading. My parents were getting on a bit when I was born and when I look back now, I realise they didn't have much idea about the demands and expectations of modern-day children. Luckily I wasn't normally any trouble – and they were far too busy with parish commitments to worry about entertaining me.

The first thing that hit me when I went to Sam's house for tea – after the fact that it was twice as big as my own house – was the noise. It seemed to me – coming from my quiet little family where the most noise ever generated was when the ladies from Mum's Bible group brought their tambourines with them to a meeting – that the Pattersons' house was actually alive, vibrating, *pulsating* with sound. There were three different types of music being played – one downstairs, two upstairs – and a cartoon blaring forth from the TV, which nobody was watching. Mr Patterson was shouting up the stairs at Sam's twin brother David, who was shouting at Sam. Sam's little sister was crying in the kitchen and her mum was telling her to shut up, whilst trying to have a conversation on the phone. The kettle was boiling. The washing machine was rattling and shaking. I rang the doorbell four times before anybody heard me, apart from the cat, a predecessor of Toffee called Blackie, who meowed and squealed until I was finally let in; and then shot around the house like a mad thing, knocking over cups and lamps as he went, and being hollered at by everyone. I stood in the hallway and stared. It was bedlam, but I seemed to be the only one who was aware of it.

Even now I sometimes feel like I'm watching the Pattersons acting out their lives like it's some kind of bizarre TV reality show. I imagine myself touching the screen and finding they're not real. Not any of them, not even Sam, with her shock of auburn hair and her laughing and her singing and her dancing. Least of all Sam, really. She's so vibrant, so *much* somehow, I often wonder how life can even hold her. One day she'll break right out of it. Right through the screen! But of course, I'll be there to catch her.

I wait till after seven o'clock. I can hear someone up and about already – probably Christine, Sam's mum, down in the kitchen. She never has a lie-in – she says it gives her a headache. I think to be honest if I woke up next to Brian every morning I'd have a permanent headache. That man starts moaning the minute he opens his eyes, and carries on till he either goes back to bed or passes out drunk.

I need to go to the loo, anyway. I open my door and creep across the landing. When I come back out of the bathroom, something brushes against my legs and makes me almost shout out loud with fright.

'Bloody cat!' I scoop Toffee up in my arms and carry him back to bed. 'There you go, you big fat furry lump,' I tell him affectionately, dumping him on the bed and then pulling on my dressing gown. 'You can sleep there while I go and make a cup of tea.'

'He had a mouse,' Christine tells me nonchalantly in the kitchen. 'Bloody big'un, it was. Brought it in through the catflap, all its legs still wriggling.'

'What did you do?' I'm trying not to shudder. It's the only reason I can't have a cat myself. I'd die at the first sign of wriggling mouse legs.

'Do?' Christine laughs – a throaty, smoker's laugh that ends in a coughing fit. 'Chased the bloody cat round the house with the broom till he dropped the bugger, picked it up and ...'

'Was it dead?' I can't hide my disgust now. I'm getting mugs and tea bags out of the cupboards, waiting for the kettle to boil.

'Didn't look too healthy!' She laughs again. 'Had to finish it off though, poor little sod. Would've died of shock. Or died of a mangled head. Whichever got him first!'

I can't ask. I just can't ask how she *finished it off*. I don't want to know, but my mind's making ghastly, horrific, pictures.

'Never mind, love,' she says as if I've spoken. She

9

shrugs. 'It's only nature, isn't it, at the end of the day? You can't help nature, love.'

Nature explains, and excuses, everything for Christine. It's *only nature* when men get drunk and shout at their wives and kids. It's only nature when Troy, her five-year-old grandson, throws his toys across the room and stamps his feet and screams if he doesn't get his own way. It was only nature, come to that, when David got his girlfriend pregnant five years ago and they ended up with Troy despite the fact that they had nowhere to live and all three of them moved in with Christine and Brian for two terrible, traumatic years, which nearly brought the whole family to the point of collapse and disintegration.

Nature, from the point of view of the Patterson women, can be a bit of a bastard if you ask me.

'Want a cup of tea?' I ask Christine to change the subject.

'Lovely, dear. Been up since five o'clock, I have. Couldn't get a wink of sleep. Too excited, love. Big day, isn't it?'

'It is.' I smile at her. 'And it's beautiful, too – look at the sunshine.'

'Rain forecast later,' she says without an ounce of regret as she bustles off to put the rubbish out.

Well, I suppose it's only nature.

I carry a tray up to Sam's room with two mugs of tea.

'Did I wake you up?' I ask her anxiously.

'No. I've been awake ages. Reading. Trying to stop myself panicking!'

I plonk myself down on the bed and she sits up and takes a mug of tea. Her mobile phone's lying next to her book on the bedside table. I remember the conversation I overheard, and a shiver of anxiety runs through me as the thought flashes briefly – What now? Which member of this bloody family is causing trouble? Why today? What's *wrong* with them?

'What's there to panic about?' I ask her brightly. 'Everything's going to be absolutely fine ...'

'You are *such* a bad actress, Abbie!' she says with a toss of her hair and a peal of laughter. 'You always were! You know as well as I do that there's never any guarantee of everything being "absolutely fine" with this crowd!'

'There isn't anything worrying you, is there, Sammy? Anything ... in particular?'

Anything that makes you call your husband-to-be at four in the morning and talk about the possibility of a family upset? Just for instance?

'Don't be silly. Of course not. I'm just being realistic.' She sips her tea, watching me over the rim of the mug. 'I know what they're like, Abbie. Dad'll get drunk. Mum'll be loud and embarrassing and probably cry. Granddad will talk nonsense, fall asleep in church and probably ask Phil who the hell he is – again. Troy will have a tantrum and kick the other children. What's new? They're all unbearable. They drive me mad.' She puts the mug down and gives me a funny, lopsided smile that makes me think she might actually cry. 'They're my family, though,' she adds in a whisper. 'And I love them all!'

Ah, well. I suppose someone has to!

11

Eight o'clock

The whole family has gathered in the kitchen for breakfast. This is unusual, and pretty ridiculous in itself, as there isn't room for us all.

'Why don't I get breakfast for me and Sam, and take it into the living room so we're out of the way?' I suggest brightly, trying to be helpful.

Good bridesmaid, thoughtful bridesmaid.

'Absolutely not!' retorts Christine, sounding shocked and almost offended. 'That wouldn't be right at all, Abbie!'

'For God's sake, woman,' says Sam's dad, Brian, irritably. 'Let them go and eat their breakfast wherever the hell they like. What's the problem?'

'Brian!' Christine sounds even more shocked. 'What are you like? Did you not see that booklet I brought home about wedding etiquette? It said it doesn't matter what form the wedding breakfast takes, as long as it's a special social occasion for everyone. It's not a *special social occasion* if Sam and Abbie take their plates through to the other room and sit on their own watching TV, now is it?'

Sam's sister Chloe is doubled up with laughter.

'Mum!' she snorts. 'The "wedding breakfast" is the

meal after the wedding! Not your toast and cereal in the morning! Didn't you know that?'

Christine drops her spatula into the pan of eggs and bacon she's frying and stares back at her. 'That's daft, that is! We're not having breakfast after the wedding, are we! We're having dinner! Soup, and chicken, and . . .'

'Yes, Mum,' says Sam, calmly, putting an arm round her mum's shoulders and rescuing the spatula with the other hand. 'Don't worry. The meal's all booked. They won't be fobbing us off with cornflakes. They just *call* it the wedding breakfast. It's just a name.'

'Daft!' repeats Christine unhappily, turning bacon so that it spits fat over the hob.

Chloe's still laughing.

'Grow up,' Sam tells her sharply. 'It's not that funny.'

Actually, I thought it was. But I love Sam for not laughing at her mum.

In the event, we all take our breakfasts into the living room and sit at the table.

'Let Mum have her social occasion,' Sam whispers to me as we're putting out knives and forks. 'Keeps her happy.'

'You shouldn't be worrying about keeping everyone happy,' I remind her gently. 'It should be the other way around today.'

'Can't change the habits of a lifetime,' she says cheerfully.

Brian sits at the far end of the table, his usual place, with the morning paper spread out, waiting for his eggs and bacon to be put down in front of him. I stifle an urge to tell him to put the paper away, take

13

his elbows off the table, make an effort, make conversation – it's his daughter's wedding day! I stifle the urge because he's actually less trouble while he's reading the paper. Maybe once he's had his breakfast he'll cheer up and be pleasant company for the rest of the day. Hmm. Pigs might fly.

'Thanks, Mum,' says Chloe chirpily as Christine brings in her eggs on toast – no bacon as she's vegetarian this week – and passes her a cup of tea. 'Cheers, everyone! Happy *Wedding Breakfast*!'

She goes into another fit of giggles at this, and Christine looks away, biting her lip anxiously.

'All right, Chloe! Enough!' snaps Brian, coming to life and throwing the paper on the floor. 'Don't try to be clever with us, miss. Not everyone's had the benefit of your education, remember.'

This is a well-worn theme in the Patterson household. To be honest – I kind of sympathise with it, too.

Chloe, you see, is the Brains of the Family. Not only that, she's also the spoilt baby of the family. She's only eighteen – ten years younger than Sam and David. Christine and Brian must have taken a long time to recover from having the twins before daring to try for another baby – and I reckon that by the time Chloe was born, they'd forgotten how to be the proper strict parents they were before, and just let her do what she wanted. And it certainly shows – she's a right little madam. Fortunately for everyone else, she's only at home now in the holidays – she's in her first year at Durham University, where she's doing a degree in something very intellectual that I can never remember the name of. It begins with a 'P' – it's psychology, physiology or philosophy, I'm not sure which and I refuse to ask her yet again and give her

14

the satisfaction of raising her eyes at my ignorance.

As you can probably tell, I am *not* a graduate – not of anything beginning with a P, not of anything at all. I'm not stupid either – definitely not stupid enough to be talked down to by that precocious minx – but I left school after my GCSEs because a fantastic opportunity had come up for me to do what I'd always wanted to do – work in the local library. One of Dad's parishioners was a library assistant there and she was retiring. I spent half my spare time in the library anyway and it was as if my dream job was just sitting there waiting for me to take it.

Mum wasn't happy.

'If you must *insist* on working in a library,' she said in pained tones, 'please, Abigail, at least go to university first. Get a degree. Go to library school and become a proper, qualified librarian.'

'I don't want to.' I shrugged. 'I don't want to be in charge. I just want to work there. I love it there. It's what I want to do.'

'But there are so many opportunities open to girls these days,' sighed Mum. 'Don't you have *any* ambition, Abigail?'

'Yes! My ambition is to work in the library!'

'To be honest, Susan,' said my dad quietly, 'I think it's quite admirable that Abbie knows what she wants to do. I see too many young people drifting, wasting their lives. Let her go out into the world and be useful! *You* never needed to have a career, my dear.'

'No,' agreed Mum, managing to convey a whole world of regret with that single syllable.

'You married me,' he reminded her, as if she might have forgotten.

'Yes,' she said.

For some reason they didn't discuss it any further. But I got the job.

We're halfway through breakfast when Sam's granddad wanders into the room, looking puzzled. Christine's been calling him.

'Where have you been, Dad? Your egg and bacon's getting cold.'

'Where have I been?' he repeats, looking at her with annoyance. 'I've been at work. Where do you think I've been?'

He retired from the docks fifteen years ago.

'All right, Dad. You're home now,' says Christine calmly. 'Sit down and eat. I'll make you a nice cup of tea.'

'Tea? Bloody tea? I'm going out for a pint. A man doesn't want a cup of bloody tea after he's been at work all day.'

'Sit down, Frank. It's half past eight in the morning,' says Brian without looking up from his plate. 'Pubs aren't open.'

'Bloody pubs,' says Granddad, sitting down nevertheless. 'Never open. What's the matter with them? War's finished, hasn't it?'

Chloe raises her eyebrows and starts to get up from the table.

'Sit and talk to your granddad,' growls Brian, pushing away his plate and picking up his paper again.

'*You* talk to him,' she retorts evenly. 'I can't talk about the war, can I? I wasn't born.'

'Think yourself lucky,' says Christine. She looks thoughtful for a minute and then adds, 'Neither was I,' as if it's only just occurred to her.

'You've heard enough about it, though, haven't

you, Mum?' says Sam with a smile and a nod at Granddad. 'I bet you feel as though you've lived through it!'

'I do,' she agrees with a heavy sigh. 'But never mind, Sammy. He can't help it, love. He's a bit vague nowadays.'

'Vague?' says Chloe, half under her breath as she leaves the room. 'He's totally lost it, if you ask me.'

'Nobody did,' Sam hisses at her departing back.

'Piss off,' Chloe whispers back, without turning round. Just loud enough for Sam and me to hear.

I feel my jaw tighten and the muscles in my fingers clench into fists. If Chloe was my sister, I think I'd have to kill her. A nice thought for the wedding morning.

Christine tries again with Granddad when he's finished his cooked breakfast.

'Do you remember what's happening today, Dad?'

He stares at her for a minute.

'Today? What day is it? Monday?'

'It's Saturday. It's the wedding today, Dad. Our Sammy's getting married.'

'Sammy.'

He's quiet now; you can see him concentrating. He looks around the table, his eyes resting on me and suddenly lighting up.

'Sammy? Little Samantha?'

I push Sam towards him, in front of me. He always does this; it must be so hurtful for her.

'Here's Sammy, Frank. I'm Abbie – remember? Abigail – Sam's friend.'

'Little Abbie,' he repeats, looking unsure. 'You were always such a good girl, weren't you? Always did your homework. Always looked after your mum.

17

Shame you had to marry that miserable bastard.'

'No, Dad,' says Christine, closing her eyes for a minute and sighing – a pale, tired wisp of a sigh, hardly even a breath's worth of energy. She picks up a stack of plates and starts towards the kitchen door with them. 'No, that wasn't Abbie, bless your heart, you're getting muddled again. That was me.'

Nine o'clock

Sam and I are alone in her room again. Thank God.

She's got the wedding dress out of the wardrobe and we're sitting on her bed, staring at it, hanging on its hanger under its polythene cover. We spent several hours of several days together in bridal shops, choosing this dress, with Christine crying fresh torrents of tears with every one Sam tried on.

'Oh, yes, this is it! This is the one! Oh, oh – you look so beautiful!' she'd cry, every time Sam emerged from the changing room in a different style, a different colour or a different fabric. Strangely enough, by the time we got to the one that Sam and I actually agreed was *The One*, which was (scarily) the third dress she tried, on our third visit to our third shop, Christine was totally speechless and couldn't even manage a tear. It's a strapless fitted gown in pale-ivory satin with embroidered detail on the bodice and a short billowing train, and Sam looked *so* beautiful in it, we were all stunned to silence.

'Can you believe it?' she says now. 'Can you really believe this is actually *it*? The day I get to wear this dress *for real*?'

'Yes!' I laugh. 'Yes, unless this is all a dream and

we're going to wake up in a minute, fourteen years old and still at James Radford, doing our biology homework together and giggling about Noel Cartwright!'

'*Noel Cartwright!*' she screams, looking at me in amazement. 'Oh my God! How the *fucking* hell did you remember *him*?'

'How could you possibly *forget* him? He was absolutely drop-dead gorgeous! The best-looking boy in the class!'

'You're right! He was! Oh my *God*, Abbie, I haven't thought about him for a million years! I wonder whatever happened to him?' She screws up her face. 'I bet he's gay. He was much too good-looking and gorgeous to be straight.'

'That's crap. He's probably not gorgeous any more, anyway. I bet he's gone fat and bald and boring. That would be only fair.'

She's frowning into the distance, trying to remember. Shit. Why did I start this conversation? Because it's only now, now it's too late and we've begun down Memory Fucking Lane, that I remember . . .

'Didn't he go out with Julia?' says Sam, suddenly remembering too.

I knew she would.

'Did he?' I ask, innocently. 'Can't remember. Anyway, what about Stephen Large? Remember him? How we used to joke about whether he was or not? Large?'

'He did, Noel Cartwright. I know I'm right – he went out with Julia – you must remember. In year eleven, I suppose – or maybe in the Sixth Form.'

'Yeah, well. I wasn't there for the Sixth Form.'

She ignores this. Always does.

'They did! They went out together – they were

together at the Leavers' Ball! I can remember it clearly now – Jesus, how could I have forgotten that?'

How could I have reminded you?

'Typical!' she says, laughing. 'Best-looking boy in the school, she went out with him. Julia always did have her pick of the boys. She was so popular, so pretty too.'

'But let's not talk about that now,' I tell her. Desperate. I'm desperate to get her off the subject of Julia. Today of all days! How could I be so stupid? 'It's your *wedding day*, Sammy – it's going to be a fantastic day, isn't it?'

'Yes,' she agrees smiling at me happily.

Is she faking, or what? I remind her of *Julia*, on her wedding day, and she laughs about it? I just wonder how much she's hurting inside. As if she can read my thoughts, she gives me a little shake and tells me quietly: 'It's all in the past, Abbs. It doesn't matter any more. Today's about the future – mine and Phil's. Come on: get your arse in gear. We've only got five hours to make ourselves totally, unforgettably beautiful!'

'Shit! We'll never make it!'

'Sod it, then – let's just go as we are!'

We're laughing now, rolling on the bed, high on hilarity and excitement. But the spectre of Julia Johnson has been raised, and I've got a horrible feeling it's not going to go away. And that's my own stupid fault. Some bridesmaid.

We're just getting out all the make-up, the brushes, sponges, tissues, nail varnish, sprays, pots and potions we're going to need for the Big Beautification, when the doorbell rings with a jolly triple ding-dong and, as if we didn't have enough to worry about, up the stairs two at a time bounds Heather the Hair.

Heather is David's girlfriend – mother of the terrible Troy – and she's actually a really talented hairdresser, which comes as something of a surprise when you don't know her very well, because her own hair is absolutely outrageous. It looks permanently like she's had a dreadful shock, or like she's plugged into an electric socket with about a thousand volts coursing through her body and sending her hair mad. I think, to be honest, she's given up with it. Maybe spending so much time making everyone else's hair look lovely, she can't be arsed with her own at all – a bit like interior decorators who don't ever lift a paintbrush in their own house, or chefs who go home and live off takeaways and microwave dinners. What she *does* do, though, is colour it. Currently, Heather's hair is a kind of chestnut with copper highlights, which at least suits her complexion. Over the years I've seen it black, bright red, platinum blonde with pink streaks and, on one unforgettable occasion, mauve. I've sometimes wondered whether she uses up the odds and ends of colour left in the tubes at the end of the week in the salon, in much the same way that I use up what's left in the fridge for Friday night dinner before I go shopping.

'Hello, *BRIDE*!' she squeals as she charges into the bedroom, flinging herself at Sam and almost knocking her over. 'How are you, darling? Nervous? Yeah?'

Sam hugs her and grins.

'Not too bad.'

Heather steps back again and looks her up and down, her head on one side, an artist contemplating the blank canvas.

22

'Get enough sleep, did you?'

Sam hesitates for a fraction of a second, and I feel my chest tightening with apprehension, remembering again the four o'clock phone conversation – the anxiety I'd heard in Sam's voice – the worry about what she's not telling me.

'Oh, you know,' she says lightly. 'Once I got off to sleep, I wasn't too bad. Bit of a heavy night last night, wasn't it!'

This isn't actually true at all. We went out for a quiet meal and a few drinks – just Sam and I, and her family. Phil was spending the evening with his own family – some of them have come over from Surrey for the wedding – so he was having a meal with them at the hotel where they're all staying. Nobody had more than two or three glasses of wine and we were all in bed by eleven o'clock.

'Nice night, I thought,' says Heather evenly, putting her bag of tools down on the bed and kicking off her shoes. 'Nice restaurant, Abbie – good choice. I always say Italian food is good for lovers.'

Heather talks a lot of crap, in my opinion. It flows out of her mouth like a babbling brook, with no obvious pretence at sense or logic. I've given up arguing the toss with her – it's a waste of time, it just stops her in her tracks and leaves her blinking in confusion, and somehow it doesn't seem fair. So I just smile and nod and let her get on with it. She's only twenty-four; she'd had a child by the age of nineteen and she already seems to have more common ground, conversationally, with Christine than she does with Sam or me. It's the big divide, bigger than a bloody mountain range – mothers on one side, childless women on the other. If you've never had a conversation lasting more than ten minutes about different types of nappy, you don't really qualify as a grown-up.

Sam doesn't want children.

She didn't tell me this until about six months ago. I suppose, because I harbour my own sweet little unlikely dream, tucked away somewhere discreet where it won't be ridiculed, that one day I'll get married and have lovely babies and live happily ever after, and because I automatically think that's what other people want too, and that the only difference is that they're more likely to achieve it, I was somewhat taken aback.

'What – not ever?'

'No.'

'Not even after you've done everything else – got the house, got the mortgage, got the wedding ring . . .'

'No.'

I paused for a minute, wondering. But we're best friends, after all – so it's no good wondering, you have to ask.

'Why not?'

She sighed. 'I just don't want them. I don't understand the attraction.'

'But you're *good* with kids!'

'That doesn't mean I have to have one myself. They just seem to cause problems, if you ask me.'

'Of course they can cause problems, but they make people happy too, don't they?'

'Do you think so? All I see is that having kids complicates things.' She paused, sighed, and then looked up at me. 'Troy . . .'

'Oh, come on!' I laughed. 'He's a particularly bad

example! I know he's a handful, but you still love him.'

'That's not what I meant.'

'Then what . . . ?'

'Oh, I don't know, Abbie!' She shrugged and laughed. 'Forget it. Let's just say I'd be useless with one of my own. I'd murder it. I'd stuff it in the dustbin.'

'You wouldn't!' I laughed out loud. 'It'd be *yours*, and you'd love it, because . . . well, that just happens automatically, doesn't it?'

'Not to me, it won't,' she said, closing her lips around the subject.

'OK,' I said lightly.

Privately, I thought she'd change her mind in time. Privately, I still think she probably will. But I try to keep off the subject.

'Right!' says Heather, rubbing her hands together and contemplating the brushes and spray bottles and scissors she's unpacked onto Sam's dressing table. 'Right: Sam – bathroom – now! Better do you first, in case we run late. Don't want the bride walking down the aisle with her hair in a wet towel, do we?'

'Don't even joke about it!' I say, laughing but shivering with sudden nerves.

'No worries, Abbie,' she says, turning to me. 'You can have *your* hair in a towel if we're not finished! No one will mind too much about the bridesmaid!'

Well, thanks a million. Seems like there's nothing like a wedding for making everyone except the bride feel totally insignificant. But to be honest, that's how I've always felt beside Sam. And I've never really minded before, so I'm not going to start minding today, am I?

25

Half past ten

Christine keeps making everyone cups of tea. I don't think she knows what else to do.

'Mum, stop! Enough tea!' groans Sam when yet another tray appears through the bedroom doorway. 'I'll be weeing all day long!'

'And you know what it's like,' says Heather, waving her hair straighteners at me in the mirror. 'When you know you *can't*, you suddenly need to, like desperately. You don't want to be standing up there in front of the vicar, just as he's waiting for you to say "I do", and all you can think about is how soon you can get to the loo. Especially not when you're wearing that long dress and everything. Could take a while to get your knickers down ...'

'Heather!' screeches Sam. 'For God's sake! Do you realise, that's what I'm going to be thinking about now while I'm walking down the bloody aisle?'

'No you won't.' I try to soothe her. 'Of course you won't. You'll be looking at Phil, and he'll be looking at you, and you'll be thinking: Soon you'll be husband and wife, and ...'

'Ah, listen to her!' says Heather, smiling at me. 'Love's young dream!'

'Leave her alone.' Sam smiles at me too. 'Abbie likes to be romantic, don't you, Abbie?'

'Well, that's what a wedding is supposed to be about, isn't it?'

'Glad someone realises that, Abbie,' says Christine, who's still standing in the doorway with the unwanted tray of tea, watching Heather working on my hair. 'All this talk of weeing and getting knickers down – not nice for a wedding day, is it, love?'

'No, Christine,' I reply obediently, ignoring Heather's sniggers. 'Good job you weren't on the hen weekend, though!'

'I can just imagine.' She smiles indulgently.

I bet she can't.

Sam's hair is finished. It looks lovely. I have to say, it isn't difficult to make Sam look lovely. She's tall and slim, with this main of thick, lustrous auburn hair that can be put up, down or back, waved, woven, twisted or twirled, seemingly without any effort or the use of more than a handful of pins, and always ends up looking superb. Today it's up on top of her head with a few wavy tendrils hanging, just perfectly, as if she's stuck it up herself without even looking in the mirror, and it just happened to look wonderful. Of course, I realise Heather's skill has a lot to do with it. I suppose like a good chef, half the art of good hairdressing is probably in making something very difficult and complicated look like you've just slung it together in a careless moment. Whereas my cooking tends to look like it's been slung together, as does my hair, because they both actually have been.

But not today. All right, it's not going to be so easy

for Heather to make me look lovely; trust me, I tried to do it myself for years but the combination of thin, mousy blonde hair – that just hangs there staring back at you no matter how much you try to persuade it into some sort of a style – pale skin, freckles and such small features that people call me 'baby-faced' has driven me to the conclusion that I'm better off with what I like to think of as my Natural Look. The Natural Look lets me off the hook. I use it as my excuse for not trying too hard. *I prefer the natural look*. It means just getting up in the morning, showering and dressing and *that's it*. But not today.

'Keep your head still, Abbie,' says Heather, only slightly crossly. 'I need to get this *just right*.'

And she doesn't need to say how difficult that is. I'm watching her as she takes a few strands of my hair and twists them, sprays them and tries to poke them into position. Tufts drift obstinately out of place and she tuts and sighs. I'm *so sorry* to be such a problem to her. I'm tempted to suggest she leaves it as it is, but I can't spoil things for Sam. For the photographs. It wouldn't do for the chief bridesmaid to be pictured standing next to the bride, all neat and demure in her aquamarine dress, posy in her hands, smiling nicely for the camera, with her straggly hair hanging round her face in nasty rats' tails, now would it? And as for the other bridesmaid . . .

'Isn't Chloe supposed to be coming in now?' I remind Heather.

'Yes – give her a shout, can you, Sam? If she hasn't washed her hair yet, she needs to do it right *now*. We haven't got all day.'

'Or she'll be the one walking down the aisle with her hair in a towel,' I suggest, privately thinking that no, she

28

wouldn't, because she'd just whip it off her head, stamp on it, kick it out of the way and go into the church with her hair all wet and mussed up, or else (God help us) throw a fit and refuse to go into the church at all.

'Chloe!' bellows the bride, opening the bedroom door and leaning out of it across the landing. 'Chloe, get your arse out of that bed and wash your hair! Heather's waiting.'

The door at the end of the landing opens and Chloe bellows back: 'Shut up, shit-face.' It's probably just an affectionate sisterly term. 'I'm not in fucking bed. I'm fucking studying.'

'Well, you can *stop* fucking studying, just for one day in your life. You're a bridesmaid today, right?'

'Yeah, yeah. OK, keep your hair on; it's not even eleven o'clock yet for God's sake. What time's this shindig kicking off?'

I clench my teeth. This is her sister's wedding she's talking about. That girl so needs a good slap!

'Keep your *head* still!' says Heather again, beginning to sound shrill.

'I can't help it. She's annoying me!' I hiss back at her.

Sam has gone out to the landing. 'Two-thirty! Two-thirty at the church, as you know damn well!' she's telling Chloe. 'But we have to be ready . . .'

'Chill out, sister! OK, OK, I'm washing my hair. I'm in the shower. I'm out of it. I'm ready. I'm beautiful.' Chloe pushes past Sam and appears in the doorway of our room. 'Bloody hell, Heather. What are you doing to Abbie?'

'What do you think I'm doing?' replies Heather calmly. 'I'm doing her hair. Obviously.'

'She looks like a hedgehog.'

'No she doesn't!' retorts Sam quickly – but not before

29

I catch the wobble of hidden laughter in her voice.

'Don't worry,' I say lightly, pretending not to care that even Heather is stifling a grin, and if *she* thinks it's funny that all her stylist's art can produce out of my mop is a hedgehog, what chance have I got? 'Don't worry about it. I'm having flowers in my hair. That'll hide the mess.'

'Mess?' retorts Heather, finally taking offence. 'Your hair is *not* going to be a mess, Abbie. You and Chloe are going to be beautiful bridesmaids. I'm making you identical.'

Ha! That certainly wipes the smirk off Chloe's face! Pretty little younger sister and wispy-haired baby-faced friend – identical? I don't think so! Not without using trick photography!

It's surprising, though, what modern technology can achieve. Somehow, with the use of things that mois- turise, thicken and repair, things that enliven, protect and nourish, and devices which blow, curl, crimp and seal, Heather produces a style for me eventually that neither looks a mess nor resembles any form of small rodent, prickly or otherwise.

'Thanks. How do you do it?' I finger my fringe gently, surprised that it's not stiff as a board.

'Don't touch it!' she screeches. 'How? With great difficulty. It'll probably all fall apart halfway through the reception. Chloe! Your turn.'

'I don't want my hair like that,' says Chloe sulkily, looking askance at mine. 'I don't want to look like Abbie.'

'You won't,' I assure her cheerfully. 'Trust me. You'd need ten more years and a lot of practice.'

And less of a scowl might help.

Half past eleven

Heather's doing Christine's hair now, in her own room, and Chloe's sloped back off to her den to sulk about her hairstyle making her look like a fucking prat. Sam and I are sitting at her dressing table, doing our make-up. She's put on some music and we're singing along, getting all bubbly and excited.

'In a few hours' time,' I say, looking at her in amazement as if this wasn't the whole point of everything – all the planning, all the waiting, all the worry and anticipation, 'you're going to be Mrs Reynolds!'

'Mrs Reynolds,' she repeats softly, staring at herself in the mirror. 'Samantha Louise Reynolds. God, it does sound strange.'

'Get away with you. You've been practising that name for the past three and a half years! Ever since you met Phil. Don't look all wide-eyed innocence at me, girl – *I'm* the one who had to sit through all the sighs and dreamy looks and listen to all the "*Oh, I love him so much! I've never loved anyone like I love him.*"'

She throws her mascara at me and we both fall around laughing for a few minutes.

'OK,' she admits. 'I know. I always wanted to

marry him. But it's still a funny feeling, actually becoming a *married woman*.'

'Why? What did you think you were going to become? A married man? A married fish?'

'Stop it! Listen, I'm trying to explain. Getting married, the wedding, being together forever – lovely, lovely, lovely. But being a *Mrs!* It sounds so ... scary!'

'So grown-up?' I suggest with a smile.

'Yes! I'm not sure I'm ready, Abbie! How can I change overnight from being a *girl* – going shopping for outrageous clothes and clubbing with my friends, sitting up till three in the morning watching DVDs, drinking too much and eating silly things – to being a *married woman*?' She shudders. 'I don't even like the sound of it. *Married women* have conversations about interest rates and prices of vegetables, and wallpaper. They wear slippers and aprons.'

'They don't! Don't be ridiculous! Look at Kirsty. Do you think *she* wears slippers and aprons since she married Andrew? Or Ruth? I can't quite see *her* talking about vegetable prices and ...'

'OK, OK. So some people don't seem to change.' She stares at herself in the mirror again. 'I know it sounds silly.'

'You're scared you're going to change?' I ask her softly.

'I suppose so. I don't want to become ... settled, and ... and boring, and ...'

'You'll never be boring! Never in a million years! What's brought all this on, suddenly? You've never talked like this before.'

'I know. I kept it to myself. I thought everyone would laugh at me, but it's not funny, Abbs! It's a phobia!'

32

'A phobia.' I'm trying to keep a straight face. 'As in – an irrational fear of something.'

'Yes! That's it exactly! An irrational fear of . . . of recipes, and budgets, and . . . and mortgages. Home-made cakes . . . DIY . . . gardening!' She shudders. 'Don't laugh – I'm sorry, but they all terrify me. I have nightmares, Abbie – nightmares where I'm wandering, lost, in a giant B&Q superstore looking for a colour of paint that I've forgotten the name of! And I have panic attacks when I'm doing the food shopping if I see someone of about our age, with a trolley piled high with proper family food, sixteen pints of milk and two horrible kids crying in the trolley seat.'

'Is that what this is all about? The thing about not wanting a—'

'I hope you're not going to mention the "B" word,' she interrupts, shooting me a warning glance.

'But if you don't want them,' I persist, earnestly, 'if you're not having babies, Sam, then why would you have to grow up? Change? Live any differently than you are now? Just because you're getting married?'

'It's just people's expectations, I suppose. Come on – marriage is still thought of as a rite of passage, isn't it? As soon as I get back from the honeymoon, people will be asking me when we're getting a mortgage, when I'm having the curtains dry-cleaned, when I'm planting things in the garden for next spring, when I'm starting a family . . .'

I *knew* this was what it was all about.

'Just tell them, Sam. *Tell* people you and Phil don't want children.'

'I just want us to carry on as we are,' she continues

33

as if she hasn't heard me. 'We want to be together – married – together forever – of course we do. But not all that grown-up stuff! I want to carry on being young, and irresponsible, living in a furnished flat and eating pasta, chips or curries every night, having *fun* . . .'

'And you can! You will! You know you will – you and Phil have the most fantastic fun together. Nothing's going to change that. You're just having an attack of the jitters, that's all. Wedding day nerves.'

'Do you think so? It'll be all right? I won't turn into something dull and unattractive in an overall cleaning the oven?'

'Never!' I lean over and give her a hug. 'If you do, I'll shoot you!'

'Promise?' She begs me with her eyes. 'Seriously! Promise you'll tell me?'

'Sam, don't be *silly*. You're *not* going to change. I'm beginning to think you really *have* got a phobia!'

She sits up straight at the mirror again, pouts at her reflection, picks up a lipstick and tries it out, but doesn't answer me.

'Sam? Come on – you're not serious, are you.' I don't make a question of it. 'You're going off to Portugal tomorrow for two weeks and, when you come back, it'll be – well, just the same, but *better*! That's what it's all about! You'll still be *you* – you'll still do your job, see your friends, you'll still sing in the pub . . .'

She doesn't look convinced, so I add: 'You surely don't think Phil would try to change you? Stop you being yourself . . .?'

'Of course not!' she retorts immediately, with a flash of her usual spirit. 'He'd never . . . of course not! He's not like that!'

34

'Exactly. So what are you worrying about?'

'Everyone else. The family, I suppose. Their ... expectations.'

'Bugger their expectations!' I tell her vehemently. 'Stuff them, Sammy! Why don't you just *tell* them this is how you and Phil are going to live your lives. *Tell* them you're not having kids, that you're not going to—'

'That's all very well,' she interrupts calmly, throwing down the lipstick and turning to face me. 'Yes, you're right, but it just isn't that easy. You know what they're like. It was bad enough, in their eyes, David and Heather having Troy without getting married, let alone Chloe behaving as though she doesn't even belong to this family. *I'm* the one they're counting on being conventional. Toeing the line. Doing everything *normal*.'

Normal? I suppose I shouldn't laugh, but *normal* is the last word I'd ever think of using in relation to the Patterson family.

35

Quarter past twelve

I venture downstairs to the kitchen to pinch a chocolate biscuit. The florist has delivered the bride's bouquet and the bridesmaids' posies. They're lying on the kitchen worktop next to the dirty coffee cups.

'Oh,' I say, surreptitiously moving them aside slightly. 'Aren't they lovely!'

Christine looks up from buttering a huge stack of sliced bread. 'Yes, beautiful, aren't they, Abbie? I do love ponies, don't you?'

'Peonies . . .', I murmur, trying not to smile.

'Yes, dear, lovely, aren't they? Anyway, I'm glad you're here. Where's Sammy? Tell her it's nearly ready.'

'Nearly ready?' I repeat, watching her in confusion. Have the caterers suddenly decided they can't manage it today? Are we taking our own buffet with us?

'Lunch!' she says briskly. She pushes the bread mountain to one side and starts hacking at a family-sized lump of Cheddar. 'Come on, Abbie, give me a hand. There's ham in the fridge. And tomatoes. I do like a nice sliced tomato in a sandwich, don't you, dear?'

'Yes, but ... I don't think, really ... ' I stare, bemused, at the pile of bread that's now so high it looks as though it might topple off the kitchen table. Then I look back at Christine, whose hair seems to be wrapped in a plastic bag.

'I don't really feel like I want any lunch, right now,' I say, without much confidence. 'Wouldn't you rather be finishing your hair, Christine?'

'No lunch?' she squawks indignantly. 'Don't be ridiculous, girl! It's going to be a long day – you do realise that, don't you? A very long day. You need some good food inside you.'

My breakfast is still actually lying quite heavily on my stomach and I'd be quite happy, personally, with a couple of chocolate digestives but how can I say that when she's just single-handedly buttered the bread mountain?

'Give the others a call, there's a good girl,' continues Christine, slapping thick wedges of cheese between slices and thumping them together with the flat of her hand. 'I can't do any more with my hair, love, till the stripes are cooked.'

'Stripes? Cooked?' I echo weakly. Oh my God. Please, no.

'Cooked, done, whatever.' She pats the plastic bag on her head lovingly. 'Heather's done me some nice blue stripes.'

I resist the urge to pull the bag off, shove her head in the sink and run the taps.

'Streaks?' One can only hope. 'Highlights?'

'Blue ones,' she says with a nod. 'Apparently they look lovely on hair like mine. You know, dear – just beginning to show a few signs of grey,' she adds in a whisper as if it's not quite nice to talk about.

37

'I'll go and tell the others about lunch,' I say some-what hoarsely.

I take the stairs two at a time and burst into the bedroom where Sam's still curling her eyelashes.

'Heather's given your mother blue fucking streaks. For fuck's sake! Where is she?' There still might be time to rinse it off. Mightn't there?

'Don't worry about it,' says Sam without so much as a shake of her hand or a blink of the eye. 'A few streaks will look good. It'll suit her.'

'But . . . *blue*?'

'It'll match her dress.' Sam gives me a wicked grin. 'Relax, Abbie. Heather knows what she's doing.'

Christine, on the other hand, hasn't got a clue.

'We've got to go down and eat a ton of sand-wiches,' I tell Sam tonelessly, 'or we won't have the strength to get through the day, apparently.'

Actually I think a couple of swift brandies might do a better job of it.

The telly's on in the lounge. Brian's stretched out on the sofa, a plate of sandwiches balanced on his stomach, a can of beer in his hand, watching horse racing and muttering 'Yes! Go on! Yes, yes, go *on*, my son!' at the screen.

Granddad's already wearing his best suit. He's got crumbs on his trousers from the cheese sandwich he's shredding into pieces.

'Eat it, Dad,' says Christine. 'Don't take it apart.'

'I don't like this stuff inside it,' he tells her irrita-bly. 'You know I don't like it. I don't know why you keep giving it to me. What are you trying to do? Kill me?'

'It's cheese, Dad. You love cheese,' she says calmly. 'Have a ham one, then, if you don't want that one. Here.' She slaps a ham sandwich on his plate and takes the mangled cheese one out of his hand. 'Eat it up.'

'I don't know why you keep forcing him to eat,' says Chloe with a bored sigh. 'It's not natural.'

'He'd waste away if I didn't make him eat,' says Christine with obvious satisfaction.

Chloe gives us a look that says *Exactly My Point*.

I want to slap her so much I have to sit on my hand for a minute.

'Eat your lunch, now, girls!' Christine turns to Sam and me, with an excited giggle. 'Not long now till the Big Moment, eh?'

She manages, somehow, to make Sam's wedding sound like a giant-sized chocolate bar.

I take a ham sandwich from the plate and nibble at it half-heartedly. Can this get any more ridiculous? None of us are hungry. I can't believe this is how other families carry on just a couple of hours before their daughter's wedding – horse racing on the telly, piles of sandwiches in the lounge, arguing over cheese and ham – for God's sake! Why doesn't Christine tell Brian to get off his fat arse and turn the TV off, instead of waiting on him hand and foot? Why did she let Frank put his best suit on before handing him a sandwich to squash and letting him spurt tomato all down his front? Why doesn't she tell Chloe to take that sneering, superior look off her face and start acting as if she's part of this family today, for once in her spoilt little life?

'Thanks, Mum,' says Sam, putting a couple of sandwiches on her plate and giving Christine a beaming smile. 'Thanks for everything.'

39

Which immediately makes me think instead: Why am I such a bitch?

Heather strolls into the room just as Brian knocks his beer over. His horse came in, apparently, at ten to one, and he was so excited he actually jumped up at the crucial moment when it passed the finishing line. At least it made him move.

'The champagne's on you, then, Brian,' says Heather, helping herself to a sandwich and standing back as Christine rushes for a cloth to clean up the beer from the carpet.

'Bloody champagne,' he retorts. 'Rather have a bloody beer.'

'Have you got your speech ready, Brian? Your father-of-the-bride speech?' she teases.

I feel a familiar cold shiver go down my spine. This is no laughing matter. Brian's speech has been the subject of many tense conversations in this house during the past few weeks.

'Don't you worry about my speech,' he says, tapping his nose.

It's a secret. He's written it, he says, on two sheets of A4 paper torn from one of Chloe's student work pads. She offered to type it up for him on the computer but he refused point-blank, and has since kept it hidden somewhere known only to him. Christine's looked in his underwear drawer (no one else would), under their mattress and on top of the bathroom cabinet where he used to hide his fags when he was pretending he'd given up smoking. She says she can't think of anywhere else he could hide anything, and she's got a point, to be fair, as he doesn't go anywhere else in the house or do anything

40

else in it. I'm wondering if he's actually written one at all. The worry of finding out that he hasn't written one is considerably less than the worry of finding out, too late, what he *has* written. Neither really bears thinking about.

'Suit yourself,' says Heather equably. 'We don't care what he says, do we, girls? Everyone will be too pissed by then, to listen! Come on, Christine. Your streaks will be cooked by now, love. Come and get unveiled!'

Maybe I do need another sandwich after all.

Sam's talking on her phone.

'See you later, then,' she says as I sit down next to her. 'Yeah, you too. See you there!'

She's smiling.

'Phil?' I ask.

'Yeah. Just checking he still wants to go through with it,' she jokes.

'That's unlucky, that is,' Christine calls out from the kitchen where Heather is apparently unveiling her streaks. 'Talking to each other on the wedding day – supposed to be very unlucky!'

'Unlucky any bloody day,' mutters Brian.

But it's never going to be unlucky for Sam and Phil. No: Sam and Phil are perfect together.

They met in the Dog and Duck one evening when she was doing a gig there. He was with a couple of his mates, celebrating West Ham's win against Arsenal. They were lively, but not lairy. Loud, but not loutish. They were drinking, but they weren't drunk.

She was singing: two sets of forty-five minutes each with a break of thirty minutes in between, and some extra time at the end for encores. Easy listening, 60s and 70s stuff, numbers the punters could tap their feet to, turn and smile and nod their heads to. Requests taken for birthdays and anniversaries, a bit of chat between numbers. Two hundred quid for the night. A regular booking.

He caught her eye when she was singing "Big Spender". It's one of her best numbers – it suits her voice. She really lets it rip. I was there with her – I'm always there with her – and I've probably heard her sing 'Big Spender' at least a hundred times, but it still gives me shivers down my spine.

I saw the moment when they made eye contact. It was just as she was singing the bit about wanting to have fun I saw him turn to look at her. It was instant. He didn't look away again – not for the whole of the rest of the evening. Probably not ever since. It was like one of those sequences in films – you know? – when everything else fades away and there's just this couple, shining in a kind of white light: him staring at her, her staring at him. I knew he was going to come and talk to her in the interval. I knew they were going to go out together. Any fool could have seen it.

Sam looks beautiful when she's singing. She's a natural – she hasn't just got a superb voice, she's also got a kind of charisma about her. She holds the audience in the palm of her hand. She sings to them as if she knows them; smiles at each individual as if she's singing specially to them. I've seen her begin to sing in a pub where the patrons started off almost hostile in their disregard for her; they turned their backs, leaned on the bar or across their tables, lifted their pint mugs as a barrier between themselves and her music, pretended not to hear her, not to see her. She

was an unwelcome violation to the sacred peace of
their local. What bloody fool invited this woman here
to screech at them and drown out their gentle conversation over their dominoes games? But by the time
she'd sung the first two songs, they were melting.
They were putting down their beers, turning in the
chairs, staring at her in surprise. By the interval they
were telling the landlord with enthusiasm what a
bloody good idea it was of his to have some live
music in here for a change, and at least this young
woman could actually *sing*. And by the time they
went home to their wives, most of these middle-aged
men were more than a little in love with her.

That night, the night she met Phil, Sam was
wearing a dark-blue shift dress, split to halfway up
the thigh. Her hair was loose and glinted like spun
gold in the low lamplight. She was sparkling.

Phil bought her a drink and sat down opposite us.

'That last song,' he began, looking at her with a
light in his eyes, 'it was ... amazing.'

'"Big Spender"?' She laughed and gave me a wink.
It was a little joke between us – there was always at
least one guy, every time she included that number,
who believed she'd sung it especially for him. 'Is it
your favourite song?'

'No. I never really liked it before. But I liked it
tonight.'

'And are you?' she continued, teasing him with her
smile. 'A Big Spender?'

'Not in the least!' he laughed. 'Do I look like I am?
I've just spent my last one pound-fifty on your grape-
fruit and tonic! Don't drink it too fast!'

There was an easy, immediate rapport between
them. By the end of the interval they'd given each

other a potted version of their life histories: how she worked by day as a secretary in an advertising agency and sang in pubs in the evenings – not just to supplement her earnings but because she loves to sing; how he worked as an IT consultant and spent his weekends walking other people's dogs because he couldn't have one of his own in the flat where he lived.

'What sort of dogs?' she asked, warily.

'All sorts. At the moment, I walk a Border collie, two corgis and a German shepherd. Why?'

'Yikes.'

'Not all at the same time, though! You don't look very impressed,' he added.

'Sam doesn't really like dogs,' I explained. 'She's more of a cat person.'

'My little Toffee had a nasty experience once with a cocker spaniel.'

'Really? What – it chased him? Did it hurt him?'

'No. It kind of fell in love with him. Seriously – don't laugh! It lived next door, and it used to run up and down by the fence, barking at him and getting really excited whenever poor Toffee went outside for a pee. In the end, we had to get him a litter tray because he was too scared to go out.'

'Stalked by a cocker spaniel! Poor little bugger.'

'Yes. Fortunately the spaniel's family moved away. We were on the point of asking the vet for tranquillisers.'

'And you haven't liked dogs ever since?'

'I'm just a bit nervous around them. Especially if they're big and scary.' She looked up at Phil over the rim of her glass and I saw something flash between them. Something raw and new, something that flickered on their faces and hovered in the air like electricity. 'I probably wouldn't be nervous,' she added with a smile that was a flirtation, 'if I was with someone else. Someone who was good with dogs. Who could control them.'

She sang to him in the second half. He sat with me, and we watched her, together, in silence. He looked at me occasionally and smiled, as if he was sharing something with me. His mates watched him, nudging each other and making the occasional lewd comment. Of course, they couldn't take their eyes off Sam, either.

'Lucky bastard,' I heard one of them mutter as he left with us at the end of the evening.

I still hear them muttering it from time to time.

One o'clock

Suddenly, there's not much time left.

I'm trying not to panic. Heather and I are helping Sam into her dress when we hear David arriving downstairs. Actually, it's not strictly true that we hear David arriving. It's Troy we hear first, shouting something about shoes and ending up bursting into loud and furious crying.

'Those *bloody* shoes!' exclaims Heather, letting go of her side of the wedding dress just as we're straightening it over Sam's hips. 'I've heard nothing else from him all week!'

'What shoes?' I ask, smoothing my side of the dress and moving round to the side Heather has abandoned. 'How does it feel, Sammy?'

'The *bloody* shoes I bought him for the wedding. Jesus, Sam. You look totally fucking beautiful.'

She does.

She looks so totally fucking beautiful that all three of us are struck dumb, staring at her reflection in the mirror. She smiles at us.

'Is it OK, do you think?'

'OK?' I retort. 'You're *gorgeous*.'

'Amazing!' echoes Heather.

The yelling starts up again downstairs.

'*Horrid shoes! I hate the horrid shoes! Don't want the horrid shoes!*'

'What's the matter with his shoes?' says Sam, turning to try and get a look at her back view in the mirror. 'What's he screaming about?'

'Just this once,' says Heather, sighing with exasperation, 'I thought I'd like him to look like a nice, smart little boy instead of some filthy urchin living rough in the gutters. Is that too much to ask for?'

'Depends who you're asking,' I suggest.

The yelling's getting louder. It's getting closer. There's a knock on the bedroom door and David appears, in his suit, holding Troy by the arm none too gently and calling out to Heather above the child's shrieks: 'See? I *told* you! What's the point?'

'The point is, David,' she returns irritably, stalking across the bedroom and snatching Troy from his grasp, 'that he has to *learn*.'

Troy's red in the face. His miniature smart trousers and shirt are already looking crumpled and he's trying desperately, even whilst being thrust from parent to parent like an unwanted and dangerous parcel, to pull the laces out of the shiny black shoes on his feet which are obviously the source of his misery.

'Well, he's not learning anything at the moment, is he?' says David. 'Where are his trainers? Hello, girls. Sorry about this. Bloody hell, Sam: you look fantastic.'

'Thanks.' Sam's trying to smile but I'm quite sure Troy's screaming is setting all her nerves on edge.

'Take him back downstairs, would you, please, David?' I ask, more calmly than I feel. 'Heather? Maybe David's right about the trainers. We don't

47

want him screaming all through the wedding. He can *learn* some other time.'

'Come on, Troy. Downstairs. We'll take the shoes off,' says David. He gives me a grin as he goes.

I like David. If you ask me he's the only half-normal person in this family, apart from Sam of course. I don't like getting between him and Heather like this. If it wasn't the wedding day, and I wasn't Sam's bridesmaid, I'd keep right out of it. But it has to be said: Heather hasn't got a clue, sometimes. The kid's a lot better behaved, a lot calmer, when David's looking after him and Heather's not around. When she wants Troy to do something, eat something, wear something – like with these shoes – she won't ever back down and admit she's wrong. No wonder the boy's so hell bent on having his own way. If you ask me he takes after his mother! But then – what do I know about children? The only ones I've ever had any dealings with, apart from the half-dozen docile tots in the kindergarten class I used to run at Sunday school when I was a teenager, are the kids who come to the library. There, it's not the little ones who give us grief, it's the older ones: fourteen- and fifteen-year-olds, who turn up after school because they don't want to go home, and mess about on the computers or pretend to be doing homework while they're carrying on their raucous courting rituals. That's when I hanker after the old-style libraries of my childhood, with notices everywhere saying SILENCE, and people tiptoeing around and whispering. God, I sound like my father!

Thankfully, Troy's gone quiet downstairs now, so I can only hope for all our sakes that David's put his trainers on him and hidden the black shiny shoes well out of sight. Bless him, I know he's a holy terror but he's going to look quite cute in his little trousers, shirt and tie as long as he's not screaming. No one's going to worry about the trainers. Heather's gone quiet too; I know she's sulking because David's overruled her, but she'll get over it. *She's* not five years old, is she. Sometimes, when I see the way some parents carry on, I think they must forget that.

'You need to be getting into your own dress, Abbie,' she reminds me a bit grumpily. Like it's *my* fault she bought her kid a stupid pair of shoes? 'I'll go and give Madam a shout. I suppose she's still *studying*.'

Surprisingly, Chloe is actually already dressed and even more surprisingly, she's smiling. Maybe there's hope for today, after all.

Our bridesmaid dresses are beautiful – a very pale turquoise. I don't think anyone could look *really* bad in this shade, but it looks particularly stunning on someone with the Patterson family's colouring. Neither Chloe's hair, nor David's, is quite as striking as Sam's; but when you see them together there's no doubt that they're siblings. David's hair is a paler, sandier shade of auburn while Chloe's is a reddish blonde. They all have golden skin and green eyes and they're all very good-looking. There's only one possibility – they must all take after their mum.

'You look lovely,' Sam tells her little sister generously, going to give her a quick hug.

'You too,' says Chloe quietly. She actually looks quite choked. I think she means it. 'You look a bit better than usual too, Abbie,' she adds with a spiteful grin at me.

Gee, thanks.

'The photographer's here!' David calls up the stairs to us.

Well, good job I look a bit better than usual, then, I suppose.

I go ahead of Sam down the stairs. I'm worried about her tripping on her dress. Near the bottom, I nearly trip myself. How ironic would that be? Bridesmaid hobbling down the aisle on crutches. I think I need to calm down. I think, to be honest, I need a drink.

In the lounge, the major players are assembled, looking excited and not a little self-conscious in their finery. Brian is fidgeting with his collar and muttering about it strangling him. Frank keeps hitching up his trousers and has a worried look on his face. I'm sure he's forgotten again why we're all here. Troy, his little striped shirt tucked neatly into his pressed black trousers, is giggling with pent-up anticipation, bouncing around the room and pointing out the trainers on his feet to anyone who cares to look. David beckons him to his side, warning him to be quiet and not to run around. I glance at David and find myself thinking how well he scrubs up. But before I have time to think any further along this line I catch sight of Christine. Or, to be more specific, Christine's hair. It would be difficult to miss it.

'They're blue,' I mutter faintly to Heather, who's followed me and Sam into the room. 'They're actually stripes. And they're actually *blue*.'

'Good, eh?' She nods with self-satisfaction. 'What do you think? Suit her, don't they? Make her look younger.'

They make her look *terrible*. They make her look like a clown. But this is hardly the time to throw a fit about it.

50

'They ... um ... do match her dress well,' concedes Sam. 'Very nice, Mum,' she calls to Christine, pointing at her head.

Christine grins.

'Thank you, dear. Glad *someone's* noticed.'

Oh, don't worry. The whole world will notice. The only reason they won't comment is that they'll be too stunned to think of a damn thing to say!

The photographer is arranging us in groups on the sofa. The bride with the two bridesmaids; then with her dad; with her brother and sister; with her mum. *Smile, please!* Flash. Christine's stripes captured for posterity. I feel sad for her. How's she going to feel when she looks at the photographs of her daughter's wedding in five years' time? When her grandchildren grow up and show the photos to their children, their children's children, and fall about laughing at the blue stripes in Great-grandma Christine's hair? Why? Why did she do it?

'Abbie.' Troy's tugging at my dress. I look down at him. He does look cute today. Butter wouldn't melt in his mouth.

'Yes, sweetheart?'

'Why did Nanny paint her hair blue?'

You see? It's started already.

I smile at Troy. 'It's the fashion. Like your trainers.'

He nods happily, understanding this immediately. He pulls at my arm so that I lean down closer to him, and whispers urgently in my ear: 'Did Nanny scream and scream?'

'No, darling. It didn't hurt her at all. It's just like having your hair washed ...'

Troy stares at me with his head on one side. 'But when *I* want the fashion,' he says, thoughtfully, '*I* scream and scream till I get it.'

Whereas, in the case of his nanny's hair, it's everyone else who screams and screams . . .

Only joking.

'Right!' says Christine in a businesslike tone when the photographer's finished and gone off to wait for us at the church. 'Who wants a nice glass of cheery brandy?'

'Cheery brandy?' retorts Brian incredulously. '*What?*'

'Calms the nerves,' she tells him with an air of authority.

'Is that right, Christine?' asks Heather politely, accepting a glass of sticky red liquid. 'I never knew that.'

'Of course it does! Why do you think it's called cheery?'

'But I thought it was supposed to be called—' begins Heather, frowning, but David stops her with a nudge. He's smiling at me. I catch Sam's eye, and she's smiling too. It's a nice moment. I'm glad Chloe's gone out of the room.

'Not for me, thanks, Mum. I'm too scared I'll spill it on my dress!' says Sam.

'Same here,' I agree, although privately I'd like nothing better than a gin and tonic right now.

'How about a quick g and t?' David whispers to us both, going to fetch some glasses.

'You're a lifesaver,' I tell him gratefully.

And then the doorbell rings.

'We're not expecting anyone else to go from the

52

house, are we, Brian?' asks Christine, pausing with her glass of cherry brandy halfway to her lips.

'Buggered if I know,' he says with a shrug.

'It's OK!' shouts Chloe, charging down the stairs and running – actually *running* to the front door. 'It's OK, it'll be for me.'

We all look at each other in surprise. Chloe didn't mention bringing a friend to the wedding.

'Perhaps it's a new boyfriend!' says Christine with evident excitement.

But Chloe hasn't mentioned a boyfriend, either. Come to that, she never does. I don't think I've ever heard her talk about any boyfriends.

And a couple of minutes later we all, finally, understand why.

Half past one

'I'm Eva,' says the rather large brunette with a faint Welsh accent. 'Pleased to meet you all. I'm Chloe's other half.'

There's silence for a few seconds longer than there should be. Chloe is standing behind Eva, looking at the floor and shifting uneasily from foot to foot.

She could have chosen a better time to come out to her family. I'll rephrase that. She couldn't have chosen a *worse* bloody time to come out to her family than her sister's wedding day! What's the matter with her? I mean, fair enough, fine, who cares? But why *today*?

'Chloe's friend?' says Christine, missing the point completely. 'Hello, dear. Nice to meet you. Would you like a nice drop of cheery brandy? We were just . . .'

'No, Mum,' says Chloe, darting in front of Eva and taking the bottle roughly out of her mother's hands. 'No, she doesn't want any bloody cherry brandy. Eva's coming to the wedding with me today, all right?' She looks round the room defiantly, daring any of us to respond. 'She's coming because . . . well, because . . .'

Who's she kidding? This is all a big act. She's not defiant at all. She's terrified of how we're going to react. Why have I never noticed before how childlike she is – how very immature, and insecure, and *frightened*? The rudeness and the arrogance are just a cover. She's shaking inside.

Eva steps forwards again. She has a wide, open face. An engaging smile. She looks nice.

'What Chloe's trying to tell you,' she says gently, glancing around the room at us all, 'is that she's asked me to come with her today – to support her today – because I'm *with* Chloe. We're a couple.' Her soft brown eyes rest on Christine, and she adds quietly, 'I hope you're not too shocked.'

'*Shocked!*' shouts Brian, getting out of his chair and putting his beer glass down unsteadily. 'You ... you come in here today, my daughter's wedding day, and you try to tell us you're ... that our Chloe's ... well that she's *like that*?' He shakes his head and turns away. 'Shocked? No. I don't fucking believe it. You're talking fucking *shite*. Get out.' He belches, aims a kick at the cat, who runs squealing out of the room with his ears back, and repeats, more viciously, 'Get *out*.'

'Dad!' squeals Chloe, starting to cry. 'Don't *talk* to Eva like that!'

'Brian,' says Christine simultaneously, taking his arm, 'there's no need to be rude. Don't mind him, Eva. He's tense about the wedding, you know, and ...'

'Tense? About the fucking wedding? I'm not; I'm fucking *tense* about this ... this *person* turning up in my own fucking house, telling me my little girl is ... some sort of ... some kind of a ...'

'A lesbian, Dad. That's what I am. I'm a lesbian, that's all, and it's about time you knew.' Chloe sniffs back her tears, wipes her face carefully with a tissue and then, very deliberately, reaches for Eva's hand and holds it firmly. Eva smiles at us all as if this is a moment of triumph. Oh boy, has she got a lot to learn about this family.

'That's nice, dear,' says Christine faintly, blinking very fast. 'Would you like a nice cup of tea? We've just about got time before we leave . . .'

'Are you OK?' I ask Sam quietly.

Chloe and Eva have gone out to the kitchen, whether to get a 'nice cup of tea' or to compose themselves and fix Chloe's make-up, we haven't asked. Brian is standing at the window, his arms folded across his chest, glaring.

'*I'm* OK,' says Sam pointedly.

'Take no notice of your dad,' whispers Christine, her mouth twitching with her own distress. 'He'll come round. He'll be fine when he walks you down the aisle, you'll see, darling. He'll be fine.'

Nobody's asked her whether *she's* fine. As usual, I suppose, she'll just have to square her shoulders and get on with it. I find myself wondering, rather inappropriately, whether she's going to say 'It's only nature' this time.

'Trust Chloe,' says David grimly. 'Always the drama queen. Always wanting to steal the show.'

'I don't think so, actually,' I admit reluctantly. 'Not this time. I don't think it was her idea to come out with it today. It was probably Eva's.'

'Why?' Heather's shaking her head in much the same way that Brian did. 'What's the matter with her?

Why couldn't she just come along as Chloe's *friend* and leave it at that?'

'Why should she?' says Sam, unexpectedly. 'I'd feel miffed if I was asked to go to a family wedding with Phil and pretend to just be his *friend*.'

Not that Eva *was* asked, actually.

'But for your mum and dad . . .'

'It's a shock for us all,' she agrees. 'I had no idea. Poor Chloe. What a shame she couldn't have confided in one of us.'

But my thoughts are running more along the lines of what a shame it is that 'poor Chloe' couldn't have realised, for once in her spoilt little life, that today was about Sam, not her, and left her lesbian lover at home.

There's a scream from the kitchen at exactly the same moment that Brian finally turns away from the window and sits back down in his armchair. He shoots out of the chair again as if he's been burnt.

'What the . . .?' he starts.

Christine and I are jostling each other in our hurry to get out of the door.

'What's the matter?' Christine's shouting back at Chloe. 'What's happened?'

'What *now*?' mutters David.

'The flowers!' screeches Chloe. 'The cat's jumped on the fucking flowers!'

'Keep your voice down, for God's sake.' I reach the kitchen just ahead of Christine, and manage to wrestle the bride's bouquet away from Chloe, who's been holding it aloft, staring in horror at the squashed blooms. 'Don't let Sam hear you.'

Fortunately, Sam and Heather are back upstairs

having a final check from all angles before the finishing touches – shoes and *bouquet* – are added.

'It was my fault,' says Eva, looking distraught. 'I said hello to the cat, and he just bolted across the room and jumped straight up there. I don't know why it is, but cats always seem to be petrified of me. I should stop trying to talk to them. It never works – I should have learned by now . . .'

'All right, don't worry, of course it wasn't your fault,' I interrupt her snappily. It's a quarter to two. There just isn't time for anything other than drastic measures. I grab the three or four biggest, most squashed flowers by their heads and tug them out of the bouquet.

'Oh! Oh!' wails Christine. 'The lovely ponies!'

'Bugger the lovely ponies,' I tell her in a heartfelt hiss. 'I don't want Sam to know anything about this – OK? A nice bouquet, only slightly squashed, without the ponies . . . the *peonies* . . . is a much better proposition than a really bad bouquet, totally smashed ponies and a bride in tears. Agreed?'

'Agreed,' says Christine at once, taking the remaining bouquet out of my hands and fluffing it up like a flattened cushion. 'You're so clever, Abbie.'

Chloe's still standing with her hand over her mouth, her eyes large with horror.

'But the posies . . .' she mutters through her hand. 'The bridesmaids' posies?'

'They look fine,' I tell her cheerfully, giving them both a shake. 'Toffee must have missed them.'

And we've already had the flowers for our hair pinned into place by Heather.

'Thank God for that.' She sinks down on a kitchen stool, looking close to tears.

'I'm surprised you're that concerned,' I say, frankly. 'I didn't think you liked the idea of carrying a posy down the aisle.'

She actually told me the other day that it was going to be the most embarrassing moment of her entire life when she had to prance through the church carrying a stupid bunch of flowers *like a poxy fucking fairy*.

'That's the whole point,' she says, very quietly, fixing her eyes on the floor. 'I wished for it.'

'Wished for what?' She's irritating me now. As usual.

'The stupid flowers!' she spits back at me. 'I *wished* for something bad to happen to them. So how do you think that makes me feel now?'

Oh! So whose fault is that, then? The *flowers'* fault?

You know what they say, don't you? Be careful what you wish for! And never leave bouquets lying around where cats are liable to jump.

Everyone's starting to leave for the church. David and Heather are taking Frank with them. Chloe and I will be going in the first wedding car, with Christine.

'What about Eva?' says Chloe petulantly. 'I said she could get a lift with us.'

'Well, you shouldn't have,' I tell her quietly but firmly. 'All the arrangements were made months ago. We didn't know Eva was coming.'

'Yeah – and can you imagine if I'd told you?' she sneered. 'You'd have freaked out.'

'Of course I wouldn't have. Have I "freaked out" now? I'm just saying that we weren't expecting an extra one in the cars.'

'It's OK. I'll walk,' says Eva calmly. 'It's not far, is it?'

'Eva doesn't know the way!' says Chloe, beginning to sound a bit hysterical. 'She doesn't live round here. She's come specially, all the way from Cardiff . . .'

More fool her.

'Where's she staying?' interjects Brian, refusing to look at Eva.

'Here. Where d'you think?' retorts Chloe.

'That's what you think, miss. She's not . . .'

'She *is*!'

'All right, calm down . . .' I try.

'She's *not*!'

'She *is*!'

'She can!' agrees Christine.

'She *can't* . . .!' insists Brian.

'She *is*!' shouts Chloe.

'Shut *up*, all of you!' Blimey, I've surprised myself. I don't think I've ever actually shouted at the Patterson family before, especially not in their own house. There's a chilly and uncomfortable silence.

'I'll just walk, then . . .' begins Eva, putting her jacket on.

'No you won't.' Jesus, is this really me, taking charge of everyone? 'You can come in the car with us. There'll be room. I wouldn't recommend getting in the back seat with Troy and Granddad. Anything could happen.'

'But she's not staying here . . .' begins Brian again, scowling.

'We'll discuss that later, thank you, Brian,' I say, in the quiet-but-deadly tone I use on the teenagers in the library. 'See you at the church, then, David? Are you all right, Frank?'

60

Frank turns back to gaze at me in bewilderment as he's being shepherded out of the door by Heather.

'Where are we going?' he says, without much enthusiasm.

'To the church, Dad,' calls out Christine. 'I'll see you there in a minute. Just sit nicely in the car and don't keep undoing your trousers.'

'Don't undo your trousers, Granddad!' repeats Troy, squealing with laughter. 'Don't undo your trousers, don't undo your trousers . . .'

'All right, Troy, that's enough,' says Heather quickly.

'Don't undo your . . .'

'That's *enough*, Troy!' I tell him, severely. 'Behave yourself!'

Blimey, I think I've actually frightened him. He ducks his head, looking up at me warily through his fringe, and holds onto David's hand as he leads him out to the car.

'Well done,' David tells me quietly. There's a twinkle in his eyes, a flicker of admiration – or amusement? 'Well done for *all* of it, Abbie.'

But we haven't even started yet – have we!

Two o'clock

So I'm sitting in the back of this wedding car with Chloe and her girlfriend. Christine's in the front. It's only a few minutes' drive to the church.

'Isn't this great?' says Eva, looking genuinely excited. 'I've never been to a church wedding before.'

This makes me smile. I wish I could say the same, but I must have notched up well over a hundred church weddings myself when I was a kid – often singing in the choir. It's different today, though – I have to admit I've never been a bridesmaid before.

'Yes,' I tell her, smoothing my dress down and trying to stay calm. 'It's exciting, isn't it?'

'I'm all of a fluster!' admits Christine, giggling and checking her hair in the passenger mirror. Still bright blue. I've given up praying for a miracle at the eleventh hour to make it fade. 'I hope I'll have enough time for a quick smoke when we get to the church.'

'Can't you wait till afterwards, Mum?' says Chloe irritably. 'I thought you were trying to give it up.'

'Too much stress at the minute, Chloe, what with this wedding and everything. I'll give up next week.

62

Doctor keeps on nagging me but he doesn't know the stress I'm under – living with your father and your granddad.' She coughs pitifully and then shrugs and concludes, 'Still, it's only nature, isn't it, at the end of the day?'

So is dying from smoking-related illnesses, but now's probably not a good time to get into that. We're pulling up outside the church.

There are crowds of people milling around in the churchyard. All Saints is a pretty Norman church set opposite the village green of Little Tunbury – which has won the Beautiful Essex Village title three times in the last five years. It's only two miles from Chelmsford town centre but it's an idyllic little village, spoilt only by the A12 dual carriageway passing within eardrum-perforating distance of its row of neat little stone cottages. This has been my dad's church for the past eight years – since the Diocese moved him on from the rough job over the other side of town at St Luke's. The congregation here is no bigger, but the parishioners are a lot older than at St Luke's, and a lot less hostile – until Dad tries to introduce anything new or faintly charismatic into the services, apparently.

'Hi, Dad.' He's standing in the church doorway, talking to some woman in a purple hat. He looks round, gives me a wave and excuses himself from her.

'Ah, Abigail. Good, good. I was thinking you were running late.' He checks his watch. 'Time's getting on. Where's the other bridesmaid?'

'Chloe. She's here. Don't fuss, there's plenty of time. How's Mum?'

'Much the same. She sends her love.'

'I wish she could have come. She loves weddings.'

I'm not saying it, but more to the point, she'd have loved to see me as a bridesmaid. First time in my life. Her only daughter.

'Yes.' His eyes cloud over. 'But she's not up to it.'

Mum's nerves have never been the same since the days at St Luke's. The kids from the estate used to hang around outside the church and call her 'Bible Basher' and chant stupid, crude rhymes: 'Mrs Vicar, lost her knickers ...' She coped with it for years, holding her head up high and saying, 'Sticks and stones may break my bones!' – but inside she was apprehensive, nervous of going out after dark. Late one winter afternoon, leaving the church after a women's prayer meeting, she was taunted by a couple of them playing on skateboards in the car park. In the gathering dusk, she thought an arm raised for balance was raised in threat, that she was about to be physically attacked. She ducked, tripped and fell heavily to the ground. The bruises, grazes and even the broken kneecap healed in due course, but the worst thing was her broken spirit. She's not good at going out of the house any more.

'Never mind,' I tell Dad, giving his arm a squeeze. 'We'll show her the photos.'

'You look lovely,' he says, smiling. 'I hope you're not going to outshine the bride.'

'No chance of that!'

I'm laughing, but I'm getting nervous now, what with his constant checking of his watch. Friends and people I vaguely recognise as distant members of Sam's or Phil's families are nodding and waving to me on their way into the church. It must be packed in there by now.

'Hello, Abbie,' mutters a familiar voice close to my ear. 'Have you sobered her up? Is she OK to go through with it?'

'Phil!' I lean over and plant a kiss on his cheek. 'You're here!'

'Don't sound so surprised! I've been here for ever! Gary and I were so nervous of getting held up in the traffic or breaking down or being abducted by aliens halfway out of town, we've been lurking in bushes down the lane for about half an hour!'

'Well done, Gary,' I tell his younger brother, patting him on the shoulder. 'First objective achieved. Now all you've got to worry about is whether you've got the ring safe.'

He pats his pocket, a look of anxiety in his eyes. 'It's here. Don't even joke about it.'

'Shouldn't you be in the church by now?' I remind them. 'You don't want to get caught hanging around out here chatting up the bridesmaids when Sam arrives, do you?'

'Talking of chatting up the bridesmaids,' says Phil, staring around him, 'Where's Chloe?'

'She's here somewhere. And don't bother trying to chat her up,' I add sweetly to Gary.

'Why?'

'She's with her partner.'

And that's all I'm saying on the subject.

Chloe and I are waiting in the porch for the bride to arrive; everyone else is inside the church. I can almost feel my knees knocking together. Chloe's staring out into the sunshine and looking bored.

'Here they are,' she announces suddenly, standing up a bit straighter and involuntarily patting her hair

65

and checking the flower's still in place.

David, in his role of usher watching from just inside the church, nods at us and gets ready to give a signal to the vicar. Suddenly, as he turns back to survey the congregation, I see a look of panic cross his face.

'Where's Mum?' he hisses to us.

'She's in there, isn't she?'

Please, God, tell me she's in her place in the front row, and not wandering around the church showing off her blue stripes to all and sundry.

'She's gone for a fag,' says Chloe languidly, 'hasn't she?'

'Not *now*, though!' Chloe almost jumps backwards at the tone of my voice. 'Not fucking *now*, Chloe, surely to God. Sam's just getting out of the fucking car!'

'No need to get arsey with *me*, Abbie,' she retorts crossly, 'Just because you're chief fucking bridesmaid.'

'Don't be ridiculous. It's nothing to do with ... Oh, forget it. Look, we need your mum to be in the church, that's all, and quickly.'

'I'll go ...' starts David.

But it's too late. The wedding car door's open; Sam's leg appears out of the car as we're all rooted to the spot, staring at each other. Brian takes Sam's arm, helps her out of the car and they turn to smile at us. Yes, even Brian's smiling.

The bride's about to walk down the aisle, and her mum's not even in the church. Please don't tell me she's going to miss her daughter's wedding while she's somewhere in the graveyard copping a crafty smoke.

'We need to go in,' says Chloe, and she's right. Sam's approaching us, radiant and beautiful on her father's arm. If we stop her at the church doorway she's going to think the bridegroom hasn't turned up. 'She won't notice.'

'Of *course* she'll bloody notice!' I whisper crossly. Surely to God every bride looks for her mum as she walks to the front of the church – looks to catch her eye and share a smile. Blue stripes or not.

'Do I give the signal?' asks David urgently.

'Yes. Yes, go.'

The familiar opening chords of the 'Bridal March' fill the church. I can almost hear everyone in the congregation shuffling in their seats, turning to look at the door, whispering, *'Here she comes!' 'Here's the bride!'*

'You look wonderful,' I say to my best friend, swallowing back my anxiety and pasting on a confident smile. 'Let's go get you married.'

We're actually walking down the aisle when we hear the sound of a toilet flushing and see Christine creeping, red-faced, from a door at the back of the church along the side aisle to her seat at the front.

Like we said – too much bloody tea this morning!

Half past two

I spent a large part of my formative years in a church.
It's been probably nine years now since I stopped
going, but as soon as I step inside one I'm back there
– the little girl sitting on the hard wooden bench next
to my mum, learning the rules from a very young age:
*Ssh, Abbie. Be quiet, Abbie. Don't fidget, Abbie.
We're in church now – sit still and be a good girl.* I
knew the hymns and prayers off by heart long before
I could understand a word of them, so I often got
them wrong.'Our Father, Witch-heart in Heaven' had
me puzzled, whereas 'All Things Brighton Beautiful'
made perfect sense because we often went to Brighton
in the summer holidays and it *was* beautiful so I could
see the point of singing about it. But even when I was
old enough to discuss these things with my dad, I
couldn't get to grips with the part of the service where
everyone confessed their sins.

'But I haven't been naughty,' I used to protest
when Dad tried to explain it to me. 'Why do I have
to say sorry, if I haven't been naughty?'

I still have a problem with that one. It was partly
why I stopped coming to services. After Mum's accident, I resented the injustice of it. It wasn't *me* that

tormented my mum and ruined her life – and *those* little bastards weren't in church grovelling on their knees pleading that they were poor sinners, were they? *I* was! How could that be fair?

Everyone's smiling at us as we move slowly towards the front of the church – well, to be accurate, they're smiling at Sam, of course. Chloe and I are just here to complete the picture. On one side – Sam's friends from work; our friends Kirsty and Ruth and their husbands; a couple of neighbours; and then Sam's family, aunts, uncles, and cousins, and, nearer the front, Granddad, looking hostile and confused next to Heather who's holding Troy down in his seat. On the other side – Phil's lovely mum and dad; his grandma; his workmates and old school friends; and the guys he goes to football with. The place is packed. Standing room only.

I catch Chloe's eye as we finally arrive in front of my dad. She looks petrified. I feel tense with nerves myself, but it makes me smile for a minute to realise that Hard-Case Chloe is suffering from serious performance anxiety. It reminds me, just for a moment, of when she played an angel in her school nativity play when she was about six, and cried with fright all the way through it. Maybe, underneath it all, she hasn't changed so very much, despite all the brashness, crudeness and snotty superiority. My dad always says that people never really change very much, they just pretend to. Come to think of it, he does say a lot of really wise stuff, my dad, even if he never has been able to convince me about Confession.

He's smiling at the congregation now as the music dies away and an expectant hush descends. With my back to the crowd, I'm conscious of every little sound – every cough, every rustle of the Order of Service sheets, every childish voice being hushed.

'Mummy, why are we . . .'

'Ssh!'

'But Mummy . . .'

'Ssh!'

Silence now. Finally. It's beginning.

'Hello, everyone, and welcome to All Saints, on this beautiful summer afternoon – this very *special* afternoon for Samantha and Philip.'

We start with a hymn. "Love Divine, All Loves Excelling". It's a nice choice – lots of people have it for weddings, and Dad says he doesn't see the point in ramming home the fact that it's actually about God's love, not human love. He says the one can lead to the other in any case. He doesn't ever refuse to marry people in church because they haven't been baptised or attended services, either – he'd rather have people in church for a wedding, he says, than never at all.

Sam and Phil are stealing glances at each other while they're singing. It brings a lump to my throat. Phil's hand is shaking slightly as he holds the hymn sheet. They're trying to keep singing and looking ahead but they can't help it – the little turns of the head, the little smiles. They can't keep their eyes off each other. Behind me, the congregation struggles to keep up with the organist, who's going at a rate of knots; male voices fail in the attempt to reach the higher notes; some woman who's a good singer is showing off by warbling a descant that I've never heard before. But all I can see are the bride and groom; all I can feel is the tension of their excitement, the importance to them of

70

this next half-hour, above all other half-hours of their lives. I can't let anything go wrong. I find myself mouthing a silent prayer to the God I've neglected for so long: Please, please, don't let anybody *dare* make anything go wrong!

As we finish the hymn and everyone behind us is sitting down, Sam turns and hands me her bouquet.

'Thanks, Abbie,' she whispers.

She's smiling, wide-eyed with excitement. She looks like a little girl just about to open all her Christmas presents. I give her a shaky smile back, and Chloe and I make silently for our seats in the front row.

Sam and Phil went through the wedding ceremony with Dad and chose how they wanted to adapt it. They've kept the traditional opening:

'Dearly beloved, we are gathered here together . . .' but wisely took out the bit about men's carnal lusts and brute beasts, and substituted some lovely words about a wife and husband being best friends, lovers and listeners, who comfort and nurture each other through the stresses of life and forgive each other's mistakes.

I'm dwelling on the thing about forgiving mistakes rather longer than I probably should do, when I first become aware of the sniffs. Next to me, Christine is holding a hankie to her face and shaking. Crying already! I thought she'd at least hold out till the ring goes on the finger. I nudge her gently, catch her eye and shake my head at her. *No – don't cry*. This just seems to set her off even worse, so instead I take her hand and hold it. She pats mine comfortingly as if we're both going through some unthinkable trauma together.

71

Dad's got to the bit where he asks the congregation if anyone knows of any reason why Sam and Phil can't be married. He laughs and says he hates those few seconds of silence that follow, and everyone laughs too, breaking the tension.

'Why're you laughing, Mummy?' pipes up a little voice that carries all too well, echoing and bouncing off the ancient stone walls like an affront to their dignity.

Troy! He'd been so quiet, I'd almost forgotten to worry about him. There's a ripple of mirth through the congregation. *No!* I want to shout. *No, don't laugh! You're encouraging him!*

'Ha, ha, ha!' squeals Troy very loudly, delighted with himself. 'Funny!'

'Ssh!'

I can just picture Heather's face, red with embarrassment. She's probably putting her hand over Troy's mouth to quieten him. He's probably trying to bite her fingers. Any minute now he's going to scream blue murder. Shit! Why did they have to bring their hell-child into the church?

And then I catch sight of Dad's face and suddenly it's back – the same helpless humility I used to feel when, as a child, I threw one of my rare tantrums, or as a teenager if I lost my temper or swore or called somebody names, and then I'd look at my dad, expecting him to be angry with me – to reprimand, shout, punish me like any of my school friends' fathers would have done – certainly like Brian would have done. But instead, he'd give me this sad, patient smile – a look that said he knew how I felt, he understood, but it was no good carrying on like that. He never had to say anything, he'd just wait, and I couldn't bear it.

I always ended up apologising.

Now, he's smiling in Troy's direction and waiting for him to quieten down, for the congregation to quieten down. It only takes a minute. Heather's hand's probably bleeding by now.

'Suffer the little children!' he says, with great irony, and there's another flurry of amusement – muffled, cut short by the corporate fear of provoking a further outburst from Troy.

'Now,' says Dad, turning to Sam and Phil, 'I have to put the same thing to you two: If either of you know of any reason why you should not be joined together in marriage, you must declare it now.'

They turn and grin at each other.

'I think we can take that as a "No"!' says Dad with a smile. 'So . . . Philip: will you take Samantha to be your wife: to live together in holy matrimony . . .'

Oh, God. Christine's bawling again.

I'm watching Brian closely to make sure he's paying attention. I don't want him to miss the bit where he has to give Sam away. He's more than likely to be daydreaming about the FA Cup or the win he had on that horse this morning.

'Who gives this woman to be married to this man?'

Here we go. I fight the urge to jump up and push him forward. Come *on*, you dozy oik! For Christ's sake, this is the *only* thing you have to do – please, please, can you get it right?

'I do.'

Finally. His voice rings out, surprisingly strong and confident, as he steps forward and takes Sam's hand. She turns to give him a smile but he's looking straight ahead, his back like a ramrod, his shoulders squared, standing to attention. I feel a rare flicker of warmth for him. He's an old-fashioned man, an ex-policeman. Christine has told me how, when he left the police, he gave up on life and kind of folded in on himself. Looking at him now, it's possible to get a brief glimpse of the man he once was: proud, groomed, disciplined. He could still be that man – couldn't he?

'There you go, mate – all right?' he says roughly to Dad as he hands Sam over to him.

Well, maybe not.

You could almost hear a pin drop in the church now, as Phil's repeating his vows.

'I, Philip, take you, Samantha ...'

I can feel the church pew vibrating beneath me. Next to me, Christine's shaking – her body heaving with silent sobs.

'... for better, for worse ...'

I grab her hand again and squeeze it. She shudders and sits up straighter, trying to compose herself. Thank God.

'... to love and to cherish ... as long as we both shall live.'

Christine gulps and shudders again. I give her hand another squeeze. It's Sam's turn now. She takes Phil's hand and looks into his eyes and that's it. Christine lets out a wail. I nudge her, hard, lean closer to her and whisper fiercely in her ear,

'Ssh! Come on!'

It's inadequate, but what else can I say? I want to tell her for fuck's sake to pull herself together, to think of her daughter, to not spoil her day and make a spectacle of herself. I'm knotted up inside with the strain of *not* clamping my hand over her blubbing trembling mouth, like Heather does with Troy, or grabbing her by the elbow and frogmarching her out of the church.

'I, Samantha, take you, Philip . . .'

Wail, wail! Christine rocks herself back and forth on the pew. I give up and let go of her hand, shaking myself free of her as if I don't want to be associated with her. I *don't*. I realise I'm disgusted by her. Why doesn't she have any self-control? I've seen more restrained behaviour at drug-crazed rock concerts.

'. . . in sickness and in health . . .'

Sob, wail! Sam has to raise her voice.

'. . . as long as we both shall live.'

'My little girl!' mumbles Christine through her tears. She unfolds her scrunched-up hankie and blows her nose into it, noisily, before going into a fresh bout of loud crying.

I want to shrink into my seat. People are shifting uncomfortably, looking around, coughing with embarrassment. Worse, I realise that Dad's stopped the proceedings and is waiting, calmly, for silence – like a teacher who knows that his disruptive class will settle down eventually and he's not going to waste his energy telling them to be quiet.

I, however, have had enough.

'Shut *up*!' I hiss at the quivering wreck of a woman next to me. 'Pull yourself together! You're holding up the service!'

The look of horror and humiliation on her face makes me almost regret it. But it works. She blots her red eyes and puffy cheeks with the disgusting, saturated hankie, shuffles herself into an upright position and swallows hard.

'I'm sorry,' she says out loud, her voice thick from crying. 'But I'm so happy!'

There's a shiver of laughter from those close enough to hear.

Dad turns to rest his eyes on her for a moment. He's smiling gently, the way he did when I stopped screaming as a child. The way he did when I stopped crying over Jamie.

'We need to express our feelings sometimes,' he says, addressing the whole congregation, 'and a wedding is a very emotional occasion, isn't it?'

In the seconds of silence that follow, punctuated by nothing more than a couple of grateful sniffs from Christine, I can feel the heartbeat of my shame. Am I such a cold-hearted bitch these days that all I care about is my own embarrassment?

'Sorry, Abbie,' she whispers to me shakily as Dad returns to Sam and Phil and the completion of the ceremony.

'It's OK,' I reply, and I take her hand again, trying to ignore the swift tucking up her sleeve of the soaking hankie.

After all, I suppose it's only nature.

Gary, shaking visibly with nerves, nevertheless plays his part perfectly, stepping forward with the ring and laying it on Dad's prayer book for him to hand to Phil. As Phil then places it on Sam's finger I realise I'm actually holding my breath. This is *it*. The crucial moment – the one they'll both remember for the whole of their lives. The enormity of its significance brings a lump even to *my* throat. God knows how Christine's holding on; I guess she's all cried out.

'With this ring, I thee wed; with my body, I thee worship . . .'

I glance around. Everyone's silent now, caught up in the moment. Something makes me look behind me. Eva, sitting at the end of the row, directly behind Chloe, is staring wide-eyed at the back of her head, with tears in her eyes. She doesn't even notice me looking. I turn back again, quickly, ducking my head. For some reason, the tears in Eva's eyes have affected me more than any amount of bawling from Christine.

And that's when I notice the bouquet. Lying on the rail in front of me, its ribbons splayed out like colourful birthday garlands across the dark of the old wood, it looks wrong – like a graceful swan that's laid down and died, its feathers ruffled and tired and neglected and . . . oh, shit. It's falling apart.

'Those whom God has joined together, let no-one tear apart.'

Taking out those crushed flowers – the three or four biggest blooms in the bouquet – must have loosened everything else. Everything has slipped. It looks a mess! How did it stay together as Sam walked down the aisle? In fact . . . *did* it stay together?

'Now that Philip and Sam have made their vows to each other, and now they have declared their love for each other by the giving and receiving of a ring . . .'

I look down at the floor of the church. I shift my feet. I've been standing on a sprig of greenery. There's a crushed lily in the aisle, next to our row. I strain my neck to look further back.

'In the name of God, I pronounce them man and wife. Phil, you may kiss the bride!'

The congregation shifts, sighs, lets out its collective breath and begins to applaud.

Halfway back down the aisle, a movement catches my eye and almost stops my blood in my veins. Troy's kneeling on the cold stone floor, his miniature shiny jacket spread out beside him. In his hands is what was, once, the last remaining peony in the bride's bouquet. He's peeling off the petals, one by one, and dropping them onto his jacket, where there are already a collection of flowers, leaves, and broken bits of stem. As I watch, he gets up and trots further down the aisle, following the trail of pink and white floral droppings, grabs another trophy and takes it happily back to his cache. All around him, adults are trying not to laugh.

I'm surprised at myself. I'm almost laughing too. No wonder he's been so quiet.

Christine, distracted from clapping the happy couple by the stirring of others looking round in their seats, smiles indulgently at her little grandson and nudges me, all thoughts of crying forgotten.

'Bless him!' she whispers to me. 'It's only nature, isn't it, love?'

Thank the Lord for nature.

Three o'clock

The relief, as we walk back down the aisle and out of the musty darkness of the church into the brilliant afternoon sunshine, is making me feel weak. It went OK. A few minor hiccups, sure, but in retrospect, nothing too terrible. Nothing to ruin the day, nothing to spoil the memories. They'll be able to laugh when they look back at their wedding album, remembering how Christine stopped the proceedings with her crying, how Granddad slept through the entire service, waking up at the end shouting about the Germans coming; how Brian said 'Righto, mate!' when Dad announced that it was time to sign the register; and, of course, how Troy screamed when Heather tried to move him and his flower collection out of the aisle so that the bridal procession could walk out without tripping over him.

He's sulking now, sitting next to Heather with his thumb in his mouth, his jacket screwed up on his lap with his petals stowed safely inside it and a glare of thunderous warning to anyone who goes near it. I smile at him as we pass his aisle. I feel gracious enough now to smile at anybody. He sticks his tongue out at me.

In the entrance porch, the photographer greets us with an explosion of flashes.

'This way, Sam! Look this way! Now turn and look at Phil. That's right. Now, carry on walking – towards me, outside now, come on. Hold his hand like you were before, and turn your face ... that's lovely. Hold it! Yes, and again ... hold it! Now the bridesmaids. Either side of the bride and groom, please, look at the bride, smile please! Now hold your hand up, Sam – bridesmaids, hold her hand and look at the ring, please. That's it! Look happy! Yes, good – hold it! Now, bride's mum and dad. Over here, please. Groom's mum and dad? Where are the groom's mum and dad? Over here – either side of the bride and groom, lovely, yes – smile please ...'

There are people I want to talk to, but it seems like I'll be posing for this photographer for hours, being captured for posterity and the wedding album with the happy couple and everyone else. Christine with her face red and blotchy from crying, her blue streaks glinting in the sunshine; Brian, loud and self-important now the scary bit's over, ordering everyone about; Chloe and Eva, arms linked, sniggering; Heather, holding onto a fractious Troy by the back of his shirt collar; David, watching them with an inexplicable sadness that suddenly pulls at my heart-strings. I want to talk to Sam, tell her how wonderful she was, how calm, how confident, how happy and smiley and beautiful and how proud I am of her. I want to talk to Phil, too, and give him a kiss and say all that stuff that people say – congratulations and welcome to the family ...

But it's not even my family!

Sometimes I kind of forget. Even though they drive

me mad, I have this horrific feeling sometimes that I'm almost a part of the Pattersons. God forbid.

'Right, bridesmaids! And all the bride's friends. Where are you? Come on, girls – all her mates, that's it, all the girls line up behind the bride – good, good. Now then, Sam, you know what to do: hold up the bouquet – that's it, love, and get ready to throw it over your shoulder . . .'

'Oh, no. Excuse me, but no, you can't.'

'What's the matter, Abbie?' Sam, holding the remains of her bouquet aloft, is looking at me, wide-eyed in surprise.

'Don't throw it!' Everyone's looking at me in confusion. Why? Are they all blind? Haven't they noticed? Where did they think all those flowers came from, that Troy collected from the church floor? Dropped from heaven? Can they not see that Sam's bouquet, even though I did my best with it while the bridal party were signing the register – untying the ribbons, pushing everything together and tying them up again – is looking scraggy and, at best, a trifle *fragile*. At worst, it's going to fall apart completely as soon as she lets go of it.

'Don't throw it,' I repeat, desperately. 'I think it's unlucky, Sam.'

Everyone laughs. They think I'm joking.

'It's traditional, Abbie!' says Sam, gaily. 'OK, everyone: get ready! Here goes!'

The photographer, half crouching, is preparing to take his super action shot. The other girls giggle and jostle each other for position. Who's going to be the winner? Who's going to be the butt of all the jokes for the rest of the day – *Ooh, so it's your turn next, then . . .*?

I was never any good at sports. I never got picked

for netball or rounders teams at school; I couldn't catch. I never had that elusive thing they called 'an eye for the ball'. I suppose I wasn't interested enough; I didn't really try. Who cared whether the other team got a goal or not? Who cared whether I got the batsman out? I never understood the importance of it. But now – suddenly – I'm faced with making the catch of my life. It matters. It matters because if anyone else catches that bouquet and experiences it collapsing into a mess of broken blooms and tattered leaves in their hands, they won't see the joke. Or even if they pretend to, they'll wonder about it, at home on their own in their beds at night. They'll read something into it. If they were meant to be the next bride, why did the bouquet disintegrate as soon as they touched it? What did it mean? Was it a sign? Should they avoid getting married at all, in case the whole thing falls apart like the flowers?

'One, two, three . . .' everyone chants together, as Sam swings the pathetic-looking remains of her flowers in a wide arc, up and over her head, and finally flings them backwards to a volley of applause and whooping from the crowd.

I throw up my arms and dive.

'Abbie!'

My eyes are closed. I'm on the grass, in an ungainly heap, my aquamarine dress up round my knees, one shoe off, my hair – Heather's work of art – unpinned and spread across my face in untidy strands full of dirt. But held tight in my arms is the horrible bundle of squashed flowers that was once Sam's beautiful bridal bouquet. Petals have stained the front of my dress. Bits of stalk have broken off

82

and found their way down my cleavage. But I've held onto the bouquet. Nobody's noticed.

'Abbie, what on *earth* are you doing?'

It's David, holding out his hand to me, looking at me with a mixture of amusement and affection, as if I'm a silly puppy who's got itself in a mess.

'Talk about desperate!' I hear Chloe giggle to Eva as I struggle to my feet, still clutching the ruined flowers. 'As if it's going to make any difference to whether *she* gets married!'

'Don't be a spiteful little bitch all your life, Chloe,' says David. 'Sorry, Eva, but ...'

'He's right, Chloe,' says Eva. 'That wasn't kind, was it. Poor Abbie might have hurt herself.'

Chloe pouts, looks away from Eva and drops her eyes.

'Sorry, Abbie. Are you all right?' she mutters.

Blimey. Wonders will never cease. Thanks, Eva. We may get Chloe tamed yet!

'So tell me.' Sam and I have managed a quick hug and a few words while the photographer's concentrating on Phil and Gary and their mates. 'What was that all about – the little stunt with the bouquet?'

'Stunt?' I rub the top of my leg ruefully. I think I'll have a bruise where I landed. 'It wasn't ...'

'I knew it was going to fall apart,' she says, smiling at me. 'Is that what you were worried about?'

'It was Toffee's fault. He sat on it. We weren't going to tell you. I had to take half the flowers out.'

'Bloody cat!' She's laughing. 'Thanks, Abbie. For trying to preserve the ... dignity of the occasion!'

'Bugger the dignity. I just wanted to be the next one married,' I lie outrageously.

'Well, my love,' she responds perfectly seriously,

giving me a kiss on the cheek, 'maybe you will be. Wouldn't that be nice?'

Nice? More like a bloody miracle!

It's not that I don't like guys. I really do. But they're not usually particularly interested in me. As a teenager, I wasn't outgoing and flirty like Sam, or Julia. Especially Julia. I hardly ever had a boyfriend and, when I did, they quickly got bored with me – I was too shy, too quiet, and they moved on to someone more naturally vivacious and charming like Sam, or more obvious and predatory like *Julia*. I didn't have a sexual relationship until I was twenty – with Jamie. And the rare occasions that have happened *since* Jamie have been awful – as awful as I deserved for being desperate enough to go for a one-night stand.

'What's the matter with me?' I ask Sam sometimes. 'Am I going to end up old and lonely with knitting and a cat?'

'Of course you're not!' she retorts stoutly. 'You haven't got a cat!'

And I pretend to laugh.

But it's not really funny.

'Over here please! Sam! Bridesmaid!' The photographer's beckoning us urgently. 'Last one now, love – big group photo. Everyone in. Squash in together – that's it, girls. Family in the centre, please. Kiddies in the front. Put the jacket down, sonny, or put it on him, can you, Mum? Where's his mum? Can he put the jacket down for the photo? No? He's going to scream? OK, OK, no, fine, forget it, let him hold it. All right, sonny, hold the jacket. Now then, everyone smiling?'

84

'Where's the coffin?' says Granddad.

'It's a wedding, Dad. Not a funeral. What did you think? Think we're all dressed up for a funeral, bless your heart?'

'Well, what you been bloody crying for then, woman?' he snaps, reasonably enough I suppose. 'Who's dead?'

'No one's dead, Granddad.' Sam's trying now. 'I've just got married! Me and Phil!' She pulls her new husband by the arm and prods him in Frank's direction. 'We're Mr and Mrs Reynolds now. Look!'

She's trying to show him her wedding ring, but he ignores her completely, staring instead at Phil with a rudeness that wouldn't be tolerated in anyone under the age of eighty.

'Who the bloody hell are you?'

'I'm Phil, Frank. Remember? Sam and I . . .'

'Phil. Young Phil. I remember. I know who you are. You're the bugger who went off with that floozy Julia Johnson!'

The clarity of the occasional window of amazing, concise memory in an otherwise blank and confused mind is frightening. So frightening that I shudder, physically shaken beyond speech. Sam gasps; Phil sighs and closes his eyes. For a moment, it feels as though time has stopped. Rewind, rewind. Make it not have happened! Make him not have said it! But the old man's nodding, pleased with himself, satisfied that he's got it right. For once in his life he's got it right.

'That *floozy*!' he repeats with a toothy grin. He looks around him, suddenly confused again. 'Where is she?'

And, as in all good stories, the sun promptly goes behind a big, black cloud and it begins to rain.

Half past three

'Quick! Under the umbrella!'
  'In the car! Come on, quickly, Sam ...'
  'Mind your dress doesn't get wet!'
  'Mind your hair doesn't get ruined!'
  'Wait! What about the confetti?'

It's pandemonium. Aunties and cousins are squealing
and darting for cover, their hands over their heads to
protect their expensive hairdos. A couple of friends
are chucking handfuls of confetti in the general direction of the happy couple as they run towards the
waiting car. It lands in pink and blue soggy blobs on
the big black umbrella being held over their heads by
the best man. There's an anguished scream from
behind me as someone, with the best of intentions,
wrestles Troy's jacket out of his hands and puts it
around his shoulders to keep him dry.
  'My flowers! My flowers!'
I look round to see him scrabbling about on the wet
ground, crying loudly as he tries in vain to pick up
his trophies before they get trodden on by the hurrying crowds.
  'Troy.' I squat down next to him and try to make

myself heard above his yelling. 'Look, I've got lots more flowers for you. Nicer ones.'

This is a lie. The remains of the bouquet are horrible. They're not only squashed, they're soaking wet too, but he jumps to his feet, immediately distracted from his trampled collection.

'Can I have them?' he asks, quite shyly, holding out his hand. 'For me?'

'If you're a good boy and get in the car with Daddy, now – quickly, 'cos we're all getting wet.'

'Thanks, Abbie,' says David, quietly, taking Troy's hand. I pass the mangled bouquet to him.

'Daddy will hold it for you while you get in the car,' I reassure him.

So maybe Troy's going to be the next one to get married after all. Wouldn't surprise me.

'At least the rain held off for the photos,' says Christine with satisfaction as our driver turns onto the road ready to head off to the reception.

It's not just raining now. It's belting down against the windows in torrents. Within minutes the sky's turned from bright summer blue to black, and there's an almighty crash of thunder as the last few stragglers run from the churchyard to the car park, yelping and trying to protect their heads, their hats, their best new clothes. Two girls in identical white minidresses with identical tans hold on to each other as they leg it, screaming hysterically, through the puddles to a waiting purple Corsa. I look out sadly as we glide away, leaving the melee behind us. What a shame. What an abrupt ending.

'Never mind, Abbie,' says Eva, surprisingly. 'It was a lovely wedding. The rain can't be helped.'

'No,' agrees Christine. 'You can't help nature, love.'

She's hardly one to talk about nature, sitting there with her wet blue striped hair.

'And the reception's going to be lovely, too,' goes on Eva, trying desperately.

Chloe's staring moodily out of the window. 'Is it?' she returns, without looking round. 'I'd say that depends on whether we can shut Granddad up, really.'

Years ago, before he started to completely lose touch with reality, Frank had a bit of an eye for the girls. He wasn't exactly a dirty old man – not quite – but he used to like to chat up Sam's friends, have a joke with them, compliment them on their clothes or their hair or whatever and tell them, 'Oh, if only I was twenty years younger, my dear . . .', until they'd be squirming with embarrassment and Sam would wade in and tell him to stop showing off, leave her friends alone or she wouldn't bring them home any more. He never did it with me; I think I was too much a part of the furniture – he probably didn't even think of me as a girl. But Julia . . . well, she was a prime target. And the thing with Julia was that it didn't bother her in the least. If anything, I used to suspect that she almost encouraged it.

'She's a lovely girl, that Julia,' Frank would say, with a glint in his eye.

'You shouldn't be looking at her. You're *four times* her age! Behave yourself!' Sam used to say, pretending to be shocked but laughing at him.

But Julia would give him a coy look from beneath her eyelashes and simper, 'Thank you, Frank. You're looking very good yourself.'

Flirting – even with an old granddad! I was scandalised, disgusted. What was the matter with her? She had practically every boy in the whole school drooling after her, men turning their heads to stare after her wherever she went, and that *still* wasn't enough for her! She had to flirt with geriatrics!

'She's only humouring him,' Sam would say, nonchalantly. 'It's only a bit of fun and it keeps him happy.'

'It's not normal,' I insisted. 'You read about things like that in the Sunday papers. It leads to all sorts of stuff.'

'Abbie,' said Sam with great severity, 'my granddad is quite safe!'

We were probably about sixteen at that time. Soon after that I left school, and Julia and Sam went into the sixth form together to work for their A levels. Inevitably, they became closer, while I gradually became more and more marginalised. I used to sit in Sam's bedroom with the pair of them, feeling like a spare part as they discussed their lessons and the boys in the sixth form. They were the same boys that I'd hung around with the previous year and all the years before, but now, it was as if I didn't know them any more. I wasn't part of it all.

I wasn't sorry that I'd left school; I wasn't sorry that I was working in the library, part of the grown-up world, instead of still sitting in a classroom, listening to a teacher, like an overgrown child. But I was jealous of Julia. I was jealous of her intimacy with Sam – their shared confidences about sixth-form love affairs, their in-jokes about teachers and their conversations about homework and exams that I could never join in.

Frank might have thought she was lovely, but he had her measure, even in those days. It was when she was going out with a lad called Ben Edwards that he first called her by what became his nickname for her. We all used to meet up at Sam's house for our nights out. Ben was a quiet boy who used to sit in the lounge making polite conversation with Christine or Frank while he waited for us girls to get ready. He used to look at Julia, when she came downstairs dressed for the kill, with huge puppy-dog eyes full of admiration – mixed with a sort of fear. She wasn't kind to him. She played with him. Her favourite game was to flirt with David in front of him. David knew her too well to take any notice, but she'd sidle up to him, slide her arms round his neck, tickle his ears, plant playful kisses on his cheeks and all the while she'd be watching Ben squirming with unhappiness in his chair beside Granddad.

One evening, Frank couldn't stand to see it any more.

'Take no notice of her, young man!' he declared boldly to the hapless Ben, offering him a cigarette. 'She's a *floozy*, that's what she is!'

He always called her The Floozy after that – not that she minded. In fact I think she quite liked it. But I'm amazed he still remembers it. I wish to Christ he didn't!

It's still chucking it down when we turn into the entrance of the Dudley Park Golf Club. We drive through a puddle the size of a small lake, water sloshing up the sides of the car and spraying the windows. Lightning sears across the darkened sky, trees toss their heads in distress and the thunder rolls and crashes in angry spasms. I can't believe it was such a pretty day of warm sunshine when we set off for the church this afternoon.

'We're going to have to make a dash for it,' says Chloe, her hand on the car door.

'Hang on – there's a guy with an umbrella ...'

But Chloe and Eva have gone – jumping through the puddles hand in hand, shrieking and laughing, mud splashing their legs and rain drenching their hair. Poor Heather. All that work.

Christine and I get out of the car a little more sedately, accepting the shelter of the proffered umbrella and hurrying, faces screwed up against the torrent around us, to the entrance of the Tudor Barn.

It's a magnificent place for a wedding reception. Of course, it's no more Tudor than it's a barn. This whole place was only built when the golf club opened about ten years ago – I remember seeing it going up – but I think there was a barn just about here originally, all traces of which have gone, of course, apart from the name. The wooden beams and plasterwork owe more to twentieth-century craftsmanship than to anything from any bygone era. But they've done a good job on it. It's impressive.

Everyone's crowding into the bar, dripping rain into the champagne being handed to us by the serving staff. It's a shame, really: the plan was actually to do this bit outside in the sunshine, another photo opportunity and a chance for the children – especially a certain little boy I could mention – to run around and use up some energy before the sitting-down part.

'Hello again!' trills Sam, throwing one arm round my neck and the other round Christine's. 'Are you

OK, darlings? You didn't get too wet, did you? Have you got champagne? Do you want a top-up?'

'Don't worry about *us*, Mrs Reynolds!' I tease her. She still looks amazing – she'd never let a little thing like a thunderstorm get her down. 'Go and enjoy yourself, go on – it's your party!'

'Bloody weather!' comes a familiar voice from the doorway just as we're relaxing and sipping our champagne. 'Bloody soaked, I am! Bloody great, isn't it – father of the bride ends up cadging a lift in the back seat with the bloody kid, getting flowers all over me, and Frank going on and on about the Floozy ...'

'All right, Brian,' says Christine hurriedly, as people begin to turn round and smile. 'You're here now, no harm done.'

'Yes, I'm here *now*,' he says, crossly. 'But look at me! Soaked!'

'Brian,' I say, warily, moving towards him. I recognise the signs. He's going into a major strop. Please, no! *Not* today. 'Come on, have a glass of champagne. Doesn't Sam look gorgeous? Wasn't it a lovely wedding?'

'Lovely? Yes, of course it was lovely,' he says, and I start to breathe again. I didn't realise I'd been holding my breath. Thank God for that. He's not going to make a scene. Silly of me to think he would; even *Brian* wouldn't do that, not on his daughter's wedding day. I start to turn away again, smiling at Eva, who's taking a lobster canapé from a silver tray held by a solemn-looking teenager in a tiny black skirt and huge white shirt.

'Yes, lovely,' continues Brian suddenly, 'till I get left behind at the church, getting soaked in the bloody rain because *that dyke* takes *my place* in the bloody wedding car!'

Shit. Eva's dropped the canapé. Troy's picking it up off the floor and suddenly, out of nowhere, Heather's screaming from the other side of the room: 'Put it down! Troy! Put it down! Don't let him eat it! Don't let him ... no! Troy! He's allergic! He's allergic to shellfish!'

Like I say. Shit. Just when it was going so well.

Quarter to four

The ensuing panic is mainly about Heather rather than Troy. She's got herself into such a state that there's a moment when, in between shrieks of hysteria, she looks as though she's forgotten to breathe. I'm just about to wade in and slap her round the face when she begins to gasp, flailing her arms like a fish out of water, her eyes growing round with fear. Blimey! Now what? Is *she* the one having an allergic reaction? David, pushing his way through the well-meaning but totally useless crowd, takes her by the shoulders, gives her a little shake and says, very calmly, 'Quick puffs *out*, Heather! Has anyone got a brown paper bag?'

Yeah, like it's the sort of thing everyone brings with them to a wedding.

'To be sick in?' asks Christine, looking like she's going to be sick herself.

'No – for her to breathe in. It's a panic attack – she's hyperventilating.'

Even as one of the catering staff runs out to the kitchen and comes back with some sort of greaseproof paper affair that seems to serve the purpose, I'm watching David with admiration and wondering where he learned his first aid.

'She does this sometimes,' he says. There's a note of weariness in his voice. Poor Heather – it's not her fault, surely? 'Where's Troy?'

That's great, that is. We're all so concerned with Heather not breathing, we've forgotten who it was she was panicking about.

'Er . . . I think . . . he was over there . . . with Eva.' I look around me wildly. Where's Eva? Where's Chloe? Where the hell's Troy? Bloody hell, he could be having a fit, or an asthma attack, or whatever the hell he has when he eats shellfish, while we're all standing around watching his mother breathing into a paper bag.

'This is *typical*,' says David tightly, half under his breath, abandoning Heather on the floor and pushing his way back through the crowd and surveying the room.

'Hello, Daddy!' sings a little voice suddenly. I never thought I'd be so relieved to see the little sod. He skips towards us, looking the picture of health, if a little red in the face. 'I did go upside down!'

'You did . . . *what*?' says David, crouching down to pick him up. 'Troy, listen to me. Did you eat any of the lobster? The fish – the red stuff – you picked up off the floor?'

'Yes, Daddy,' says Troy very solemnly. 'Sorry, Daddy.'

'What do we do?' I'm asking, trying not to frighten Troy by sounding too frantic. 'Do we rush him to hospital? Does he have to have an injection? Will he be OK?'

'Let me look in your mouth, Troy. Is your tongue swelling up? Did you eat very much of the red stuff?'

I can't believe how calm David's being. I suppose he's used to it.

'But Daddy!' Troy's giggling as David's trying to look down his throat. 'Daddy, I did go *upside down*!'

'It's OK, David.' Chloe has appeared out of the ladies', accompanied by Eva, who she pushes forward, looking at her with a proud smile. 'Eva's saved his life.'

'Eva?' David looks at her, confused. 'What . . .?'

'I just turned him upside down,' she says modestly, 'and slapped him on the back, that's all. It was only a tiny bit of lobster. He'd only just swallowed it.' She unwraps a piece of toilet paper and displays a gruesome piece of red slime, about the size of a fingernail. 'Would it have done him any harm?'

'No.' David smiles, setting the child back down on the floor. 'No, I'm sure it wouldn't have. I think, to be quite honest,' he adds, lowering his voice, 'he'd have to eat a whole lobster to even so much as come out in a rash.'

'But . . . !' I protest. That can't be right. Heather was beside herself! 'But . . . I thought he had an allergy! A dangerous one!'

'He's got a few . . . slight sensitivities. Like most kids. His face and lips came up a bit red and swollen once when Heather gave him a crab stick.' He shakes his head. 'He was only a baby. She shouldn't have been giving him crab at that age, anyway.'

'It's worrying, though, isn't it?'

'Abbie,' he says quietly, watching Troy running off to play with some other children, 'bringing up a child is a constant worry, one way or another, if that's how you choose to look at it.'

I don't know what he means, really. I'm glad

Troy's all right. But Heather's still puffing away into the paper bag.

'You should apologise!' Chloe's saying fiercely to Brian, who's doing his best to ignore her and pour champagne down his throat. 'You were *so rude* to Eva! It's all your fault!'

'How do you work that out?' he retorts crossly. 'How come everything's always my fault?'

Because you're a bad-tempered, foul-mouthed, fucking ignorant male chauvinist pig? springs to mind but it's probably not up to me to tell him.

'You made Eva drop the lobster canapé. If Troy stopped breathing it would be on your conscience for the rest of your life!' she says dramatically.

'Perhaps,' says Brian, 'you shouldn't have brought her here. Then she wouldn't have had to drop the bloody thing.'

'I'd rather have Eva here than you! I hate you! You're the most miserable, horrible father in the world!' Chloe shoots back, beginning to cry.

Oh dear.

'Come on, Chloe, don't cry.' I try to console her, but I'm beaten to it by Eva, who takes her arm and leads her away, wordlessly, to the other side of the bar, where they sit down together with their hands entwined and their heads touching. I watch them for a minute, thinking that perhaps it makes sense. If I had a father like Brian, perhaps it would have put me off men for life. Perhaps I'd feel safer with a nice girlfriend. I'd like to say as much to Brian, but what's the point in antagonising him any further? It'd only ruin the day.

When I glance round at him, though, he's staring

97

at Chloe and Eva himself. And there's a strange expression on his face. If I didn't know him better, I'd think it was a look of regret.

We all feel a bit distrustful of the canapés now. The teenagers in black skirts and white blouses seem to be on a mission to get us to scoff the whole lot in as short a time as possible. Maybe it's an attempt at a record-breaker. There's a record for most things these days, isn't there? It wouldn't surprise me at all if there was one for the most canapés devoured in an hour at a wedding reception.

'Anchovy and olive, madam?'

'Cream cheese and red pepper?'

'These are smoked salmon, madam.'

I feel obliged to take one from every platter, for fear of offending anyone. Who knows? They might get paid by results. A fiver for every empty platter. I'd feel terrible if the Anchovy girl went home with less pay because I'd stuffed myself with too many from the Cream Cheese girl. I don't even like anchovies, but she doesn't seem to be having much luck getting rid of them and I feel sorry for her.

'Don't look so worried!' says Phil. 'It can't get any worse!'

'It can!' I say gloomily, before I can stop myself. 'Oh, sorry, Phil. I'm only joking. It's going marvellously.'

'You're a rubbish liar, Abbie!' He laughs. 'But actually I *do* think it's going marvellously, though. Can I take one of those?'

He helps himself to an anchovy canapé from the pile on my paper plate. 'Mm. Lovely. Why are you hoarding anchovies, Abbs?'

'I've no idea. I can't stand them. I just felt sorry for the girl. Here,' I add as he gives me an odd look, 'take the plateful. Please!'

'You're a funny girl, Abbie,' he says in quite an affectionate tone. 'I wonder if you'll be the next one married? Eh?'

'Don't be silly,' I say, shrugging uncomfortably. 'I haven't even got a boyfriend.'

'I know. But that's only because you haven't moved on yet.'

'Moved on?' I ask him, frowning. 'Moved on from what?'

'Jamie!' he says, shaking his head at me, his mouth full of anchovy. 'As you know perfectly well!'

I don't, actually. I don't know it at all.

I've moved on from Jamie. I have! I've *so* moved on, I can hardly even remember him!

Let me think, now. Let me try to think what he looked like. OK. He was tall, and dark, and he had those very dark brown eyes that go almost black in certain lights – low lights. He had a little mole on his neck, the left side. He wasn't too skinny, quite kind-of chunky. Muscular. His arms were strong and brown – lovely arms, he had, actually. He smiled a lot. He used to look at me with his head on one side – like he was considering me carefully – and smile that slow, lazy sort of smile at me, and I'd just melt inside . . .

But I'm over all that now. Ages ago – years ago, in fact. I never even think about him now. I don't know what Phil's talking about.

'Jamie?' I say, giving him an incredulous look like he might have suggested I was hankering after Tony Blair or Mickey Mouse. 'Don't be ridiculous. I've forgotten all about him.'

'Ah,' he says lightly. 'Ah, but have you *forgiven* him?'

That word again. I mill around the bar area, talking to an uncle here, an old school friend there, trying to avoid the platters of canapés, thinking all the time: *Forgiveness*. Why can't I ever get away from it? Why does it haunt me? Didn't I hear enough about it, sitting through a million church services, chanting words I didn't understand?

'Hello, dear.'

'Dad!' I start in surprise. How come he appears just as I'm picturing him at the pulpit, giving one of his sermons about forgiveness?

'Haven't missed too much, have I?' he asks, shaking rain off his hair. 'Just had to tidy up the church a bit and lock up . . .'

Missed too much? Only a couple of arguments, a panic attack and the forcible regurgitation of a lobster canapé. Nothing out of the ordinary, really, for the Patterson family.

'Hello, Vicar!' calls Phil before I can reply. He and Sam are elbowing their way across the room to greet him. Phil shakes his hand and Sam kisses him on the cheek.

'Thanks, John. The service was just perfect.'

'You look stunning, my dear.' Dad's very fond of Sam. We've spent so much of our lives together, after all, that Mum and Dad often say it's been like having an extra daughter. 'And you, young man, you look stunning too!' he adds, giving Phil a playful punch on the arm. 'Congratulations to you both'. He raises his champagne glass. 'I'm quite sure you'll be very happy.'

'I'm glad you came,' I tell him quietly as the bride and groom move off to talk to someone else. 'I think it means a lot to them.'

'I won't stay for the meal, though,' he says, his smile fading slightly.

'Because of Mum. No. Of course.'

We're both silent for a minute. I look at him, watch the shadow passing across his face as his sips his champagne. It's not fair! I feel the old resentment filling me up again. Why should he have to suffer? Why should my mum have to suffer? Why should she still be having flashbacks, and needing counselling, and having to skulk in the house, afraid to go out, afraid to face new people, afraid of crowds? It isn't *fair*!

'How can you bear it, Dad?' I blurt out, suddenly exasperated by the whole thing. 'Those kids ruined Mum's life. It's not fair!'

We've had this conversation before, many times before.

'I know it's not fair,' he says, sighing. 'Don't you think I feel that too, Abbie?'

'So how can you do it? How can you stand up there on Sundays asking people to "forgive those who trespass against them"? You *shouldn't* have forgiven those yobs, Dad! They didn't deserve to be forgiven!'

'They called the ambulance,' says Dad, giving me a very direct look. 'They sat with your mum till it came. They were only *kids*, Abbie. They didn't mean for it to happen. She fell.'

'It was their fault!'

'Not directly.'

'If they hadn't called her names ...'

'I know. But they were sorry. And they weren't to

101

know that your mum had such a nervous disposition.'

'Only because of *them*,' I mutter, feeling the anger swelling again.

'No, Abbie. She was *always* afraid to go out. It was always ... a problem. She coped with it as best she could. She was incredibly brave; it was so hard for her. But after the accident – she just couldn't do it any more.'

I stare at him. I'm thinking back to my childhood. Remembering my mum getting ready to go out to church. Seeing her shaking as she put on her coat. Seeing my dad holding her arm, encouraging her, supporting her.

'You knew that, Abbie,' he says, more gently. 'You've always known that.'

Of course I have. How have I managed to distort it in my mind over the years? Turned it around so that I was convinced it was all the fault of those kids? How have I let myself become so horribly vindictive?

'You need to let it go. For your own sake,' says Dad, giving me a quick hug. 'I know you hate the word, Abbie, but there's a good reason for forgiveness – a selfish reason, if you like. It makes you feel better.'

He grins cheerfully as if he's told me something really good, and I stand and watch him as he walks away from me to talk to Christine and Brian.

I love you, Dad. But I'm sorry. You're talking crap.

102

Quarter past four

Heather looks pale and shocked. She's sitting down with her head resting in her hands.

'Do you want a drink of water?' I ask her.

Nobody else seems to be looking after her.

'Thanks, Abbie.' She still sounds breathless. She's clutching the paper bag as if it's all that stands between her and an early demise. 'Yes, water would be good. Thanks.'

I wonder if I should have offered wine, or brandy. What are you supposed to do with people who've just had a panic attack? Buggered if I know. Why did I never learn any first aid? One of our librarians, Corrine, is our nominated first-aider. She's a right bossy cow, but I have to hand it to her – she knew exactly what to do when a kid had an asthma attack in the library a couple of months ago. And when an old lady collapsed with pains in her chest last year. Me – all I'd be able to do if anyone's taken ill and Corrine's not around is get them a drink of water. And look up their symptoms in the *A–Z Emergency Medical Directory*, I suppose. At least I know whereabouts it is in Non-fiction.

'Here you are. Drink some of this.' I sit down next

to Heather and pass her the water. 'Are you feeling any better?'

'Not too bad,' she says, shakily. 'Sorry.'

'Don't be silly. It's not your fault.' I'm not sure what to say. I never knew she suffered from this sort of thing. 'Troy's absolutely fine. He's playing with the other children over there, look.'

'I know. I heard what Eva did, Abbie. She saved his life.'

'Well ...' I don't want to sound uncaring, but on the other hand – let's not get this too much out of proportion. Before we know it, The Saving of Troy's Life will be taking over from Sam and Phil's wedding as the event of the day. It'll be reported in the local paper and Eva will be nominated for a Lifesavers Award. 'Actually, Heather, I don't think his life was in any danger there to be honest. He'd only eaten a tiny crumb of lobster, and it didn't seem to have done him any harm ...'

'Oh, that's your opinion, is it?' she retorts, spitting her mouthful of water at me. 'Your considered opinion, Abbie? And remind me again – how many children have you brought up? Eh?'

'Sorry ... I, er, look – I wasn't saying I was an expert or anything, just that he seemed ...' I tail away awkwardly. 'He seemed fine.'

'*Seeming fine* is just not good enough, though, Abbie! Children can *seem* fine, but you never *know* what's going on inside them. Troy has all manner of medical problems – problems you wouldn't even *begin* to understand.'

'God! I'm sorry, Heather. I ... I honestly had no idea. You never said! What sort of problems?' I'm watching Troy, now, tearing the petals off the last few flowers from the bridal bouquet and trying to stuff them down the neck of a little girl, who's screaming in terror and crying for her mummy. He certainly doesn't give the appearance of a sickly child. In fact, I've often thought that a few well-placed non-accidental injuries might improve his behaviour. Now I feel really bad. 'It's not anything serious, is it?'

'He's *delicate*.' Heather sniffs and starts to tremble again. 'He ... He's prone to *illnesses* and *accidents*.'

'Illnesses?' I prompt her. 'Accidents?'

'Come on, Abbie!' she exclaims, giving me an impatient glare. 'You *know* he had chickenpox a few months ago!'

'But ... surely all children have ...'

'And as for coughs and colds! He's *always* got the sniffles.'

'But that's not ...'

'*And* he fell off the climbing frame when he was at playgroup. Right from the top! I was furious! They don't supervise the children properly, you know. He should *never* have been allowed up there. I've warned his teacher, now he's at school, that he's not, under any circumstances, to be allowed to do anything potentially dangerous. He's far too delicate!'

I can't believe this. I mean, I know Heather's always seemed a bit of a fussy mum, and I've heard David moaning often enough about how she won't let the kid do this, that, or the other. But ... *delicate*? Troy?

'Sometimes,' says Heather, shaking her head sadly to herself, 'sometimes, Abbie, I wonder how other parents manage. I mean – it's a constant worry, bringing up a child.'

'Well,' I reassure her with a smile, 'at least you've got David. He's very calm and sensible, isn't he?'

Even if you're not.

To my surprise, she snorts with laughter at this.

Is she drunk? That's definitely only water I've given her, but what else has she already had today? One glass of champagne? Surely Christine's cheery brandy wasn't that strong?

'What's so funny?'

But she just shakes her head as if it's a private joke she can't possibly share with me. I can't make her out. She's a nice enough girl, Heather, but we've never been particularly close. This sounds awful – in fact it makes me sound like a total bitch – but I've never really understood what David sees in her. They've never seemed the slightest bit suited to each other. David's very clever. He didn't have a university education like Chloe but he's got a very scientific mind; he works in a pharmacy. He's taken all his exams while he's been working. I've got a lot of respect for David. He's so different from his father; he works hard, looks after his family, doesn't go out on the booze or lose his temper. He's kind and funny, and interesting to talk to, and I just can't imagine how he can sit and listen to Heather prattling on and on, the way she does, about shopping and the telly and what's wrong with the royal family. I suppose love's like that. You can't help who you fall for. Perhaps it's that thing about opposites attracting.

'It's all a bit complicated!' Heather says, when she finally manages to stop laughing for a minute.

'What is?' I've lost the thread of this. 'Troy's allergies?'

At this, to my consternation, she throws back her

106

head and begins to laugh again, uproariously. Did I say something funny?

Actually, she's looking quite dangerous. She's laughing her head off, but she doesn't really look as if she's the slightest bit amused. What do you do about someone who's going hysterical? I've already done the glass of water bit. Where's the bloody *A–Z Emergency Medical Directory* when I need it?

'Calm down!' I try, looking around me desperately. People are beginning to notice. She'll be carted off and locked up if she keeps this up. 'Shall we go outside? Get some fresh air?'

It's still pissing down with rain, but I'll risk it.

'No. I'm OK.' She sits up and stops laughing again as abruptly as she started. 'I'm sorry. I'm just feeling a bit overemotional, Abbie – what with it being a wedding day, and everything.' She smoothes down her skirt, fiddles with her hair, gets a tissue out of her bag and blows her nose. 'Take no notice of me.'

Just like that?

'But ...'. I lower my voice. 'Is everything all right? Have you and David had a row or something? Was it the thing about Troy's shoes ...?'

'No. Everything's fine,' she says brusquely as if nothing's happened. As if she hasn't just been sitting here laughing like a madwoman on drugs. 'Just forget it, OK?'

'OK,' I mutter unhappily, looking at her out of the corner of my eye. I can't help wondering if she's suddenly going to start up again. You know, tear her clothes and thrash around. I once saw a woman doing stuff like that in church when Dad was preaching about the Holy Spirit. It freaked me out so badly I wouldn't go the next week, but Dad said she was having a nervous breakdown and it had far more to do with her husband sleeping with the au pair, than with the demons she'd been yelling about taking over her body.

'Sorry,' says Heather again, quietly.

She sounds a lot more calm now, at any rate.

I think I could do with a drink.

At the bar, Frank's sitting on the corner stool, leaning against the wall, looking as though someone's propped him up there and left him. He's got a pint glass of beer in his hand and his eyes already look glazed. Not good.

'Hello, Frank. Are you OK?' I ask him, warily, as I wait for my glass of wine to be poured.

'Julia?' he says, his eyes lighting up.

Bloody hell, he needs his eyesight testing.

'No, Frank. I'm Abbie.'

And I'm short, thin, mousy and plain. Could I be any more different from the gorgeous Julia if I walked around disguised as the Hunchback of Notre-Dame?

'Where's Julia?' he says, looking around wildly. Shit, not this again. Why, when he hasn't mentioned her for at least six months, does he have to start raving on about bloody Julia today, of all days, when he doesn't even know what day it is, let alone whether it's a wedding or a fucking funeral?

'Not here,' I snap. 'She's not here, OK?'

'Is she dead?'

'Dead?' I feel like screaming. How do I get myself into these conversations? Aunties and uncles are looking on with interest, obviously listening. A cousin of Phil's stops in mid-gulp of his beer, nearly choking. 'Dead? Of course she's not dead!'

108

'Where is she, then?' He looks at me anxiously, his eyes seeking reassurance. He doesn't even know who I am and he's looking at *me* to reassure him. Suddenly it hits me: he's frightened. It must be so frightening to be over eighty and unable to remember who anyone is – unable to remember your own family; where you are, what you're doing here. Poor old bugger. Everyone's so impatient with him, and all he wants is to be *told*.

'Julia's not living around here any more, Frank,' I tell him much more gently. 'She ... moved away.'

He regards me solemnly for a few seconds. Takes a sip of his beer. Nods wisely to himself. Good, good – I think he understands. I think I can walk away now; talk to someone else. Try to have a conversation with someone who *isn't* barking mad, before I end up like it myself.

'Moved away, you say,' he repeats calmly.

'That's right. Yes.'

'Bloody good job too!' he cries, so unexpectedly I nearly drop my wine. 'Good riddance to her! The *floozy*!'

'He's not wrong, though.'

I didn't realise that Brian's been listening. Although, to be fair, most of the crowd in the bar must have heard that last outburst.

'Let's not start on all that,' I say. 'Please, Brian! Today –'

'Is a special day. Do you think I don't realise that, Abbie?'

I look at him in surprise. He sounds ... well, he sounds sober. And almost normal. Not like Brian at all.

'Do you think I don't realise I've already upset one daughter?' he continues, looking away from me, looking down at the carpet. 'I'm not about to do anything to spoil the day for the other one.'

'Well, good . . .'

'Of course I'm not. What did you think? That'd I'd make a scene? Start a row? Cause trouble?'

Well, er . . . yes, I'd have to say that those were the kind of things that had been going through my mind, yes.

He looks back at me, clocks the expression on my face and shakes his head sadly. 'I'm not about to ruin my own daughter's wedding. What do you take me for, Abbie? Some kind of fucking *lout*?'

Well, now. That's a tricky one, isn't it?

Quarter to five

'I knew I shouldn't have come,' says Chloe sulkily.

Eva's gone to get another drink and I've stopped to ask Chloe if she's all right now, after the contretemps with her father. Big mistake.

'Don't be ridiculous. You had to come. You're Sam's sister. You're a bridesmaid.'

'I hate it. I hate being a bridesmaid. I hate weddings. I hate ...'

'Chloe! This is *not* about you. It's ...'

'Sam's wedding. How could I possibly forget? Seems like it's all anyone cares about in this family. Sam's boyfriend, Sam's new flat, Sam's engagement, Sam's hen party, Sam's wedding – is Sam the only person in the universe, or does it just feel that way?'

'I can't believe you're saying this. For once in your life, Chloe Patterson, the world is *not* revolving around you ...!'

To my surprise, instead of shouting back at me or going into a mega sulk, Chloe looks down and wipes away a tear.

'Don't *you* have a go at me too, Abbie.'

I'm not fooled by the pathetic little voice.

I am a bit taken aback by it, though, to be honest.

111

'Well, I'm sorry, Chloe. I know your dad hasn't been very fair ...'

'That's putting it mildly, isn't it?'

'Yes. Yes, you're right: he's been a complete arse.'

She looks up at me with surprise in her eyes.

'Well, I mean about Eva,' I amend. 'But on the other hand, *you* weren't very fair, were you? Springing it on them? *Today*?'

'Eva wanted me to. She didn't want us to have to pretend. She's ... quite big on honesty and openness.'

'That's good. That's great, yes. But she probably wasn't reckoning on your father being so ...'

'Homophobic, I think is the word you're looking for.'

'No. I don't think he is, really. Just old-fashioned. And easily shocked.'

Why am I defending Brian, all of a sudden?

'Well, I hate him. He's ruined my life. Eva's probably going to finish with me after this.'

'I don't think so.' I smile at her. It's not easy. God, she's a self-obsessed little madam, isn't she? 'Eva seems to have a bit more staying power than that, I think.'

'Do you like her?' asks Chloe, almost shyly.

Chloe? Being coy? This is a first.

'She ... seems nice. I've only just met her, haven't I?'

'She's been so good to me. She's so much more mature than I am, of course. I've grown up a lot since I met her.'

I wish I could say it shows.

*

112

Chloe was always like this. I've known her since she was a baby and she hasn't changed. Attention-seeking, from the moment she could sit up in her pram: arms outstretched, mouth wide open, scream-ing. *Me, me, me*! I think it was the first word she learned.

When Chloe was about twelve, Brian was retired from the police on medical grounds. He was only fifty but he'd developed diabetes and arthritis; he was offered a desk job but his pride wouldn't let him accept it. It was a difficult time in the Patterson house. Christine worked four mornings a week in Tesco but she had to go full-time because Brian's disability money wasn't enough to live on. She told me, much later, that actually she'd gone full-time because she couldn't stand being in the house with him in his permanent foul mood. To make matters worse, it was around this time that Frank had a couple of strokes and started to become vague. When Christine came home from a long shift on the check-out, it would often be to an atmosphere of furious resentment. Chloe would be trying to do her home-work, Brian would be slobbing out on the sofa with the football or the racing on the TV, loud enough to shake the walls, and Frank would be sitting in his pyjamas with his hat on, looking bewildered.

I was round there one evening, waiting for Sam to come home from work, when Chloe flounced down-stairs, her cheeks flushed. She slammed doors, threw her books down and shoved past me in the kitchen where I was talking to Christine and helping her with the dinner.

'I can't work like this!' she stormed. 'I've had enough!'

113

'Brian!' called Christine, wiping her brow from the heat of the cooker. 'Turn the TV down!'

'It's no good, Mum,' retorted Chloe. 'It'll just be the same thing tomorrow, and the next day – he has the telly blaring, and shouts at me if I try to turn it down, and Granddad keeps wandering into my room in his underpants asking who I am, and Sam comes home and plays her music and you keep asking me to lay the table, or wipe the dishes, or feed the cat ... and *I'm trying to revise*!'

'I'm sorry, dear. I know it's difficult, but it's a bit hard for *all* of us at the moment ... we all have to try ...'

'No, Mum! *You* can try! I'm not! I'm going!'

'Going where?'

'To live at Vanessa's house. I've just phoned her. She's got bunk beds in her room. It's quiet there. *Her* parents don't shout. *Her* granddad lives in a home.'

'Don't be silly, dear. Look, I'll talk to your father about the TV ...'

'I don't care! I'm going!'

It lasted for two days. Apparently Vanessa's parents objected, not surprisingly, to having another mouth to feed. There was a huge fracas, Chloe refused to speak to Vanessa ever again, and after a mega session of door slamming and stamping up and down stairs, things gradually returned to normal.

Afterwards, Sam laughed and said it was the quietest two days they'd ever had at home. But, if you want to know the truth, it wasn't really like that. Far from being relieved and happy that she was gone, there was a lot of crying, blaming and soul-searching going on amongst the rest of the family during those

114

two days. There was a new rule about the TV volume enforced by Christine afterwards, and Brian took on responsibility for making sure Granddad got dressed properly and stayed out of Chloe's room.

So she got her way, again, as always.

But when I think about it now, I wonder if actually she had a point.

Like now, to be perfectly honest.

'Where's Julia, Abbie?'

Jesus, if I hear that name one more time I think I'll scream.

'She doesn't live round here any more ...' I start to explain to this auntie of Sam's, trying to be polite, swallowing back the temptation to retort *What's it to you?*

'I know that, dear. Moved to Eastbourne, didn't she?'

'Bournemouth.'

'Same difference. Not very far away, really.'

'Well, actually ...'

'I mean, surely she could have come over for the wedding? You three girls were always such *great chums*, I can't believe she wouldn't have come, just from *Eastbourne*! I mean, it's not as though it's the end of the earth, is it?'

'Bournemouth. It's a bit further ...'

'Yes, but really! Malcolm!' She turns to her husband, who's been standing beside her nursing a glass of champagne and looking fed up. 'Malcolm, Bournemouth isn't *that* far, is it, dear? I mean, in terms of coming to a wedding – one of your best friends' weddings—'

Oh, *why* doesn't this bloody woman shut up? I feel

115

an almost irresistible urge to rip off her silly green hat, feather and all, and stuff it into her stupid mouth.

'Actually she didn't want to come,' I interrupt her bluntly.

'Oh!' She takes a step backwards. 'Did you hear that, Malcolm?' Malcolm nods dejectedly. 'That pretty girl Julia! The one who moved to Eastbourne! Abbie says she didn't want to . . .'

'She was invited,' I add quickly. 'But she didn't reply.'

'Well!' The feather is quivering in indignation. She turns to her husband again. 'Young people these days,' she says in a stage whisper as if I'm not supposed to hear it. 'No manners! *Fancy* not replying to a wedding invitation! I'm *very* surprised at Julia.'

Ah, but did you really know her?

Did anyone?

David's talking to Sam when I finally manage to join her.

'She's just overwrought,' I hear him saying, holding his sister's hand reassuringly. 'Please don't worry. You know what she's like.'

'Heather?' I assume.

'Yes. Troy's absolutely fine,' he continues to Sam. 'Look at him!'

We all look. Troy is chasing another child in and out of the legs of the adults, tumbling and giggling and red-cheeked with juvenile vitality.

'Certainly doesn't look like there's much wrong with him,' I agree, smiling.

'There isn't. Heather . . . worries too much.'

'Isn't that normal, though? For a mother?' There's a fleeting look of something like pain in David's eyes.

116

I don't know what I've said to cause it, but I'm horrified. 'Or a father!' I add quickly. I know he loves the boy. Perhaps I've offended him. 'Any sort of parent, really. Isn't it all part of the whole thing – parenthood – the anxiety, the worry?'

I'm gabbling, now. This is *so* not helping, Abbie. Shut up before you dig yourself in any deeper!

'Not that I know anything about it, of course,' I say desperately. 'I realise I'm hardly qualified to talk about parenthood, what with not having any children of my own, or even *knowing* any children, really, other than Troy.'

This time there's a look that passes between David and Sam. It's a look of sorrow. For a moment, it makes me shiver.

'What?'

They both blink and look at me as if they've only just realised I'm there.

'What have I said?'

'Nothing,' says Sam, laughing quietly and squeezing my arm. 'You're fine, Abbie – don't worry about it.'

'But . . .'

'Everything's fine, Abbie,' says David firmly. 'We're going through for the meal soon. Do you want another drink?'

'I don't really want to go back to the bar,' I admit. 'Your granddad's propping it up and he keeps asking me about . . .' Oh no. Don't mention Julia. 'He keeps embarrassing me.'

'Surely not!' says Sam with a burst of laughter. 'That doesn't sound like Granddad!'

'As long as he keeps his trousers on,' says David, 'I can forgive him anything, today.' Don't speak too

117

soon. 'I'll get you a drink, Abbs. What do you want?'

'Is he OK?' I ask Sam as I watch him making his way to the bar. 'He seems a bit . . . sad.'

'Oh, he'll be all right. He'll survive.'

'Is it . . . Heather? Have they had a row?'

'Well, you know what it's like. Relationships,' she says vaguely, waving her hand at me as if she could wave away my anxieties.

If only it were that easy. I'd wave my hands and make the anxieties of the whole world disappear. I'd do anything, right now – anything at all – to make today free of anxieties for Sam. And for David, I realise suddenly. And for David.

I've always been fond of David. He's Sam's twin brother, of course, so it goes without saying that they're quite similar in many ways so, obviously, I'm going to find the same characteristics likeable in them both. That's all.

There was a time, when we were all about fourteen, when I decided I fancied him. I'd never had a boyfriend, not even the type of boyfriend that you sat next to in the classroom, learned how to kiss with at lunchtime behind the bike sheds and wrote his name all over your school stationery to show off to your friends. David was in a different class from Sam and me – the teachers thought it was a good idea, for some reason, to separate twins – but he was always nice to me, unlike most of the boys in my own class. It was just brotherly, really, but I was desperate to be able to say I was 'going out' with someone – so I started writing 'David' with hearts and arrows on my rough notebooks and pencil case. Of course, Sam thought it was hysterical.

'You fancy my brother?' she screamed, attracting the attention of Julia and all the other girls, who crowded round to get in on the gossip. *'Really?'*

'So?' I said, going red and doodling some more hearts on my English file. I couldn't back down now. 'So what if I do?'

'Does he know?' squealed Julia. 'Shall we tell him?'

No! I wanted to scream. *I'd rather die and be chopped up into pieces and be fed to the school goldfish!*

'OK,' I said, trying to sound nonchalant. 'If you want.'

The deputation to David's form room after school was led by Sam and Julia, followed by half-a-dozen giggling girls, with me bringing up the rear, burning up with embarrassment, sweating like a pig, dragging my feet, feeling like someone going to their execution. If only!

'Hi, David!' crooned Julia in the honeyed, flirtatious tone she'd managed to acquire even at that tender age.

David looked up from his huddle of raucous mates and their animated discussion about the big match. Imagine it. A fourteen-year-old boy, confronted in his own form room, in front of his own gang, by his sister and her horrible friends, suspecting he's about to be shown up in some unforgivable way.

'What do *you* want?' he aimed viciously at Sam.

'Just to tell you something,' she giggled, trying to nudge me to the front of the group.

'Piss off, stupid. Tell me at home.'

'We want to tell you *now*, though, don't we, girls?' sang out Julia, to an answering chorus of more giggles.

'Go on, tell him, Abbie!' taunted Julia.

119

'*You* tell him,' I said, miserably, wishing I'd never started this. Wishing I'd gone straight home, or even gone to the detention room (even though I hadn't got a detention) – anywhere, anywhere in the world rather than agreeing to come here with this lot.

'Piss off,' said David again. 'Stupid cows.'

'Abbie Vincent fancies you!' sang out Julia. 'She *lurves* you! She wants to marry you and have your babies!'

'I never said that!' I shouted, feeling tears of humiliation pricking behind my eyes. But nobody could hear me above the din from the other girls, shrieking with laughter and excitement.

'Well?' persisted Julia, finally managing to yank me to the front and pushing me in front of her like an exhibit. 'Well, do you want to go out with her?'

I wasn't one of the prettiest girl in the class, or one of the cleverest, or even one of the best at sports or art or music – the saving graces for many otherwise unremarkable pupils. The boys were all watching David with expressions that could only be called derision. *Go out with HER*? I could see it written all over their faces. *Er . . . I think NOT!*

I stood, like a rabbit in the headlights, waiting for the crushing retort David was bound to deliver. The retort his mates would expect. Sam took hold of my arm and gave it a tug.

'Come on, Abbie. Let's go. This is stupid.' Her face was screwed up with concern and regret. It'd started off as a bit of fun, but as usual, Julia had taken it too far.

As we turned to go, accompanied by groans of disappointment from the other girls, there was a sudden shout from behind us.

'OK!' It was loud, it was clear, and it sounded . . . well, it sounded sincere. 'OK, I'll go out with her.'

'Fucking hell, Patterson,' sneered one of his mates as I turned back in amazement. 'Are you *sure*?'

He told me later, during one of the few walks round the playing field that constituted our 'going out' – before exams, football matches and teenage life in general took over and it fizzled out the way these things do – that he'd always fancied me anyway. But I knew it wasn't true; he'd done it to be nice to me. He'd seen how humiliated I was and he'd helped me out, even though it meant running the gauntlet of his classmates' teasing.

I liked him better for that than if he'd actually fancied me.

Five o'clock

Sam didn't want a traditional 'Top Table' – she didn't like the idea of sitting awkwardly staring out across the room with nobody sitting opposite her to talk to. So the top table is a round one like all the others, the middle one of three that have been set on a raised area at one end of the room – a lovely idea, putting the bride and groom where everyone can see them.

Everyone else has been shown to their tables before Sam and Phil walk in to the function room. A cheer goes up then, and everyone starts clapping as if they've only just seen them for the first time. They're sharing their table with Christine, Brian and Phil's parents Duncan and Helen. Frank's being looked after by a couple of aunts and uncles on another table, and I'm on the table nearest to the bride's – with David on one side of me, next to Troy and Heather, and Gary on the other side, next to Chloe and Eva, for whom an extra chair and extra place setting have been hurriedly fitted in thanks to some discreet words to the caterers from David. We're a bit squashed, although Troy fortunately doesn't take up too much room.

'What's this, Mummy?' shouts Troy as soon as he's

sitting in his place, with a napkin tucked firmly into his shirt collar.

'It's a camera, Troy. Put it down.'

There's a disposable camera on every table – a nice touch. One of Phil's ideas. A good lot of informal pics of the reception for the happy couple.

'*I* want the camera,' says Troy in a deceptively pleasant voice. 'Please, Mummy.'

Here we go.

'No, Troy.' Heather's voice rises only slightly. 'Put it down. Now.'

'But what's it for?'

'For grown-ups to take pictures.'

Bad mistake.

'*I* want to take pictures. Let *me* take pictures. Daddy, *I* want to take pictures!' The tone of his voice is definitely not quite so pleasant now.

'Troy,' whispers David, 'nobody is allowed to take pictures until the bride and groom have said it's OK to start. All right?'

'Who? Sammy?'

'Yes. Sammy's in charge today. That's why she gets to wear the big posh dress.'

He thinks about this for a few minutes. Good. At least it's keeping him quiet.

There are bottles of red and white wine on the table. David and Gary pour for everyone while we're waiting for the soup.

'Where's Troy?' asks Heather suddenly. We all look around. He must have slipped off his chair while we were all concentrating on the wine. Well, look – priorities, OK?

'He can't have gone far,' says David reasonably, but Heather's on her feet, her forehead creased with concern, gazing from table to table.

'I'm here, Mummy!' calls an excited little voice. 'Look!' There's a click and a flash as Troy runs towards us from the top table, holding a camera above his head and firing it indiscriminately without looking through the viewfinder. 'Sammy said I could,' he adds defensively, seeing the look on his mother's face.

'It's the camera from the bride's table,' I mutter to David. 'He'll use up all the bloody film.'

'Give it to me, Troy,' says Heather.

'But Sammy said!' He stamps his feet and holds fast to the camera, his arms wrapped around it.

'I said he could take one picture,' calls Sam. 'Sorry!'

'OK, Troy, you've had your one picture, now give back the camera,' demands Heather.

This is turning into a major confrontation. I knew it. I just knew we couldn't get through the whole day without this happening. He's going to have one of his screaming turnouts, probably just as the soup's arriving. There'll be spiced tomato and basil soup all over the place. I can see it now.

'Come here, Troy,' says David quietly. 'Come and show me the camera.'

He considers this for a minute and then sidles over to David, still clutching the camera tightly. David pretends to look at it with him for a minute or two. 'Yes', he's saying calmly. 'Nice camera, Troy. I bet you took a really good picture. We'll be able to see it in a few days' time.'

The waiters are approaching our table with their bowls of steaming soup borne delicately aloft like offerings to the gods.

'OK, Troy – tell you what – you've taken a picture on Sam's camera now; after dinner you can take a picture on our one? Yes?'

The waiter leans across Troy to place a bowl of soup in front of David. Please, please, don't let him jump up and down and throw a strop right this minute.

'So let's give this camera back to Sam – OK? And let's sit you down ready for your soup, right? It's tomato ... your favourite. Good boy.'

David's got his arms round the kid now, steering him into his own seat. He takes the camera coolly out of his hands and passes it back to Christine, sitting behind him, to put back on their table.

'Phew,' says Heather, who looks like she's broken out into a sweat. 'I was really panicking there, for a moment.'

I catch David's eye.

'Yes,' is all he says.

Troy's already tucking into his soup.

'So,' says Chloe, leaning past Troy to attract Christine's attention on the next table. 'How are you enjoying your *wedding breakfast*, Mum?'

If she's expecting a reaction, she's disappointed.

'It's lovely, thank you, Chloe,' says Christine with great dignity, sitting up straight and sipping her soup from the side of the spoon.

I notice Brian giving Chloe a fleeting glare, and wonder whether he's going to go into one of his 'We Haven't All Had the Benefit of Your Education' speeches, but fortunately Sam is holding him in conversation. Phil's parents look slightly puzzled, seeing Chloe sniggering to herself and David looking like he wants to kick her under the table.

'Family joke,' I say, with what I hope is a charming smile in their direction whilst managing a steely frown at Chloe. 'Take no notice!'

'Oh, a "family joke"!' laughs Helen. 'We have *lots* of those, don't we, Duncan?'

The mind boggles.

Duncan looks as though his mind's boggling too, to be quite honest. 'Do we?' he says, sounding totally bemused.

'Yeah, you know,' joins in Phil, winking at me, 'we joke about weddings, and receptions, and speeches . . .'

Suddenly this isn't funny. I've been trying not to think about the speeches. I look across the 'top table' at Brian. Where *is* his speech? In his jacket pocket? Tucked down his trousers? In his shoe? *Why* is he being so secretive about it?

'Have *you* got your speech prepared?' I ask the best man, who's sitting next to me, to take my mind off Brian's.

'Kind of,' says Gary, knocking back his second glass of wine.

Blimey, he's not even going to be able to talk, at this rate, especially considering the champagne and the beer he was drinking before the meal.

'What do you mean, "kind of"?'

'Well, I've kind of thought about it, yeah, but I kind of thought I might as well kind of ad-lib it.'

Kind of ad-lib it?

I watch him in horrified fascination as he pours himself another full glass of red wine. This is *not* going to be good. Ad-libbing is bad enough. Drunken ad-libbing is just a recipe for disaster. He might just as well stand up there, burp, fart, get a cheap laugh and sit down again for all the sense he's going to make.

I know Gary quite well, but probably not really well enough to do what I'm going to do next. He's nearly four years younger than me. That makes it feel more acceptable.

'Don't drink that,' I tell him, quietly but very sternly – the tone I use on those annoying children in the library. 'Don't drink any more until after your speech.' I pick up his glass of wine and move it away from him to the other side of my plate. 'And really, Gary, I think you ought to be giving your speech a bit of last-minute thought. Is it fair to your brother to stand up there on his wedding day and "*kind of ad-lib it*"?'

He sits back in his chair, putting down his soup spoon and staring at me in surprise.

'Bloody hell, Abbie,' he says. 'Give it a break!'

'No! No, I'm serious, Gary. It's important! You should have *worked* at it.'

'I didn't think it was a bloody assignment, Abbie. What's the matter with you?'

'I don't want today spoilt. That's all.'

He pushes his soup bowl aside, looks around for his glass, sees that it's out of his reach and shakes his head at me. Then he starts to laugh, very quietly.

'Well, I have to hand it to you. You should have been a fucking schoolmistress. Or a fucking police-woman. OK, OK, I'll ease off the wine. Let me have the glass back.'

I don't want him to make a scene. I pass his wine glass back to him and he puts it down, very deliberately, a little further away from him than before.

'And think about your speech,' I remind him,

'while you're eating your dinner.'

'Yeah, yeah, OK, fair enough.'

He's still shaking his head. I don't think there's a chance in hell of him thinking up a decent speech, not at this eleventh hour. His thoughts are more likely running along the lines of what a bossy, interfering cow I've turned out to be.

'You just need to say what a wonderful brother he is,' I tell him more gently. 'And how pleased you are that he's marrying such a lovely girl as Sam. And say how lovely the bridesmaids look, of course,' I add jokingly.

'Bridesmaids, yeah,' he says, morosely, as if the thought of them makes him feel physically ill. Well, thanks for nothing.

But he's looking straight at Chloe.

Chloe, as we speak, is staring at the plate in front of her as if it's going to jump up and bite her.

'I can't eat that!' she says accusingly to the waiter who's just served her main course. 'It's chicken!'

'That's right, madam. Chicken with lemon and tarragon sauce. Is there a problem?' asks the waiter politely.

'I'm a *vegetarian*!' she retorts, as if the waiter should have known this just by looking at her. 'I *can't* have this . . . this carcass on my plate! It's repugnant.'

She hands her plate back to the waiter, holding it at arm's length, averting her eyes from the offending poultry.

'I'm sorry about that, madam. I'll check with the kitchen about the vegetarian option.'

'Thank you –' she begins, but David, who's been listening to this exchange (it would be difficult not

128

to), interrupts: 'Chloe, did you *order* a vegetarian option?'

'Well, of course, it's *obvious* I have to have a vegetarian option, isn't it, if I'm a vegetarian?'

'But you weren't vegetarian last week,' I remind her. It's a job and a half to stop myself adding that if she continues to take that tone with David I'll push her face into the chicken with lemon and tarragon sauce and see how she likes *that*.

'Well,' she says, with a smug look at me, 'I am *this* week, aren't I?'

'Then it's tough,' I say without bothering to pretend any sympathy or politeness. 'You've got no dinner. You can eat the vegetables. That's what vegetarians do.'

The waiter's hovering, looking from one of us to the other, obviously not sure what to do.

'You surely must *have* a vegetarian option!' she accuses him.

'We'd certainly have one if you'd ordered it, madam.'

Chloe looks like she's about to explode. 'Abbie, why didn't you order me a vegetarian dinner?' she demands.

I'm just about to give her the dressing-down of her miserable little life when Eva suddenly, and silently, places her hand over Chloe's and waits for her to turn to look at her.

'Leave it,' she says very quietly but very firmly. 'It's your own fault. Just leave it. You can have extra veg. You can have mine.'

For a moment nobody speaks. The waiter, shifting uneasily from foot to foot with the discarded plate of chicken in his hands, looks to me and David for guidance and I nod at him to take it away. He brings her back an empty plate on which to serve her vegetables; she hangs her head and stares at the plate as if she's a poor starving little orphan girl in the workhouse who's not going to get any gruel.

'Good girl,' says Eva, squeezing Chloe's hand, talking to her like a child. 'No more fuss.'

There's not another sound out of her as the waiter judiciously serves her with extra-large portions of glazed carrots, sauté potatoes, French beans and braised courgettes. Amazing. I feel like asking Eva if she'd like to stay with Chloe on a permanent basis. It might be worth it just to see Brian's face.

'Mu*mmee*!' wails a little voice suddenly just as everyone's hoping to get tucked into their meals. 'Mummy, I *don't want* it. It's *repuggerant*.'

'That's enough, Troy,' says David with an edge of steel in his voice. 'Eat it.'

Troy, to be fair, eats it.

There's an unnatural silence around our table as we begin the main course. I don't think there's anyone left, including the kid, who's not pissed off with someone else. As for me, I'm pissed off with the whole damn lot of them. I almost wish I'd sat with Frank.

Half past five

There are flashes going off all round the room as people use the table cameras to take pictures of each other posing, raising their glasses, eating their meals, generally being merry. I keep a wary eye on Troy and tuck our camera out of his sight but he seems to have forgotten it for the moment.

'How's my favourite little grandson?' calls Christine somewhat tipsily from the next table.

'Troy's doing OK, Mum!' David calls back. 'Getting on with his dinner. You all OK over there?'

I can hear Sam and Phil laughing together. It lightens my heart and makes me forget my forebodings for a minute.

'Yes, dear. We're all *chunky-dolly*.'

'Hunky-dory, Mum.'

'What?' Her blue stripes glint in the light as she cranes her neck to look at David. 'What did you say?'

'Never mind.'

I think I prefer chunky-dolly.

As I'm getting stuck into my chicken I look around the other tables and catch sight of Frank, who's trying to get up out of his chair and is being restrained by

Sam's Auntie Barbara. He's looking in our direction with an expression of pure panic on his face. Barbara looks as though she's fighting a losing battle.

'Won't be a minute,' I tell David quietly as I slip out of my chair and make my way across to their table.

'Julia,' mutters Frank as I approach, 'there you are.'

'Abbie,' I correct him automatically. 'Is everything all right, Barbara?'

'He keeps wanting to get up and wander around,' she says, sounding exhausted. 'Keeps asking for Julia.'

Why the bloody hell has he got such a fixation about Julia, today of all days?

'Frank,' I tell him, holding him still by both elbows, 'look at me.' His eyes are clouded with confusion. 'Julia isn't here. Now, come on – sit down and eat your dinner. You've hardly started it. It's chicken. You like chicken.'

Actually I haven't got the faintest idea whether he likes chicken or not and, as long as he sits down and doesn't keep on about Julia, I don't even care if he's another bloody vegetarian.

'All right, all right,' he retorts. 'Keep your hair on, woman.'

That's more like the Frank I know. I smile at him as he sits back down in his place and picks up his knife and fork.

'You always were a right little madam,' he says, giving me a lopsided grin with his mouth full of potato, 'Julia.'

Sam was right, you know, when she said that Julia

132

had her pick of the boys, all through school and beyond. Julia's reputation preceded her as she became older, even more beautiful, even more popular. The boys were practically lining up to go out with her. Sam was lovely herself, of course – bright, bubbly, charming and talented. When the two of them walked into rooms together, you could see the heads turning and the guys' mouths dropping open. But whereas Sam and I, without Julia, were as comfortable and easy together as a favourite old pair of shoes – hanging out together, laughing and chatting and joking like the best friends we still considered ourselves to be, even after I'd left school – when Julia was with us, it wasn't the same. It was like the mixture had been stirred and spoilt. Like too much salt had been added to a tasty dish. I *liked* Julia all right. I just felt wary of her; I didn't completely trust her. Not without reason, as it turned out.

After they finished the sixth form, Sam and Julia both got jobs in London. They were almost as excited about the idea of commuting together every day, and meeting for lunch in the city, as they were about their new working lives. Once again, for a while I felt left out and frankly jealous.

'Why don't *you* look for a job up in town?' suggested Sam. 'There are plenty of vacancies ...'

Perhaps there were, for girls with degrees, or even the three good A levels each that my friends had achieved.

'I've only got five GCSEs,' I reminded her, suddenly feeling sorry for myself.

'But you're so clever with your English literature, and your history, and ...' She stopped, probably aware that she was unintentionally sounding slightly patronising. 'There are libraries in London where you could apply, aren't there?'

'I like my job, though,' I said, sulkily. 'I don't really want to work in London. I just want to be able to meet you and Julia for lunch.'

She threaded her arm through mine. 'Don't be sad, Babbie,' she said teasingly, using her old nickname for me. It was a contraction of Baby Abbie and I hated it. I smacked her and we both started laughing. 'We can meet you after work. We can have lunch on Saturdays. And Sundays. And in our holidays.'

'If you don't forget about me.'

'I'm never going to do that, stupid,' she said, stopping laughing and looking at me with real concern in her eyes. 'Don't ever think that. You're my best mate. We don't have to work together to prove that, do we?'

Of course, I got over it and got on with my life, and Sam was true to her word. If anything, we probably saw each other more than ever, because Julia always had a boyfriend. Never the same one for very long, it's true – but she didn't like to be without one, and if anything, she preferred to have an overlap. 'Hedging my bets', she used to call it, apparently thinking it was hilarious and very clever. I secretly thought it was cruel. She'd keep the old boyfriend – the one she was bored with, the one she'd started to treat with a weary impatience bordering on contempt – hanging on whilst she investigated the new possibilities (which, for Julia, were endless and waiting hungrily in the wings). I asked her once why she didn't do the decent thing and finish with the existing guy *before* starting a new relationship. She looked at me in horror.

'But then,' she cried, 'I might be left with *nobody*!'

Which was not only a rather tactless thing to say to somebody who spent her entire life *with nobody* – but was also as unlikely as the oceans freezing over and the sun falling out of the sky.

'She's actually quite insecure,' said Sam one day, phoning me to tell me that Julia's three-week-long latest romance with a *Darren* was off, and that she was now seeing a *Michael*.

'I don't know how you work that out!' I scoffed.

Insecure? I'd seen more insecurity in a fox confronting a tasty meal of terrified rabbit than I ever saw in Julia making a play for her next conquest.

'She's afraid of being single. To be honest, I find it quite pathetic, in a way. Sad. She needs to get herself a life.'

If, in my permanently single state, I learned from Julia everything I needed to know about how *not* to conduct relationships, from Sam I learned exactly how I wanted my own life to be – if only I could ever meet anyone. Sam shared it all with me – the excitement over the first few dates; the build-up to spending the first night together; the steadying down (sometimes) into a serious relationship; the cooling off, the arguments or the unexpected, traumatic bust-ups. I was always there for her with the tissues, the wine and the chocolates. And always, no matter how madly in love she might have been with her man of the moment, we had our girls' nights together. Sam, unlike Julia, was perfectly happy without a man on her arm.

'Maybe you're right,' I said doubtfully. 'But she never *seems* insecure.'

'She's *so* insecure, she's afraid to admit it, even to us. That's why I feel sorry for her. That's why I'm still her friend, even though she behaves the way she does.'

It was a rare piece of insight. Sam was right, of course, and I felt insensitive for not seeing it myself. I made an extra-special effort, for a while, to think more charitably about Julia. After all, it was up to her who she went out with, and what she did. It wasn't for us to criticise or condemn her. It wasn't as if she was hurting *us* in any way.

Not at that point in time, anyway.

Quarter to six

When I return to my own table, Eva's missing.

'Gone to the loo,' says Chloe, still sounding sulky. She's eaten about half of her plateful of vegetables and pushed the rest deliberately to the side.

'Is Granddad all right?' asks David.

'Well, not bad,' I say with a sigh. 'He's just unsettled. It's all a bit much for him. Your Auntie Barbara's got her work cut out. And he keeps on calling me Julia.'

I don't know why I'm telling him this. It's *so* not what I want to be talking about. I also don't like the way he's grinning at me about it.

'How could he possibly make that mistake? I knew Granddad was getting senile, but even for him ...'

'Well, thanks a million!' I retort, stung. It's one thing to know perfectly well that I couldn't hope to look like Julia even if I spent my entire life undergoing cosmetic surgery. It's very much another thing to be told that, and told *laughingly*.

David's looking at me strangely. He shakes his head.

'Would you *want* to be confused with Julia? It's hardly a compliment, Abbie.'

137

'Oh, yeah, right!' The petulant teenager in me rises to the surface. 'Like I'm supposed to *prefer* being plain, and boring, and unpopular . . .'

'No. You're supposed to prefer being *you*. You're not any of those things. Why are you feeling sorry for yourself?'

'Well, how would *you* feel, if . . .'

I don't know what I was going on to say. Perhaps – how would you feel if you were an old maid, on the shelf, with nobody to love you? And if you wanted nothing more than to fall in love, get married and have a family but it was never likely to happen? Whatever – I don't get any further because he stops me with a sigh, looking away and running his hand across his forehead as if he had a pain.

'Being single's not the worst thing in the world, Abbie. It's better than being with the wrong person.'

The noise of the party goes on around us. Troy's conducting a monologue to Chloe, telling her what a good boy he's been, eating all his dinner up – look, he's even eating the horrid green things that look like caterpillars. Heather's leaning back in her chair, chatting to Christine, behind her, about how awful it was that the bouquet fell apart like that – honestly, it just goes to show, even when you use the best florists in town, they can't manage to get it right, can they? And a little thing like a cat sitting on the flowers really shouldn't have caused that much damage, not if they were *good* flowers in the first place. Further down the room, two girls from Sam's work are screeching with drunken laughter and a guy's voice is saying, loudly: 'All *right,* it's not that funny, Miranda. How much have you had to drink already?'

Between David and me, there's a hiatus of pure-bred

138

silence, like the moment of quiet between two thunderclaps. It trembles, light and fragile as a bubble.

'What do you mean?' I ask him, finally, on a breath of a whisper. 'Who's with the wrong person?'

He toys with his fork and shrugs. 'Lots of people. Relationships aren't always perfect.'

'Of course not!' I raise my voice only very slightly, but it's enough to make the bubble burst. Heather turns and looks over at us with a puzzled expression; Troy gives up talking to an uncommunicative Chloe and throws his spoon into the middle of the table to create a diversion; Gary reaches for the wine bottle and pours another glass of wine to replace the glassful he wasn't going to drink, his hand so unsteady that he slops some onto the tablecloth, just as the waiter appears to begin to clear the dinner plates.

'Of course not,' I say again, dropping my voice back down to a murmur. *Nothing's* perfect, David. *Nobody's* happy all the time.'

So they've definitely had a row – him and Heather. Maybe it was a bad one.

'Never mind,' I encourage him – although to be fair, for someone who's had a row with his girlfriend, he doesn't really look too upset about it. 'You know what your mum says: "It'll all come out in the wash!"'

He gives me a smile. 'You know what happens, don't you, when it all comes out in the wash? White things go pink. Some things shrink; some stretch. Nothing's ever right again.'

While we're waiting for dessert I nip out to the ladies'. I'm a bit concerned that Eva's taking so long.

139

Chloe doesn't seem bothered – or if she is, she's refusing to say so, but then, she's been refusing to talk to anyone at all, since the episode with the chicken dinner.

'Oh, there you are.' Eva's standing at the sinks, staring at herself in the mirror. 'Are you all right?'

She sighs at her reflection. 'I suppose so. Sorry.' She turns to face me. 'I'm being antisocial.'

'Not at all. I just thought someone should check if you were OK.'

I put a heavy emphasis on the 'someone'.

'Thank you, Abbie. And I take your point – but Chloe wouldn't have done, of course. Not while she's in one of her moods. I could be lying unconscious, or dead and bleeding with a dagger through my heart and she'd pretend not to notice.'

'I'm sure that's not true, Eva. I get the impression she likes you a lot.'

'Not half as much as she likes herself. But you don't need me to tell you that, do you?'

God, not another couple in crisis, please. Maybe David's right about relationships.

'How do you put up with her?' I ask mildly, having a half-hearted attempt at straightening my hair in the mirror.

'I love her, obviously,' she replies instantly, matter-of-factly.

'Despite everything? The selfishness? The childishness?'

'She *is* still a child. I love that about her – her freshness and her certainties – the way she sees things as black or white. She hasn't started to get into the habit of *greyness* and nonchalance that comes with growing up . . .'

140

'I wish she *would*, to be quite honest. She can be an absolute pain in the neck.'

'I know. That's the negative side. This sulking, these . . . tantrums. Her family must be sick of her.'

'It's partly their fault. She's the baby. They spoiled her.'

'Did they?' Eva looks up at me, sharply. 'I've never got that impression. I thought they pretty well ignored her.'

'Is that what she says?' I feel a momentary flash of anger on behalf of Christine and Brian, before I suddenly find myself wondering: Is that true?

'No, she doesn't say much about them at all. Just that she never felt like she belonged. That she was born too late, when everyone else was grown up and no one was interested in children. I presume she was an accident?'

'Why do you presume that? Actually I think Christine and Brian might have tried for a long time to have her.'

I don't know any such thing. I also don't know why I'm leaping to their defence. It just irritates the shit out of me to think that Chloe's gone through life with this self-conceived idea of herself as a poor unwanted little orphan.

'She wasn't unloved,' I add, thinking of all the toys, all the presents she used to get at Christmas – all the comments Sam made to me over the years about how she got so much more than she and David ever had. 'But she *was* bloody ungrateful.'

There was this particular time – it was her birthday, probably her fourteenth. The family had clubbed together to get her a computer. Christine and Brian still weren't well off, but Sam and David were both at work, bringing in a decent wage, so between them they managed to get the whole package – computer, printer, scanner, the lot. I was round there the evening before her birthday; Chloe was in bed and they were setting it up for her so it'd be a surprise in the morning.

'Do you think she'll be pleased?' Christine asked me anxiously as David was connecting up the various leads. 'Do you think it's a *good* one, Abbie?'

'I'm sure it is. She'll be over the moon.'

But who could tell with Chloe? She was just as likely to throw a strop and say she wanted a different one.

'Only, the teachers said at the parents' evening that she has great potency,' added Christine proudly.

'Potential,' Sam corrected her.

'Yes. So we have to try to provide her with all the right things. She might even go on to university.'

'Good,' said Sam. I saw her exchanging a look with David.

'Yeah, good,' said David tonelessly.

He'd thought about going to university himself, but at the age of eighteen he'd been told by his father to go out, be a man and get himself a job.

I wasn't there on the morning of Chloe's birthday, but I asked Sam the next day whether she'd been pleased with the computer.

'Not really,' she said, barely containing her annoyance. 'She asked if that was all.'

'*What?*' I'd been genuinely shocked. Even Chloe, I'd thought, wasn't that greedy. Was she?

'Yes. She thanked Mum and Dad, and then asked what David and I had bought her. We explained that we'd helped to buy the computer.'

142

'Actually you paid for most of it!'

'Yes, but that's not the point. She just gave us this sour look as if to say we'd as good as not bothered with a present at all.'

'The spoilt little . . . !'

'I know. I was so sorry for Mum. It ruined everything. She kept saying she and Dad should have got her something else.'

'Sam, Chloe isn't stupid. She knows how expensive these things are! She needs to be *told*.'

'Yes, and she was. By Dad! He gave her such a lecture about being spoiled and ungrateful, and sent her to her room. Wouldn't even let her use the computer!'

'Serves her right!' I said with feeling.

It's only thinking about it now, nearly five years down the line, that I also find myself thinking, despite myself – poor kid. Some birthday.

'Sometimes,' Eva's saying, leaning against the sinks and folding her arms, 'she tells me how they bought her really expensive presents . . .'

'Like the computer?'

'For her fourteenth birthday. But what she'd really wanted was a CD.'

'A *what*?' I stare at her. 'A CD?'

'Yes. Christina Aguilera's. She'd apparently been asking for it for weeks.'

'But . . .'. I'm flabbergasted. 'But that's *nothing*, compared to a computer!'

'I depends whose perspective you're looking at it from, though, doesn't it – the person whose birthday it is, or the people buying what they *think* that person should have?'

'*I* could have bought her the damn CD! I bought

143

her floppy disks or something, for the computer! I thought that was what she'd have wanted . . .' I tail off, uncomfortably. Did I ask her? Did any of us?

'I don't think she was ungrateful,' says Eva with a shrug. 'I think she was actually upset that her family had spent all that money.'

And that no one had listened to what she'd really been asking for?

'Don't get me wrong, Abbie,' she adds quickly. 'You've known her a lot longer than I have. And I'm not disputing what she can be like. I've had to come out here to cool off or I'd probably be giving her a right mouthful!'

'It might do her good.'

'Don't worry,' she laughs. 'We do have our arguments. I do tell her, frequently, that she's acting like a baby. But . . .' She hesitates.

'But?' I prompt her, gently.

'She's had a rough time, the last couple of years.'

'How d'you work *that* out?'

The Chloe I know hasn't had a rough time at all. Far from it. While the rest of the family are working, keeping the home together, looking after Granddad and the cat and fighting amongst themselves, she's been living the life of Riley up at Durham doing whatever it is that begins with a 'p', as well as apparently meeting Eva and keeping it a secret from everyone.

'You see?' says Eva sadly when I say this to her. 'None of you have even bothered to find out what subject she's studying.'

'It's a long word,' I say, feebly, awkwardly. 'It's either physiology, or psychology, or . . .'

'It's philosophy, Abbie. And you're a very intelligent girl – you were a top English student, Chloe says . . .'

144

'Chloe says?'

It's news to me that she had any idea what subjects I took at school.

'Yes. So don't try to pretend to me that you don't know the difference between *words beginning with "p"*.'

I feel, suddenly, terribly ashamed of this. It was a joke between me and Sam. We delighted in it – pretending we were too stupid to know. But Eva's right – we weren't. We were just too stupid to care.

'She's had a hard time,' repeats Eva firmly, 'because she's been trying, ever since she was about fifteen, to come to terms with her sexuality.'

'Perhaps she should have told someone. Her mum, or her sister.'

'She didn't feel like they'd be interested.'

Ouch.

'So yes, I get angry with her sometimes. But I'm trying to be patient, Abbie. I'm waiting for her to grow up, and grow into her own identity.'

'And what if she never does?'

'Oh, she will. I'm sure of it.' She gives me a sad smile as she straightens up and we turn to go back out to the party. 'And when she does, she'll probably be ready to move on, spread her wings. She'll probably leave me.'

Quarter past six

Everyone's eating their black cherry cheesecake by the time Eva and I sit down again.

'Yum!' Troy's scraping his plate enthusiastically. 'Can I have some more?'

Heather cuts off a slice of her own dessert and passes it to him. 'Eat it nicely,' she warns him. 'Slow down. Or you'll get a tummy ache.'

'Yummy yummy, in my tummy!' he giggles, rubbing his stomach happily.

I can't help smiling. Kids don't change much, really, over the years, it seems to me. I remember saying that myself when I was little. Not that we ever had black cherry cheesecake, to be quite honest. Home-made apple crumble, almost every bloody Sunday, from what I can recall.

'Where have you two been, anyway?' asks Chloe suspiciously.

Well, at least she's started talking.

'Toilets,' says Eva. 'And having a chat.'

'What about?'

'Philosophy,' I say, quickly.

Chloe gives me a look of surprise. 'I didn't think you knew what it was, Abbie,' she says, narrowing her eyes at me like a cat.

'Of course I did. I was just joking. A stupid joke.'

She shakes her head at this, as if it's the most ridiculous thing she's ever heard. Maybe it is. 'Strange sense of humour you've got,' she remarks lightly as she picks up her spoon and contemplates her dessert.

'It's good, Chlo,' says Eva, who's already getting stuck into hers. 'Try it.' She gives her a smile, and I can see Chloe visibly relax – the tension of her earlier sulk lifting from her shoulders as she smiles back and takes a mouthful. 'You do look lovely today,' Eva adds in an undertone that I'm not supposed to hear.

Chloe flushes slightly and bends her face over her dessert, but not before I see the leap of joy in her eyes.

I don't know why, but it makes me ache inside.

I'd forgotten about Gary. I turn my attention to him now, and see to my horror that he's not only been drinking more wine, he's actually slumped in his seat, his eyes half-closed, looking like he's either going to fall asleep, or fall off the chair, if not both.

'Gary!' I say sharply, nudging him so hard that he actually does overbalance for a minute, and has to hold on to the table to keep himself upright.

'Whassamatter? Whassup?' he slurs. He looks at me as if I'm several miles away and he's trying to get me into focus. 'Abbie?'

For Christ's sake! He's as pissed as a newt.

'Gary, I thought you were going to stop drinking? Why couldn't you just try?'

Oh, what's the point? It's a bit late to start nagging him now.

'Try? Try what, Abbie?' he asks, sounding like a

147

pathetic sick child. 'What d'you want me to try? Mm? Try to eat my pudding, shall I?'

He sways slightly as he picks up his spoon and aims it vaguely in the direction of the cheesecake. It misses and hits the table. Looking surprised, he tries again but this time he knocks over his wine glass, which, fortunately or unfortunately depending on how you look at it, is empty. He swears softly to himself, beginning to look as though he can't remember what he's trying to do anyway, and throws the spoon back on the table.

'Fuck it,' he says loudly to me, giving me a crooked smile.

'Ssh.'

'Bucket!' repeats Troy at once, laughing. 'Bucket, bucket, put it in the bucket!'

Gary laughs too, although it's quite obvious he has no idea what the joke is.

'I think,' I say with exasperation, pushing my untouched dessert to one side, 'that you need some fresh air, Gary.'

'I'll take him ...' begins David, who appears to have suddenly, and much too belatedly, become aware of the state of the best man.

'No – you'd better try to keep the peace here,' I tell him, as Heather tries unsuccessfully to get the overexcited Troy to sit down, stop waving his spoon around and stop shouting 'Bucket'! at the top of his lungs. 'Gary – come on – let's take a walk.'

''Sall right, Abbie.' He pushes back his chair. There's a perilous moment, as he struggles to his feet, when it looks like he might overturn the whole table. He grabs my arm, steadies himself, a look of panic on his face, then smiles stupidly and continues: 'I'm

148

going. I'm going to have a piss.'

I don't think I'll go with him in that case.

As I watch him totter shakily down the steps to the lower floor and then weave his way across to the doors, David leans over to me and says quietly: 'Shit, I'm so sorry, Abbie. I just didn't notice.'

'Well, you wouldn't expect to have to *babysit* the groom's brother, really, would you? For God's sake! I did ask him to stop drinking till after his speech.'

'The speech! Shit!' He claps his hand to his head. 'Is he going to be able to do it?'

'Your guess is as good as mine. He was talking about ad-libbing it. And that was *before* he was totally out of his head.'

'What a prat. What with him, and Dad . . .' He tails off, looking over his shoulder at the top table. 'Talking of which, has Dad said anything about *his* speech yet?'

'No. I just hope *he's* managed to stay sober,' I say tersely.

David leans back in his chair and taps Christine's arm. 'Mum. Is Dad OK?'

'OK, dear? Yes, I think so. Brian, David says are you OK? Yes, he's fine, dear. Having a lovely time. Isn't this pudding nice? Are you enjoying yours, David? Is Troy being a good boy?'

'Bucket!' squeals Troy. 'Bucket, bucket!'

'Ah, bless him! Isn't it lovely, Troy! Eat it all up, there's a good boy. Isn't he being good, Heather? Like a little angel. Why does he keep saying *bucket*?'

It's on the tip of my tongue to shout '*BECAUSE IT RHYMES WITH FUCK IT!*' I think I'm losing the will to live.

*

149

The dessert dishes have been cleared away and the waiters are serving coffee.

'Where's Gary?' I whisper to David. 'He's been outside for ages.'

'Maybe he *has* gone for some fresh air. Let's hope he's sobering up.'

'I'm going to look for him. He needs to be here. Everyone will be expecting the speeches any time now.'

'I'll come with you, then. You can't go looking in the men's toilets.'

No. Last time I did that, I was nine years old and went in the wrong door by mistake. The shock stayed with me all through my teens.

We find Gary, as it happens, asleep at the bar. He's got his head on the counter and he's snoring.

'I thought it was probably best to leave him there,' says the girl behind the bar, apologetically, 'to sleep it off.'

'But he's the best man,' says David grimly. 'Gary! Come on, man. Wake up!'

'Does he want a glass of water?' asks the girl, watching with interest as Gary raises his head slightly and tries to open one eye.

'He can have it poured over his bloody head for all I care, as long as it sobers him up,' I retort.

Have you ever regretted saying something?

Before any of us have even realised she's got a full glass in her hand, the girl's lifted it and tipped it. Gary, catapulted awake by the shock of it, jumps to his feet, spluttering, rubbing ineffectively at his wet hair and his wet jacket, while the water runs down his face and drips off his chin as if he's just surfaced from a swim.

'What the *fuck*?' he yells, gasping and staring at us furiously. 'What the *fucking hell*?'

Neither David nor I can speak. The sight of him is just too much.

'Did you not mean it, then?' asks the girl, still holding the empty glass in the air. 'Was it a joke?'

'A *joke*?' repeats Gary. 'I'm fucking *drenched*!'

'Come on, Gary,' says David, and I can hear laughter in his voice. It's making me want to laugh myself. 'It was only a pint of water. You're not going to drown.'

'My fucking *suit*!' He grabs a towel that the girl's passing him across the bar and begins to dry at his jacket with angry swipes. 'I'm the *best man*!'

'Well,' says David, and now the laughter's gone, 'perhaps you should have thought of that before you got pissed and passed out at the table.'

'I wasn't pissed. I was just having a little rest. For God's *sake*!' He starts to rub his hair dry.

'Let's not argue about it, Gary. The point is, are you OK now?' I look at his dishevelled appearance. 'Can you straighten yourself up a bit and come back in for the speeches?'

'Oh, Christ.' He suddenly slumps back down in his seat again. 'Oh, shit – the speech. I forgot about the fucking speech. How long have I been ... out here ... resting?'

'Long enough. Don't worry about it. As long as you're OK now.'

'I've let everyone down,' he says, mournfully, holding his head in his hands. 'I've ruined the wedding. Sam will never forgive me. My brother will hate me for ever.'

Oh, Jesus. I think I preferred him being angry.

'Don't be a wuss,' retorts David. 'You had too much to drink – it happens. Get over it, and get your arse in gear now and no one will be any the wiser.'

'But *she* will. *She'll* know.' He shakes his head, a pitiful look in his eyes.

'Who – Sam? No, she's much too busy enjoying herself,' I say, briskly.

'No,' he says, still shaking his head. I'm surprised he can do that. The amount he's put away, he deserves to have a crashing headache. 'No, not Sam.'

I wait, but he obviously decides not to enlighten us any further.

'Who?' I prompt him.

'Doesn't matter.'

'Well, whoever she is, she won't want to see you looking like a bit of limp lettuce, so why don't you get yourself into the gents and spruce yourself up a bit. Quickly. We'll wait for you.'

I'm talking to him like I'm a mother, and I've never even been one.

'She won't care *what* I look like,' he mutters morosely to himself as he shoves past us on his way to the toilets. 'That's the problem.'

'Who?' asks David, staring after him as the door to the gents' swings shut. 'Who's he going on about, d'you think?'

'I haven't got a clue.' I look at my watch and sigh. 'I'm a lot more concerned with how late we're going to be with these speeches than I am with his love life, or lack of it, to be quite honest.'

'Chill, Abbie.' He puts his arm casually across my shoulders. 'It's cool. No one will mind. Who goes first, anyway?'

152

'He does. He's supposed to introduce the speakers. Then your dad makes the first speech, God help us.'

David grins. 'You're right there.' He looks at me curiously. 'Where d'you learn all this stuff, Abbs?'

'The internet. *Wedding etiquette*. There are so many websites about it, you could spend all day reading it up.'

I did, actually – at work in the library.

'You can get addicted, you know,' he says, smiling at me. 'Next thing, you'll find yourself trawling through dodgy websites, getting proposed to on line by rich weirdos in foreign parts . . .'

'I should be so lucky!' I laugh. 'The nearest I get to that is a ton of spam emails every day, trying to sell me drugs to enhance my sexual performance . . .'

I trail off, suddenly blushing furiously. He pretends not to notice.

'And do you ever buy them?' he asks me, softly, still smiling.

'Piss off!'

Luckily, at that point Gary comes out of the toilets – looking smarter, and drier, and, thank God, relatively sober. In fact, so much more sober than before that he marches ahead of us back into the function room, where he leads the way to our table and stands, holding his empty glass and tapping on it with a spoon to get everyone's attention.

'Ladies and gentlemen,' he says, as the chatter begins to die away and people turn expectantly in their seats to look at him. 'I hope you've all enjoyed a very pleasant meal. And now we've come to the part of the evening that I'm sure you've all been looking forward to. It's my duty and my great pleasure to call upon the bride's father – Brian Patterson –

to propose the toast to the bride and groom. Brian? Over to you.'

'Well done, Gary,' I whisper as he sits down. I try to say more, but I can't. I'm watching Brian heave himself to his feet, shaking out the sheets of paper he's had hidden God knows where for the past couple of months, and my throat is taut and dry with foreboding. What the *hell* is he going to say?

Half past six

BRIAN'S SPEECH

OK, here we go, then.

Apparently this is the bit where the bride's father finally gets his own back on her for all the years of sleepless nights, teething, nappies and all those kind of things. I have to be honest – I can't really say that. I'm not exactly your New Man. I wasn't a hands-on father – I left all that icky stuff to her mum. In fact, to be *really* honest, I left the whole damn child-rearing job to Chris – I admit it. And from where I'm standing here tonight, I don't think there's anyone in the room would disagree with me, folks – she made a bloody good job of it, didn't she?

But before I go any further into that, though, there's a couple of things I'm told I'm supposed to say. You see, Abbie? I *was* listening! I wrote down all this stuff you got off the internet – see?

First of all, I need to welcome everyone here today and thank you all for turning up – it's turned out to be a lousy day, weather-wise, and you could have said 'Nah, let's give it a miss and watch the football,' but here you all are – yeah, I thought that'd get a

155

laugh out of you blokes over there! – you've all made
the effort, and I know Sam and Phil really appreciate
you all being here with them on their big day. I
specially want to welcome Phil's parents, Helen and
Duncan, and the rest of their family who've trekked
over here from wildest Surrey. Hope it's worth the
journey, eh! Seriously – lovely to have you all with
us today, and especially of course Phil's great-auntie
Enid who's come all the way from Toronto for the
wedding. Hope you've got over your jet lag, love,
and don't worry if you fall asleep over the coffee.

Apart from that, of course, I'd like to welcome all
our own mob – some of you I haven't seen for a fair
few years, probably since the last wedding in the
family – buy you all a drink later on, OK? Only I've
been nagged senseless about staying sober till I've
done the speech, like. Only joking.

And then I have to say hello and welcome to all
Sam's and Phil's friends here tonight. All the rowdy
lot at the back there – yeah, the champagne was good,
wasn't it mate? – enjoy yourselves, all of you – make
the most of it, the bar shuts at midnight. No, seriously
– it's great that they've got such a good lot of friends,
isn't it? Let's face it, you're born into your family
and much as you love them, sometimes they drive you
round the bend and sometimes the different genera-
tions don't quite understand each other the way they
should. But your mates are your mates because
you've got stuff in common – some of you went to
school with Sam, or Phil, or you've met them at work
or down the pub or whatever – and, well, what I'm
trying to say is, we always need our mates, don't we,
even after we meet someone and get married? You
know what I mean?

Now then, what about young Phil? I tell you what, some fathers might find it difficult, handing over their daughter to some young bloke. They might look at him and think: Who the bloody hell do you think you are, mate? Just because you're young, and good-looking, and fit, and intelligent, and you work hard and you've got a good job, you think you're good enough to marry my daughter, do you? Well, let me tell you – Phil's all of those things. Yeah, it makes you sick, doesn't it? And yes, sure, I'm jealous as hell – here I am, maybe still good-looking but not quite as, you know, fit and *sexy* as I was a couple of years ago, not as young and thrusting if you know what I mean. But I'm *glad* Phil's taking Sam off my hands – someone had to do it, she was getting too expensive for me – and if anyone had to do it, I'm glad it's Phil, 'cos he's the best bloke for the job and that's a fact. Phil – it's my pleasure, mine and Christine's, to welcome you to our family, mate, and to prove it I'll buy you a double Scotch on the rocks at the bar later on, OK?

Finally – well, what can I tell you about my Sammy? My little girl? I don't need to tell any of you, for a start, that she's beautiful – I mean, just look at her! She obviously takes after her mother in that respect. She's also clever – that's the bit she gets from me – and, as any of you that have heard her singing will agree, she's got talent. I don't know *where* she gets that from, but it's amazing, and I tell you what – she ought to go on one of those TV shows, what do you call it? *Pop Idols*? I keep telling her. She'd win hands down, not that I'm biased or anything.

Like I said earlier, I'm not one of your modern

hands-on fathers; OK, you all know that. What you might *not* know is, I actually regret that. Yes, I'm not too proud to admit it – I wish I'd got more involved with my kids. I wish I could've stood up here today and talked to you about how I fed Sammy her bottles or how she ran to me when she fell over and grazed her knee, or to tell me when she got her first date. But of course, she didn't – she ran to her mum for those things, and that was only natural, because I was either too busy working, or feeling sorry for myself after I lost my job. Phil, mate, if there's one piece of advice I'm gonna give you tonight it's this: if you and Sam have kids, get stuck in there, mate. Don't be the token father, watching from the sidelines, thinking all you have to do to be a dad is to bring home the bacon. There's a lot more to it than that, and if anyone should've learned that a long time ago, I should have. Most of you probably know how we almost lost our Sammy a few years back. It's the most terrible thing a parent can go through – having to face that possibility – you don't ever want to experience that, believe me. Seeing her here, today, beautiful and happy and ... and everything ... well, sorry, but it brings a lump to my throat, and that's a fact.

Anyway, before I have the lot of you in tears – what's that? Chris is crying already? Well that's nothing new! Stopped the bloody wedding service, didn't she! Let's all get on with the celebrations, everyone, and for starters, let's have everyone raising their glasses for a toast to the bride and groom, for health and happiness in their lives together. *Sammy and Phil*, everyone. Cheers.

Twenty to seven

It happened on my sixteenth birthday – a bitterly cold January day, a Saturday.

Sam and I had plans. We were going to be out all day. Shopping first, then lunch in Pizza Hut, and then on to Kirsty's house with Julia and the other girls, where we were all going to watch a video until it was time to get changed and go out for the evening. I called for Sam at half past ten in the morning, wearing the new coat and boots Mum and Dad had bought me for my birthday and with my hair in a new, experimental style. I probably looked like a yeti.

'You look great!' said Sam generously as she flung open the front door and gave me a hug. 'Happy birthday, Babbie! Come in while I get ready. Shut the door, quick – it's freezing out there!'

We had a cup of tea while Christine disappeared upstairs, rustled some paper and reappeared with a hastily wrapped present for me.

'It's a Saint Peter, Abbie,' she told me happily as I unwrapped a charm on a silver chain. 'It's supposed to protect you.'

'Saint Christopher, Mum,' Sam corrected her. 'He protects travellers.'

'Well, there you go then. You're travelling on the bus today, aren't you? So he'll protect you!'

'Thanks, Christine.' I gave her a quick kiss on the cheek and she fastened the chain around my neck for me. 'I'll wear it all the time.'

'You're welcome, dear. Have a lovely birthday. Now then, what time are you girls off out? 'Cos you can take Chloe with you, and drop her at her dancing class, if you don't mind.'

Mind? I'm ashamed to say I almost gave her back the necklace and said forget it.

Chloe was five and a half at the time, and already a right little madam. Her favourite trick, if she didn't get her own way, was standing rooted to the spot and screaming at the top of her lungs until you gave in to her rather than risk serious and lasting damage to your eardrums. Come to think of it, I've seen Troy doing exactly the same thing recently so maybe it's a family trait.

That particular morning, she was playing up because she couldn't find her ballet shoes.

'It doesn't matter. You can wear your plimsolls,' Christine tried to console her.

'No! I *can't* wear my *plimsolls*!' she shrieked in disgust. 'Only *babies* wear plimsolls.'

She'd been in the 'babies' class' at the dancing school herself until she turned five. The three- and four-year-old tots weren't expected to be kitted out in the full ballet regalia in case they decided after a term or two that they didn't like dancing classes after all (as kids that age are prone to do). Progressing into the 'big girls' class', with its attendant pomp and ceremony and wearing of pink nylon tutus and proper ballet shoes, was obviously a huge event in any little

160

girl's life. But Chloe wasn't old enough, or maybe careful enough, to look after her things properly – and Christine was too busy to notice where she put them. Ballet shoes, books, swimming bags and pencil cases went missing on such a regular basis that nobody turned a hair any more – until the screaming started.

'Look after your things properly, then,' Sam told her ruthlessly that morning. 'It's your own stupid fault.'

Needless to say this only intensified the volume of the screaming. I put my hands over my ears and wished I was family, so that I could justifiably give her the bloody good hiding I privately thought she badly needed.

'Don't be mean, Sam,' said Christine, sighing as she pulled a load of washing out of the machine with one hand and emptied a can of cat food into a dish with the other. 'Chloe, you probably left them behind at the dancing school last week. OK? They'll be in Lost Property. Ask Mrs Fanshaw when you get there.'

The screams subsided and Chloe wiped her nose on her sleeve. 'You ask her. I don't want to ask her. She'll tell me off.'

'I'm not taking you this morning. I've got to wait in for the gas man. Sam and Abbie are taking you.'

'Do we have to, Mum?' put in Sam, crossly. 'We'll miss the bus.'

'Get the next one, then,' snapped Christine. 'Don't be selfish. Abbie's not complaining, are you, Abbie?'

'No,' I said, as I could hardly say anything else. Some bloody birthday.

'I want *Abbie* to ask Mrs Fanshaw for my ballet

shoes,' said Chloe, suddenly becoming all sweetness and cuteness as she snuggled up to me and lisped in my ear. 'Please, Abbie, can you ask Mrs Fanshaw? Sam's being horrible to me.'

'No more than you deserve,' muttered Sam. 'Come on, Abbs, we'd better get going, then, if we've got to traipse round to the stupid dancing school first.'

It wasn't like Sam to be ungracious, but on this occasion I didn't blame her. It was my sixteenth birthday: my *sixteenth*! I'd been dreaming about this day ever since I was about Chloe's age. Sixteen had such a magical ring to it – in all the fairy stories the beautiful princess had something fantastic happening to her on her sixteenth birthday. A handsome prince on a white charger, or at the very least a fairy godmother offering to grant her three wishes. Now, of course, my hopes and dreams had less to do with fairy stories and more to do with getting a birthday kiss off Martin Butler, but it was still the most special and exciting birthday of my life so far. I had fifteen pounds that I'd saved from my own allowance, and a voucher for twenty-five pounds from my gran, burning a hole in my purse, and a new hairstyle to show off. I was itching to get out and get on with the day. And instead, we had to take a crying brat to her dance class and find her missing bloody ballet shoes into the bargain.

'You're going too fast!' whined Chloe as we dragged her along the street, holding a hand each, to stop her from playing about on the icy pavements. 'Wait! You're giving me a tummy ache.'

'It's just a stitch,' said Sam brusquely. 'It'll go when you get to dancing and start doing your stretches.'

'I'm telling Mummy!' she snivelled. 'You're a horrid pig, Sammy. I hate you! I want Mummy.'

'Mummy's busy. Abbie and I are being very kind to you, Chloe, taking you to your dancing class when it's Abbie's birthday and we're supposed to be going out. So stop bloody moaning and get a move on.'

'You said "bloody". I'm telling Mummy.'

'Big deal. Come *on*, Chloe. What's the matter now?'

She'd stopped dead, digging her heels in, wresting her hands free from ours. 'My tummy hurts.' She was gasping for breath. 'I can't walk any more.'

'Sam, I think we're making her go too fast,' I said, suddenly panicking. How was it going to look if we delivered Chloe to her dance teacher, pale and wheezing, clutching her stomach and crying that we'd been horrible to her? Come to that, what would Christine say? I felt a wave of shame. 'It doesn't matter if we miss another bus.'

'All right, suit yourself,' retorted Sam, by now thoroughly rattled. 'Do what you like, then, Chloe. Take your time, see if I care. Mrs Fanshaw's already going to be cross about your shoes, so why not be late too and really piss her off?'

As she was saying this she was marching ahead of us without looking back. I was actually quite shocked. Yes, Chloe was irritating beyond belief and, yes, I was cross too about the delay to my birthday treat, but I knew Sam was overstepping the mark.

'Come on, Chloe,' I said, quietly, offering her my hand. 'We'll go more slowly. OK?'

The next few seconds are burned into my mind like a horror film. Even as Chloe shrugged me off, shouting 'No! I don't *want* to be late! Wait! Sammy!'; even

163

as she shot ahead of me, sliding on the icy ground as she ran after Sam, who'd begun to cross the road in front of us; even as I saw the red car turn the corner and heard the screech of brakes, I was thinking: No, no, no, this can't be real, this can't be happening, it's a nightmare, it's going to stop in a minute, everything's going to be all right.

But it didn't stop. It wasn't all right. I must have frozen to the spot; I must have closed my eyes for a second because when I opened them, the stillness and silence were terrifying. The car was skewed across the icy road, the driver slumped over his steering wheel, out cold with shock. Someone was lying in the road, half under the car. Then the screaming started. I began to shiver violently and it wasn't until I actually collapsed and threw up in the gutter and the screaming stopped that I realised it had been me.

When I came round, the stillness and silence had given way to mayhem. There were people everywhere. Other cars had stopped at the scene and their drivers were holding up the traffic. A man and a woman were bent over the figure slumped in the road. I could hear sirens in the distance.

'The kid's OK,' someone was saying. 'Just shock and some bruises, I should think. Ambulance is on its way.'

'Chloe?' I croaked, my throat tight with fear. *Please God, Please God, let her be all right, I promise I won't ever complain about her again. Please – I'll be good, I won't ever smoke another cigarette, I won't even kiss Martin Butler . . .*

'The little girl's fine, love.' A lady was leaning over me, looking at me with grave concern in her eyes. 'Your friend . . . she pushed her out of the way.'

'Sam?' I tried to stand up but the pavement tilted beneath me so that I swayed, hanging onto the stranger. 'Where's Sam? What happened? I can't remember . . . I didn't see . . .'

'She dived in front of the car. She probably saved the little girl's life.'

The lady must have seen it happen. She was trembling with shock. A solitary tear ran down her plump cheek. She was probably a mother herself. I imagined Christine finding out that her child had nearly been run over while Sam and I were supposed to be looking after her, and I began to cry myself.

'Is Sam hurt? I want to see her. Please . . . ' I stopped short, terrified by the expression on the kind lady's face. 'Please can I see her?' I finished in a whisper.

'They're giving her first aid,' she said, looking away and wiping her eyes.

Just then the ambulance roared up the road, its sirens screaming, its lights flashing, and everyone was suddenly running to help, to tell their version of what happened. Someone came out of a house with a blanket, wrapped it around me and took me into their living room where I was made to sit down in front of a fire and given a strong cup of tea with sugar. Like an automaton, I did as I was told. I drank the tea, I warmed myself, I let them wash my face and rub some life back into my frozen hands, and all the time I never stopped shaking, and I never stopped crying.

I was taken to hospital later, after the *serious casualty* had been dealt with. I heard the words being whispered around me. 'Serious casualty.' 'Multiple injuries.' 'Life-threatening.' I listened, and I shud-

165

dered, and I cried. At hospital, they gave me an injection, and I slept – I don't know how long for. When I woke up, Mum and Dad were there, and I immediately started to cry again. Held in my mother's arms, I told her it had all been my fault – because it was my birthday; because I was selfish and impatient, and hadn't wanted a five-year-old spoiling my fun, my best friend had jumped in front of a car to save her sister's life and now she was going to die.

My mum hugged me and soothed me and promised me that none of it was my fault, that everyone got cross with five-year-olds when they were being difficult, that Chloe had run into the road of her own volition, that it was an accident, a terrible accident, nobody's fault. And I was taken to see Sam in Intensive Care, where she lay, as pale and still as a corpse, surrounded by bleeping machinery. I sat by her side, talking to her unresponsive body, telling her what we were going to do when she was better – how we'd go shopping again, and go dancing, and if she was better in time for *her* sixteenth birthday in a couple of months' time I'd buy her the Oasis CD she wanted. And eventually the day came when she blinked, and then the next day she moved her lips, and twitched her fingers, and, finally, she opened her eyes and smiled. And we knew she was going to recover.

'Forgive yourself, Abbie,' said my dad a few months after the accident, when I was still refusing to talk about it. 'You can't go through your life carrying that burden of guilt.' He knew the whole story by then, of course. Everyone did, and everyone had put it behind them. Everyone except me, apparently. 'It wasn't your fault. If anything, it was Sam's. She knows that.'

166

Even Sam gave up, eventually, trying to discuss it with me. Everyone said what a fantastic recovery she'd made – both physically and psychologically. She talked it through at great length with her family; she talked it through gently with Chloe until her little sister, eventually, stopped having nightmares, wetting the bed and being unnaturally quiet and withdrawn, and gradually went back to her normal annoying behaviour – admittedly to everyone's relief. But with me, she had to give up, because I *wouldn't* talk about it. I couldn't handle the fact that Chloe could have died because of our selfish attitude; that Sam nearly *did* die because of it, so I buried it all away and pretended not to think about it.

Four years later, my mum's accident brought it all back up to the surface, but it only served to unleash a kind of anger in me. Why did these things happen to us? Why did God allow them? What was the point of going to church and saying all those prayers, and trying to be good, if He still let horrible things happen to my friends and family?

Basically, my dad's right about me. I'm no good at forgiveness. I can't even forgive God.

As for Sam's accident, I still never talk about it. And I'm certainly not going to start today, just because Brian thinks it's a good idea to bring it up at her fucking *wedding*!

Quarter to seven

There's been a lot of clapping, and a lot of patting Brian on the back and saying well done, good one mate, brilliant speech, didn't know you had it in you.

'It was in the garage,' he says, grinning at Christine as he waves the pages of his speech at her. 'Under the engine.'

We should have guessed. He's had an engine from one of his old cars out there in the garage for as long as I can remember. He's going to do something with it one day, he says. I think everyone's got so used to seeing it there, they don't even notice it any more.

'I'm surprised he did that,' says David, quietly, toying with his cutlery on the table in front of him.

'I'm not. It was obvious, really. Where else would he hide it?'

'I don't mean the engine, Abbie. I'm surprised he said that about Sam's accident.'

I look away, trying to pretend I haven't heard him.

'But then again,' David goes on, without bothering to try to make me listen, 'it's probably a good thing. What with that, and the stuff about not being a hands-on father – maybe Dad thought this was an opportunity to say some things he can't normally find the words for.'

'Maybe,' I say with a shrug.

I'd like to ask him whether a wedding is really a good time for family history to be raked up. It wouldn't happen in *my* family – but then, we're not likely to have any weddings so what would I know?

'Sam likes things out in the open,' David says simply as if he can read my mind.

Me, I prefer to bottle things up and try to forget them. I know.

'After all, it was twelve years ago,' he goes on. 'It was an accident, everyone survived, and Dad must feel very grateful about that today.'

'Of course! We all do!'

Nobody's more grateful than me. I just can't bear to think about what *might* have happened.

'Be happy then, Abbs,' says David unexpectedly, giving me a smile.

He's a good one to talk!

I look across the table at Heather, who's pink-cheeked and flustered from trying to keep Troy quiet during the speeches. She's a strange girl in some ways, but she's friendly and outgoing and can be good fun. OK, she seems to find motherhood a strain, but who doesn't, especially at such a young age, and especially with a demon-child like Troy?

I wonder what's going on between them. Maybe they haven't just had a row – perhaps they're really not very happy together. But Heather doesn't seem particularly upset. Wouldn't she have said something when she came to the house earlier? Or even if she tried to keep it to herself because it's Sam's wedding day, wouldn't we have been able to tell something

169

was wrong? I like to think I'm as reasonably percep-
tive as any other female when it comes to people's
feelings. And I can't imagine Heather being that great
an actress.

David glances across at Gary, sitting on the other
side of me, and raises his eyebrows at me. 'Give him
a nudge! He's supposed to be introducing the next
speech.'

It's true. Brian is back in his seat, everyone has
fallen silent again and they're all looking in Gary's
direction. Phil's hovering, half in and half out of his
chair, obviously wondering whether he should just
stand up and get on with it without waiting for his
best man to introduce him. There are a couple of
meaningful coughs and a murmur of laughter from
around the room. Gary's gone back to sleep at the
table, his head resting on his hand, twitching occasionally as if he's in a lovely dream.

'Hey!' I hiss in his ear, nudging him so hard that
his elbow slips off the table and he jerks awake.
'Wake up!'

'What?' He stares at me, takes in the scene around
him and then jumps to his feet, muttering 'Oh,
Christ!'

There's a hush now, as everyone settles down to
listen.

'Sorry. Sorry, everyone, I ... er ...' He glances
nervously at me. 'I just lost the thread for a minute
there.'

'YOU WAS ASLEEP!' shouts Troy joyfully.

There's another burst of laughter. Heather flushes
almost purple and leans across Troy, trying to cover
his mouth. David puts his finger to his own lips,
whispering 'Ssh!' at him across the table.

170

'Anyway, ladies and gentlemen, it's time now to hand you over—'

'YOU *WAS* ASLEEP!'

Troy has almost bitten through Heather's fingers in his determination to be heard. I suppose, if I'm really honest, I can understand where he's coming from. If *he'd* dozed off at the table he would have been told off. How come adults can do stuff like that and get away with it? No wonder he sounds so indignant.

'Troy,' says David, sternly, 'that's enough.'

'It's time to hand you over,' repeats Gary, a little louder to overcome the competition, 'to the bridegroom – the only person who's ever beaten me in a conker fight and got away with it – my big brother Phil. Phil, over to you.'

He sits down, looking across the table ruefully at Troy, who's meanwhile gone into a mega sulk at being told off by his father.

'Don't like weddings,' he announces huffily as, at the next table, Phil stands up and prepares to begin his speech.

And then, in the expectant silence that falls as everyone sits back to listen to the bridegroom: 'I WANT A POO!'

Ten to seven

PHIL'S SPEECH

Ha, ha, ha! I know how you feel, mate – I'm so bloody nervous I might just follow you out there! Is he OK, Heather? Take him out, yeah, don't worry, love. Kids, eh?

Well, now. Hello all! Like Brian said, Abbie downloaded all this info off the internet about wedding speeches. Bless her – there was reams of it. No, no – I'm grateful Abbie, honest! I'd never have got round to it. I'll tell you the truth, I only got round to looking at it the other day – sorry, Abbs! – and it was a bit late at night, you know, and I'd had a couple of pints, so I don't know how much of it stuck, if you know what I mean. So let's see.

Well, first off, I know I'm supposed to say thanks to Brian for his good wishes and for welcoming me into the family. Brian, I would've said it anyway – even without the internet, OK? Cheers! And, Christine, thanks for everything, Chris – all the help with the flowers and everything, and traipsing around the shops with Sam, choosing her dress – doesn't she look stunning? I must admit, like most blokes I suppose, I couldn't understand all the fuss – how does it take so long to choose one dress for God's sake? But when I saw her coming down that aisle – well, let's just say it was well worth it. I'm a very lucky guy.

Now, I also have to say thank you to two very special people – that's my own mum and dad, Helen and Duncan. I'd like to say they had a hard job bringing me up, but of course, I was such a nice well-behaved kid, I was no trouble at all – was I, Mum? What? Get away – I never got up to any mischief! That was our Gary! Well, OK, I guess in retrospect there might have been one or two little incidents – like that time when I poured red paint over Veronica Smith's hair because she laughed at my trousers. Oh, and that other time when I fell off the school roof and ended up in hospital ... Yes, I thought you would remember that! You've never forgotten it? No, neither have I – I've been scared stiff of heights ever since! And I don't care what the teachers said – I only climbed up there to get Gary's ball back for him, didn't I, Gaz? Gaz? You awake now?

But the thing is, I had a good upbringing, and it's a hard job, isn't it – bringing up kids? I can't imagine how anyone ever manages to do it and get it right. All the decisions you have to make, all the times you have to say no when you want to say yes, or say yes when you want to say no – I think it must be a harder job being a parent than running a bloody multinational company. No wonder people are terrified of taking it on, eh, Sammy? No wonder we're thinking about not bothering with it, eh? If we ever did, though, well, all I can say is I hope we'd make as good a job of it

173

as my mum and dad, that's all. They gave me a bloody good start and I'm grateful for it.

What else? Well, of course, I need to thank everyone for all the terrific presents. We did say not to bother and we meant it, didn't we, Sam? You know, these days, people live together, they get their homes together and everything, before they get married, so it's not like we *need* all the basics for wedding presents – you know, toasters, cruets, tablecloths. My mum and dad said they were driven home from their wedding reception with an ironing board sticking out of the car window – present from some friends who took it to the wedding, wrapped up in silver paper and all! Bizarre. We don't need that kind of stuff, thank goodness, but your generosity has been mind-blowing, despite what we said and Sam and I want to thank you all from the bottom of our hearts. It was enough just to have you all here with us today. But presents too – fantastic!

As I say, Sam and I have been together for a few years now. Some of you might not know the story of how we met. She was singing in the pub – The Dog and Duck. Yeah, that's right, Nick, you remember, don't you! West Ham's win against Arsenal, cup match, three–two after extra time. Good game, yeah! We were celebrating! And suddenly, there was this . . . this *angel* in a blue dress, singing to me. To *me*! I fell in love that night. Yes, and I'm still as much in love as ever, and I still can't believe my luck; not only did I *find* the love of my life, but she's marrying me. It can't get better than this, can it?

Don't cry, Chris! Someone give her a tissue, for God's sake!

Anyway, just to finish off – last thing, I promise –

I've got to say thank you to another two very special people: the bridesmaids. Sam's 'little' sister, Chloe, and her best friend Abbie. Abbie was with Sam that night in the Dog and Duck, by the way, so you can't accuse me of making it up! Girls, you've done a fantastic job today. I know how much help you've given Sam, how much you've put into making the day go smoothly, and just to show our appreciation, here's a little present for you both from me and Sam.

The bridesmaids, ladies and gentlemen – Abbie and Chloe!

You can relax now, Abbie! It's nearly over and nothing's gone wrong yet, has it?

Seven o'clock

It's a beautiful silver necklace with a filigree heart emblem. It's gorgeous. Chloe's fingering hers, almost lovingly, and I think I see the glint of tears in her eyes. It surprises me. Eva leans towards her, takes the necklace from her hands and gently puts it around her neck and fastens it. Suddenly, as if I'm watching myself in the mirror, I feel the same thing happening to me; I feel the necklace being lifted from my hand, I feel it being laid, light and cold, against the skin of my throat; I feel fingers at the back of my neck, working the clasp. For a minute, I hold my breath.

'There you go,' says David lightly.

'Thank you,' I reply automatically. I'm not sure why my voice comes out as a croak.

'It looks lovely,' he adds, turning me to face him.

There's a split second of hesitation between us. My breath still feels strange in my throat, as if I've got a heavy cold.

'*You* look lovely,' he adds, so quietly that I think I must have misheard him.

I think I *did* mishear him.

Obviously.

*

And anyway. What was all that about kids? Since when was there any question, between Sam and Phil, of 'thinking about not bothering' or 'if we ever did'? Eh? It isn't that she's *thinking* about it, or that she *might* – she doesn't want any! Full stop! It was only this morning – this very morning, the morning of her wedding day! – that she told me how worried she was about other people's expectations, her *family's* expectations; how she was afraid that they'd ask her how soon she was going to have a baby, but that she just wanted to stay the same, and not turn into 'something dull and unattractive in an overall cleaning the oven'!

Look, I've known about this for six months. Sam told me. I'm her best friend. She hasn't changed her mind – if she had, I'd have known about it. So what the hell's Phil doing, standing up there, grinning at her and laughing and saying all that stuff about 'if we ever did'? Does *he* think he's going to change his mind one day and want kids? And does he think that when he does, she's going to suddenly laugh and say, yes, OK, fine, I'll have a baby now, I was only joking, I'm fine about it really?

This is making me feel sick with apprehension. You can't get married with such a huge misunderstanding hanging over you, can you? I need to talk to Sam. Badly.

Up till she told me all this about not wanting children, I not only assumed that Sam *would* want them, I also thought she'd make a great mother. It's true that Troy isn't exactly the ideal model on which to base your views of parenthood, but she *has* been patient with him – despite what she says – just as she was always patient with Chloe, apart from that one terrible time.

After the accident, Chloe was different. For a long while, she was quiet, well behaved and disturbingly withdrawn. When Sam came out of hospital she spent about a month at home before the doctors said she was well enough to go back to school. During that time, I watched the two of them together and it was strangely moving to see the little girl, who was barely speaking to anybody, lie down on Sam's bed with her or snuggle up to her on the sofa, under her duvet. They'd watch the TV together in silence, Chloe sucking her thumb while Sam plaited her hair. Or Sam would read to her from one of her favourite books while Chloe held her battered old teddy bear on her lap, endlessly stroking its tatty ears.

It was a phase, and everyone agreed it was a good one, a healing one – one that they both needed to go through. It didn't last for long. By the time Sam was back at school, Chloe had found her feet again – and her voice, unfortunately, although I could understand that the family was massively relieved that she was back to normal.

Over the years, the memory of Chloe as a silent, traumatised little waif faded into incredibility, but even during her worst tantrums, Sam was usually able to pacify her. As she got older, when she reached the point where she wanted to leave home, and then went into her troublesome teenage years, of course, *nobody* could get through to Chloe – not Sam, not David, not her parents; she was a law unto herself.

And then there was Troy.

David hadn't been with Heather all that long when he announced to the family that she was pregnant.

'Are you pleased?' asked Sam automatically.

178

'Pleased?' He looked surprised, as if he hadn't considered this. 'Yes. Yes, I am.'

'You don't sound too sure,' said Brian with heavy sarcasm. 'It's a bit late to have doubts, lad, isn't it?'

David flushed. 'Yes, Dad, I am sure. We're both happy.'

'But you didn't want to bother with getting married first?'

'Brian!' Christine remonstrated. 'Don't start! Not everyone gets married these days, you know. And having a baby isn't a crime. At the end of the day, it's only nature.'

'And I don't suppose you thought about finding somewhere to live,' went on Brian, ignoring her, 'to bring up this baby?'

'She is keeping it, is she?' interrupted Sam, since no one else seemed to have liked to ask.

'Yes, she's keeping it and no, we're not getting married. And yes, we've looked for somewhere to live.' David, at the time, was renting a room in a house, sharing with three other guys. The room was barely even big enough for him, never mind a girlfriend and a baby. And the late-night drinking sessions and general lack of hygiene in the house might have been a great lifestyle for a group of young men but we all knew it would hardly be a good start in life for a child. 'But we can't find anywhere we can afford.'

'She'll have to stay with her parents, then,' said Sam, practically. 'Won't she.'

'They've only got a three-bedroom house and they've got other kids . . .'

'Tough!' said Brian with feeling. 'You should have thought about all this, son, before you forgot your johnnies.'

179

'I didn't *forget* anything,' retorted David. 'We *chose* to have this baby.'

'Well, in that case you're both bloody stupid. Nowhere to live . . . '

'Stop it, both of you,' said Christine. 'What's done is done, and there's no point arguing over it. There's a baby on the way now, and that comes before anything else. Do you love this girl, David?'

The directness of the question took us all aback slightly.

David blinked and thought for a moment, as if it was a new idea to him.

'Yes,' he said eventually. Nobody seemed to notice that it had taken him much too long to answer. 'Yes, I love her.'

'Then she'd better move in here with us,' said Christine firmly. 'And that's settled.'

'*WHAT*?' Chloe, who was thirteen then – and who'd been keeping quiet so that no one realised she was still in the room, listening – exploded with indignation. 'A *baby*, here, in our house?'

'That's what *we* thought when *you* were born,' David reminded her a bit unkindly, although I couldn't blame him.

'It'll be screaming all night! I won't be able to sleep! I won't be able to concentrate on my homework! What about my exams? What about if my friends come round?'

'This isn't about you, Chloe,' Christine told her with unusual firmness – at which Chloe burst into tears and went running out of the room. 'She'll come round,' she added calmly. 'She's at a funny age. *Hormiones*. It's only nature.'

*

180

So Heather and David moved into his old room. Heather, to be fair to her, fitted easily into the Patterson family. Even Brian had to admit she was a good cook, and everyone got their hair cut for free. When Troy was born, they all rallied round to begin with. Even Chloe forgot her tantrums and pleaded to be allowed to hold him, to feed him, to take him out in his pram. It was a novelty, of course – and it soon wore off. Within months there was a constant stream of complaints. The baby cried every evening, just when everyone wanted to watch TV. There were nappies everywhere. The house smelled of sick, and milk, and poo. The washing machine was always on. The dryer was gobbling up electricity. Heather was too tired to help with the housework any more. Then Troy started crawling, and eventually walking, and things got even worse. Everything had to be put out of reach, or it got picked up, broken, or worse – possibly swallowed. Toy cars, teddies, balls and picture books were spread around the house, tripping people up. Granddad stepped on a piece of Lego and nearly fell down the stairs. Brian picked up his pint mug to drink his beer and found a well-chewed rusk floating in it. You know – the sort of things that happen in all households with a baby. Except that in this household, the baby hadn't been an intended addition in the first place and the whole experience was beginning to sour. Rapidly.

Before too long the family was split down the middle. Brian and Frank made no secret of the fact that they wanted their house back the way it was pre-Troy. Chloe, finding she now had adult allies, was naturally vociferous in her agreement. Christine, who'd fallen in love with her little grandson and also

181

enjoyed Heather's company around the house, was equally determined that they should stay, and Sam backed her up.

'I know it's difficult,' she told me with a sigh, 'but what are we supposed to do? Turn them out on the street? David's working flat out to save up for a place of their own. If they have to spend everything he earns on rent for some crummy poky flat, they'll *never* get on their feet. And it's not Troy's fault.'

It was never Troy's fault. It wasn't Troy's fault that he screamed so much; that he refused to be potty-trained; that he wouldn't eat anything but bread and jam; that he wouldn't go to sleep; that he had a habit of throwing things across the room ... I could go on and on.

Eventually, it was his bed-hopping that was the last straw. Once he was old enough to climb out of his cot, he'd get up in the middle of the night and clamber into his parents' bed. Then one night David left their bedroom door open and when Frank woke up in the morning, there was a toddler in a wet nappy sitting beside him on his pillow, playing with his false teeth. It might have been 'only nature', but even Christine had to admit that perhaps the time had come for this particular branch of the family to put down its own roots.

It was dramatically quiet in the Patterson house after they finally moved out and into their own place. Chloe was smug in her gratification. Frank and Brian stretched out their legs, turned on the TV and sighed with the pleasant anticipation of uninterrupted evenings. And Sam? She jumped into her little red Mini and drove round to her brother's flat to babysit. She was the only one prepared to do it. The only one who could handle the demon-child, with the same brand of quiet patience she'd used years before on Chloe.

That's why I always thought she'd want to be a mum.

Beside me, Gary is rising to his feet. While I've been sitting here daydreaming, I'd almost forgotten what's coming next. I take a deep breath, wondering who's the more nervous – him or me? The best man's speech is supposed to be the highlight of the wedding reception. It's supposed to be bright, interesting, funny, witty. It's *not* supposed to be given by someone who's poured so much alcohol down his throat that he's had to be sobered up, and has then fallen asleep at the table.

'Are you OK?' I whisper fiercely to Gary.

There's a lot more I want to say. *Are you capable of this? Or are you going to forget what to say, or worse – say something stupid, something vulgar, something offensive? Are you going to ruin the whole bloody day for your brother? For Sam?*

'I'm fine, Abbie,' he whispers back, giving me a look that tells me he knows exactly what I'm thinking. 'Stop worrying.'

If only I could.

'Can you all hear me at the back?' he begins. 'OK, good, good. Now, we've heard from the bride's father, and we've heard from the bridegroom, but before we move into the main attraction of the day – no, not the wedding, don't be silly – *my* speech! – I'm just supposed to ask whether anyone else wants to say a few words. Of course, I realise you're all going to

183

say no, so I'll be able to move swiftly into ...

'What?

'Who?

'Christine?

'I ... er ... well, yes, of course she can. No, Brian, no, that's fine. Of course you can, Chris. Protocol? We don't care about that, do we, every-body? I think the bride's mother's *certainly* entitled to talk at her daughter's wedding.

'So here you go then – slight change of plan. I'll hand you over now to Christine, mother of the bride, who wants to say a few words. Christine!'

As she gets unsteadily to her feet, the blue stripes in her hair glinting in the light, I close my eyes and rest my head in my hands. I feel a sinking in my heart. After all the planning, all the hard work I've put into ensuring that this day goes according to plan! Christine saying a few words? Please, please tell me it's just a bad dream.

'It's cool, Abbie,' whispers David. 'She'll be fine.'

I wish I shared his confidence.

Five past seven

CHRISTINE'S SPEECH

Thanks, Gary, love. Thanks, everybody. Sorry, I'm a bit nervous. Sorry ... whoops, that's my drink I've just knocked over. Oh dear.

Well, I know this is a bit ... you know, not quite the normal thing. And I don't want to take up too much of your time. I know it's Gary you want to hear, really, what with him being the best man, and probably he's got a lot of jokes and all! That's only nature, isn't it? The best man always has to have a laugh, it was the same at my wedding – mine and Brian's – wasn't it, dear? Tony's speech? Remember?

Anyway, as I say, I'll keep this very short. I just wanted to say a little bit, as it's, you know, my daughter's wedding day – a little bit about love, really.

You young people, I know what it is: you don't think your parents know anything about love. I suppose you look at us, and, well, we're not young and beautiful any more, are we? We might have been once, when we were your age, but we lost that along the way, somehow, what with giving birth and going through the hard times, looking after the kids, and not having enough money and everything. Anyway, sorry, enough of that – I'm not talking about hard times and misery, not today – it's a wedding, not a funeral.

What I'm trying to say is this. At your age, it's easy to be in love. It's only nature, at the end of the day. It's lovely, isn't it – seeing my Sammy happy, marrying her lovely young man? Don't laugh, he *is* a lovely young man, aren't you, dear? I couldn't wish for a happier day. It's what every mother wants.

Now, on the other hand, when you get to our age, well, it's a different thing altogether. You think you're always going to feel the same way you do today. Of course you do. That's what it's all about, isn't it?

But you won't.

I'm telling you: you won't feel like you do today, when you get home late from work because the trains are playing up, and you've run out of milk, and the central heating's gone wrong. Or ... let's say the baby's been crying all night and you've got a headache and all the bills come in on the same day. Yeah, we've all had some of that. Or if you've had a row about the ironing, or the housework, or, like, he says you never listen to him and you say he never says he loves you. That's life, isn't it? It happens to all of us. It's only nature.

What I'm trying to say is be kind to yourselves. Don't think it means you've fallen out of love. Don't think, if you stop feeling weak at the knees when you see each other, or you don't want to jump into bed every other minute of the day, that it's all over. Don't think because you might grow old, and grumpy, and sit in silence in front of the TV sometimes because you can't be bothered to talk, that the love's gone out of the window.

Fact is, the way I see it, marriage isn't the same thing as a love affair. It's not about just staying together till the passion wears off. It's for life, or that's what it's meant to be about, isn't it, Brian, dear? And, to be quite honest, well, if you look at each other in thirty or forty years' time and think: he's a miserable, ugly old bugger but he's what I picked so I'm sticking with him, then I reckon *that's* love.

That's all I wanted to say, really.

Sorry to take up your time.

Have a lovely day, Sammy darling. Thank you. Whoops – sorry – nearly knocked my chair over. Thanks. All right, Gary?

Ten past seven

For a few heart-stopping moments, there's total silence.

Then the whole place erupts.

People at the back are standing up, clapping, cheering, like it's a football match instead of a wedding reception. Sam's hugging her mum and looks like she's crying. Great! On her wedding day! Brian has his arm round Christine's shoulders and I catch him running his hand over his eyes as if he can't see properly. Phil's smiling, his parents are holding hands across the table and looking gooey at each other, and all round the room, couples are kissing each other and aunties are wiping tears away.

This is a fine carry-on, isn't it!

This is *exactly* why it wasn't a good idea to let the mother of the bride say her 'few words'. I could have told you this was what it'd be like – a lot of nonsense about 'only nature' and some sentimental twaddle about loving each other when you're old and miserable. She should know!

'Well done, Mum,' I hear David calling across to her, above the commotion around us. 'Well said.'

There's a break in his voice. I turn to look at him

and he gives me a quick, kind of apologetic smile.

'It must have taken a lot of nerve for Mum to get up and say all that.'

Or a lot of champagne, more likely.

'It was lovely,' says Heather, blowing her nose loudly.

David ignores her and turns back to me. 'She means it, you know.' He shrugs. 'My dad hasn't always been a miserable, bitter old git. Life does that to people, sometimes.'

He's right, of course. Even I remember Brian in the old days, before he lost his job. He was never exactly my idea of Prince Charming, and because he was about as far removed from my own father as Homer Simpson is from Father Christmas, I've never been close to him. I just put up with him because he was Sam's dad. But I have to admit, I remember him having a sense of humour, and playing rounders with us kids in the park, and making us laugh with his raucous singing of the latest pop songs and impersonations of TV stars. He did used to have a bit more life to him. He didn't always spend all his time sprawled on the sofa with a beer in his hand.

Life does that to people.

'So we just accept it, do we? We carry on, and love them regardless?'

Maybe I shouldn't have said that to David – not when there's possibly something wrong between him and Heather. I'm not exactly going to get the first prize for diplomacy.

'Sorry ...' I begin. But he's looking at me with a strange, wistful sort of smile.

'Yes,' he says. 'Yes, that's exactly what we do – carry on and love them regardless.'

189

I don't know what to say to this. I suppose I should be pleased for him, that he's able to say, in effect, that he still loves Heather despite whatever's happened. I *should* be pleased, but for some reason I'm finding it kind of irritating and annoying.

I look at Gary, wondering if he's going to take for ever to stand up and get control of his audience again. I think, the sooner we get his speech over with now, and get on with the dancing, the better. At least everyone can relax then, including me, and if anyone else wants to get overemotional at least the whole bloody room won't be listening.

But Gary's staring moodily at Chloe, who's leaning against Eva and holding her hand as they whisper to each other, blocking out the rest of the world.

'Gary,' I prompt, again. 'Are we going to get on with the show now? Unless anyone else wants to stand up and pour out their heart?'

But before he can answer, there's a shout from the other side of the table, where Troy's been allowed to get down from his chair and play with his toy car on the floor.

'MUMMEEEE! I've got a tummy ache! I'm going to be ...'

Fortunately or unfortunately, depending on how you look at it, the word 'sick' is lost in the retching.

But as Heather grabs her son and runs for the toilets with him in her arms, his overindulgence of cheesecake and orange squash is all too evident down the front of his nice little shirt. And down the front of her flouncy pink dress.

'I suppose,' says David with a sigh, 'I'd better go and help her.'

But he doesn't. He sits, watching the double doors

190

swinging closed behind her.

'Shall I go?' I ask him. 'It might be easier ...'

'Would you mind, Abbie? Thanks.'

I follow Heather outside and find her in the ladies' toilet, in floods of tears. Troy's playing with the roller-towel, looking as right as rain now his digestive system's sorted itself out.

'Are you OK, Heather?'

Stupid question. She looks at me resentfully.

'Look at me! I've tried wiping it all off but it's hopeless! I can't go back in! I stink!' She sniffs and wipes her nose. 'I'll have to go home!'

'No you won't. Take your dress off. Quickly! It's not as bad as it looks. Troy, come here, darling. Let's take that mucky shirt off, shall we?'

I peel the disgusting smelly garment off Troy's unresisting body, dampen some paper towels and give his chest and tummy a brisk rub-down which leaves him collapsed on the floor in fits of giggles. Heather's stepping out of her pastel-pink summer dress as I rinse Troy's shirt under the taps and leave it soaking in one of the sinks.

'Where's his waistcoat?'

'It's here. I brought it out.' I turn and see Eva, standing in the doorway with the miniature waistcoat in her hands. 'He'd taken it off and left it on his chair. I thought you might need it. Can I help?'

'Thanks.'

I turn my attention to Heather as Eva holds Troy still and buttons up the waistcoat over his naked top half.

'It's so warm in here anyway, Troy,' she tells him conversationally. 'You don't need all those clothes

191

on, do you? You're as warm as toast.'

'I'm as "warm as toast"!' he repeats happily, looking at her in awe. 'I *like* toast.'

'You won't be eating anything else this evening, young man!' Heather snaps.

I watch his face crumple and his little mouth form itself into a sulk. I catch Eva's eye and she raises her eyebrows at me. Suddenly I feel, instinctively but with an absolute certainty, that this girl who's still a student and is actually a couple of years younger than Heather, has so much more common sense and substance to her that I feel sure she's going to be good for Chloe. However it ends up.

'OK, Heather,' I tell her. 'Get me a few more paper towels. If we just get the worst off ... this material is so light and flimsy ... we'll be able to rinse it off and dry it under the hand-dryer.'

'There'll be a *stain*,' she says mutinously, passing me the paper towels.

'The pattern will hide it.'

'Anyway, Heather, thank goodness it happened after the photos,' says Eva brightly.

Heather manages a tight little half-smile in response.

I feel more like telling her that she's not the bride, no one's going to be looking at her and if she wants to go home do we really care? But I suppose that's not really helpful. And she *did* do a good job on my hair – even if her prediction has turned out to be right. It's already all come down and is hanging round my face in its normal straggly rats' tails.

Ah, well. Some things just can't be helped. But I've done pretty well with the flouncy pink dress, even if I do say so myself. If you don't look too closely, you'd never know the slightly damp splodge just to the left of the white flower between Heather's boobs is not part of the pattern, but the remains of a vomit stain.

And by the time we creep back into the room, of course, Gary's already on his feet and is launched into his speech. At least I haven't had any more time to worry about it.

Twenty past seven

GARY'S SPEECH

... so yes, as I say, thanks, Sam and Phil on behalf of the bridesmaids, Abbie and Chloe – ah, there's Abbie now. Anyway. Right.

Like Phil and Brian, I've had my orders from Abbie about this speech. And I actually spent weeks sitting at the computer trying to compose something suitable. But you know what? This is what I'm going to do with it – yep, that's right: I'm ripping it to shreds! This speech that I've toiled over, agonised over, long into the lonely nights when everyone else was in bed asleep – I'm binning it. There. It's gone. Don't look so shocked! It was rubbish. You see, all the tips I picked up on the internet, all the rules Abbie told me, all the protocol I tried to learn off by heart – they were rubbish because this, today, is about *one special couple*. A special couple who chose *me* to deliver something *personal* about them on the most important day of their lives. You can't get that off the internet, 'cos where love and marriage are concerned, sorry but One Size doesn't Fit All.

So, where do I start? Maybe by telling you a little

bit about Phil – my big brother. The year he was born – 1979 – I hadn't even been considered, never mind conceived, so I can only rely on what I've been told. Apparently it was a crap year. "YMCA" was the number one hit of the year – I think that tells you all you need to know about the culture and tastes of the time – and funnily enough it's still the only thing Phil can dance to. It was his favourite song all the time we were growing up. Mum says they were the first four letters of the alphabet he learned, so maybe it's not surprising his spelling's a bit suspect.

Of course, it was only his favourite song till the night he met Sam. I know some of you guys had the misfortune to be with him that night in the pub, and I've heard what a pathetic sight he was. Don't worry, he was even worse by the time I saw him. I actually thought he'd had a stroke or something. He had this strange look in his eyes and he kept making a growling noise in the back of his throat that sounded vaguely like a very bad rendition of "Big Spender". I wasn't sure whether he'd fallen in love or won the lottery.

Phil and I had our share of fights, like any brothers. Being five years younger, I had to resort to fighting dirty. I learned a lot from Phil. There was the time we were playing over the park, and he got mad at me and pushed me in the lake, so I pretended I was drowning. He was so scared, he stripped off his belt from his jeans and dangled it over the edge for me to grab hold of. You notice he *didn't* jump in after me? So much for brotherly love! Anyway, there he was, balanced on his knees on the edge of the lake, screaming at me. The lake was deep but I was treading water. I got hold of the end of his belt, gave it a sharp yank and toppled *him* into the water. We both got a telling-off from Mum that day, from what I remember.

By the time I was fifteen and he was twenty I was as big as him, but it was too late then – I had to accept that he was never going to give me back my yo-yo, or the packet of Jelly Tots he stole from me in 1989. So my first piece of advice to you, Sam, is don't let him play with your yo-yo and keep a tight hold on your Jelly Tots. But I'm sure your mum's told you that already, hasn't she?

She also told me that it only seems like yesterday that she sent you off to bed at night with a dummy. And now . . . here she is doing the same thing all over again. All right, I admit it – that's one of the ones I *did* get off the internet!

I know you're probably all expecting me to regale you with stories of booze, drugs and wild women. But I'm not supposed to be talking about myself here! As you probably know already, Phil isn't much of a drinker. His stag weekend was the most expensive I've ever been on – not because of where we stayed (honestly, Dirty Mary's Bawdy House was the only place in Edinburgh where I could get any rooms at the last minute). No, it was because we kept on getting another round in, in the hope of getting the bride-groom drunk, but apparently he was passing his drinks round the table so everyone *else* got slaughtered while he was still nursing his second pint. That's Phil for you! What other guy comes back from his stag night more sober than he went away? You're a lucky girl, Sam. Love might be blind, but at least he's not getting blind *drunk*. Unlike some of the rest of us. It's all right – I've sobered up a bit now!

Well, Phil's a lucky guy, too, isn't he? Again, being my big brother, he was always held up as a kind of shining example to me. *Work hard at school like Philip. Do your homework properly like Philip. Play fair like Philip. Be good like Philip. Eat up your greens like Philip.* God, I can't tell you how much it got up my nose! I used to go to bed and dream of the day that someone would tell him to: *Fail your exams like Gary; Spit out your cabbage like Gary; Wet your bed like Gary.* Well, now for the first time I can honestly say I hope I follow in my brother's footsteps. *Find a lovely, talented, beautiful girl to marry, like Philip* sounds like a bloody good idea, except that I doubt whether there are many more around quite like her. And even if there are – well, they wouldn't be interested in me, that's for sure. Trust Phil – he always did win the first prize! Sam's a lovely girl and she deserves a good husband. Luckily for you, Phil, she didn't find one so she's ended up marrying you!

Finally, well I couldn't really finish without the traditional embarrassing story about the bridegroom, could I? OK, so maybe Phil isn't much of a boozer but he always had a bit of an eye for the ladies ... you know what I mean? He was probably about fifteen when he first brought a girlfriend home. I was only ten and like a lot of boys at that age I thought girls were horrible. It really got on my nerves that he preferred to hang out with that stupid giggly creature instead of playing computer games with me. But it didn't last long, did it, Phil? She was scared of dogs. Animals, you know, have always been Phil's first love, but he shut his Alsatian, Rolo, in the garage when this bird came round. So I did what I had to do – let him out. You know what dogs are like – if someone runs away from them, they think it's a game. They run after them! We never saw her again. Of course, I thought it was hilarious.

I didn't set the dogs on *Sam*, you notice. I'm not sure whether that proves how much I like Sam, or how scared I am of getting another kicking from my brother.

Anyway that just about wraps it up, so thanks for listening. I think in a little while they'll be moving the tables ready for the evening, but in the meantime let's just raise our glasses one last time: to Sam and Phil, everybody – may they always be as much in love as they are today. Sam and Phil.

Half past seven

I'm so horrified, I can hardly lift my glass.

I try to catch Sam's eye, but she's looking the other way.

Why? Why the bloody hell did Gary need to do that? It was a great speech, up till he had to go and mention . . .

'That was Julia,' I hiss at him, angrily, as he sits down.

'Sorry?' He looks at me with complete bewilderment. He's flushed with the relief of finishing his speech. 'What was?'

'That girl. Phil's *first girlfriend*.'

'Really?' He gives a snort of laughter. 'What, that stupid bird in the micro-miniskirts? I don't remember that being Ju . . .' He stops and frowns. 'So you're telling me . . .'

I sigh. 'Gary, we were all just kids then. You were just a baby. You only remember it because you enjoyed setting Rolo on her.'

'But I never realised he went out with her back then! Before . . .'

'It was only once or twice. She went out with everybody. He was just one of many,' I say, with feeling.

*

199

The boys were practically queuing up for her with their tongues hanging out. It wasn't that she was *easy*. She wasn't even a tease. She used to tell me and Sam that she actually only really liked kissing, nothing more, and she couldn't understand why they all seemed to think she was up for it. I understood it, though, even then, and even though I never got asked out myself. Julia was just one of those girls who *look* as though they want sex. It wasn't just the good looks and the short skirts; it was something inherent in her nature. Her walk, her laugh, the way she tossed her hair. It took me many years of jealousy and resentment before I realised that she wasn't doing it on purpose. But I still wished she'd stop doing it.

She said she didn't want sex, but she certainly wanted boyfriends. Sam was probably right – she must have been insecure at some level. She needed everyone to see how popular she was, so she went from boyfriend, to boyfriend, to boyfriend, with ruthless haste and abandon. She told us she kept a list. She didn't give them marks out of ten or anything vulgar like that – she didn't stay with them for long enough to care whether they were kind, or fun to be with, or even if they were good kissers. She just wanted names for the list. Names, and numbers. My dad once told me that people equate numbers with power. He was actually talking about the sizes of church congregations but I remember thinking that it was equally true of Julia's list of boyfriends.

At that time, we didn't know Phil. He went to a different school, but he lived near Julia. Sam and I didn't get to meet him – she wasn't with him for long enough – he was just another name in her notebook.

We both laughed when she told us about the incident with the dog, of course, although Sam didn't laugh quite as much as me because she's a bit scared of dogs herself.

'I bet his little brother got into trouble about it,' I remember pointing out to her. 'He won't do it again, Ju.'

'No, he won't, because I'm not going round there again!' she retorted vehemently. 'I was getting fed up with him anyway.'

After two dates. Typical.

When Sam and Phil met, almost ten years later, and they started going out, there was obviously a moment of instant recognition when Sam introduced him to Julia, but neither of them said anything. I suppose that to say 'Oh yes, I remember him. I snogged him on the sofa when we were fifteen, and he tried to get my bra undone,' wouldn't be entirely appropriate when you're being introduced to the love of your friend's life. It wasn't until much later that we found out they'd met before. And by then it was too late.

'Are you OK?'

It's no good. I've had to get up and come over to Sam's table. I couldn't bear to think how that story of Gary's might have upset her. Fortunately, Phil's wandered away to chat to some friends at the other side of the room.

'I'm fine,' she laughs, getting up and giving me a hug. 'How are *you*?' She holds me out at arm's length and touches my cheek, suddenly looking concerned. 'Chill out, now, Abbs. The worst is over!'

'Sorry. I . . . just . . . I was worried.'

'You've worried *far* too much. You've been such a

darling, taking all this strain on-board; I know how much agony it's been for you. Now, all you need to do for the rest of the evening is relax and enjoy yourself. Right?'

'This isn't about me,' I protest, miserably. 'That isn't the point.'

She drops her voice and takes hold of my hand, looking into my eyes. 'Abbie, it was funny. OK? The story about Julia, and the dog – I'd forgotten all about that. It made me laugh.'

'Really?'

'Really. And don't blame Gary – he didn't even realise who she was.'

'I know. But . . .'

'I'm over it, Abbs. The only thing that upsets me about the whole Julia business is that she didn't come to the wedding. I'd have liked to have drawn a line under it.'

'Perhaps she realised it wouldn't be exactly tactful.'

'Perhaps. But let's not dwell on it, eh?'

'I agree. Absolutely. Onwards and upwards, Mrs Reynolds!'

'Eek!!! I'm a *married woman*!'

'And a gorgeous one, Sammy.'

'Remember what you promised? You won't let me wear aprons and . . .'

'No knitting patterns. No jam making. I promise!'

'Thanks, Abbie. I mean . . . for everything. I'll do it all for you, you know, when . . . '

'When I get married? Ha! You'll have a long wait.'

'I don't think so!' she says, tucking her arm through mine affectionately. 'After all, it *was* you who caught the bouquet, wasn't it?'

Yeah. The *tatty*, *crumpled*, *squashed* bouquet. Just about right!

I've actually sat down in Phil's seat next to Sam and we're having a nice girlie chat about the speeches, and the other guests, who's wearing what and who's already had too much to drink, when we suddenly become aware that Gary's getting back to his feet.

'What?' My throat tightens with anxiety again. Not another unscheduled person wanting to give a speech? Please, not Chloe, for God's sake?

'The cake,' Sam reminds me.

'Oh, God, yes! I'd almost forgotten!' I glance at Sam. 'What's funny?'

'Nothing.' She tries, unsuccessfully, to wipe the smile off her face. 'Nothing at all.'

'The cake looks gorgeous,' I comment, but this just seems to start her off laughing again. 'What?' I repeat. 'They didn't drop it, or something, did they?' From this distance, it looks absolutely fine – the traditional three tiers, with the little bride and groom figures on top – but maybe there's a squashed bit round the back, or something. Sam had it made by a shop in town, so it's not as if it's an amateur job. What's the joke?

'OK, ladies and gentlemen,' calls Gary, tapping his glass with a spoon again. 'My final official duty this evening is to ask the bride and groom to make their way over to the table at the side there, please, for the cutting of the cake. Sam and Phil?'

Sam gets to her feet, still smirking to herself, and joins Phil, who's brandishing the cake slice casually as if he's about to do a spot of knife throwing. He looks at Sam and they both grin widely at each other.

203

Whatever the joke is here, they're obviously the only ones in on it. Is the cake going to fall apart when they cut into it? Is it the wrong cake underneath the icing – a Black Forest gateau instead of rich fruit? A jelly? A meat pie? My imagination's working overtime. No one else seems to have noticed the happy couple giggling together as they pose in the traditional way for all the photographers, their hands entwined over the handle of the knife. They hold the pose for a few minutes, smiling at the cameras, and then ease the knife through the icing to make the first ritual cut before allowing the maître d' to carry the cake back to the kitchen for slicing.

'What was all that about?' I ask Sam as she and Phil walk, hand in hand and still giggling, back to their table.

'What?' she asks innocently.

'Come off it. The grins, the giggling, the whole in-joke there. Am I missing something?'

'You and everybody else!' She's laughing out loud now. 'But don't worry about it, Abbie. I just said to Phil – if nobody notices anything, then it obviously doesn't matter, does it?'

We don't get a chance to discuss it any further because at that point Frank shuffles up to us with his trousers undone, calling me Julia and asking whose wedding it is.

'Come and sit with me now, Dad,' Christine calls, and I lead him over to her, trying to whisper discreetly to him about his trousers. 'And do your trousers up, for God's sake!' she adds in a screech that sets Troy off in a hyperactive fit of jumping around screaming with laughter.

I sit down on the other side of Frank. 'Does he

really not know whose wedding it is?' I whisper to Christine.

'Of course he does! Dad – you know who's just got married today, don't you?'

'Julia?' he says, looking at me hopefully.

'No, I'm Abbie, Frank,' I try, patiently. 'I'm a bridesmaid, but Sammy's the bride. It's Sam and Phil's wedding.'

'Where's Julia?' he persists, gazing around the room.

'She's not here,' says Christine, giving me a wary look. 'Bless his heart, Abbie, he can't help it, love. He can't remember things. He gets a bit muddled.'

'I know. It's all right.'

'But she *should* be here,' Frank's going on. 'Sammy's wedding, is it?' He gives me a look that's only slightly less than hostile. *'Julia* should be the bridesmaid. She's our Sammy's best friend.'

Thanks a million. I can feel the smile freezing on my face.

'Sorry, Abbie, dear,' says Christine, looking pained. 'He doesn't mean it.'

'I know. Don't worry.' I try to force myself to say 'It's all right' again, but the words are stuck in my throat.

It isn't all right, not really. Because the fact is, however much I don't want to admit it, she *should* be here. Not because she's Sam's best friend. She's not her friend at all now, and hasn't been for a long time. No – she should be here because Sam wanted her to be.

But I thought I knew better.

Twenty to eight

The tables have been moved to the sides of the room, leaving the floor free for dancing. Troy and two or three other small children are playing a raucous game of running at full pelt across the floor, throwing themselves down on their knees and rolling over and over. Any minute now, one of them's going to get hurt and all hell will be let loose.

'He's been *quite* good, though,' says Heather, seeing me watching them. 'It's a long day, and they do have to let off steam.'

'I know.' It's a shame they can't go somewhere else to let off steam but there you go. 'I just hope he doesn't make himself sick again.'

'No. I haven't let him have any more to eat. He'll probably fall asleep later on.'

We can only hope and pray.

'Are *you* all right?' I ask her, with a sudden flash of sympathy. She's a nice girl really, and it must have been hard for her, coping with a child at such a young age. I don't suppose she's made a worse job of it than anyone else. Troy's just a normal little boy, isn't he?

'Yeah, my dress doesn't look *too* bad, does it? Thanks for that, Abbie. I just panicked.'

206

Actually I wasn't talking about her dress. I was wondering about her relationship. But I guess it's none of my business.

'Where's Chris?' Brian asks me – as if I should know. I might be the chief bridesmaid, but am I supposed to keep a constant check on where everyone is, doing a headcount every five minutes like a teacher on a school outing?

'Gone to the loo?' I suggest.

'Go and hurry her up, then, Abbie, will you? They're waiting to do the first dance.'

Great! Teacher's on toilet duty now. I push open the door to the ladies', where two aunties are powdering their noses in the mirror and a colleague of Sam's from work is leaning against the sink whilst her mate splashes cold water on her face and asks her whether she thinks it was the champagne or the cheesecake that did it?

'Christine?' I call, tapping on the two closed cubicle doors. 'Are you in here?'

'There's an old granny in that one,' says the girl doing the water revival, nodding at the first cubicle. 'And,' she drops her voice to a stage whisper, 'one of those *lesbians* in the other one. So watch yourself!' she adds with a giggle.

I can actually feel the expression on my face hardening to something like granite. I catch sight of myself in the mirror and I almost frighten myself.

'Sorry,' says the girl with a shrug. 'But she *is* old ... look ...'

Phil's nan, who might be over eighty but walks with a sprightly step and is as bright as a button, comes out of the cubicle and chats to the aunties as

207

she washes her hands. I continue to stare angrily at the girl with the sick friend, who's now stopped splashing her face and turned to stare back at me.

'What?' she says, as the three older women go out. 'You all right, mate?'

I don't know why I'm so mad. This stupid girl and her throwaway prejudiced remarks are nothing to do with me. We all hear pathetic jokes like that all the time, don't we, and normally I'd just sigh and ignore it. But I feel *outraged* that she seems to think it's OK to come to a friend's wedding and insult the other guests.

'The people you're being so rude about,' I tell her, calmly but quite loudly, 'are Sam's sister and her girl-friend. So I think perhaps you might like to apologise.'

As I'm saying this, Eva has opened the cubicle door behind me. She meets my eyes in the mirror, and shakes her head at me.

'It doesn't matter,' she whispers.

'Hilary,' says the sick girl leaning against the sink, 'say sorry. That wasn't very nice, what you said.'

'Didn't mean anything by it,' says Hilary, shrugging again. 'Takes all types, doesn't it? Just don't think they should be holding hands, really, to be quite honest. Not at a wedding.'

'So you don't think weddings are about love?' I retort, my anger still clipping my words and making my voice sound harsh and strange to my ears.

I don't often get angry. I don't like feeling out of control. Part of me wishes I hadn't started this; but I can't just let it go. It's not *right*.

'Yeah, 'course!' says Hilary, beginning to sound bored. 'What's your problem? It's about *love*, innit, but not *that* sort of love. You ask the vicar! I know what *he'd* say!'

'Actually, you don't,' I say, smoothly. 'But I do. He'd say that we should *all* love each other and that none of us should judge each other. Only God can do that.'

I'm shocked at myself. What am I thinking of – spouting Christianity to a couple of half-cut birds in a toilet? Even Dad would have told me to walk away. 'Walk away with your head high,' he used to tell me, when kids at school teased me about being the vicar's daughter, a Bible-basher. But I'm on a roll now. It's like all those stupid girls in the school playground, jeering and pouring out their inane misconceptions, are suddenly embodied by this one spiteful, ignorant person in front of me. And now I'm *not* walking away.

'The vicar would say,' I carry on boldly, 'that God would look more favourably on people who show love to each other – no matter what sex they are – than on those who make nasty, hurtful comments.'

'Fuck off!' retorts Hilary, finally deciding she's had enough. 'Who the fuck asked you, anyway?'

'And what makes you think *you* know what the vicar thinks?' adds her mate, who's perked up a bit now things are getting heated.

'I know what he thinks,' I say, smiling at last, 'because I used to live with him.'

There's total silence as I take Eva's arm and open the door. We walk out with our heads held high.

'That was brilliant,' she says, laughing. 'Their faces were a picture!' Then she sighs and adds more seriously, 'But you shouldn't have bothered. It's not worth it.'

'Normally I wouldn't have,' I admit. My knees are feeling wobbly now it's over. 'I'm usually too scared – I hate confrontations. But it just made me mad. How dare she come to Sam's wedding and insult you and Chloe?'

'You're a funny girl, Abbie,' she says, smiling at me with an affection that seems out of proportion to the few hours we've known each other. 'I always got the impression from Chloe that you didn't have a lot of time for her. But actually, you care a lot about their whole family, don't you?'

'Of course I do,' I say, feeling suddenly, inexplicably, like I've been stripped naked. 'They're Sam's family.'

'And yours too?' she suggests gently.

I don't bother to answer. She's already seen far enough into my soul.

One year, when I was about thirteen or fourteen, Sam asked me to spend Christmas Day at her house. It was probably the most exciting invitation I'd ever had. I knew, from spending so much time at the Pattersons' during the lead-up to the big day, how different it was from the quiet festivities in our own home. Our Christmases followed the same predictable routine: getting up early for church, a glass of sherry with a few of the most faithful parishioners, the exchange of modest gifts, a nice dinner which avoided any undue excesses, either of calories ('Think of those less fortunate who'd be happy with a crust from our plates') or of alcohol ('Everything in moderation, Abbie – pleasures should be savoured, not guzzled'), and a quiet afternoon playing Scrabble or watching innocuous TV programmes.

Christmas at the Pattersons', I knew, would be rowdy, exuberant and fun. For a start, there'd be no church – and I couldn't feel guilty if nobody went, and nobody even offered to take me, could I? There'd be alcohol – and plenty of it. There'd be loads of brightly wrapped, extravagant presents; there'd be tins of biscuits, bowls of nuts, chocolates, lashings of cream with everything and lashings of brandy *in* everything. They'd play noisy argumentative games and probably shout and swear at each other, but they'd also hug each other, kiss each other, try to dance with each other, laugh and shout and tell rude jokes. The Pattersons didn't *savour* their pleasures. They opened up their arms and dived into them. I wanted to be part of it. I wanted it more than anything else in the world. I wanted it so much, it didn't even occur to me that even *asking* for it would hurt my parents' feelings.

'Christmas Day,' Dad told me quietly, while Mum left the room dabbing her eyes with a tissue, 'is for family. You can see your friends every other day of the year, Abbie.'

'They've invited me,' I said, stubbornly. I wanted to add that if he wouldn't let me go, I'd hate him for ever, but I wasn't allowed to hate anyone, and anyway I knew I wouldn't really mean it.

'Have they? Sam's parents have invited you, have they?' He looked at me with his level, knowing gaze that made me drop my eyes.

'Sam has. Her parents will say yes.'

'Well. Shall we see what her parents say first?'

This was confusing. On the one hand, it seemed like I'd won: after all, Christine and Brian were certainly not going to refuse to have me for

Christmas. On the other hand, I didn't *feel* like I'd won. I felt uncomfortable, as if I'd done something vaguely wrong – picked my nose in church, or broken a plate and hidden the pieces – and was waiting to be told off about it.

The next day, I went back to Sam's house with her after school.

'Abbie's mum and dad want to know if it's OK for her to come over for Christmas,' said Sam to Christine.

Christine put down the carrot she was peeling and wiped her hands. She looked at Sam, then turned to look at me. For far too many seconds, she didn't say anything. Then: 'Sam, go and tidy your room.'

'But Mum! Abbie's here.'

'Your room needs tidying,' insisted Chris with a steely glare at Sam, who slunk off upstairs with a hostile hunch of her shoulders and a pitying lift of her eyebrows in my direction.

'Now, then.' Christine put on the kettle and pulled out a chair at the kitchen table. 'Let's have a talk about this.'

I was already taking fright. This sitting down at the kitchen table and talking woman to woman wasn't something I was used to. It didn't happen in my family. If there was any important, serious talking to be done, it was done by my dad, and it was done while we were working together on my bike, or while we were walking to church, or I was helping him with the garden – allowing us both to pretend that the issues of morality or behaviour or life-affecting decisions that we were discussing had just come up in the course of conversation, along with the weather, rather than being broached in an embarrassingly formal way, face to face over the table. My mum had never talked to me about morality or behaviour or life-affecting decisions at all, apart from continually expressing the opinion that I should have gone to university and shouldn't be working in the library.

I hung my head and stared at the table.

'It doesn't matter,' I said, lying through my teeth, 'if you don't want me to come for Christmas.'

'Abbie,' said Christine gently, pushing a mug of steaming tea towards me and opening the biscuit tin, 'there's nothing I'd like more.'

My spirits lifted. I looked up at her eagerly. 'Really? So I can . . .?'

'There's nothing I'd like more,' she repeated, 'if you didn't already have your own family to spend Christmas with.'

'But I do spend Christmas with them,' I said, sulkily. 'Every year. What's wrong with having a change?'

'Nothing wrong with change, love, as long as it doesn't hurt people.'

The uncomfortable feeling of having done something bad crept over me again. I tried to push it away but it pricked at the back of my eyes and made me kick the table legs to stop myself from crying.

'It's not fair,' I said childishly. 'Why can't I do what *I* want to do, for once?'

'Because it's Christmas,' said Christine simply, 'and you belong with your family. When you grow up and leave home, you can do what you want to do, love, but at least until you get yourself a husband or a partner, I bet you a million to one you'll still try to spend Christmas with your mum and dad. And that's the right thing to do, and you know it really.'

'Why?' My lower lip was wobbling and I knew I'd already lost the battle.

'Because that's how it is,' she said, with a broad shrug. 'You're very special to us, Abbie, love, and you're always welcome at this house. But you've got your own family and I'd be disappointed in you if you didn't want to be with them at Christmas.'

'So I can't come?'

'Only if your mum and dad want to come too. They'd be very welcome,' said Christine generously.

I didn't appreciate her generosity. I knew perfectly well my dad wouldn't leave his church, my mum wouldn't be able to face a rowdy Patterson Christmas, and both of them would feel awkward and uncomfortable if I persuaded them against their better judgement to accept this invitation.

'That's OK,' I muttered ungraciously. 'Don't worry about it. I'll stay at home.'

'Good girl,' she said, patting my hand and getting up to get on with her vegetables. 'Come over on New Year's Eve instead. We're having a bit of a do. You can stay over, Abbie. Your mum and dad don't celebrate New Year, do they?'

She knew perfectly well they didn't. They went to bed early.

'All right, then. Thanks,' I said, remembering my manners even as I stomped off upstairs to tell Sam how unfair all parents were and how much I wished I'd been born into her family instead of mine.

But from that year onwards, I've always spent New Year's Eve with the Pattersons. My second family. I love them both.

214

Ten to eight

'Did you find her?' Brian bursts through the double doors of the function room, looking from left to right with great agitation. 'Where is she?'

'Who?'

I've forgotten what I was supposed to be doing, but fortunately, just at that moment, Christine saunters in from outside, putting her cigarette packet away in her handbag.

'It's stopped raining now!' she announces cheerfully. 'I think it's going to be a lovely evening.'

'Never mind about all that, woman!' says Brian with unnecessary irritation. 'We're here for the bloody wedding, not for a picnic or a bit of bloody gardening.'

Eva, standing next to me, sniggers quietly at this and Brian glares at her.

'They're waiting for you!' he adds, pulling at Christine's arm to hurry her up. 'They want to start the dancing. The DJ can't get started – I told him you'd want to be there for their first dance, and where are you? Outside having a bloody fag.'

'Well, sorry,' she retorts. 'I didn't know, did I? And don't you start getting all holier than thou about my smoking, Brian Patterson, just because you've given up yourself. Everyone knows you give up every other week but you never stick to it, so you've got nothing to be all *superfluous* about.'

'Supercilious,' I mutter automatically, but she's already following Brian back through the double doors, tutting under her breath and tossing her blue-striped head.

'So much for married love,' laughs Eva.

'All part of it, I'd say,' I reply with a smile. 'And anyway, you couldn't live with him without giving him a mouthful every now and then, could you?'

'I couldn't live with him at all,' she says fervently.

I know how she feels. And I even *like* men.

'So, let's get right on with the dancing, everyone,' the DJ is booming, at a volume guaranteed to do serious damage to our hearing, as we walk back into the room. 'And of course, Sam and Phil – your bride and groom for this evening—' Who does he think are going to be our bride and groom for tomorrow evening? '—would like to start the dancing off for you. Sam? Phil? Here they are, everyone – your very own *Bride* and *Groom*!'

There's a round of applause as I'm thinking what a prat this guy is. He's introducing them as if they were a second-rate stand-up comedy act at a cheap holiday camp.

Then he starts their chosen music for the first dance and everyone falls silent.

I've been to quite a few weddings in recent years – friends of about my own age are steadily getting married off – and the same songs come around, fairly predictably: "Beautiful Tonight", "Can't Take My

Eyes Off You", "Everything I Do (I Do For You)"
... They're all lovely songs, and I guess it must be
hard to choose, if you haven't got a particular
favourite. But Sam, being a singer herself, *has* got
her favourites – and almost as soon as the engagement
ring was on her finger, she was telling me about the
music she and Phil had chosen for the reception.

'My love ...' croons Lionel Richie, as they hold
each other tenderly and begin to circle the dance
floor.

"Endless Love". Beautiful.

Diana Ross is responding to her 'first love', as Sam
and Phil smile into each other's eyes and, as I look
around the room, several of the women are rummag-
ing in their bags for tissues, and by the time the two
voices merge to sing about two hearts beating as one,
I'm having a problem with the lump in my own throat
and Christine is actually bawling her eyes out.

Halfway through the song, Sam breaks away from
Phil and leads his father onto the dance floor, while
Phil takes the weeping Christine into his arms.

'This is our moment,' says a voice in my ear,
making me jump.

'Sorry?'

'The best man's supposed to dance with the chief
bridesmaid now.'

'Oh. Yes, OK, I suppose so.'

'Don't sound too enthusiastic, will you!' jokes
Gary as he holds me loosely round the waist. 'I won't
tread on your toes, don't worry!'

'I'm sure you're a *wonderful* dancer, Gary.'

'Now you're just being sarcastic.'

I laugh. 'Come on, cheer up. What's the matter?
You've done all the difficult bits now – your speech.'

217

'Yeah.'

'And are you feeling OK now?'

'You mean am I still pissed? No, I'm all right, Abbie. Don't worry. I'm not about to start singing, or pass out on the dance floor.'

'Well, that's a relief, anyway.'

He gives a faint smile.

'So what *is* the matter?' I ask again. He's staring broodingly over my shoulder. Anyone would think it was a wake, not a wedding.

'I've made a complete fool of myself, that's all.'

'What? The drink? Don't worry about it, Gary. Everyone does it. Nobody was any the wiser. It was fine.'

'I'm not talking about the bloody booze, Abbie. I'm talking about the *reason* why I drank so much in the first place.'

'Well, after all, it's your brother's wedding. It's a big, stressful occasion, isn't it? I should know! I was *so* stressed, this week, I . . .'

'I haven't been stressed. I've just been a prat.' He suddenly stops dancing and stands still, making me almost overbalance, and gives me a very direct look. 'Over a girl.'

'Oh! Well.'

I shrug, awkwardly. I'm not sure I'm the best person for a twenty-three-year old man to talk to about his problems with his love-life. How am I supposed to help? What do *I* know about such things? Then again, I suppose it's my own fault for keeping on asking what's wrong with him. The song's coming to an end. Lionel and Diana are giving it some welly about their endless love. Christine's still crying on Phil's shoulder and Gary and I are standing stock-still

218

in the middle of the dance floor, staring at each other uneasily.

'Chloe,' he says suddenly. 'It's Chloe.'

'*Chloe*?'

'Yes, Abbie. I didn't realise. Not till today.'

And I think the only thing to say to that, really, is 'Oh fuck'.

We go out to the bar together and get another drink. I think I need one almost as much as he does.

'I didn't know until today either,' I tell him, although I can't really imagine that this is going to make him feel any better. 'None of us did.'

'You don't think it's just a phase, then? A sort of ... I don't know ... experimentation?'

Is it? Perhaps a teenage rebellion – an attempt to shock her father (and a very successful one at that)? Well, no – not from what I've heard from Eva. Anyway, Chloe's nearly nineteen – even if she does act like a moody twelve-year-old half the time.

'Who knows?' I say, watching Gary's face, trying to be kind to him. But is it kind to give him false hope? 'I don't think so, though,' I add, more truth-fully. 'How long have you been ... feeling like this about her?'

'Since her birthday last August. Her eighteenth – you know, the party at the pub. It was the first time I'd talked much to her. I just thought of her as Sam's little sister, you know, but ...'

'You got talking?' I prompt him. Do I really want to hear this? He's gulping back his beer now. It won't take him long to get pissed again – he's just topping up.

'Yeah. We ... like ... well, we got on really well.

219

She told me she didn't have a boyfriend, but she never said she had a *girlfriend*.'

'She didn't. She didn't meet Eva till she started at uni.'

'So after the party, we started emailing each other.'

'Oh. But ... you didn't meet up again?'

'No. Well, she was going on holiday, wasn't she, and then she started up at Durham, so really, it just never got off the ground. At least, that's what *I* thought. And we've carried on emailing, all the time she's been up at Durham, and she's been, like, "Really looking forward to seeing you in the summer" and "Lots of love, Chloe" – and all the time she's been having it off with a *bird*!'

'I'm really sorry, Gary. But I think you just read too much into it. I don't think she was leading you on. I don't suppose she realised you thought ...'

'Yeah, she did! She knew what I was thinking, all right, 'cos I fucking *told* her!' He covers his eyes with his hand and sighs. 'I feel such a prat. I was, like, "I really like you a lot, Chloe", and "I haven't felt like this about a girl before, Chloe". They must have been having a right laugh about it, her and her girlfriend. Probably printed out my emails and stuck them on the wall and threw darts at them.'

'No. I'm sure she wouldn't have laughed.'

'She talked about her friend Eva, you know, but I just thought it was ...'

'A friend.'

'Yeah.' He looks at me, miserably. 'What a plonker.'

'Just a misunderstanding, Gary. Easy enough mistake to make.'

220

I don't know what else to say. I can't believe Chloe's deliberately encouraged him. She might be a pain in the neck but surely even she wouldn't be that cruel?

'I actually thought,' he tells me confidentially, putting his empty glass down on the bar, 'for just a little while, I might have done it.'

'Done what?' He's lost me now.

'You know.' He manages a rueful smile. 'Like I was saying in the speech. Done as good as Phil. Found a beautiful, lovely girl, like he has. I couldn't do much better than Sam's younger sister, could I? I had visions of being like him – being with one of the Patterson girls. Might have known it was too much to hope for.'

'Don't put yourself down. You'll meet someone. If you stopped trying to compete with Phil, just be yourself.'

'Abbie, you're an only child. You don't know anything about it,' he says impatiently. 'Competing with Phil *is* being myself. I've never known anything else.'

Maybe that's why Chloe had to be so drastically different from Sam. She'll never have to compete, will she? She's taken herself out of the game.

There's been another romantic slow dance while we were out of the room, and now the DJ, wisely, is announcing that he's going to warm things up a bit with a livelier number. Sam and Phil beckon everyone to join them on the dance floor and within minutes there's a heaving throng of bodies up there, with most people glad to get moving after sitting down for several hours.

'Are you OK?' I ask Christine, finding her standing beside Brian, nursing a gin and tonic.

'My little girl!' she sobs, her eyes still fixed on the bride (who's now strutting her stuff to "Dancing Queen"). 'All grown up and married! I can't believe it!'

'Come on – don't cry,' I encourage her. 'It's a happy day!'

'I *am* happy!' she wails, wiping her eyes with her hanky. 'I'm so happy! Isn't she beautiful, Abbie?'

'Of course she is,' I tell her, squeezing her hand. 'She takes after her mum.'

Brian raises his eyebrows at me but, fortunately, decides to say nothing.

I'm just about to join in the dancing when I become aware of a group of people at the edge of the dance floor huddled together and convulsed with laughter. I can hear them shrieking even over the music. I can't contain my curiosity. I get to them at the exact same time that Sam and Phil stop dancing to come over and see what's going on themselves.

'I can't believe nobody noticed!' laughs a tall willowy girl – the girlfriend of one of Phil's workmates. 'How funny is that!'

She's holding a digital camera, which seems to have been passed round the group.

'Shit – turn it off, quick – Sam's coming over,' says someone urgently, grabbing the camera out of her hands.

'What's up, guys?' asks Phil. 'Got some funny photos of the wedding?'

'No, no, nothing like that, mate,' says his friend much too breezily. 'Come on, let's get on with the

222

dancing, everyone, yeah?'

'Is it the cake?' asks Sam.

There's a horrible silence for a minute. Everyone looks at each other uncomfortably. I'm just wondering whether to demand what the hell's going on, or whether to think of some kind of diversion, when Sam bursts out laughing and Phil slaps his mate on the back and says that he was beginning to think no one had noticed.

'What *is* so funny about the cake?' I ask Sam, feeling a bit aggrieved at being left out of the joke.

Someone turns the camera back on, flicks through the pictures and hands it to me with a close-up photo of the wedding cake in view.

Oh my God.

I can't believe this has happened.

More to the point, I can't believe they're all *laughing* about it! Or that Sam and Phil were almost collapsing with the giggles while they were cutting the damn thing!

'You *knew* about this?' I ask her weakly. 'How the *hell* did it happen? Are you going to sue them?'

She ordered the cake from an upmarket bakery in town and it was delivered straight here yesterday.

'No, of course we're not suing anyone, Abbie,' says Sam, starting to laugh again. 'It's just one of those things. It's not the end of the world. Look – nobody even noticed till they started looking at their photos! People mainly see what they want to see, don't they?'

'To be honest,' says Phil, 'It was my fault really. Sam asked me to pick up the cake yesterday and bring it over here. I should have done, then I'd have seen it in time and they might have been able to change it.

But when they offered to deliver it ... well, I guess it was the easy option.'

'But it was my fault in the first place,' argues Sam. 'I should have just left it the way we ordered it originally. But Mum said we should really have our full names on the cake.'

'Well, you've certainly got full names!' chortles the tall girl with the camera.

'What *happened*?' I persist. I can't help it. I just can't see the joke. I *knew* something awful was going to go wrong today. It had to be the cake, didn't it? The one thing it never occurred to me to check for myself.

'Well,' says Sam, still giggling, 'when I ordered it, originally, I asked them to write "Sam" and "Phil" on the top. But as I say, Mum persuaded me – you know how she is. "It's a formal occasion, Sam. It's your wedding day!" I was a bit reluctant really because as you know, I don't really like *Samantha* – but anything for an easy life – and Mum offered to phone them for me and change the order. So I just let her get on with it. I remember her saying that the woman she spoke to at the bakery sounded really stressed and rushed, but ... well, I'll be honest: it didn't occur to me that Mum would just ask for the names to be in full, without actually spelling them out.'

'That's *ridiculous*!' I say, crossly. For God's sake! I'm furious with Christine, but why the hell did Sam ever think it was a good idea to leave something so important to her anyway? 'They should have phoned you back! Checked it with you! They should have asked for it in writing! I mean – there could be dozens of different variations.'

'I know. I know all that, Abbie.' She stops laughing

and looks at me seriously. 'But I'm not having Mum upset about this. She did her best, and it's not worth spoiling the whole day over.'

'Sam's right, Abbs,' says Phil quietly. 'We're not worried about it. Actually, I quite like the name.'

'Me too,' laughs Sam. 'I prefer mine to Samantha, to be honest.'

I stare morosely at the photo for a minute. I think about the cake, by now being sliced up in the kitchen for guests to help themselves later on, and for absent friends to be sent a piece after the event. Unless they see photographs as close-up as this one, nobody ever needs to know. And, well, if I was waiting for something to go wrong, today, we've kind of got off lightly, haven't we, if this is the worst that's going to happen? This and a squashed bouquet?

'All right, then, "Philippa" and "Samuel", I suppose you're right,' I say with a forced smile.

'Come on, Samuel,' says Sam. 'Let's dance.'

'OK, Phil,' says Phil.

It crosses my mind, just briefly, that it could even be seen as a good omen ... that they're so much in love, so much a part of each other that even their names are interchangeable.

But I can't really be doing with all that kind of crap.

Ten past eight

I've been dancing near David when the DJ slows the pace again. "Just the Way You Are". Without saying a word David reaches out for me and gets me in a kind of clumsy waltz hold.

'How you doing, Abbs?' he says.

His breath smells of beer. He's taken his jacket off and loosened his tie; his shirtsleeves, unbuttoned and turned back slightly at the wrist, feel rough against my bare arms. I've been jumping around in my usual ungainly fashion to "Love Shack" so I'm quite hot, but I feel a sudden shiver as he moves his arms round my waist and pulls me closer.

'I'm OK,' I say. I decide not to say anything about the cake. 'It's all going well, isn't it?'

He laughs softly. 'Oh, Abbie, little Babbie,' he says, looking at me as if I'm a cute little puppy. 'I know you too well.'

'What's that supposed to mean?'

It doesn't sound like a compliment, somehow.

'It means you're not fooling anyone. You've been so stressed about this wedding, I could almost see the steam coming out of your ears. And you're *still* stressed, aren't you?'

'No. I just . . .'

'You just found out about the names on the cake. Don't worry – I noticed it as soon as they brought it in! Sam's not upset about it, Abbs, so . . .'

'I know she's not. She thinks it's funny. Fine, OK, just one more thing to laugh about, or maybe cringe about, when we look back at the day.'

'Like what else?'

He's still smiling at me. I feel like I'm being patronised. I feel like telling him: 'Like your mother's blue stripes; like your son's allergic reaction and his vomiting up of the cheesecake; your wife's panic attacks and your sister's sulks; your granddad's tactless comments and the best man getting drunk.' Should I go on? Instead, and because it's David, and I like him even when he patronises me, I just shrug and say: 'Oh, I don't know. I suppose the whole thing about Julia's still hanging over everyone, isn't it.'

I don't know why I said that.

Why bring up her name at all? Just when nobody's asked me, for at least twenty minutes now, why she's not here today. I'm expecting David to be irritated that I've even mentioned her, but instead, and to my complete surprise, he touches my cheek very lightly with one finger and says gently, into my eyes: 'You need to let it go, Abbie.'

'What? Let what go?'

I'm so flustered now, I can't even look at him. My cheek feels red hot where he touched it. What's the matter with me? This is David, for God's sake – not George Clooney, not some rock star or TV star. He's like a brother to me. We've known each other since we were eleven. Why is he suddenly looking at me like he's going to . . .

227

I move my face away, quickly, before he gets any closer.

'Let what go?' I repeat, shakily.

'All that old bitterness and resentment.'

'What? Well, thanks very much!'

I'm annoyed now. It's almost a relief.

'I'm not insulting you, Abbie.'

'Just calling me bitter and resentful?'

'No. Of course you're not – never – not normally. Just about Julia.'

'I'm *not*.'

'Be honest with yourself. You've never forgiven her, have you?'

That word again. If one more person talks to me about forgiveness today, I'm probably going to jump on them. 'It's not exactly up to me to forgive her, is it. It's up to Sam.'

'Sam *has* forgiven her. That's not what I'm talking about. I'm talking about Jamie. See! I knew it.' I've turned away from him. 'You can't go on for ever refusing to talk about it, Abbie! It happened! You have to move on!'

Not again! As if I haven't had this already today from my dad, and even from Phil! What's going on? Is there some kind of conspiracy afoot? *Let's all try to get Abbie on her own and bend her ear about forgiving and moving on*?

Well, that's what I'm doing right now. Moving on, out of this room, away from this music, these sick, sad lyrics about loving someone just the way they are, and this dancing much too closely with the man who's supposed to be my pseudo-brother who's got his face practically touching mine and telling me what I should or shouldn't talk about and who I

228

should or shouldn't forgive.

I can't hack it. Not today.

Or maybe, as he says . . . not ever.

I met Jamie when I was twenty, going on twenty-one. He was a regular at the library – an engineer, studying for some further qualifications. He borrowed books with titles that might as well have been in a foreign language. Sometimes he sat at one of the tables in the library, with two or three of these big black books open in front of him, scanning through them as if his life depended on it, making notes on a lined pad before closing the books with a thump and rushing out of the library with barely a smile in my direction. But other times, he'd come in late, just before we closed, take out a book and then chat to me while we closed up. It wasn't long before he suggested we went on for a drink.

I thought all my dreams had come true overnight. I actually woke up in the mornings and pinched myself in case it wasn't really true. Me – little, mousy Abbie who never even got noticed by boys, never mind asked out – going out with this gorgeous man? I could hardly breathe for excitement. Even when we'd been together for months, the excitement never wore off. I was like a kid, waking up every day expecting to have to get up for school, and then realising it was still the summer holidays. And the summer went on, and on, and on until I was almost dizzy with it.

I was still living at home with my parents then, but Jamie had his own flat, right in the town centre, in the new development by the river. A typical bachelor pad – one living room, one bedroom, a tiny kitchen and bathroom. It was furnished with leather sofas and lots of rugs. I told him it needed cushions and he laughed and let me buy them for him. We had sex for the first time propped high on his bed on a pile of my cushions. He told me I was the sweetest girl he'd ever made love to. I didn't tell him that for me, he was not only the sweetest, but the first. I also didn't tell him that he'd be the last; that I'd never want anyone else because I was so terribly in love with him; that I wanted to be with him forever; that he'd changed my life; that I'd die if he left me.

I didn't tell him any of these things because, inexperienced though I was, I understood instinctively that it would scare him off. I wanted to move in with him, but he never asked. I thought it was just a question of waiting; I mustn't rush him, mustn't make him think I was desperate or needy. He told me I was beautiful, lovely, charming, sweet, but he didn't say he loved me. So I waited. He'd say it in time. He just didn't want to be rushed.

We'd been seeing each other for quite a while before he met my friends. He was too busy studying for his exams to go out, so I'd just go round to his flat and sit with him, make him coffee or cook him meals while he sat hunched over his books until late in the evening, and then we'd go to bed. Who cared about going out? Who cared about friends? The walls of Jamie's flat became the boundaries of my universe.

'I haven't seen you for weeks,' Sam complained on the phone. She bombarded me with emails at work, telling me where she'd be singing that night, or who was having a party, or which pub everyone would be in at the weekend.

'I'm worried about you,' she admitted, at length.

'You shouldn't be spending *all* your time with Jamie.'

'Can't you just be happy for me?' I retorted. It rankled that she and Julia and all our other friends could have as many boyfriends as they liked, but as soon as I had my first ... my only ... they were all on my case about getting away from him.

'Of course I am,' she said, softly. 'You know better than that, Abbie. *All* I care about is you being happy. That's why I'm worried. You know what they say about *eggs* and *baskets*.'

'I know you mean well, Sam. But you don't understand.'

Ha! When we first fall in love, we think we're the only one it's ever happened to, don't we? That no one else can possibly imagine how we feel? Where do those blinkers come from? And how sad that once they've been shattered, we never get to wear them again.

'I can't bear to be apart from him,' I admitted.

'Then bring him with you. I'm singing at The Plough tonight. Loads of people are coming.'

'His exams ...'

But I couldn't use them as an excuse any more. He was taking his final paper that day. He'd be glad to go out and celebrate ... wouldn't he?

'I'd rather stay here and celebrate in bed, babe,' he murmured, nuzzling my neck. 'We'll get a bottle of champagne and ...'

'Please, Jamie. My best friend's singing ... you've never heard her; she's terrific. And all my friends want to meet you.'

'Do they?' He gave me a quizzical look, the flicker of amusement in his eyes making my heart jump and thud. 'Why's that, then? What have you been telling them about me?'

'That you're wonderful . . . of course.'

'That I'm a sex god? A raging shagging machine? A fantastic f—'

We were tearing each other's clothes off before he'd even finished asking.

But we did get up and go to the pub later on.

If I say that everyone turned and looked as we walked in, you have to believe that it wasn't me they were staring at. Jamie had that effect on people. He was so gorgeous-looking, I never understood what he saw in me. He had an easy, confident manner. He smiled and chatted and bought people drinks, and I sat back, enjoying the glow. It was new for me, you understand? I'd never been the one, before, that other girls sneaked envious glances at, trying to weigh up what it was about her – what secret weapon she had that had attracted this ace specimen of manhood to her, rather than to themselves. For the first time in my life, I felt like *I* was one of the beautiful people.

How naïve and pathetic can you get? I wasn't one of the beautiful people at all. I was still skinny little mousy Abbie Vincent and I always would be.

I was so carried away with myself, basking in this rosy glow of imaginary admiration, that I didn't even notice Julia flirting outrageously with Jamie. And if I had, I'd probably have just laughed to myself and thought: Not this time, love. This one's mine, all mine. If only.

We went out with them all again – several more times after that. But it wasn't until about two months later that I called round to Julia's place one Saturday,

232

in the middle of the day, to take back a DVD I'd borrowed, and found the curtains drawn. And I knocked, and I rang the bell, and, as I finally gave up and turned to go, I saw the curtain twitch, and Jamie looked straight out at me. Jamie, naked.

He didn't even try to make excuses.

'I couldn't help it,' he said, with a shrug as if it didn't matter.

Maybe he couldn't. After all, I'd been watching the effect Julia had on boys ever since she was about twelve years old. She seemed to reduce them to jelly. They became powerless, as if she worked some fatal magic charm on them.

But *she* could have helped it! She could have stopped herself, just this once, from taking what she wanted. From screwing around, not because she even wanted to, not because she even *liked* it, but just to add another name to her list, another notch to her belt – another top-up to her self-esteem. With *my* man! Call herself a friend? You must be joking.

I finished with Jamie. I shut myself in my room and cried, and cried, and cried. Sam came round every day, and just sat with me. She didn't try to tell me to pull myself together, or get over it, or even to stop crying. She just passed me tissues, and chocolates, and hugged me, and waited for me to come through it. She didn't even tell me what I found out much later – that Jamie had already been unfaithful to me with two other girls; that he was a total waste of space who'd never loved me and that I was better off without him. It hurt when I found that out. But nowhere near as much as Julia hurt me.

She cheapened that first love affair for me, so that instead of looking back and remembering how much

I was loved and desired, I can only remember that he 'couldn't help' wanting Julia too.

And I'm supposed to move on from this? I'm supposed to *forgive* her?

I think not.

I think not *ever*.

Twenty past eight

David finds me on a bench outside by the lake.

It's a pity it was raining when we arrived here from the church. It's beautiful out here. It would have been lovely for some photos. It's still light. It'll be the longest day of the year in another week or two, and it'll still only be dusk at ten o'clock.

'Should we bring Sam and Phil out here and take a few photos by the lake, do you think?' I ask David as he sits down next to me.

'Abbie ...'

''Cos it's such a lovely evening, and it'll still be light for a while, you know. It'd be good to have some photos in such a nice setting.'

'Abbie, I'm sorry. I shouldn't have said that. It's none of my business; I had no right.'

'Let's go and ask them, shall we? I think they'd like to—'

'Abbie!'

He shouts it. It makes me flinch. And then I feel like I'm going to cry. I screw up my eyes, tight. Whatever happens, I mustn't cry. I can't be that selfish: today is *not* about me, not about my feelings, or my hurt, or my pathetic refusal to let go of something that happened seven years ago.

It's while I've got my eyes shut tight that I become aware of David's arm round me. For a moment I just sit there, feeling the weight of his arm lying gently across my shoulders. I'm conscious of his warm breath tickling my ear, and of the hairs suddenly standing up on the back of my neck. For some reason, I don't want to open my eyes.

'I didn't mean to upset you,' he says much more softly. 'I'd *never* want to upset you. You're so special, so important to me.'

At this, my eyes do fly open.

'You're Sam's best friend,' he adds quickly, looking into my eyes. 'And ... well ... you're a best friend of the whole family, Abbs. You know how much you mean to us all.'

David never talks like this. It's weird. It's making me feel very uneasy.

'I'm sorry I walked out on you,' I say, to change the subject. 'I suppose it just all got a bit much ... You're right, I've been quite stressed about today.'

'You've been absolutely brilliant.' He tightens his hold, squeezing my shoulder and pulling me closer to him. I'm beginning to feel like I can't breathe. 'I don't know what we'd have done without you.'

It's nice of him to say so. But to be honest I feel like I haven't been much help at all. I didn't manage to keep the bouquet safe and stop the cat squashing it. I didn't think to check the cake and see whether it had the right names on it. I didn't manage to stop the best man from getting drunk, or the bride's mum from crying her eyes out. I'm just about to tell him this, when I see a shadow moving towards us and,

236

suddenly, there's Heather, standing next to us. I push David's arm off my shoulders as if it's burning me. I feel flustered and embarrassed as if I've been caught with my knickers down.

'Hi,' says David, not sounding in the least perturbed. 'You OK?'

'All right. You?'

This does not sound at all like the conversation between two lovers. I'm definitely right – they've had a row and they're trying not to let it show.

'Nice out here, isn't it?' says Heather to me.

'Yes. I was just saying to David . . . maybe we should ask Sam and Phil to come out and have some photos taken by the lake. Before it gets dark.'

'Good idea,' says Heather, gazing out across the lake.

'I'll go and ask them, then.' I get to my feet.

'Where's Troy?' David asks, looking round and behind Heather.

'I left him with your mum for a minute. I wanted some fresh air. I'm just having a walk round the lake.'

'I'll go and see if he's OK,' I say. I want to leave these two together – to sort things out, or discuss what's wrong, or whatever. I don't want to be around them while they're talking to each other like this, in this strange, distant tone as if they've only just met. It's embarrassing, and awkward.

I'm almost back at the outside doors of the golf club when Christine comes hurtling out, panic in her eyes.

'Have you seen Troy?' she almost screams at me.

For a minute I can't understand what she's talking about. Troy's with *her*. Why's she asking me if I've seen him?

237

'He ran off! One minute he was here, right here with me, grumbling about wanting his mummy, and the next minute he ... was gone.'

'Well, he can't have gone far,' I say, trying to sound reasonable and calm. I don't feel calm. He's five years old. He can sprint like a greyhound. He could be anywhere.

'I've looked everywhere inside,' she says, her voice shaking. 'Under the tables, in the toilets ...'

'Did he know Heather was going outside?'

'Yes. He heard her say she was going for a walk round the lake. That's the trouble. He kept on and on about wanting to go round the lake with his mummy. So I said I'd take him. I said, "Just hang on a minute, Troy, while Nanny finds her jacket" and when I looked round ...'

It's a warm evening. The doors have been left open.

'Did anyone see a little boy come out of these doors a few minutes ago?' I ask the people hanging around outside smoking. 'A little boy in just trousers and a waistcoat?'

There's a general shaking of heads and a few people stare out across the grass, craning their necks as if they're going to find him without even moving, without even stubbing out their cigarettes.

'I wouldn't let him run around out here if I were you, love,' says a little tubby man with a big bushy beard.

'No. We're not *letting* him. He's run off.'

'Better find him quick,' advises the woman leaning against the wall next to him, blowing a cloud of smoke towards me. 'Only it'll be getting dark before too long.'

238

'And there's the lake,' adds her friend ominously. Thanks for nothing.

'Go and tell David and Heather,' I tell Christine. 'They're over there. Get them to start looking that side of the lake. I'll start on the other side.'

'You don't think ... ?' Christine's voice tails off, the air trembling scarily around her.

'I don't know. He could be anywhere. He might be hiding ... We need to shout. Troy!' I cup my hands around my mouth and bellow as I start to run towards the lake, rounding a bend and into a clump of trees at the water's edge. 'TROY!'

If you've never been a *shouting* sort of person, it's surprising how much it hurts. By the time I've hollered his name a dozen times, I'm already feeling like I've been punched in the throat and my vocal cords are sore, like they've been rasped with a metal file.

'What?' says a little voice, right beside me, just as I'm taking a deep breath ready to let rip with another yell. He's squatting on the bank, dangling a stick in the water.

'Oh, my God!' I reach out to grab him but he wriggles out of my grasp. 'Where have you been? You naughty boy!'

'I'm *not* naughty!' he protests, backing away from me.

The edge of the lake is right behind him. It might be a nice clear evening now, but the grass is wet and slippery from the early downpour.

'OK, OK, you're not naughty,' I agree immediately. 'But we were worried. We didn't know where you were.'

'I came to find Mummy,' he says, looking at me as

if I'm stupid. 'Nanny said.'

'Right. Look, if you give me your hand, Troy, we'll go and find Mummy together. Yes? And Daddy?'

'Are you cross?' He turns towards me, folding his arms and looking at me warily. 'Is Nanny cross?'

'Nobody's cross. We just didn't want to lose you. Now, give me your hand, there's a good boy, only it's muddy and . . .'

He offers his hand to me; I'm just about to take hold of it when there's an almighty cacophony behind him. A rowdy gang of squawking, jabbering ducks zoom across the water at a rate of knots, skimming the centre of the lake, and splashing to a halt, quacking and complaining to each other at the tops of their voices, just feet from where Troy's standing. I watch his face register surprise, then delight, as he spins around to look at them.

'Ducks!' he shouts happily.

And promptly falls in.

I don't know who's more surprised – Troy, or the ducks, or Heather, David and Christine, who turn up just in time to see me clambering back up the bank on my hands and knees, clutching a bawling, muddy child.

'You jumped in?' says David incredulously.

'I'd call it more of a flop than a jump,' I reply through the chattering of my teeth.

'Let me go!' screams Troy, who's far more upset about the indignity of being hauled out of the water by me than he was about the possibility of drowning.

David bends down and grasps him by both arms, swinging him onto the ground where Heather

240

immediately picks him up like a baby, crying about how he could have died.

Great. Just what he needs to hear.

'Let me *go!*' he shrieks again. 'I want to see the ducks!'

'You nearly joined them,' I tell him without much sympathy.

'Actually, Troy, I think you frightened them all away,' adds David. 'Here—' he helps me to my feet and peels off his jacket '—put this on. You're freezing.'

'I'll make it all wet and muddy,' I protest. 'Anyway, you should put it on Troy.'

'Troy's all right,' says Christine. She's already wrapped him up in her own jacket. 'Aren't you, my lovely?'

'Wanted to see the ducks,' he sulks, looking at the mud squelching out of his shoes. He rubs his eyes with a dirty fist. This has shaken him up, frightened him, but there's no way he's going to admit it. Five years old and already acting the macho man. He'll probably tell his mates at school that he jumped in on purpose, swam a couple of times round the lake and gave the ducks a run for their money.

'Let's get you inside,' says David. 'You're shivering.'

He's talking to Troy. But he's looking at me.

We must look an odd little procession going back into the Barn: two of us dripping wet, covered in mud and dressed in jackets that are much too big for us.

'I'm going to have to go home and get changed,' I say. I don't know whether the shock or the reality has suddenly hit me, but as well as shivering all over, I now feel like I could sit down and cry. My lovely

241

bridesmaid's dress – ruined. This lovely day – ruined. And now it might as well all be over. What am I supposed to do? Come back in my jeans and a jumper?

'You can't drive,' says David reasonably. 'I'll call a taxi. I'll need to take Troy, too, and clean him up and get him some clothes.'

'No, I'll take him,' says Heather. 'I can change out of this dress at the same time. There's still a stain; I've just been hoping no one notices. And now I'm all muddy from Troy.'

'Well, we don't *all* have to go,' I'm saying, wearily, just as Sam wanders out of the function room to see what all the fuss is about.

'Go where?' she demands. 'Nobody's going anywhere yet.' And then: 'Oh, my *God*! Abbie! What happened? Did you fall in the lake?'

'No.' I'm finding it hard to see the funny side of this. 'No, your nephew did. He wanted to be a duck.'

'Abbie rescued him,' says David, patting me on the back as if I'm a good kid. 'She's soaked, and freezing. They both are.'

'You poor darling!' She swoops towards me, but I back away, afraid of her getting mud on her dress. 'Come on – upstairs! Straight away!'

'Upstairs?'

'Yes, come on, Abbie, don't mess around. Heather, bring Troy. Quickly – he'll catch cold, poor little thing!'

'Where are we going?' I ask, stupidly, as she leads us towards the stairs.

'The showers!' she says, laughing at me. 'Obviously!'

Obviously. I look at Heather, whose face is as blank as mine.

242

'Didn't you think there'd be showers here? In a golf club? For the golfers?'

Sam throws open a door marked LADY CLUB MEMBERS ONLY, and it's as much as I can do not to gasp. I thought the toilets downstairs were nice – you know, clean, with hot water and soap dispensers that actually work – but this is more like a bathroom in a glossy homes magazine. The floor's carpeted. There are chairs – *armchairs* – and hairdryers. There are little frilly boxes of tissues and dispensers of moisturiser. And that's just in the ante-room. Kicking off our shoes, we follow Sam through to the shower room. Heather's already stripping Troy's muddy clothes off as I stare in surprise at the spacious shiny shower cubicles, complete with complimentary little bottles of shower gel, shampoo and conditioner like you get in hotels. On a rack on the other side of the room is a pile of thick, fluffy white towels.

'But we're not lady club members,' I point out to Sam. I realise I'm whispering and looking over my shoulder, just in case any lady club members should come striding in with their golf bags over their shoulders and order us out of their boudoir.

'They said I could use it. To get changed, later – you know, into my going-away gear.'

Sam and Phil are only going away as far as a hotel at Stansted Airport tonight. But fair enough, she still had to have a going-away outfit.

'Will they mind?' I ask doubtfully, still whispering.

There's a bit of difference between a bride slipping out of her bridal gown and into something more comfortable, and two muddy women and a muddy child showering half the lake off themselves in their pristine shower cubicles.

'To be honest, Abbie, with what we've paid for the hire of this place, they shouldn't mind if we bring everyone up here and hold the bloody *party* in the showers!'

Not till I've cleaned up a bit, please.

It's such utter bliss to be under the shower, feeling the hot water washing away the mud and the chill from my skin, luxuriating in the steam and the scent of the shampoo, that I haven't given a thought to what I'm going to wear when I'm finished, until I turn off the water and step out, wrapping myself in a towel and seeing Heather, also with a towel around her, drying Troy off and telling him to stand still while she puts his 'jamas on him.

'Pyjamas?' I echo.

'Yes – thank God, I put them in the car, in case Troy fell asleep later on, so I could get him changed and he'd be ready for bed by the time the taxi comes.'

Nobody's driving home tonight. Anyone who brought their car here is leaving it to pick up tomorrow. There's a fleet of taxis booked to take us all home.

'So what the hell are *we* going to wear?' I muse, looking sadly at the pale turquoise bridesmaid's dress lying soiled and crumpled on the bench.

'Well, we could always try washing it in the shower – and doing my dress again at the same time,' suggests Heather half-seriously.

'Here we are, then. Take your pick!' sings Sam, coming back in and flourishing an armful of clothes at us, like a conjurer who's produced them out of mid-air.

'What ...? Where ...?' I'm stuttering like a fool

244

while Heather excitedly holds up a pair of cream linen trousers, a long white cotton skirt, a blue crinkle top, an orange-and-white dress ...

'You know what I'm like,' says Sam with a shrug and an apologetic smile. 'I *always* pack too many clothes.'

'These are out of your *trousseau*?'

'Abbie, what a gorgeously old-fashioned word. I haven't heard that since my gran talked about her honeymoon one Christmas when she got drunk.'

'But they are, aren't they? Heather, put them down. We can't wear these things! They're Sam's *honeymoon* clothes.'

'They're my excess luggage, Abbs. I've packed *two* pairs of cream trousers because I couldn't decide which ones to take. I've packed twice as many tops as I need, twice as many skirts ... Please, do me a favour. Help me make the decisions.'

She holds the blue top up against me and smiles into my eyes.

'It's just your colour. It'll look great on you. We always did like sharing our clothes, didn't we? Aren't we lucky that we're the same size?'

She's being generous. Yes, we both wear the same dress size, but Sam fills out the clothes perfectly in all the right places, whereas on me they just hang. I haven't got much of a figure. I could get away with wearing a size smaller, but I don't, because that would just accentuate my shapelessness.

'Are you *sure* you don't mind?' squeals Heather, who's already got her underwear back on and is excitedly zipping herself into a dress.

'I'm positive. That looks *so* good on you, Heather.'

I forget I'm only wearing a towel. It drops to the

ground between us as I run to Sam and hug her tight. It doesn't matter. She's the only person I don't care about seeing me naked. The only person who's never judged me, always loved me the way I am, always been the very best friend anybody could ever, ever have.

I'm just telling her this, in fact, when there's a knock on the door and a worried male voice calls: 'Are you all OK in there? Only the DJ's calling for the bride . . . are you coming, Sam?'

'Yeah, I'll be right there, David!' laughs Sam.

She's laughing because, even though there's a closed door between us, I've grabbed the towel back round me and flushed scarlet as soon as I heard his voice. Whereas Heather hasn't even turned round.

Quarter to nine

The only person on the dance floor is Frank. He's got his shirtsleeves rolled up and an unnatural gleam in his eye and he's boogieing, all on his own, to "Rock Around The Clock".

They always play a couple of these old rock 'n' roll numbers, don't they? I think it's purely for those people, mostly in their sixties now, who learned to jive in the 1950s and are still so bloody good at it, they like a clear dance floor so they can show off their routine. Right now, though, nobody wants to jive because Frank's up there, and he's all over the place – swaying, grinning, jumping, spinning on the spot, nearly falling over. I don't think anyone would risk sharing the dance floor with him, and certainly not to do the swings, swirls and lifts necessary in a good old rock 'n' roll session.

'And here she is, everybody!' cries the DJ excitedly as we walk back into the room. 'Our very own bride, Samantha!' Or Philippa, whichever you prefer. 'Are we going to see you back on the dance floor, Sam?'

Sam takes the hint immediately and glides over to her granddad, taking him in a waltz hold and moving him smoothly to the side of the floor. Apparently Christine, several of the aunties and even Eva have already tried to do this but he's fought them all off, continuing to dance like a demented clubber on drugs, almost knocking one of the aunties out in the process. She's apparently outside now with a bleeding nose.

'I don't know what's got into him,' says Christine, scratching her blue stripes in agitation. 'He's *never* been aggressive. A bit peculiar at times, granted, but never *aggressive.*'

'Has he been drinking?' I ask her.

'Not much, love. One or two, I suppose. I hope they kept an eye on him over dinner – maybe he had too much wine. It might not mix with his medications, you know.'

'Well, it looks like Sam's got him under control now. Don't worry. I'm sure he didn't mean to hit Auntie Joan on the nose. He's just kind of . . . high.'

Actually I was staggered to see how much energy he had out there. It's a bit sad, really. Normally it's as much as he can do to totter from room to room, but get a bit of drink and drugs inside him and he's a raging tornado. A bit like *One Flew Over the Cuckoo's Nest* but without the lucidity.

Sam's slowed him right down now but she's still got a tight hold on him. The DJ's swiftly changed the music to a slow number, and she's waltzing him carefully round the edge of the dance floor. A few other couples are braving the floor again, giving Frank wary looks as he passes by.

'Anyway, dear, you're looking much better now!' says Christine brightly, turning her attention to me.

Better than when I was covered in mud and smelly green slime? Or better than when I was in my brides-maid's finery, with my hair and make-up done? Obviously, since the lake and the shower, there's nothing left of Heather's handiwork – my hair's hanging around my face in its normal strings. I can't deny I feel a hell of a lot more comfortable, but it wasn't exactly the plan for the evening.

'Lovely top, dear,' goes on Christine. 'That colour blue really suits you.'

'It's Sam's,' I try to explain, not that she's listening.

'I don't know if anyone else has thanked you properly,' she says, patting my hand and looking at me earnestly, 'for diving in and rescuing Troy.'

'Oh . . . no, I didn't exactly dive . . . I just sort of *slid* in. And anyway, it all happened so quickly – one minute he was about to hold my hand, the next minute, there were all these ducks, and he just lost his footing. I didn't even think about it – I just got in and pulled him out.'

'You saved his life,' she insists. 'He could have drowned. Children can drown in two inches of water, you know. Even in the bath. You hear about it all the time.'

'Well, it was just lucky I was there.' I don't want her thinking I'm a lifesaver. It wasn't exactly difficult and it certainly wasn't brave, skidding down a slippery bank and fishing a five-year-old out of a mucky lake. Compared with Sam's bravery when she dived in front of the car to stop Chloe being run over, for instance, it doesn't even merit a notch on the scale.

'You saved him from drowning,' persists Christine, her eyes suddenly filling up with tears, 'and we'll never forget it, Abbie.' She plants a kiss on my cheek. 'You know we all love you, don't you? You're just like one of the family.'

I'm still trying to make up my mind whether I

should take this as a compliment or not when the music stops and the DJ calls out: 'OK, ladies and gentlemen. Can I have your attention, please? I've got a special announcement now.'

Heather's standing beside the DJ, with Troy, in his Superman pyjamas, wriggling in her arms. What's all this, now? Request time? And what would Heather request, anyway? 'Hair, There and Everywhere'?

'Want to get *down*,' I can hear Troy complaining, but Heather tightens her hold on him and plants herself in front of the DJ, smiling. God, she's not going to sing, is she?

'Can we have Abbie up the front here, please? Abbie Vincent?' says the DJ, at exactly the same moment that I realise Heather's actually smiling straight at me.

Me?

I look at Christine, horrified. She smiles back at me.

'Go on. It's you.'

I'd never have guessed.

If it wasn't for the fact that it's even more embarrassing sitting here with everyone staring at me, waiting for me to go up to the front and get it over with – whatever it is – I'd simply refuse to go. A few people start clapping as I get up and walk, shakily, to where Heather's waiting with the DJ. They don't know why they're clapping but I suppose it gives them something to do.

'Abbie,' he says, as if to make sure he's got the right person.

'Yes.' I feel totally stupid and self-conscious standing here. Like being called out to the front of the class because you've written a good essay. It doesn't make your classmates impressed with you. It makes them call you names – but teachers never seem to realise that.

'Ladies and gentlemen, I've just been told that, while we've all been *dancing* and *enjoying* ourselves here this evening, Abbie's been performing a life-or-death operation outside at the lake! Do you want to tell us what happened, Abbie?'

He shoves the microphone in front of my face.

'No,' I whisper at him, shaking my head violently.

Unfortunately, my whisper echoes all around the room – *No, No, No* – accompanied by the crackle of static.

'I'll tell them!' says Heather bravely, grabbing the mike. 'Troy here—' she attempts to hold him up to show everyone who Troy is, but he fights and wrestles himself out of her grip, '—he wandered off and fell in the lake. Abbie found him, and jumped in and rescued him.'

There's a gasp, a few calls of 'Well done, Abbie!', and another round of clapping. I want to crawl away into a hole somewhere.

'Without a thought for her personal safety,' adds Heather, really getting into her stride. 'Or her hairdo, or anything. If it wasn't for Abbie ... well.' She shakes her head, unable to go on. Instead, and to make her point, she reaches down and puts her arms around Troy again, trying to hold on despite him scowling, stamping, shouting 'Leave me alone!' and lashing out at her with both fists.

I'm tempted to take him outside and chuck him back in the lake.

'I just wanted everyone to know: Abbie is a *heroine*,' she finishes, giving me a soppy smile.

She hands the mike back to the DJ, who tries to say something about it being a wonderful story, and isn't it a pity there aren't more people in the world prepared to sacrifice themselves to save others, but, thank God, most of it gets drowned out by the noise everyone makes as I slink back to my chair – clapping, cheering, whooping, even a drunken rendition of "For She's a Jolly Good Fellow".

'I feel a complete fraud,' I say to Sam, who puts her arms round me, gives me a hug and laughs.

'Why? You *did* save him. It's nice of Heather to let everyone know.'

'It was crap. I just slid in after him and ...'

'Abbie, I know you don't like being the centre of attention,' she says, suddenly more serious, 'but don't always put yourself down.'

'I'm not,' I grumble. 'But it's *your* special day. I don't want everyone looking at *me*.'

'Why not?' she says with a smile. 'You look lovely.'

Maybe I should wear Sam's clothes more often.

Now he's got everybody in a mellow mood, and now Frank has finally calmed down and got off the dance floor, the DJ decides it's a good time to have a father-and-daughter dance.

'Come on, Dad,' he calls in Brian's direction. 'She might be your little girl, but after tonight, you probably won't be the one dancing with her any more. You might as well make the most of it!'

This is so *not* the way to talk to Brian, who'd much sooner prop up the bar with a pint in his hand than appear on a dance floor at *any* time, even his daughter's wedding. I watch him making his way to the front, trying to force a smile in much the same way I just did, and I suddenly feel something in common with him for the first time in my life.

'OK. Brian? Sam? Are you ready? Everybody – let's hear it for the bride and her father!'

There's another ripple of applause. Everyone must be getting sore hands by now. I haven't heard so much clapping since I went to Troy's school concert. Mums and dads were standing in the aisles, clapping and cheering as if it was the best thing they'd ever seen, better than all the West End shows and all the rock concerts and big football matches they'd ever been to in their lives. But then, I suppose the first time you see your own five-year-old reciting the lines of a play, or singing in a choir, that must be how it feels.

The DJ starts the music and Brian and Sam begin to dance.

I can't believe this.

How yucky can you get?

Take good care of my baby . . .

Brian looks a bit sick, as well he might. Sam starts to giggle. Christine's dabbing at her eyes again.

'Shall we join them?' Phil asks his mum, who's sitting behind me. 'I think Brian might appreciate some support.'

Within minutes there are half-a-dozen couples on the floor, all joining in with the lyrics, which at least makes them sound a lot less maudlin.

'Come on,' says David, taking my arm. 'I've never danced with a real-life heroine before.'

'Don't take the piss,' I tell him mildly. But I'm laughing despite myself.

'Don't get me wrong. I'm as grateful as anyone.'

253

He pulls me into his arms and swirls me towards the middle of the floor. 'More grateful than you can imagine. Troy's a little sod, but . . .'

'But he's yours,' I say, giving him an understanding smile.

He doesn't reply. For a minute, I think he's getting all emotional on me too. Not another one! But then he grins quickly and says, 'Yes. And he might be a little sod, but he probably doesn't deserve to be buried up to his neck in mud with the ducks nibbling his ears.'

'Er . . . no, maybe not!'

It's a close thing, though, at times.

We're both laughing when he suddenly stops and stares at me as if he's only just noticed me.

'Christ, Abbie, you don't half look gorgeous.'

I feel myself flushing. 'You're only saying that 'cos I'm wearing Sam's clothes. She's got such good taste. They'd obviously look better on her, you know, but—'

'Shut up. You look gorgeous. It's not the bloody clothes, you fool. It's you.'

'Oh!' I don't know what I'm supposed to say to this. I'm not exactly in the habit of being told I look gorgeous. 'What have you been drinking, David? Has it affected your eyesight?'

He sighs and shakes his head. 'You never could take a compliment. Remember that time in year nine?'

'When Julia made you ask me out? Yeah, 'course I remember it. I thought I'd die of embarrassment. But you were so sweet, pretending you wanted to go out with me anyway.'

'You see?' he says, snorting with exasperation. 'You *see*? You wouldn't believe me. It was so annoying, in the end I gave up trying. You wouldn't believe it then, and you won't now! I *always* fancied you, Abbie. I always did, and I still . . .'

It's a very lucky thing that the end of this speech gets drowned out by about fifty drunken voices joining in the finale of the lyrics of this chosen father/daughter song. So many voices shouting at the top of their lungs about sending their baby right back home is enough to drown anything out, especially when most of them are horrendously off-key, but just to make completely and totally sure of obliterating what I don't want to hear, I join in myself. If I'd been Troy's age I'd have probably stuck my fingers in my ears and hummed.

David shakes his head again and smiles at me. 'Don't pretend you didn't hear me.'

But I'm singing at the top of my lungs. I keep on singing even when the music's finished, but only inside my own head. And only to drown out the thunderous beating of my own heart.

Actually I'm quite upset about it. Look – it doesn't matter how much he's had to drink. It doesn't matter how bad the argument is, between him and Heather. David should *not* be talking to me like that. He's obviously teasing me, and as my dad always said about teasing – it's not funny, and it's not kind. It upsets me, because actually I've always thought David *was* both those things – funny, and kind.

Like most only children, when I was a little girl I always wished I had a sibling, and when I met Sam, her twin brother was the thing I envied most about her. And that's really saying something, you understand, because I envied *everything* about Sam: her hair, her skin, her voice, her popularity, her house, yes, and her family, even though I thought they were all mad. I envied her these things, but I didn't *resent* her having them. It made me feel blessed and special that she brought me into her magic circle and let me share them with her.

Of course, the novelty of sharing an eleven-year-old twin brother soon wore thin.

'I can't understand why you think you'd want a brother,' grumbled Sam when David and his rowdy mates in their muddy football gear interrupted our Secret Dream Diary Club meeting for the umpteenth time. We'd tried holding the meetings at my house instead, because it was so much quieter, but my bedroom was too small for five or six of us to sit comfortably, and we only had one living room. We obviously couldn't read out our secret dream diaries with my mum and dad sitting there pretending not to listen. So the meetings inevitably had to move to one of the other girls' homes.

'It's always *me,* and *my* friends who have to move,' complained Sam. 'Boys get it all their own way, all the time.'

'We could always invite the boys to join in,' suggested Julia with a giggle. Even at eleven she was a tart.

'No we bloody can't!' exclaimed Sam crossly. 'You girls without brothers have got *no idea* how horrible boys can be! They shout, and smell, and make a terrible mess all the time!'

Needless to say, it was only another year or two before we started to appreciate that boys did have a few good points despite being smelly and messy. But my only-child upbringing, not to mention my own personality, made it difficult for me to talk to boys –

especially if I liked them. The only one I ever felt comfortable enough to be myself with, all the time I was growing up, was David.

But that was only because I'd made him my honorary brother.

Nothing else.

So the thumping of my heart is probably something to do with the stress of the wedding. Or maybe I just need another drink.

Ten past nine

Phil's in a huddle with a group of his mates. They've got their arms around each other's shoulders, laughing into each other's faces. Every now and then, one of them leans outside of the scrum, picks up his pint mug, takes a few gulps and then ducks back into the group to continue with the story, or the joke, or whatever it is they're all guffawing about.

I sometimes wonder about blokes. I mean, I wonder what it's like to *be* one. I'm not sexist or anything, but they do seem to have it easier, don't they? For a start – no periods, no PMT, cramps, flooding, worrying about the date whenever you plan anything. No fear of getting pregnant any time you consider having sex. No morning sickness, no baby twisting and turning inside you, pressing on your bladder, giving you varicose veins and piles and stretch marks and making you look like a beached whale with legs. No horrors of childbirth – no heaving, grunting, screaming, sweating, pushing and having everyone from consultant to trainee midwife peering between your legs, and then being repaired with an embroidery of stitchwork that makes you walk like a novice horse-rider for weeks afterwards.

No sore breasts and leaking of milk when you hear your baby cry in a crowded supermarket. And when it's finally all stopped, and things are just settling down to an acceptable hormonal level, no menopause: no hot flushes, night sweats, mood swings and loss of libido.

Of course, I don't know about any of this stuff myself, not first hand anyway – apart from periods of course, which are enough of a curse for anyone and, if you believe in the Old Testament, I can't really see why God didn't give the same punishment to Adam for eating the damned apple as Eve got just for tempting him. He didn't *have* to succumb to temptation, did he? But that's typical of the whole gender equation, if you ask me. It's always the woman gets the blame.

The pregnancy and childbirth stuff I mostly found out about from Heather, who delighted in telling the whole family every gory detail of Troy's nine-month sojourn in her womb, his journey out into the world and how it all contrived to wreck her body and her life in general. It's a wonder I haven't been scared off the whole process, but I guess none of us ever believe our own experience is going to be quite as bad as anyone else's ... until it actually happens. Christine told me once that Nature (that old friend of hers), somehow manages to make you forget how bloody awful it is to have a baby, once it's born. Otherwise nobody would ever have more than one kid. My mum only had one anyway, of course, but apparently that was because she had a whole lot of miscarriages after I was born, and my dad decided she'd been through enough.

It was Christine, too, who recounted to me with great relish, the step by step progress of her menopause. She refused to consider taking HRT because 'the Change' (whispered in hallowed tones as if it was something to be revered) was, predictably, 'only nature'.

'Why should I have to take drugs to fight nature?' she asked me rhetorically, and I have to say I quite admire her reasoning. 'Just because we're supposed to stay young and beautiful and sexually precious all our lives?'

'Precocious.'

'Exactly, dear. Why shouldn't *men* be the ones who have to take drugs to fight *their* nature? They're the ones making all the demands, at the end of the day.'

It was always kind of hard to imagine Brian making any sort of demands at the end of any day – especially as he spent most of his life either asleep or slumped in front of the TV – but I wasn't keen to get into a debate about that.

Anyway, and getting back to my original point – it isn't just because of 'nature', just because of biology, that I think men have an easier time of it. There's a social conditioning, too, which still goes on behind the scenes of today's big shop window of Equality, Role Sharing and Men Discovering Their Feminine Sides. It's filtered like piped music into places where boys gather sweatily together in testosterone-charged matiness – the football pitch, the communal changing rooms, the local pub, the snooker club. It's evident in the way they smack each other on the back, swear at each other and jostle each other around. Where we girls sit for hours over a glass of wine, listening to each others' problems, picking holes in each others' relationships, hugging and crying together, spending sleepless nights worrying about each other, sending texts and greetings cards and sweet little email messages with puppies and teddy bears on them to reassure ourselves that we love and care about each other – what do blokes do? They buy each other a beer, slap each other a couple of times and get on with discussing the football. Phone each other? For a chat? Are you crazy? Send each other birthday cards? Like . . . uh . . . *why*?

I'm thinking about this now, watching Phil throwing back his head and laughing, watching his mates slapping his arm, patting his shoulder, slurping their beers together. At least we've moved on a little, I think, this generation. At least today's young guys don't hold back from touching each other, hugging each other, for fear of being called poofters. But I can't imagine Phil lying awake just, for instance, worrying about what John's girlfriend said to John in a row, or whether Stu's wife is thinking about leaving him. It's just never going to happen. Don't ask me why.

'You OK?'

Eva's sat down next to me and I never even noticed.

'Yes, fine. Sorry. I was just sitting here wondering about men.'

'Jesus! That's a job and a half.'

'Do you like them?'

It might sound like a silly question, but I'm intrigued.

'Some of them. Same as you. You don't like the whole bloody species, do you?'

'Absolutely not. I see what you mean.'

'It's only the sexual stuff that's different, Abbie,' she says, smiling. 'It doesn't stop you liking or disliking people as *people*.'

'Sorry. I didn't mean to be crass.'

'You're not, not at all. I prefer being open about it.'

'In that case, I think you're lucky. Being gay, you're lucky.'

'Why? You fancy Chloe?' she asks me with a teasing smile.

I laugh, but actually it's a terrible thought. I'd like to say I'd have better taste than that even if I was gay, but how insulting would that be to Eva!

'No. Because girls are nicer to each other. They don't hurt each other.'

'Are you *joking*? Christ, Abbie, what kind of protective bubble have you grown up in? Have you never, ever had a girlfriend who's been a bitch to you?'

'Yes.' I look away quickly. What am I talking about? Why did I say that, even think it, even for a second? 'Yes, I have. That was a stupid thing to say.'

'*People* hurt us,' says Eva firmly. 'People hurt people, whether they're male or female, straight or gay. You can't get away from it. It's inevitable.'

'Why?'

It comes out as an anguished squawk. I take a big gulp of my gin and tonic and wonder whether I'm anguished about the inevitability of being hurt, or because Eva, at only twenty, is talking so much more sense than I seem to be able to make of things even though I'm pushing towards thirty.

'Because they can't help it. Because it's part of caring. Part of being human. Part of loving. Part of living.'

'"It's only nature",' I say morosely into my drink.

'Exactly,' she agrees seriously, and I laugh, and

hug her, because she doesn't know why it's funny but she's still laughing along with me and it makes me realise how nice she is.

'I'm glad you're with Chloe,' I tell her. I'm slurring a bit and in a funny way it's a relief to know I'm starting to get drunk. The edges of things are looking slightly blurred. It's better that way.

'So am I. But don't get carried away thinking how lucky we are, Abbie. You've got so much going for you yourself. You're a lovely girl – good, kind, caring, everyone loves you. And you've got at least one guy desperately in love with you.'

'Oh, yeah, *right*!' I laugh sarcastically. 'As if!'

'Even if you refuse to see it yourself!' she adds with a grin as she gets up and moves on.

I finish the drink off and go to get another one. I must be *really* getting drunk. I can't make out what the bloody hell she's talking about.

'OK, let's have everyone up dancing now. Come on, everyone on the dance floor, that's right . . . Come on, love, you too . . . Let's have a bit of "YMCA"!'

I know Gary was just joking, in his speech, about it being the only thing Phil can dance to, but it's still obviously one of his favourites. He was the first up. I watch him and Gary from the edge of the dance floor, sipping my g and t morosely.

'*Young man* . . . !' shouts Gary at Phil as they throw themselves enthusiastically about. I suppose they look comical, but I hate this bloody dance with a vengeance.

'What's up?' Chloe asks, leaning against the wall next to me.

'I don't understand it,' I say with a shrug. 'Why

does this song always make people act like morons?'

'You mean the fact that they feel the need to spell out four letters of the alphabet with their arms?'

'Not only that,' I agree, 'but they look so pleased with themselves about it! If they were doing the complete Russian alphabet in semaphore, sure I'd be impressed, but four letters?'

Chloe laughs. 'I didn't have you down as a cynic and a spoilsport, Abbie.'

'Oh, I wouldn't want to spoil their enjoyment. It's a bit like watching those crappy reality TV shows – harmless fun as long as you don't start thinking they're clever.'

'More like watching monkeys at the zoo, if you ask me!' She gives me a smile. 'You glad it's all over now, Abbie?'

'Well, it's not actually *over* ...'

'You know what I mean. All the serious bits. The important stuff. It all went OK, didn't it?'

Why do people keep saying that? Are they trying to reassure themselves, or what? The list of today's disasters keeps on growing by the hour, but even now we've had a near-drowning they're still deluding themselves that it's all gone without a hitch.

'It was never going to be straightforward,' says Chloe, linking her arm through mine. 'Not with our family.'

My eyebrows feel like they've shot up into my hair. This must be the first time in her life that Chloe's ever shown me any sort of affection.

'You've been a terrific bridesmaid,' she says, surprising me even more. 'I know I haven't. I've been crap.'

So once again this is all about Chloe. What does

she want me to do? Deny it? Tell her of course that's not true, she's been wonderful – we wouldn't have been able to get through the day without her?

'You don't have to say anything,' she adds, quietly. 'I'm not stupid. I know I've been a spoilt bitch. It's just . . . it was difficult. You know? Seeing Sam so happy, planning her wedding and everything.'

'But you're happy with Eva, aren't you?'

'Yes, of course. It's changed everything.' She pauses, looks at me a bit warily as if she's not sure whether she ought to go on. 'I didn't *choose* to be gay, Abbie.'

'I realise that.'

'It's not easy. I used to keep hoping I was going to wake up one morning and fancy one of the boys in my class. I wanted to be the same as everyone else.' She hangs her head. 'I guess I feel a bit ashamed of that now. You know, we're supposed to be proud of it, aren't we? Gay Pride and all that.'

'I think,' I say carefully, 'that there's nothing to be either ashamed of, or proud of, is there? Isn't it just the way you are? It's like saying you should be proud of being tall, or I should be proud of being blonde.'

'Now you *are* joking!' she teases and we both laugh.

'Oh, *no*!' I groan a second later.

The DJ's decided it's a good idea, while all the drunks are on the dance floor, to move on to that other old party favourite – "Saturday Night".

'You hate this one too?' guesses Chloe.

'Are you surprised?'

'My mum loves it.'

Sure enough, Christine, together with about half the women in the room, especially those over about fifty, are rushing to their feet with an excited gleam in their eyes, anxious to perform the same carbon-copy dance routine that they roll out at every party they ever go to.

'What they don't realise,' I say, shaking my head sadly, 'is that they're handing men, on a plate, the chance to crack the old joke about women only being good at *simple repetitive movements*.'

'I know. Even Troy can do it.'

'Well, in his case, I admire him. But older than five or six, then I'm sorry, but it's not that clever, is it?'

'And they look so chuffed with themselves!'

'Well,' I concede, laughing again, 'I suppose we just sound like a pair of mean bitches. At least they're having fun.'

'And so is *he*,' points out Chloe.

I follow her gaze. It's Gary – who's abandoned his brother in favour of a new dancing partner. She's blonde and buxom and she's holding on to Gary as if he's a rock in a raging sea. I've never actually seen anyone slow-dancing to "Saturday Night" before. Just goes to show – it can be done. It certainly shows more ingenuity than the normal dance steps.

'She's a friend of our cousin Tanya. I hope he gets off with her,' says Chloe thoughtfully.

'Why do you say that?'

'Because I feel bad about him.' She sighs. 'He thought we were going out together, just because we kind of chatted and got on well.'

'Maybe you should have told him.'

'Jesus, Abbie!' she exclaims. 'What – do I have to walk around with a sign hanging round my neck – LESBIAN. DO NOT APPROACH? I *like* men! I like their company, I like talking to them – it's not *my* fault if they can't be friendly without wanting sex, is it?'

'No, Chloe.' I watch Gary tightening his arms around the busty blonde and moving in to nuzzle her neck. 'No, it's not your fault at all.'

It's just the way of the world, it seems.

It's only nature.

Half past nine

Chloe and I are still leaning against the wall, watching the dancing together in an unexpectedly companionable silence, when Phil joins us. With the waistcoat of his bridegroom suit unbuttoned and his tie off, he looks rumpled, slightly pissed, and (I realise suddenly) very attractive.

'How you doing, darlin'?' he asks me, leaning close to plonk a kiss on my cheek. 'My bestest girl's bestest mate?'

He smells of beer and cologne. His lips are firm and his cheek's just slightly bristly.

God, I miss being kissed by a man. I'd almost forgotten what it was like.

I must be drunker than I thought. This is Sam's husband, for Christ's sake!

But he's moved on to Chloe, before I can even respond to him.

'And how about you, little Sister-in-law?' he says with a grin. 'You all right?'

'I'm great, thanks, Brother-in-law,' she says calmly.

For some reason he seems to find this hysterically funny. Alcohol has a lot to answer for, and I know he doesn't usually drink much, so it's probably having a profound effect on him.

'Lovely to see you both,' he chuckles, as if we've only just arrived, and he moves on to the next group of guests, weaving slightly as he goes.

'Prat!' says Chloe vehemently as soon as he's out of earshot.

'Who – Phil?' I look at her in surprise. 'He's just a bit tipsy.'

'That's not what I meant,' she retorts. 'I said he's a prat, and I mean he's a prat.'

I can't believe I'm hearing this. Everybody likes Phil. He's so ... well, he's just so *likeable*. Surely even Chloe can't come up with a good reason not to like him?

'Actually I think he's a nice guy.'

'Do you really? Despite what happened a couple of years ago?' she challenges me, jutting out her chin at me.

'Ah, well. If we're going to drag all *that* up again ...'

'Come off it, Abbie. Don't try and pretend you haven't been thinking about it yourself today. Every time someone's asked why Julia's not here, every time Granddad calls you Julia by mistake.'

'All right. Yes, all right – of course it's been on my mind. *She's* been on my mind. I didn't want anything to happen – anything to be *said* – today, that would upset Sam or spoil things for her. That's all.'

'If she's upset at all, it's only because Julia didn't come.'

'That's what she *says*. But do you really think she would have wanted her here, today, on her wedding day? Her wedding to *Phil*?'

269

'Yes, I do think she would. She did. She *told* me she did. She told me how disappointed she was that Julia didn't even reply.'

'Huh. I wasn't at all surprised. She never had any bloody manners.'

Chloe studies me silently for a minute. 'Don't let it eat you up, Abbie,' she says at length.

'What?'

'The bitterness. The anger. You're so full of it, it's coming out of your ears.'

How *dare* she!

Chloe, Miss Bad Temper, the Queen of Sulk, who through all the years I've known her has displayed more moods, tantrums, door-slammings and down-right *attitude* than anyone else I've ever met – how dare she, of all people, accuse me of being *angry* . . .!

'And you're such a lovely, gentle person really,' she adds, taking the wind out of my sails completely. 'You always were.'

'Never knew you cared,' I say sarcastically. Gruffly.

'Look: I know what you think of me. Or at least what you've thought of me at times. But just because I've had my own problems; my own *demons* – it doesn't mean I haven't always loved my family in my own way. They know that. And whether you like it or not,' she adds with a grin, 'you're part of the family, aren't you?'

I don't know how to answer this. I can't quite believe I'm hearing it, to be honest. 'You honestly don't understand why I still feel angry at Julia?'

'Of course I understand. But it's a shame to let it fester away forever, isn't it? Spoiling your life?'

Spoiling my life? There hasn't been a hell of a lot to spoil, in all honesty.

270

'But it's all right for you to blame Phil for what happened?'

'I'm not blaming him. I just think he's a prat.' She laughs. 'But then, *I'm* not so likely to be blinded by his stunning good looks, am I? Or his aftershave?'

I feel myself flush. 'I don't *fancy* him! He's Sam's husband!'

'I know. And as long as she's happy, I don't really care if he *is* a prat.'

'What's this?' Brian's voice booms in my ear. 'A bevy of bridesmaids?'

'Well, at least Chloe still *looks* like a bridesmaid,' I respond.

'And a very pretty one, too.'

Bloody hell. We should have a wedding in this family more often. The compliments are flowing like the champagne.

She turns her face away from him, refusing to be mollified. I don't blame her. She and Eva got it totally wrong by choosing today to drop their bombshell, but that doesn't excuse him being so insufferably rude to them. Does he really think a few pathetic smarmy words are going to make her jump up and hug him? He needs to apologise, at the very least, and that's *not* going to happen. Not in a million years.

'Sorry, Chloe, love.'

Jesus, Christ. The world's gone mad!

'*What?*'

Chloe looks as stunned as I feel. This is a first, believe me. Next thing we know, he'll be kissing babies and carrying a handbag.

'Sorry for shouting. About your . . .' He looks

271

uncomfortable. 'About . . . um . . . Eva.'

Chloe just shrugs but doesn't respond. Her whole body language is saying *It'll take more than that, buster*.

'You have to appreciate,' he says, trying to sound conciliatory and reasonable, 'that it came as a shock.'

'OK!' She swings around to face him, suddenly, her face flushed and her eyes flashing like ice. I find myself thinking, involuntarily, that without her customary black eye make-up, black clothes and black scowl, she really is quite beautiful. 'OK, fair enough, we sprung it on you. Maybe today wasn't the best timing in the world, but Dad, would it *ever* have been good timing, for you? Would you *ever* have been gracious and polite – like Mum was, like Sam and Abbie were? Like *everybody* else has been? Eh? Maybe it hasn't occurred to you that we chose today because we thought perhaps, on Sam's wedding day, you just *might* be in a better mood for once in your life – less likely to be bad-tempered and hostile and . . .'

'Is that what you think of me?' he asks, so quietly that I only just hear him above the music.

'Well.' She's run out of steam now she's got that out of her system. 'Well, you *do* know what you're like.'

There's a horrible silence. For a minute I'm afraid that Brian's either going to shout at her again, or worse – burst into tears. Then I'd *really* think aliens had taken over his body.

Then, unbelievably, he suddenly starts to laugh.

And even more unbelievably, Chloe joins in.

'I know, I know,' he says, slinging an arm round her shoulders and giving her an affectionate smile.

'I'm a miserable old bastard at times, aren't I?'

'Yes, you are,' she agrees, pretending to punch him in the stomach. 'But I suppose you can't help it. And at least I know who *I* take after!'

'You're right there, you bad-tempered little madam, you!'

'You grouchy old sod!'

'Ratty little cow!'

And they're hugging and kissing each other while the insults fly back and forth!

Sometimes I think I'll never understand this family as long as I live.

I probably don't need yet another drink. I've had enough, and it's still early, really. But nevertheless, here I am at the bar, topping up again, and drinking as if it's my first one after a month on the wagon.

I suppose it's inevitable, after all the preparation and all the worry of the last few months, that I suddenly feel very strange this evening, now the wedding's over, and most of the reception too, and we're just cruising towards midnight with all the worst cock-ups behind us. It's not exactly an anti-climax. Far from it – I feel like I'm on the verge of euphoria, despite everything that's happened. I can see the light at the end of the tunnel. I can almost believe that Sam and Phil are going to survive their wedding day unscathed. This time tomorrow they'll be away on their honeymoon, and nothing can touch them, nothing can spoil things for them. Or if it does, at least it won't be my fault.

I wish I could just sink into this feeling of relief, like relaxing against a soft fluffy pillow, but I can't. There's something holding me back ... just a niggle on the edge of my consciousness. Like that fluffy pillow's got a lump in the middle of it, and no matter how much I turn the pillow over, pummel it and push it into shape, I can still *just* feel the hard lump, in the back of my neck, every time I settle down against it.

I suppose I'm kind of hoping the alcohol will deaden my senses enough so that I stop feeling the lump of my anxiety and can finally sink into that comfy pillow of complacency. A job well done. A happy bridesmaid.

Unfortunately, the niggle that won't go away has a name. Its name, of course, is Julia, and the struggle to keep her memory out of this wedding is what's worn me out more than anything else.

And have I even succeeded? Of course I haven't.

She's here. Just as surely as if she'd come today, she's here in everyone's mind, and nothing was ever going to stop that. The sun went behind Julia's cloud on 15 May two years ago in Venice, and it was obvious since then that she was always going to rain on this parade – whether she actually turned up or not.

Venice: May 2005

'Look at it. It's just beautiful,' said Julia with a sigh. 'You can understand why people fall in love here.'

The four of us were standing on the Rialto Bridge, looking out over one of the most famous and romantic views in Europe. Unfortunately, none of us were feeling the slightest bit romantic. It was probably the wrong place for a single girl, a couple who didn't really like each other, and a girl with a broken heart, to come for a long weekend away. But that wasn't how it was meant to be.

For a start, I wasn't even supposed to be there. It had started off as Julia's treat – or bribe, as I preferred to think of it – for Sam. Julia was working for a travel company at the time and occasionally got special deals like these really cheap flights to Venice for four people. Ever since the incident with Jamie, Julia had been trying to wheedle her way back into Sam's affections. She obviously knew *I* was never going to forgive her – why did she think Sam would? It made me sick. For a long time Sam was having none of it, and I just wished Julia would give up and piss off.

We dropped her from our conversation. Sam didn't

return her calls and if we saw her in pubs or in the street we both ignored her. It suited me. I'd have been quite happy if I never saw her face again as long as I lived.

I don't know exactly when, or how – I didn't want to hear about it – but there must have come a time when Julia finally got to talk to Sam and spin her a load of pathetic lies and excuses about why she slept with my boyfriend.

'It wasn't her, Abbie . . . it was Jamie,' Sam told me afterwards.

I stared at her. What had happened to her? Why was she being sucked into this shit instead of telling that cow to fuck off?

'I thought both people needed to be involved,' I replied scathingly.

'She doesn't remember what happened. She thinks he must have put something in her drink.'

Yeah, right.

'She's so sorry, Abbie – she never wanted to hurt you. She's worn herself out with crying. You should see the state of her – she must have lost two stone, worrying about it.'

'Worn out and wasting away with too much shagging, more like.'

'I honestly don't think it was her fault. She might be a flirt, but she really didn't mean for that to happen.'

Poisonous snakes probably don't mean for you to die when they bite you, but you still do.

'It *was* Jamie,' went on Sam quite seriously. 'Think about it, Abbs – you know what he was like, now. He was a total shit. He was having it off with Andrea Farmer, and that girl Gillian from the petrol station.'

276

'I don't care about them!' I shouted. 'They might be slags, they might be cows, but at least they didn't pretend to be my *fucking friend*!'

It hurt me that Sam believed Julia's story – apparently believed I was making a mountain out of molehill over the ruination of my life. But at least she had the decency to refuse all her offers of reconciliation. Until the Venice trip.

'It's just that it's our two-year anniversary – mine and Phil's – and Venice is so special, so romantic. It'll be perfect,' she told me.

'You don't have to go with *her*, though, do you?'

She shrugged and smiled at me sadly. 'If you really don't want me to, I won't.'

I ground my teeth. Of course I didn't want her to. I also didn't want her to put me in that position. Why was she even considering it?

'She's offered us free flights, that's all. I don't suppose we'll spend any time with her when we get out there – she's going with this guy Ian. She seems really keen on him. I think she might finally be settling down, this time.'

'Good for her. Let her go with Ian on their bloody own, then.'

'She's *trying* to be nice, Abbie. Trying to make amends. She'd probably offer the flights to *you*, if you were speaking to her.'

I doubt it. I'm sure she knew perfectly well where I'd tell her to stick them.

A hotel in Venice was duly booked and I pretended not to be jealous, not to care that Sam was prepared to go away with the person I hated most in all the world, not to mind being the one without a boyfriend, the one left sitting at home alone with the TV and a stack of library books for company. Nothing new there.

I got the phone call ten days before they were due to go – at half past two in the morning. I'd been in such a deep sleep, the phone must have been ringing for about ten minutes before I finally surfaced. When I heard Sam's hysterical crying I was suddenly wide awake.

'What is it? Is somebody hurt? Tell me!'

'It's over!' she managed to get out between her sobs. 'He's finished it, Abbie! He's left me!'

'What?' I couldn't have been more shocked if she'd told me Phil was taking a day trip to Mars. He was crazy about her! He'd never looked at anyone else since the day he met her! What the hell could have happened to change that overnight? 'Look, calm down, Sam. I'm sure he'll be back. Did you have a row? It's nothing that you two can't sort out. Give him till tomorrow and he'll be . . .'

'It wasn't a row. We've been sitting here in the flat for about twenty-four hours, just talking. He's made up his mind.'

'Made up his mind about *what*? There isn't another girl, is there? I can't believe it!'

'No.' She was trying to stop crying, trying to talk without hiccupping and sobbing. 'He says he still loves me but . . . he's not ready to settle down. He says it's because I've made a big issue about our two-year anniversary – booking a romantic weekend in Venice and everything. It's all brought out all this anxiety in him.'

'That's *crap*! He can't just say . . . because of a weekend away . . .'

'I said I'd cancel it. I mean . . . for God's sake! It's just a holiday, it doesn't matter. But he said . . . he said it was too late, he was already in deeper than he wanted to be . . . he had to get out and sort his head out . . .'

'"Sort his head out"!' I spat in disgust. 'I'll sort his fucking head out for him, when I see him! What the hell . . .?'

But she was crying properly again now. I was just making things worse.

'I'm coming over,' I said, peeling off my pyjamas and looking for my jeans. 'I'll be there in five minutes.'

'No! It's half past two . . .'

'I'd come over even if was midnight on the last day of the world,' I retorted, snapping my phone shut and grabbing my car keys.

Four hours and half-a-dozen cups of tea later, there was only one thing we'd agreed on: she wasn't going to run after him and beg him to come back.

'He's having an attack of commitment panic,' I proclaimed with the wisdom of someone who's only ever had one boyfriend. 'If you phone him, crying and pleading, it'll just make him more convinced that he was right to have been scared off.'

'But I'm not *like* that! I've never put any pressure on him! I've never been desperate, or needy, or talked about weddings and babies and stuff! It's so *unfair*!'

'I know it is. He's being pathetic.'

'This is the *first* romantic thing I've ever suggested! It's always been him – *he* wanted us to move in together, *he* buys me flowers and takes me out for surprise meals and stuff.'

279

'I don't think it's anything you've said, or done,' I tried to reassure her. 'I think he's more likely frightened by his own feelings.'

'Well, he's taken a long time deciding he was frightened! *Two years* we've been together, Abbie – you'd have thought he'd have run away a bit sooner if he was that scared.'

'He's suddenly sat up and thought: Shit, this is serious. Am I ready for this? Men are so stupid. He's probably just been rolling along in his own sweet little way, enjoying the ride, not stopping to think where it was leading, and for whatever reason, he's suddenly realised that it *is* about commitment. I reckon he just needs a bit of time to get used to it and he'll come straight back saying it's what he wants.'

'I don't know,' she said, wearily. 'He talked himself round in circles in the end – I'm not even sure he knows what he wants himself.'

'Exactly.'

'Well, I'd better phone Julia and cancel Venice.'

'You were looking forward to it,' I said, sadly, feeling really mean, now, about wishing she wasn't going.

'I know.' She looked at me for a moment and then added, 'Well, actually, come to think of it – why should I cancel it?'

'Fair enough. Go anyway. Good idea. Show him you're getting on with your life. It'll do you good.'

'What are you doing the week after next, Abbie? Want to join me?'

It was a hard one. Four days away with Julia, who I hadn't really spoken to for about five years and who I'd like to push in the canal as soon as look at her. I'd rather do almost anything than spend any time with Julia. I wanted to say no. But Sam needed me. Sam needed *me* – Julia was far too selfish to bother with her if she was all loved up with her new boyfriend. We got the booking changed and I packed my case.

We spent the first day exploring, finding our way around the city. After we'd taken photos on the Rialto Bridge, we stopped for lunch at a pavement café next to the Grand Canal, watching the gondolas glide past with their cargoes of eager tourists.

'God, he's so *irritating*!' exclaimed Julia as Ian went inside to use the toilets. He'd just been telling us a long, rambling story about the times of the trains he used for his morning commute, and I must admit our eyes had all begun to glaze over.

'I thought you really liked him?' said Sam in surprise. 'I thought that was what all this was about?'

I was barely speaking to Julia. I had to force myself to bother at all. She hadn't changed one bit, as far as I could see – still thought she was God's gift – and she certainly wasn't bothering to make much effort to be friendly to me. But Sam had asked me to try to be civil and more than anything, at the moment, I didn't want to do anything to upset Sam.

'Well, I suppose I *did* think that. He was OK for a while. But Jesus, being with him twenty-four hours a day – he's so *bloody* boring, isn't he? I wish I'd left him at home and come on my own like you two.'

It didn't seem to occur to her that this wasn't exactly the most tactful thing she could say right now.

'I'm sick of men,' agreed Sam, however. 'All of them.'

I'd been taken aback by the change in Sam. After

a couple of days when she barely stopped crying, she suddenly seemed to mentally square her shoulders, swallow back the pain and harden her heart.

'If he doesn't want me,' she told me with only the slightest tremor in her voice, 'then I'm buggered if I'm going to waste my life hanging around moping over him. I'm better off on my own.'

'Good for you,' I told her, not convinced.

But she'd proceeded to prepare for the trip to Venice with every appearance of enthusiasm. At her insistence, Phil wasn't even mentioned, and I began to wonder if this was really the same girl who'd been so passionately in love only a few short weeks before.

On the Saturday, the second day of our stay, we made our way to the famous St Mark's Square and visited the Basilica, the Doge's Palace and jostled with the crowds on the Ponte della Paglia for the best view of the neighbouring Bridge of Sighs. The afternoon sun was hot as we leaned on the parapet staring out across the canal.

'Beautiful,' I sighed.

'Yes,' agreed Sam. 'But it kind of spoils it when you remember it was used by prisoners crossing the canal to the torture chamber.'

We'd already traced those poor prisoners' footsteps ourselves, walking through the interior of the Bridge of Sighs from the Doge's Palace.

'That's the trouble,' said Julia meaningfully. 'Everything starts off looking lovely till you get to know more about it.'

She gave a very pointed look in Ian's direction but he was engrossed in his guidebook, quoting facts and figures to us even though nobody was listening.

'Let's get ice creams!' exclaimed Sam, suddenly

brightening up at the sight of a stall selling dozens of different colours and flavours.

'And then let's have a gondola ride!' I added. 'You can't say you've been to Venice without having a gondola ride.'

Maybe I'd get my chance to shove Julia in the canal.

'Not here, though,' said Ian predictably. 'The guidebook warns you that St Mark's is the most expensive place for gondolas. It's all a rip-off, if you ask me, of course.'

'Oh, shut up!' exclaimed Julia. 'Don't bloody come, then, if that's how you feel! Stand on the bank and take photos!'

He did, too. I've still got a framed copy of one of the photos he took on my camera: it's of Sam, Julia and me, sprawled in the gondola, with the gondolier grinning in the background. The body language speaks volumes: Sam and I are linking arms, smiling at the camera but I've got my back to Julia, who's only got eyes for the gondolier. I've often felt like chucking that photograph in the dustbin, but something's always stopped me. I think it's because it was the last one ever taken of the three of us together.

By that evening, Julia's irritation with Ian had become mutual and they were barely speaking to each other. On the Sunday, over breakfast, she announced that they were no longer an item and he would be 'doing his own thing' for the rest of the trip. Ian passed us in the hotel foyer on his way out, wearing walking boots, an anorak and a stony face.

'Have a nice day,' I said, feeling just a little bit sorry for him. He didn't look round.

That meant we were lumbered with Julia for the duration. We took the vaporetto out to Burano, the prettiest island in the Lagoon, where we strolled down narrow streets bordered by brightly painted blue, yellow, red and pink houses. We browsed for souvenirs among little shops displaying coloured glass jewellery and lace pillowcases on tables outside in the sunshine, crossed the canals over pretty little bridges, which just cried out to be photographed, and sat in the shade outside a pink-washed trattoria to enjoy plates of sardines in tomato sauce washed down with a good bottle of Valpolicella.

We'd all caught the sun by the time we boarded the vaporetto to take us back to Venice. Sam's colouring meant that despite careful application of factor 20, instead of tanning she developed a pinkish bloom and a hectic rash of freckles. I went red and blotchy. Julia, with her glossy dark hair and olive skin, simply looked more beautiful than ever.

'What a lovely day,' she purred, stretching out on the seat of the boat. 'We don't need men, to enjoy ourselves, do we, girls?'

I remember thinking that this was a bit rich, coming from the person who'd stolen my only boyfriend, and whose eyes were, even now, constantly searching for the next male victim.

And then, when we got back to the hotel, Phil was there waiting for us.

Sam flushed in surprise, hesitated for a moment halfway in through the hotel door, and then took a deep breath and tried to walk straight past him.

'Wait!' he said, in a strangled voice. 'Please. Sam, please . . .' He followed her like a puppy at her heels

284

as she stalked across the lobby to the reception desk to pick up her room key. 'Please! Can we talk?'

'Is there anything to talk about?' she retorted icily.

'I've come all this way ... I paid a fortune for the flight ...'

'Nobody asked you to.'

I didn't know whether to be impressed or stunned by her toughness. True, he'd made her suffer ... but wasn't this what she'd wanted? For him to realise his mistake and come running back to her?

Julia was staring at them with her mouth open. I grabbed her arm and hustled her towards the stairs.

'Let's give them some privacy,' I hissed at her.

She was so bloody tactless, if I'd left it to her she'd probably have joined in with the argument.

I went to my room and had a shower, changed my clothes and sat on the bed reading my book. Within half an hour, Sam flounced into the room and threw her shoes into the corner.

'Well?' I said, smiling at her in anticipation, sure of the romantic happy ending I wanted.

'Well what?' she said grumpily, throwing herself down on her bed.

'Did he apologise? Is everything OK?'

'Yes, he did. And no, it's not.'

This wasn't going the way I expected.

'If you want me to move out of the room ...' I tried again, hinting with my eyebrows.

'Abbie!' She turned on me, sounding exasperated and impatient. Not sounding like Sam. 'Haven't you heard what I've been saying all weekend? He's blown it. I don't care how much he comes whining around me now, saying he's sorry and he's thought it all over and he's made his decision. It's too late. I've moved on.'

'But it's only been a couple of weeks,' I said in not much more than a whisper. 'And you loved him so much.'

'Did. Before I knew how much he could hurt me.'

'But if he's sorry—'

'I've made up my mind, Abbie,' she cut me off harshly. 'I don't want him back.'

There was a silence between us that I had no idea how to fill.

'If you're my friend,' she added eventually, 'you'll support me in this.'

'Of course,' was the only thing I could have said. Wasn't it?

We did our make-up and went out for dinner as if nothing had happened. Julia pleaded a headache from too much sun, and stayed in her room. I thought maybe she'd had a fit of compassion and was waiting for Ian to come back. As if!

Sam and I ate at a little *ristorante* just round the corner from our hotel. There were dozens of questions I couldn't ask: What had Phil said? How had he changed his mind? What did he say when she rejected him? Where had he gone? Instead, we talked politely about the meal, about our trip to Burano, about what we were planning for the next day (our last) and about the weather. I felt as if we were barely acquainted instead of best friends. It was almost a relief to walk back to the hotel.

Upstairs, there were voices coming from Julia's room.

'Ian's back,' I remarked. 'And at least they're not shouting at each other.'

'Let's go and say hello,' suggested Sam, knocking on the door.

'Hang on a sec!' called Julia gaily, before flinging open the door and inviting us in with a smile.

I'll never forget that smile. It was *triumphant*.

She was in her flimsy satin dressing gown. And Ian wasn't back at all.

Phil was stretched out on her bed in his boxer shorts, with a bottle of wine and half-empty glass on the bedside table beside him, grinning at us dopily as if everything was absolutely fine in his world.

To her credit, Sam didn't say a word. Not even the 'Fuck you both!' which I tried to shout, but which seemed to get stuck in my throat by the bile rising. She closed the door on them very quietly and we went back to our own room, where she got undressed, got into bed and turned to face the wall, refusing to talk to me or listen to the total crap I was trying to come up with to pass off as comfort. The next morning she and I packed and left for the airport, getting an earlier flight home.

And the odd thing was that within a week she was back with Phil as if nothing had happened.

But Julia moved to Bournemouth. And bloody good riddance.

Quarter to ten

Troy's finally fallen asleep on a pile of coats across two chairs. People walking past him stop and smile and whisper, 'Aah! Cute!' If only they knew.

I'm not sure if he's always a little demon, or if he just saves it for his family. He might have been a perfect model child at playgroup, for instance, and when he started school a couple of months ago his teacher might have gasped in delight at his exemplary behaviour. He might go to Sunday school and sit silently with his hands folded in his lap, listening to the Bible stories and closing his eyes for the prayers, like one little boy I used to have in my own class when I was a Sunday school teacher. His name was Gerald – never shortened to Gerry – and he wore a proper shirt and tie, every single week, and called me 'Miss'. I used to tell the other children off for laughing at him. Then, one day in the middle of the story about Jonah and the Whale, which was usually one of their favourites, Adam Fisher pushed Gerald off his chair. Before I could get to him, Gerald was on his feet, had grabbed Adam by his collar and landed a punch square on his nose. Mrs Fisher had to be called to take Adam home, crying like a baby with a hanky held to his bloody nose.

'Serves him right,' she proclaimed when she'd been told what happened, giving him a cuff to the shoulder that made him cry even louder.

No one ever messed with Gerald again, though, and in fact from what I remember, he and Adam Fisher eventually became best friends. Wonder what happened to him? He's probably in the army or something now.

'What you thinking about?' says Heather, who catches me standing here staring at her sleeping son.

'A kid I used to teach at Sunday school. He punched another boy's lights out in the middle of Jonah and the Whale.'

'What's Jonah and the Whale?' says Heather. 'A pub?'

'No. No, it's ... never mind.' I gaze again at Troy's tousled blond head, his perfect eyelashes resting against his round pink cheek. 'He's a sweet little boy really, Heather, isn't he?'

'When he's asleep,' she says with heavy irony.

'I'm sorry,' I add, warily, 'if I upset you earlier: when you were telling me about him being ... *delicate*. It's just that – well – you never mentioned it before. And he doesn't look it. So you'd never guess.' I'm trying to be diplomatic. What I really want to say is that she needs to get real and get over it. Troy's no more delicate than I am.

'Well, I shouldn't have snapped at you,' she says a bit grudgingly. 'It's not your fault you haven't got any kids of your own. I always say, nobody knows what it's like until you have one of your own.'

'I'm sure that's true,' I concede to this piece of perceived wisdom.

'I know he's probably not *unusually* delicate,' she admits, 'but he's such a worry to me.'

I'm not surprised, really. If he was mine, I'd be worried he was going to go out and nick cars or blow up Parliament.

'It's difficult, you know,' she adds morosely, stroking Troy's hair casually with the backs of her fingers.

'Yes. I'm sure . . .'

I've got no idea what she's on about, but at least we seem to be in agreement now.

The music has stopped abruptly and the DJ taps the mike twice to get our attention and announces:

'OK, everyone – listen: apparently there's sandwiches and wedding cake on the long table at the back there. If anyone's feeling a bit peckish I suggest you all . . . *go and fill your boots, everyone*!'

He says this last bit on a roll, with a strange pseudo-American accent that he probably thinks matches his cowboy hat and boots. He's called Big Wayne. As DJs go, he hasn't done a bad job – at least he hasn't played ABBA all night or tried to sneak in some of his own collection of Country and Westerns.

'Coming to get a bite to eat?' asks David, appearing suddenly at my side and steering me towards the buffet table.

'Looks like I am!' I joke.

I haven't spoken to David since we had that dance together. I know he's a bit pissed but I'm really wary now of what he might say or do next. It's a strange, unnatural feeling – being wary of David. We're normally so relaxed together.

'Didn't embarrass you, earlier, did I?' he mutters

close to my ear, as if he can read my mind.

''Course not,' I lie. 'What sandwiches are these? Ham?'

'It's just ... you look so lovely tonight, and ...'

'I think I'm going for the chicken rolls. Want a slice of quiche?'

'I need to talk to you, Abbie. There's stuff I need to tell you.'

'Mm. Vegetable samosas over there! My favourite!'

He sighs and follows me along the queue at the buffet table, carrying a plate but not picking up any food.

'OK. OK, I'm embarrassing you. I'm sorry. But can we talk?'

I'm not answering. I'm filling up my plate with salad and coleslaw. He can talk to me any time he wants; he knows that. What's all the sudden fuss? He's making me feel jittery and uncomfortable.

'Abbie,' he says, quietly, nudging me with his empty plate. 'I *need* to talk to you.'

There's something about the way he says the '*need*' that makes me turn to look at him. There's a pleading in his eyes. I suppose he wants someone to pour out his heart to about Heather: about their row, their lovers' tiff or whatever's gone on between them today.

'OK,' I say automatically. Abbie the Agony Aunt. I've never understood why people turn to me with their problems about their love lives – I've got less experience in that field than any of them. 'Of course. Fill your plate up, David. We've got a couple more hours of drinking ahead of us: we need carbs. Maybe we can find somewhere quiet to sit and talk while we're eating.'

291

'Thanks, Abbs. Here – do you want a piece of "Philippa and Samuel's" wedding cake?'

'I think we owe it to them, yes!' I feel myself relaxing. Fine, I don't mind listening to him talking to me about Heather. As long as he doesn't talk about *me*, everything stays normal and neutral and I don't get that scary feeling of the ground shifting beneath my feet. 'OK? Got enough on your plate? Want a sausage roll?'

I lead the way towards the door. There are a couple of sofas in the reception area outside. No one will miss us while they're getting stuck into the buffet.

But we never actually get that far.

Christine's running towards me – literally running – her mouth a big round 'o' of panic, her hair jumping about on her head as she runs, so that corkscrews of blue dance in the light, making her head look like an electromagnetic field.

'Have you seen my dad?' she gasps, almost knocking me over as she grabs me by the arm, shaking me frantically as if I might have him hidden up my sleeve.

'Isn't he with Auntie Barbara?' says David, turning and scanning the room quickly.

'No. The last she saw of him, he was going out to the toilet. He's not in there, and no one's seen him.'

'Jesus.' David runs his hand through his hair and sighs. 'Couldn't someone have gone *with* him. Where was Uncle Don?'

'I don't think they realise how much worse he's got. They've been very good, helping me out, keeping an eye on him ... he can be a handful,' she says with an apologetic shrug.

'We'd better go out and look for him, then,' I point

292

out, fear suddenly clutching at my heart, thinking of the lake.

It's dark outside now, and if we're going to have a repeat performance of Troy's rescue operation I don't think there'll be enough dry clothes to go around.

'Come on,' says David, taking my plate of food out of my hands and putting it down, with his own, on a table beside us. 'I've got a torch in the car. Let's go.'

I give the samosa a lingering look as we go. I was looking forward to that.

'Hang on.' I'm running to keep up with David. He's already been to his car and got the torch and he's charging out across the grounds towards the lake. 'Look, this is silly. There's no point us all tearing around in the same direction.'

He stops and looks at me as if he's just remembered I'm with him.

'You're right. Why don't you go down the drive in case he's gone that way and got as far as the road? Mum,—' Christine's running after us, panting, tottering on her new high heels '—go with Abbie. I'll take the torch and search the grounds.'

My heart's pounding as Christine and I jog along the main drive of the golf club, heading for the road.

'Silly old fool,' she mutters. 'I *told* him he mustn't go outside.'

'He can't have got far,' I try to reassure her. 'He walks so slowly.'

'I know. He was looking really tired, to be honest, last time I checked on him. He kept asking when we were going home.'

'That's it then. I bet that's what he's doing – or what he *thinks* he's doing – making his way home.'

'He's got no sense of direction, Abbie. He went out and got lost a few weeks ago. Did I tell you? A lady had to bring him home. She found him wandering around down at the market.'

'At the market? How the hell did he get that far?'

'On the bus, apparently. I didn't get a lot of sense out of him, of course, but I think he got on a bus at the end of the road, showed his bus pass and thought he was going to work at the docks.' She sighs, slows down and then stops to take off her shoes. 'It's no good, I can't walk any further in these.'

'Do you want to go back? I'll carry on.'

'Of course not. I don't mind walking barefoot, Abbie. It's only nature.'

We're nearly at the road now. This is worrying. I'd hoped we might have found him by now.

'We'll need to split up and go in different directions,' she tells me matter-of-factly. 'You go towards the town. I'll check the bus stops.'

'Hang on. Let me just check with David – no point us carrying on if he's found Frank already.'

'Amazing, isn't it?' she says, watching me with an awestruck expression as I flip open my mobile and scroll down to David's number. 'Phones are getting tinier and tinier. I had to leave mine at home today – it's too big for my handbag. Can you take pictures on it too, love? Isn't that clever?'

'David, hi, it's me. Yes. Any sign of him? No? Well, look, we've just got as far as the main road, so we're going to split up and . . .'

'They didn't have things like this years ago, did they?' Christine's carrying on, still gazing at my phone as if it's a prototype of an astounding new invention.

'OK, David. Yes, you too. Right, I'll call again if I get as far as the station. Your mum's going in the other direction. Should we ... Should we be talking to the police yet, do you think?'

I'm half whispering at this point. I don't want to get Christine too upset and worried just yet if it can be helped, but I'm beginning to wonder if we're going to find Frank on our own, to be honest. Anyway, she's not even listening to my conversation. She's still rabbiting on and on to herself about the wonders of modern technology.

'... and I know some people complain about them,' she's saying as I snap the phone shut. 'It's true they can be a nuisance, can't they – if people talk too loud, or don't turn them off, you know, in the cinema or whatever? But personally I think they're a *good* thing. I'm always saying to Dad: "If you go out, Dad, take your phone *with* you." Then at least, if he needs me ...'

'You what?' I stare at her, stunned. I mean – is this woman for real? 'Frank's got a *mobile phone*?' I demand.

'Yes, dear. I bought it for him a couple of Christmases ago. Of course, he wasn't quite as vague then as he is now ...'

'Has he got it on him?'

'Well, I don't know, Abbie. He drives me mad. I keep *telling* him, but ... Oh.' She stops, stares back at me. Hallelujah: I can see the light dawning. 'Oh, I see what you mean!'

'Does he know how to use it? How to answer it?'

'Well, I think so, dear. I've shown him, of course, but as you know, he does forget things from time to time.'

Like where he lives and who everyone is, for a start.

'We could try it, though,' she says doubtfully. 'He might hear it, if he's got his hearing aid switched on.'

For the love of God. I think we'd have more chance of getting in touch with him if we joined hands and held a séance.

'What's the number?' I say, flipping open my phone again.

'Oh. Well, it's in *my* phone, of course . . .'

'And that's at home. Great.' I'm trying not to sound impatient, but honestly – isn't all this just so typical of the Pattersons? I suppose people are going to start missing us soon, and before you know it, half the wedding party will be out here scouring the grounds for a deaf, daft old man who doesn't even know what day it is.

Sorry, God. If he turns up in the lake I'm going to feel guilty for the rest of my life, but *bloody hell*! Can't they *ever* act like normal people just for one measly day?

I call David again.

'Did you know your granddad had a mobile phone? No? Well, don't worry – he probably doesn't even know he's got one himself, to be honest. OK. Yes, all right – if your dad's got his phone on him, yes, give him a call and see if he knows the number. Otherwise . . . Yes, talk to you later.'

'Sorry,' says Christine quietly. 'I should have written the number down. I should have made sure he had it switched on. I should have . . .'

'Never mind,' I snap. 'Let's keep going, Christine. He could be on a bus by now, heading for bloody Southend or . . .'

'I don't *think* you can actually get a bus to Southend from round here, Abbie. The number two-three-nine only goes as far as Chelmsford, but then it turns round, past the bus garage, and if you wanted to go to *Basildon*, you'd have to get a number three-five-four, which goes—'

'All right! Shut up about the fucking buses! I'm sorry I mentioned them!' I look at her stricken face. 'Sorry,' I add quickly.

'You're right, dear. After all, he could even have got on a number sixty-two, and then he *could* have ended up at Southend, eventually, because—'

Fortunately, just before I scream at her, my phone rings.

It's David. He's found Frank wandering round the other side of the complex, staring in the windows of the restaurant with his trousers undone. He was just about to be arrested.

'Thanks very much,' David's telling the restaurant manager as we arrive. 'I really appreciate you cancelling the call to the police.'

'Just take him away and keep him under control,' says this guy, looking at Frank as if he's a nasty specimen that's crept out from under a rock. Not far wrong there. 'If I find him lurking out here again, with his . . . well—' he glances disdainfully at Frank's flies, which are now mercifully zipped up '—with his *private parts* exposed, frightening my patrons, then believe me, I shall have no option . . .'

'Yes, yes, we quite understand,' says Christine, marching up to them with as much dignity as she can manage in her bare feet, and grabbing Frank by the arm. 'Thank you, young man, and I'm sure my father would want to apologise for his behaviour if only he were able to. But as you can see, he's old and muddled and he really can't help it. So let's all be thankful we're not like it yet ourselves, and try to live and let live. It's part of growing old, I'm afraid, and it's only nature, at the end of the day.'

'Well said, Mum,' says David, putting his arm around her shoulders.

I feel like giving her a round of applause to be quite honest. Or giving her a hug and a kiss. But I'm too close to tears to do anything. It must be the relief of finding Frank safe and well – even if he did nearly end up with a conviction for indecent exposure. Or maybe it's because I feel bad for shouting at her earlier. Despite everything, I really do admire her, you know.

She lets him have it, though, once we walk away from the snotty restaurant manager.

'What on earth were you *doing*, Dad? With your trousers undone?'

'Looking for the toilet,' he retorts, staring at her as if she's stupid. 'What d'you think?'

'It's inside, Granddad,' says David. 'Come on, I'll take you.'

'Too late now, lad,' he scoffs, laughing. 'I got caught short, didn't I. I had to have a piss up the side of the wall there.'

'Outside the restaurant?' I ask faintly. No wonder the patrons got the hump. I mean, it'd be enough to put you right off your sausages, wouldn't it?

'Can we go home now?' says Frank pitifully as we go back into the function room, the lights and the music hitting our senses with a sudden double whammy as the doors open. 'I just want to go home. Please, Julia?'

'Soon,' I tell him with a sigh.

I can't even be bothered this time to tell him I'm not Julia. It hardly seems worth the effort.

Half past ten

'Where have you all been?' Sam demands, trotting across the dance floor to me, hitching up the hem of her dress with one hand.

'Don't ask.'

I sink down onto a chair at one of the nearest tables. I feel, suddenly, so utterly exhausted that I'm not sure if I'll be able to last out the night.

'Is everything all right?' She sits down next to me and takes hold of my hand. 'You look shattered.'

'Me? I'm fine. I just ... Well, I didn't get a lot of sleep last night.'

'I hope you weren't lying awake worrying, Babbie? Worrying about today?'

She's teasing. She knows perfectly well I would have been lying awake worrying. I always lie awake worrying.

'Not particularly,' I lie, with a grin.

I want to add that I was awake at four o'clock, tiptoeing into her room, hearing her talking on her mobile about something that might cause a massive family row. I want to ask her what that was all about. Maybe she'd found out about Chloe and was hoping to keep it quiet – pretend Eva was just a friend?

300

Perhaps she had prior knowledge of Christine's blue stripes and thought Brian might throw a wobbly about it (whereas in actual fact he hardly seems to have noticed)? Or perhaps it was nothing – nothing at all? Perhaps I just got the wrong end of the stick? Whatever it was, here we are at half past ten and everyone's still on speaking terms ... so far ...

'What are you looking so anxious about, then?' Sam asks me softly. 'Eh? It's nearly over now! You'll be able to relax and forget all about it!'

'Ah, don't say that! You know how important today's been for me! Of course I'll never forget it!'

'No,' she laughs. 'We'll have all those photos to look through, won't we, when we get back from Portugal!'

'Yes – I'm looking forward to that. And don't forget the table cameras – has everyone used them?'

'I should think so. I bet there'll be some dodgy ones on those!'

'And then the video.'

'Eek!' squeals Sam, covering her face with her hands. 'Not the *video*!'

We both collapse with the giggles. We've had previous experience of the Patterson family videos.

It's normally Brian's job, doing the videos. Thank God, today he passed the responsibility on to Uncle Dennis (his brother), because as father of the bride he knew he would hardly be able to lug a video camera down the aisle and film himself giving Sam away. Dennis, unlike Brian, is a quiet, unassuming guy with the manners of an old-fashioned gentleman. He's only a couple of years younger than Brian but it's hard to believe they're brothers at all. They

301

don't even look alike. I often think Brian must have taken all his parents' combined allocation of noisy, argumentative genes and left only the peaceful ones for Dennis.

Dennis has been so unobtrusive with the video camera for most of today, at times I've completely forgotten that he was filming at all, so that I've literally jumped with surprise when he's sneaked up behind me and asked me to smile for the camera.

Unlike when Brian's been filming in the past. I don't know what it is about him and the video camera, but whenever he gets behind it, a kind of megalomania seems to take him over and he thinks he's making a documentary for *BBC World News* instead of a home video for his family.

On one occasion, we'd all gone to watch Chloe in a school play when she was about nine or ten. We had seats near the middle of the hall, but as soon as the play started Brian stood up and started the camera rolling.

Needless to say, a chorus of irritated tuts erupted around us.

'Dad,' Sam whispered. 'Sit down! People behind you can't see!'

'But I'm *filming*!' he retorted, looking at her in amazement as if this obviously gave him exemption from all normal expectations of behaviour.

'Sit down, mate,' said the father sitting directly behind him. 'We *all* want to see this – you're not the only one with a camera.'

'Ssh!' called someone further along the row.

'You're distracting the children,' hissed a woman in front of me.

'Mind your own business,' snapped Brian.

302

The woman gasped and her husband swung round in his seat, red in the face, looking like he was going to throw a punch.

'Could you *please* keep the noise down, there,' stage-whispered a teacher, bustling along to the end of our row and firing a look of disdain at Brian. 'Please, sir, either sit down or go and stand at the back.'

'For Christ's sake!' muttered Brian, trampling on everyone's feet to get out of the row and go to the back of the room. 'I'm trying to make a *film* here!'

By now I'd shrunk right down in my seat, burning with humiliation and trying to pretend this family was nothing to do with me, so I couldn't believe it, when I glanced at Sam and Christine, to see them shaking in their seats, their hands clasped over their mouths to stop themselves from giggling out loud. But even I had to join in the laughter when we watched the finished result of Brian's video, which had recorded the whole soundtrack of the contretemps, while the camera had swung on his arm filming the backs of the seats in front of us, the floor, Brian's feet marching to the back of the hall, and, finally, as the camera was refocused on the stage, featured the voice of Brian saying: 'Bollocks, left the bloody thing running' over the voices of the child actors on stage.

'Chloe didn't laugh, though,' Sam reminds me now as we're chuckling together at the memory.

'No. Poor kid. No wonder she's grown up so bloody bad-tempered.'

Sam giggles again. 'What about that time in Tenerife, then?'

'Oh, Jesus, don't remind me!'

And we're off again, holding each other's arms and squealing with hilarity.

I'd been invited to join the family holiday – a fantastic opportunity for me, as up until then, my holidays every single year had been a two-week stay with Mum's cousin in Cornwall. Not that I'm ungrateful, and I loved the little village in Cornwall, which felt like a second home to me every August, but Cousin Frances was a spinster in her sixties who didn't much like men or children. Still, it was nicer sitting on the beach with my books than sitting in my bedroom at home with my books, and I was happy to see Mum and Dad relaxing. It must have done Mum good because I have definite memories of her sitting in the sunshine on the green at the top of the cliffs, which is sad to think about really as she could never do that now.

Anyway, at the time of the Tenerife holiday Sam, David and I must have been about fifteen. I don't think Brian had had the video camera very long. I remember being intoxicated by the sun, the sparkling blue sea, the feel of the hot dark sand under my feet, the scent of the air – so different, so *foreign* – and being entranced by the sounds and flavours of the little pavement cafés and bars, the background mix of Spanish and English voices I could hear when I closed my eyes, the smell of local-caught fish, the constant warmth of the sun on my arms. It was like falling in love for the first time – every experience so new and exciting I could hardly catch my breath.

Brian followed us around with the camera, recording every moment. 'And here's little Abbie, enjoying her first taste of Spanish ice cream. How's it taste, Abbie? Delicious?'

'It's a holiday video, Dad,' complained Sam, who was stretched out on the beach next to me, 'not a bloody ice-cream commercial.'

'And here's Sam,' he went on regardless, 'in a crotchety mood this morning. Too much sun, Samantha?'

'Piss off,' she whispered for my benefit, making me choke on my ice cream.

'And here's Chris,' said Brian, swinging the camera wildly, searching for her through the viewfinder. 'Wait a minute . . . where is she?'

'*Brian!*' shrieked Christine. 'Turn that *bloody* thing off, will you? I'm getting changed!'

She was crouching behind her deckchair, struggling to hold a towel round her waist while she wriggled out of wet bikini bottoms. We all know what it's like. You come out of the water, your skin goes cold and clammy no matter how hot the weather. You yank at the things to get them off but they stick to your bum. You end up doing a kind of mad dance, dropping the towel, getting sand everywhere, performing contortions to get your feet out of the bikini and dry your bottom without looking too much like you're just wiping yourself after a particularly nasty toilet incident.

'Let me hold the towel for you, Mum,' said Sam, jumping up to help her, but Brian was there before her, chortling with amusement, holding the camera at close range and zooming in even closer.

'And here's Chris, doing a striptease on the beach,' he shouted for the benefit of his target audience back home. Instead, half-a-dozen families near us on the beach sat up and stared. 'Will she drop the towel? Is she going to show us her bum?'

'Shut up, Dad!' exclaimed Sam.

'Yeah, Dad, give it a rest,' said David, looking embarrassed.

'Come on, Chrissie!' called Brian, completely undeterred, chasing Christine around the deckchair as, with Sam helping to hold the towel, she scuttled away from him, squealing in protest. 'Show us your *arse*, love!'

Wham! In one swift movement, taking him completely by surprise, Christine lobbed a fist at the camera, knocking it straight into Brian's nose. He yelped in pain, dropped the camera on the beach, and a passing child running out of the sea kicked wet sand all over it.

'At least we didn't get bothered by his bloody camera any more that holiday!' says Sam now, when we manage to stop laughing.

'No. Your dad wasn't very happy, though, was he? The camera had to go in for repair when we got home, and he walked around all week holding a hanky up to his nose, pretending it was bleeding.'

'Served him right.' She sighs, and adds abruptly, 'Wasn't it a fantastic time, though, Abbs?'

'That holiday? The best of my life. I can still remember everything about it.'

'Not just the holiday. That time. That age. We had such laughs together, didn't we? Before boys got in the way.'

I smile at her, slightly nervously. 'Not exactly the right thing to say on your wedding day, Sammy!'

'No,' she agrees with a grin. 'But you know what I mean, don't you? When it was just you and me, having fun.'

I want to add 'Yeah, without Julia'.

But that wouldn't be a good idea.

We sit together for a few minutes, watching the dancing.

'Come on,' says Sam, getting up and smoothing her dress down. 'Let's dance to the next one.'

But it turns out there isn't a next one.

'Ladies and gentlemen,' says Big Wayne as we hover at the edge of the dance floor and everyone's eyes turn to him expectantly, 'we have a special request tonight. Your very own bride tonight, your very own *Samantha Reynolds*—' he bellows her new name at her across the room as if she's not likely to realise it's her '—is a very special young lady, as I'm sure you all know. I'm sure her new *husband* doesn't need me to tell him that – ha, ha, ha! Not only is she a very special *bride* here tonight, ladies and gentlemen, but I understand she has a very special *talent* – and Sam, I've had a request for you to come on up here tonight, love, please – on your very own *wedding night*, to give your friends and family a song or two. Sam? Is that OK, love? Any song you like?'

Sam's gone a bit pink. She's used to this sort of thing, of course, but she certainly wasn't expecting it tonight. Everyone's clapping now, calling out to her – 'Yeah! Sam!' 'Come on, Sam!' 'Go for it!'

'OK!' she says cheerfully, going into performer mode with barely a blink of the eye.

She whispers with the DJ for a couple of minutes about the music and then steps up to the microphone. 'I wasn't really expecting to be doing this,' she says, smiling around at everyone. 'But all right – in the circumstances, I think there's only one song I ought to be singing tonight.'

I know what it's going to be. Everyone settles down as the introduction begins, and I reckon you could literally hear a pin drop as the bride looks directly at the groom and launches into "Big Spender".

Although it's their song, of course, because of the night they met, it's not really an appropriate song for Phil at all. He's about as far removed from the image of a Big Spender as it's possible to get. He's an easygoing charmer, but he's not materialistic, not ambitious or driven, except in terms of enjoying his life and having happy people around him. He and Sam are fantastically well suited. He told me once, some months after they got back together again following the Venice episode, that the reason he'd taken fright when he realised how serious things were getting was that he didn't ever want it to change.

'That sounds mad,' I told him crossly. He was in a confiding mood at the time, leaning against me companionably as we sat on a bench seat in a pub where Sam was singing. 'Did you think it wasn't going to change if you *left* her?'

'I was so scared,' he went on with a shrug, 'that we were going to lose the *fun* and the *spontaneity* – the enjoyment of it all – in the whole rush to settle down, grow up, buy a house, get into debt ... Yes, I actually thought we'd be better off ending it there and then, Abbie, rather than risk it turning into something that was mundane and hard work.'

Life's mundane and hard work, I wanted to tell him. But I didn't, because I could see that he meant it and, more to the point, I knew Sam felt the same. She still does – this is exactly what she was worrying about this morning, before the wedding. In some ways, they're like a couple of kids who don't want to put their toys away. He's a lovely guy. I don't know why I've forgiven him for Venice, why I've accepted his version of the event but still can't forgive Julia. I suppose I can forgive him anything as long as he always makes Sam happy.

There's a thunderous round of applause as she finishes singing.

'More!' shouts one of Phil's friends from the back of the room, and immediately there's a chorus of 'Encore! More!', a stamping of feet and some whistling, until Sam, laughing, holds up her hand and agrees: 'OK, OK. Just one more, then.'

"Yesterday".

It's one of our all-time favourites; we used to sing it together when we were walking home, slightly the worse for wear, from parties and nights out on the town when we were teenagers. Me and Sam and Julia, arms linked, swinging along the pavements, singing our hearts out. All our troubles *did* seem so far away.

Sam catches my eye and smiles as the sweet old words flow over me like memories. Christine, standing beside me now, is crying quietly again into her hanky.

'The voice of an angel,' she sobs. 'My baby!'

What happens next is so surreal, so unbelievable, that I'm never going to be able to hear the words of this song again without remembering this precise moment on this exact day – without hearing Christine crying softly next to me, and seeing Sam up there on the stage in her wedding dress, singing her heart out and smiling at me.

As I'm staring into space, lost in the song, lost in the magic of the moment – just as we get to the part about doing something wrong, and longing for yesterday – there's suddenly another voice joining in. I look up and there, standing beside Sam at the microphone, tears pouring down her face as she sings, is the one person I never wanted to see again as long as I live.

'*Julia!*' shouts Frank excitedly across the room.

And for once, he's got it right.

Quarter to eleven

Therc's something pretty spooky about the sound of fifty or more people all gasping at once.

'Julia!'

'It's Julia!'

'It's that girl – Julia,' echoes around the room like a whisper.

Christine and Brian are staring, open-mouthed. Frank's grinning toothily with excitement. Chloe's looking at me anxiously. Phil's gone white. But Sam's just carrying on singing. If anything, her voice grows stronger and higher as she goes into the final chorus. And then she turns to Julia, their eyes meet over the microphone, they join hands and sing the final line together.

I'm too shocked to think straight. But I know how I feel. *Yeuk*.

I'll tell you what Phil's version of the Venice fiasco was.

'I don't know what happened.'

'He says he doesn't know what happened,' Sam told me after they got back together. 'He was drunk.'

I gave her a look. In my limited experience (mostly

gleaned from library books), drunkenness confers a certain amount of confusion, occasionally even memory loss, but more often than anything else it's used as an excuse for bad behaviour.

'I thought you weren't going to have him back,' I reminded her carefully, 'no matter what?'

'I know. I know I said that, Abbie, but Venice changed everything.'

'How?'

'Because it shocked us both. Shocked us into seeing what we really wanted: each other.'

I didn't understand it then and, to be honest, I still don't. Of course, I was glad they were back together again because it was obvious Sam was happy. That was all that mattered.

I forgave Phil, because Sam forgave him. Because basically, I like the guy, that's about it. But Julia?

How can Sam possibly have forgiven Julia back then, without even having an explanation from her? And I know she didn't have an explanation. I made sure of that, because I had one . . . and I didn't tell her.

The applause at the end of this song practically lifts the roof off.

Sam and Julia are hugging now; I think both of them are crying, but I can hardly bear to watch. People are rushing to join in: before you know it, there's a group-hug situation going on up there. In fact it looks more like a rugby scrum. Since when did Julia become so popular with everyone? Nobody's even seen her for over two years, but suddenly it's like she's the prodigal bloody daughter.

'You're not joining in the emotional reunion, then?'

says David, coming to sit next to me.

'Don't be sarcastic.'

'I'm really sorry, Abbie.'

'Why? It's not your fault.'

'Well, actually ...' He shifts in his seat, looks away for a minute and then turns to meet my eyes. 'Actually, I'm afraid it is. I asked Julia to come.'

'You *what*?'

So is *this* what it's all about? All this stuff about needing to talk to me, needing to tell me something? And I suppose all the flattery, all the nonsense about me looking lovely tonight, was just a load of crap to try and butter me up. To try and stop me hating him for asking that *cow* to come and spoil the wedding day.

I'm so disappointed I could cry. Disappointed in David because I never thought he'd do something like this: so underhand.

'I'm sorry,' he says again. 'I knew it was going to upset you if she decided to turn up. I wouldn't want to hurt you, Abbie, you know that. Not for anything.'

'Looks like it!' I snort, angrily.

'But today isn't about you,' he adds very gently.

Well, that's telling me, isn't it.

'Thank you,' I respond with as much dignity as I can manage. 'Thanks for pointing out how selfish I am.'

'Of course you're not selfish.' He tries to take hold of my hand, but I snatch it out of his reach. 'You're the least selfish person I know. But you're so obsessed with how you feel about Julia, you couldn't see ...'

'What? See what?' I feel like hitting him. Doesn't he realise what he's doing to me? He talks about not

313

wanting to hurt me, but his words are slicing into me like knives. I can't believe I'm not actually bleeding.

'You couldn't see how much Sam wanted her to come today.'

'She *said* she did . . .'

'Abbie. She *really* wanted her to come. And if you couldn't see it – wouldn't see it – I had to sort it out for her myself. I know how close you two are,' he adds quietly. 'You're like sisters. You always know what she's thinking . . . except for in this one thing. It's not your fault. I *know* why you're irrational about Julia.'

'Irrational!'

'OK – all right, I'm sorry – I *understand* why you feel the way you do. But today – just for today – Sam's feelings come first.'

How can I argue with this? David is Sam's twin. Of course he's bound to care more about her feelings than anyone else's. Especially today, of all days. I *have* been selfish about it. Deep down inside, I know I have. More than he realises.

'So you contacted her?' I ask him flatly.

'Yes. I phoned her. It wasn't easy. Had to do some detective work to get her number.' He shrugs. 'At first she said no: she wouldn't come. She didn't think she'd be welcome. She didn't think she'd been forgiven. I told her Sam wanted her to come – that she was upset that she hadn't replied to the invitation.' He gives me a very direct look. 'She said she didn't even get it.'

He knows.

I stare at the floor, feeling the shame flooding my face. My chest hurts and I can hardly breathe. Maybe this is what it feels like to die. Maybe that's what I deserve.

'You didn't send it, did you, Abbie? You didn't post her invitation?'

'I thought it was for the best,' I whisper. I can't look at him. 'I was thinking of Sam. Honestly. I thought it would be too much for her ... to have Julia turn up today ... I thought it would ruin everything.'

'Well, you nearly got your own way. Julia told me she couldn't face coming.'

'So what happened?' I ask, ungraciously.

'I did tell her that if she changed her mind, even at the last minute, even on the day, she should just turn up. I told her it would make Sam's day.'

He touches my arm and waits for me to look up. He's smiling. Somehow, this just makes me feel worse.

'Don't feel bad, Abbie,' he says. 'Just feel happy for Sam. Please?'

'If you say so.'

What's the matter with me? Even now, I can't admit I was wrong. I remember how it felt to destroy that invitation. I tore it up into tiny pieces, screwed the pieces up viciously into a ball and threw it in the dustbin. At the time, I felt like I'd *won*. Like I'd somehow got my own back.

Now, it just feels like I was stupid, and pathetic, and vindictive. And a lousy friend.

'Maybe you and Julia should talk?' suggests David tentatively.

'Piss off.'

He laughs and gets up to move on. 'Remember,' he says quietly without looking back at me, 'I still need to talk to you. Later on, yeah?'

To say I feel confused is to make the understatement of the year. What's he want to talk to me about

315

if it isn't just my guilty secret about Julia's invitation? I suppose it's his row with Heather, after all. Great. I might be the Wicked Witch of the West, but he still can't wait to discuss his love life with me. I hope he forgets, to be quite honest. I've had enough. I look at Sam, walking from table to table now with her arm linked through Julia's, and all I really feel like doing is going home to bed and pulling the covers over my head.

'This was unexpected, then, wasn't it?'

I've drained my gin and tonic by the time Chloe has come to sit next to me, and I'm feeling slightly drunk again. I'm watching the Sam-and-Julia combo moving ever closer to my table, preparing myself to get up and move away before they reach me.

'I don't want to talk to her,' I say morosely into my drink.

'Don't, then, if you don't want to,' says Chloe surprisingly. 'But it's probably your loss.'

'Don't you start,' I say with a sniff, feeling sorry for myself. 'Everyone seems to think I should have forgiven her.'

'Nobody else's business,' says Chloe with a shrug. 'No point pretending to forgive her if you don't.'

If only life were that simple.

'But you're the one carrying the load of resentment around with you like a banner,' she adds without looking at me.

Thanks for nothing.

'You all right, Granddad?' she calls out before I can reply.

Frank's tottering past us, a pint of bitter in his hand. He lurches, grabs the back of my chair and the beer slops over the edge of the glass as he grins at us and says: 'She's back, you know! That Julia!'

'Yeah,' I say. 'We saw.'

'The *floozy*!' he snorts, laughing happily. 'I always knew she'd be back!'

'Dirty old man,' says Chloe under her breath.

'He'll have to join the queue.'

'Actually,' says Chloe nonchalantly, 'I don't think there'll be any floozying around from her any more. Not right now, anyway. Have you *looked* at her, Abbie?'

Not really. I've tried to avert my eyes.

But now I look properly. She's wearing wide-legged trousers and one of those trendy smock tops that make anyone over a size eight look about six months pregnant. But Julia isn't just wearing the smock top to be trendy. She was always only about a size eight but now ... now she actually is *pregnant*. She's probably at least five months gone. And – even more surprising – she's wearing a wedding ring.

'Looks like someone's finally floored the Flooze,' says Chloe with a snigger.

Can't help feeling sorry for the guy, can you.

Eleven o'clock

I admit it: I was always jealous of Julia.

Not of her stunning good looks, her ability to pull any guy she wanted or even her brilliance at art, music, tennis, swimming, dancing ... I didn't care about any of those things. I was only jealous of her because of Sam.

It sounds pathetic and childish to say it, but I wanted Sam all to myself. I'm not proud of it.

I had my palm read once by an old gypsy woman in a booth on the pier at Southend. I never told Mum and Dad about it, obviously, because the church frowns on any sort of fortune-telling – but show me a teenager who can resist the temptation to dabble in the unknown, to dip a toe in the vast ocean of the future and try to catch a glimpse of what's in store for them. This supposed gypsy had a tea cosy over her crystal ball and wore trainers with popsocks, but Sam and I didn't let that put us off.

'I can see only one man for you,' she intoned in a harsh smoker's voice as she removed the tea cosy and gazed into the glass. 'One man – and one true friend. And a long, happy life'.

Sam was falling about laughing. 'Only one man!'

she chortled when we got outside the booth. 'Poor you!'

'That's OK,' I said defensively.

Looks like being true, too.

'And one friend!' Sam carried on screeching. 'Only one friend! That's ridiculous! Nobody has only one friend.'

I was so hurt, I could barely talk to her for the rest of the day. It wasn't *just* the fact that she thought it was so ridiculous to have only one friend; the worst thing was that she didn't even seem to realise it was actually already true: she *was* my only friend. Oh, we hung around with Julia too, of course, and a few other girls as well. But I never saw any of them on my own. Sam was the catalyst. If it wasn't for Sam, I'd have been sitting at home with my books every day. The truth was that I didn't *want* to be friends with Julia, particularly, but I had to be, because of Sam.

I can remember the exact day when this changed. It was the summer when we were all seventeen – I'd been at work for a year by then, and Sam and Julia were halfway through the sixth form. It was a hot Saturday afternoon and we were sitting in the park together, eating ice creams and watching some lads playing football with their tops off.

'What time's the party tonight?' Julia asked Sam idly.

'Dunno. I thought we'd get there about half past eight. Yeah?'

'Whose party is it?' I don't know why I asked. It was bound to be someone from school, someone who wouldn't remember me, never mind invite me.

'Jason Lloyd's. His brother's going to be there and I *really* fancy him,' said Julia, pursing her lips suggestively.

No change there, then.

'You can come, Abbie,' said Sam, leaning back and lifting her face up to the sun.

'Can she?' retorted Julia rudely. 'Did Jason say?'

'Don't be an arse,' said Sam mildly. 'Jason won't mind. He knows Abbie always comes to anything if I go.'

I glanced across at Julia just in time to see her look down at her feet and scowl – and in a flash, I realised. *She* wanted Sam to herself too!

It was an inspiration to me. Suddenly, for me, the whole balance of the relationship between the three of us was changed. Julia didn't want *me* around any more than I wanted *her*. But Sam didn't care – as far as she was concerned, we were both her friends, and if we bitched at each other she wasn't going to take sides, join in, or even take any notice of it.

I tried being nice to Julia after that. She seemed a bit surprised at first, but it kind of worked, because we became quite genuinely friendly, and even though I was still, always, jealous of the time she spent with Sam at school and, later, commuting to London and having lunch with her, I learned to disguise it and pretend I didn't mind. Until Jamie.

They're at the next table now. Sam's introducing Julia to people, smiling, hugging her, telling everyone she's her long-lost friend. It makes me want to vomit.

'Isn't it nice?' says Christine, appearing in front of me, swaying and grinning with a huge glass of something frighteningly pink in her hand. 'Isn't it lovely that Julia decided to come along after all?'

'Is it?' I say morosely.

'Of course, I wish she'd been here for the ceremony.

And for the photos. And the meal, of course, and the first dance. And the cake-cutting—'

'Yeah, well . . .' I try to interrupt, before we get onto wishing she'd been here for the collapse of the bouquet, the shellfish allergy, the panic attack, the rescue from the lake and the disappearance of Granddad.

'Better late than never, eh? That's what I always say.'

Well, personally, in this instance, I think never would have been a whole lot better.

'It's *so lovely* to see how happy it's made Sam, having Julia turn up like this,' continues Christine cheerfully. 'I'm so glad you sent her an invitation, Abbie.'

And now I feel like shit, even if I wasn't beginning to already.

'She's married to a doctor, you know.' She leans towards me and whispers confidentially as if this is something we definitely don't want the gossip columnists to get hold of. 'Met him through her work, of course. She's retrained as a botanist, dear – did you know that?'

'A botanist?'

'Yes. A fleabotanist, she says. Must be something to do with studying insects, do you think? She always was very clever, was Julia.'

'A phlebotomist, Christine! They take people's blood.'

'Oh, my goodness. What, like some sort of *vampire*, do you mean, Abbie?'

That sounds about right, doesn't it.

By the time Julia approaches our table, Christine has guzzled down the rest of her pink cocktail and has slumped forwards in her chair, her eyes closed. I think it's probably kindest to leave her to it. I think I'll just get up and sneak away, preferably before Julia . . .

'Abbie.'

Too late. She's standing in front of me, looking at me as if she's considering something rather painful but necessary. I wonder if this is how she looks at her patients when she's just about to take three tubes of blood off them. *Left arm or right? Now then, just a tiny prick* . . . And she should know.

'Julia,' I say, not looking at her.

Sam's standing beside her, looking at Christine with some concern.

'I think I'll go and get Mum a coffee. They're serving it now, at the bar,' she says, looking from Julia to me and back at Julia again. Julia gives her an almost imperceptible nod of the head. *Go on, it's OK. I don't think Abbie's going to stab me*.

'How are you?' she asks me as soon as Sam's out of earshot.

I shrug.

'Can I sit down for a minute?'

She doesn't wait for my reply, but pulls up a chair next to me, away from Christine, and sits watching me for a moment without speaking. The DJ's playing "Oh, What A Night", and a dozen or so die-hards are still bopping on the dance floor. I'm feeling uncomfortable, sitting here not talking, with her staring at me.

'Well?' I say eventually.

'What?'

'Well, let's get it over with. Whatever it is you want to say to me.'

322

'I was hoping we could just ...'

'What?' I turn to face her, my anger finally bubbling to the surface. 'What, be friends? Make up and let bygones be bygones? Is that what you thought?'

'I was hoping,' she says quietly, 'for Sam's sake.'

'For *Sam's* sake!' I spit at her. 'It's a bit late to be thinking about Sam, isn't it? Maybe two years ago would have been a better time. In Venice, when you were deciding to go to bed with Phil, might have been a *good* time to think about Sam, if you wanted to call yourself her friend.'

'Oh, Abbie,' she says with a sigh, shaking her head at me.

Just that – 'Oh, Abbie' – as if it's *me* being unreasonable! It's no good – I can't talk to her. I'm going to have to get away from her.

'I told you what happened in Venice,' she says as I start to get to my feet. 'Phil and I didn't sleep together. Sam knows that now.'

'Sam believes you. Good for her.'

'You don't? You prefer to believe Sam's married someone who'd lie to her about a thing like that?'

'I don't care. As long as she's happy. And Phil's basically a nice guy.'

'Yes. Yes, he is, Abbie. So nice, I found him crying into his beer in the hotel bar in Venice after Sam told him she wasn't going to have him back.'

I know that. That's what she told me two years ago. It's the rest of the story I refused to believe. Knowing Julia, what could she expect?

She came to see me after we all got back from Venice.

323

'I know what you think,' she said as soon as I opened the door.

I tried to shut it, but she stuck her foot in the way.

'Please, Abbie. Sam won't let me explain.'

'Of course she won't! Leave her alone! She doesn't want to see you! Piss off!'

'I didn't have sex with him!' she shouted through the gap in the doorway. A passing pensioner stopped dead on the spot and stared. I felt like telling him to piss off too.

'I need to explain,' Julia said again. She was crying. She disgusted me. 'Look, he was drunk . . .'

'So he wasn't capable? Shame. Poor you.'

'No! He was upset. We *talked*.'

I flung open the door so that she fell in and we both stumbled against the opposite wall. I was breathing hard, trying to restrain myself from lashing out at her. I'd never hit anyone – never, in my life. My parents abhorred violence; hitting someone was so totally outside of my sphere of reference that I couldn't even think, physically, how to go about it, but I'd never felt so much like trying it as I did at that moment.

'So you *talked*, did you?' I sneered, as she fought to regain her balance, propping herself against my wall. 'In bed?'

'I was feeling sorry for myself,' she said quietly, sniffing back the tears. 'I'd been looking forward to Venice, and it was a washout.'

'How do you think *Sam* felt?'

'I know. Everything had gone wrong. Sam and Phil, me and Ian. It was supposed to be a romantic weekend, but . . .'

'Oh, spare me the tragedy,' I snapped impatiently.

'You broke up with your boyfriend, and Sam said she didn't want Phil back so he seemed like fair game. You *knew* how much that would hurt Sam! How *could* you?'

'It wasn't like that! Please, Abbie, please believe me! Please tell Sam I didn't do anything to hurt her.'

'You just happened to find yourself in bed with him? I suppose you're going to say you don't remember what happened, like he did? For God's sake! Give us a break.'

'I went down to the bar for a drink,' she said, wiping her eyes. 'I was wishing I'd agreed to go out for dinner with you and Sam. I felt fed up and lonely.'

'My heart's breaking for you.'

'Phil was already drunk. He was slumped in his seat, with a whisky in front of him. I got myself a drink and sat down with him. I tried to talk to him – I was trying to tell him to leave it for a bit longer, give Sam a chance to come around, you know – forgive him for hurting her. I knew she would. I knew she still loved him.'

'But instead, you suggested having sex with him? To cheer you both up?'

She sighed. 'If Phil and I wanted to have sex, we'd have done it years ago. Before he even met Sam.'

I stared at her in surprise. What was all this? She'd never mentioned this before.

'I went out with him once when I was about sixteen. It didn't last long.'

'They never did, did they?'

'No. I didn't see the point in telling Sam. What I'm trying to say is, I don't fancy him – right? I *like* him, but . . .'

'Just enough for a quick shag?'

'Abbie! I'm trying to tell you – I was just *talking* to him about Sam, trying to make him listen, but he started crying – really loudly. It was embarrassing. Everyone was looking at us, and then the barman came over and asked us to leave. Said he thought Phil had had enough already. Of course, he doesn't normally drink much so he'd got drunk really quickly. And he didn't have anywhere to go, so ...'

'So you took him up to your room.'

'Yes! Yes, I did, and it *wasn't* like you think! I said he could sleep in the other twin bed. I tried to just put the duvet over him, but he started getting undressed. He was totally out of it, Abbie – he didn't know where he was. I just about managed to stop him stripping completely naked. Within minutes he'd fallen asleep on top of the covers so I figured it was best to just leave him to sleep it off. I tiptoed around, getting myself ready for bed, not wanting to wake him up. I felt really sorry for him, but I was pissed off, too, to be honest. Nice way to spend the last night of the holiday, wasn't it – with someone else's ex passed out drunk in my room! And I'd only had one drink myself. Then I remembered the bottle of wine we'd opened the night before – there was still a bit left. I poured myself a glassful and sat on my bed, reading my book, wondering where you two had gone for dinner, wishing I'd gone with you.'

'How am I supposed to believe ...'

'I was listening out for you to come back, Abbie! I thought maybe I could leave Phil asleep and come into your room with you – we could have some more wine and maybe you'd let me sleep in the chair. But anyway, he didn't sleep for very long. He woke up and didn't know where he was. I was talking to him, trying to calm him down and telling him to go back to sleep, everything would be all right in the morning, I'd tell Sam how upset he was.'

'This is all crap, Julia. The look on your face when you opened the door – it was the cat that got the fucking cream.'

'Of course! I wanted a happy ending! I was sure when Sam saw him there, all upset and drunk out of his skull, and I told her how he'd been crying, and everything . . .'

Julia met my eyes and, in that moment, I saw something in them that I've denied ever since. It was honesty. She wasn't lying.

'But I forgot how it looked,' she finished faintly. 'I wasn't thinking.'

'Obviously not.' I wasn't going to give her the satisfaction of telling her I believed her.

'I know what you think of me. But it didn't occur to me that you or Sam would think me capable of being so . . .' She stopped, saw the expression on my face, sighed, and just nodded to herself. 'Oh yes,' she said, with a look of defeat. 'I see. Jamie.'

For a while, it was like the aftermath of Jamie all over again. Sam was back with Phil but she refused to see Julia, refused to take her calls, deleted her emails and texts without reading them. So I didn't tell her that Julia had been round to see me. I pretended to myself that I didn't believe her explanation anyway, so what was the point of passing on her lies to Sam, it'd only upset her. By the time Julia moved down to Bournemouth, I'd forgotten about the moment she looked at me and I saw the

327

honesty in her eyes. I forgot it because I didn't want to remember it. I wanted everyone else to hate her as much as I did.

'Sam believed me in the end,' says Julia now, picking an empty glass up from the table and twirling it between her fingers. 'I bombarded her with letters after I moved away. I couldn't just leave it.'

'I know. She told me. She tore them up and threw them away.'

'She might have told *you* that, Abbie. But actually, she did read them. She believed me. She just took a while ... because she wanted to believe *you*. She didn't want to think you were lying to her.'

'Me! Me, lying to her? That's rich!'

'She was upset that you lied to her. That you told her I hadn't talked to you, hadn't explained what really happened. But don't worry, Abbie, Sam's such a lovely, forgiving person ...'

'I know she is! Of course she is! That's why she forgave *you*!'

'That's why she forgave *you*, Abbie.'

Me? I want to protest again. *Me*? What have *I* done?

But Julia's looking at me like she can see right into the back of my mind. That dark bit right at the very back where nobody gets to see; where the guilt lurks like a horrible wound that never heals. I *know* I should feel sorry for pretending I didn't believe Julia, and for not telling Sam about it. I *know* I should feel sorry for tearing up her invitation. I *know*, if I still went to church, I'd be fooled into admitting what I'd done, asking God to forgive me, all that crap. I know it'd actually make me feel better.

But it's no good: I don't think I can feel sorry. I don't even want to.

Because *she hurt me first*.

Quarter past eleven

A few people are leaving – older relatives who aren't staying the night; a friend of Phil's whose girlfriend is eight months pregnant and exhausted; a guy who's so drunk his wife has called a taxi and is pouring him into it, looking like she's going to give him hell in the morning.

Chloe and Eva are sitting together at a table littered with empty glasses.

'Hey, Abbie!' calls Chloe as I'm stumbling past, trying to get outside. Away from Julia. 'You OK?'

'Yes. Fine. I just want to ... um ... get some air.'

'Do you feel ill?' asks Eva, looking at me with concern.

'No, no ... probably just, you know, couple of drinks too many.'

'I'll come out with you,' she says at once.

She squeezes Chloe's hand as she gets up and I find myself feeling suddenly, ridiculously, envious. I wish I had someone who squeezed my hand like that, someone who looked at me the way she looks at Chloe, the way Phil looks at Sam ...

'You don't feel sick, do you?'

'No. Just ... sorry, just a bit giddy.'

She pushes the outside door open and we step out and breathe in deeply the night air. The sky's clear – that not-quite-navy-blue colour you only ever see near midnight in midsummer. I stare up at the moon and feel the ground moving gently beneath my feet.

'Want to find somewhere to sit down?' says Eva, nodding at a nearby bench. 'You must be so tired, Abbie, after all the planning and worry about today. No wonder the drink's gone to your head.' She grins at me. 'I know Chloe hasn't been any help whatsoever.'

'She didn't even want to be a bridesmaid.'

'I know. It was all a bit too girly for her.' She laughs fondly. 'She's a bit jealous of her big sister, anyway. I can understand it. Sam's the original Golden Girl, isn't she.'

'She's lovely. I love her.' I blush, suddenly realising who I'm talking to, and add quickly, 'Not in *that* sort of way – I mean . . .'

'I know,' laughs Eva. We reach the bench and sit down, then lean back and look up at the stars. 'I know you're straight, Abbie, don't worry! That doesn't mean to say you're not allowed to love your friends.'

'Friend,' I correct her. 'I haven't got any others.'

She frowns. 'What about Julia? I thought the three of you were good mates?' She stops and turns, trying to see my face in the moonlight. 'What have I said?'

'Julia's not my friend.' I suddenly feel an urge to tell her all about it; it'd be such a relief to unburden myself to someone I've only just met, who doesn't know me well enough to judge me. 'She *used* to be,' I say, carefully, 'But she slept with my boyfriend.'

'Shit. Sorry, Abbie. Chloe never told me about that.'

331

'She probably didn't know about it. She'd only have been about ten at the time.'

'Wasn't there some kind of misunderstanding about Julia and Phil, too, or have I got that wrong?'

I hesitate. I have a choice, now. I either feed Eva the same line that I've fed myself for the past two years – or I tell her the truth. And maybe begin to feel a bit better.

'Actually,' I find myself saying, 'you're right – it *was* a misunderstanding. We kind of jumped to conclusions. Sam and Phil had had a bust-up, and Julia was trying to help, but it didn't look that way at the time.'

'And because of what happened with your boyfriend, you must have assumed the worst,' said Eva, nodding to herself. 'Understandable.'

'Is it?'

'Is it what?'

'Understandable? Do you think so?'

'Well, of course, Abbie!' she laughs. 'Who could blame you!'

'But I never forgave her,' I say, almost in a whisper, 'even though I knew she was telling the truth. I didn't *want* to.'

'Is this what it's all about?' she asks me softly. 'Is this why you needed to come outside? To get away from her?'

I can't answer. I wonder what she thinks of me now. And I quite liked Eva, too.

'Forgive *yourself*, Abbie,' she says. 'You haven't done anything so very terrible.'

I don't think there's anybody left now who hasn't told me to forgive myself.

'But I didn't want her to come tonight. I tore up her invitation.'

332

She bursts out laughing. 'Did you? Good for you! I didn't think you had it in you! Bloody good for you, girl!'

'You don't think I'm a terrible person?'

'What?! No – I quite admire you for it! Serves her right, really, doesn't it!'

I find myself laughing along with her. Laughing in surprise and relief. Maybe I'm not going to hellfire and damnation after all?

'Come on. I'm getting chilly out here,' she says. 'Are you OK to go back in now?'

'Yes. Definitely. Thanks – I feel a bit better now.'

'Good!' She pulls me to my feet and slips her arm through mine as we walk back to the entrance. 'Well done, Abbie.'

And she squeezes my hand.

'Guess what?' says Chloe as we find her at the table where we left her. Her eyes are glowing fiercely with satisfaction. 'Guess what Dad's just told me?'

Eva and I shake our heads. I can't think of anything Brian could say that would please Chloe to be quite honest. Unless . . .

'You're allowed to stay the night, Evie.' She grins at her shyly. 'I don't know whether it's just the drink, but he seems to have calmed down a bit. Got over it.'

'Blimey!' I exclaim. 'I never thought . . . '

'Well, maybe not *completely* got over it, but at least he's not being such a total *arse*,' she amends. 'You can stay, but he says you've got to sleep in Sam's room.'

'Fair enough,' says Eva, smiling. 'Can't expect him to take too much on board at once . . . '

'I think you were right,' Chloe tells her happily.

'Maybe it was a *good* idea to come out today, after all.'

'Maybe,' agrees Eva. 'But nothing's ever that cut and dried, is it, Chlo? Things always seem like a good idea at the time.' She smiles at me and shrugs. 'So we can only do what we think.'

'You were always such a beautiful little girl,' Christine's crying into her coffee. Sam's got her arm round her; she looks up at me and raises her eyebrows as I approach. 'Always so sweet, so good, so helpful.'

'No I wasn't, Mum!' she laughs. 'I was a right little cow at times! Remember when I broke the washing line 'cos I was using it as a swing? And all the sheets fell in the mud?'

'An accident. I wasn't cross, dear.'

'You went potty! You threatened to make me scrub them all clean with my bare hands!'

'Well, maybe just a *little* bit annoyed.'

'And what about when I threw the teapot on the floor and smashed it 'cos you wouldn't let me go to Stephen Watson's party? And when I kicked David 'cos he nicked my best felt-tip pens, and he fell over and broke his arm? And . . .'

'I'd say you were a right little horror.' I laugh, sitting down to join them.

'You were just as bad, Abbie,' protests Sam. 'Remember when we took our bikes over to Tweedy's Hill, and dared each other to ride all the way down with no brakes?'

'Jesus, yes!' I groan. 'I'd forgotten about that.'

We were only eleven. We'd both got new bikes for our birthdays, but they were mangled heaps by the time we'd extricated ourselves from the pile-up at the bottom of the hill. We were lucky we only had cuts and bruises. But we were banned from going out together for weeks.

'I remember that!' says Christine, 'I said to Brian, I didn't think little girls were supposed to behave like that. Bad enough with David.'

'David never gave you any trouble. I was the naughty one.'

'And now look at you,' says Christine lovingly, looking like she's going to cry again. 'All grown up, beautiful, lovely . . .'

'Married.'

'How does it feel?' I ask her. 'Scary?'

'Not yet!' She smiles at me. 'You were right. I haven't suddenly turned into a Married Woman. Have I?'

'Well, I don't see any sign of an apron.'

We laugh together for a minute, then she gets up, pats her mum's arm and turns aside to me, saying quietly, 'Are you OK? With Julia?'

Ah, shit. Don't ask me this. What do you want me to say?

'Well, if it's made you happy, I'm glad she turned up.'

I suppose.

She looks at me questioningly. I drop my eyes.

'And I'm sorry.'

'What for?'

'You know. Not telling you what really happened. After Venice. I should have said sorry ages ago.'

'Oh, for God's sake, Abbie. That's water under the bridge, isn't it? Why drag it up now?'

'I don't know. My guilty conscience, I suppose.'

335

'Get over it, love!' she laughs. 'And anyway, I don't see why *you* should feel guilty. She hurt you first.'

I stare at her. Can she read my mind? Or is it written all over my face?

'But it's all in the past now, isn't it?' she goes on cheerfully. 'No bad feelings any more, eh, Abbie?'

'No.'

None that I'm going to talk about.

'Come on, then!' says Sam brightly, pulling me to my feet. 'Let's dance, for God's sake, before it's too late!'

'Too late?' I look at the time and shake my head. 'I can't believe it. It's gone so quickly.'

'So stop rabbiting and get dancing!'

Julia's on the dance floor with our friends Ruth and Kirsty from school who are still squealing and hugging her every few minutes while they're dancing. She smiles at me as Sam and I join the throng dancing to "Walking on Sunshine". I wish I could smile back but my face won't let me.

'Where's Gary?' Phil asks, swaying alongside us suddenly as the music finishes. 'He hasn't gone home, has he?'

'I don't know,' says Sam. 'Haven't seen him for hours.'

'Is he still with that girl?' I ask.

'What girl?'

'I don't know. Chloe said she was a friend of your cousin Tanya. Blonde, with big . . .'

'Oh, that's Siobhan. She's a really nice girl. Is Gary interested?' asks Sam excitedly. 'I can put in a good word for him.'

'He looked a bit more than *interested*,' I say meaningfully.

The DJ announces the next number and before we know it, almost everyone is on the dance floor, jostling with each other and yelling along with the lyrics to "Dancing in the Moonlight". None of us give Gary another thought until the music finishes again and we stumble back to our table to have a quick breather and a glug of our drinks.

I'm just emptying my glass when I hear a whisper behind me. 'Psst! Abbie!'

It's coming from behind that nearest pillar. What the hell?

'Abbie! Quick!'

I peer around the pillar. It's Gary, looking very shifty and darting anxious glances to left, right and over his shoulder.

'What are you playing at?' I laugh. 'Are the police after you, or something?'

'Ssh!' he implores me in a sharp whisper, leaping forwards then dragging me back behind the pillar. 'Don't draw attention to me!'

'I think you're doing that anyway!' I whisper back, 'skulking around behind pillars acting like a fugitive. What have you done?'

'Oh, don't ask!' he groans, holding his head.

'What? It's not really the police, is it?' I start to look out from round the pillar, but he pulls me back.

'No! Not the police, Abbie! *Her*! Siobhan! The girl I was ... dancing with.'

'Oh, I see.' I nod at him. Poor girl. 'I suppose you've had enough of her now and want to get away from her.'

'It's worse than that.' He's not altogether sober and

not making much sense. What the *hell* has he done? 'Hide me, Abbie. Please!'

'What are you talking about, you idiot? I can't hide you!'

'Ssh!'

'I can't *hide* you!' I whisper. 'Look, if you don't want to see her any more, you'll just have to tell her. Just because you've *danced* together, or . . .'

'We've been . . . outside . . . together,' he mumbles miserably.

'OK, well, so what – just because you've had a *snog* or whatever . . .'

'I was a bit pissed.'

'Gary. Did you have sex with her?'

'No!' he retorts, looking quite shocked. 'What, after one dance and a bit of snogging by the lake? What do you take me for?'

'So you haven't tried to . . . well, to do anything she didn't want to do?'

'For God's sake, Abbie! I'm not a bloody rapist or some sort of *pervert*! I *respect* women.'

'So, what, then?' I ask, totally at a loss. 'What have you done that's so bad?'

'I asked her to marry me,' he whispers, looking somewhat shamefaced. 'I was kind of joking. But she's run off to tell Tanya. Do you reckon she thinks I meant it?' He runs his fingers through his hair. 'I only said it because I was pissed, and we were snogging, and she . . . she has nice boobs. Abbie? Supposing she took me seriously?'

Fuck. And I actually thought we were going to make it to midnight without any more catastrophes.

338

Half past eleven

'Calm down, you fool.' Phil's trying not to laugh.
I've sneaked out from behind the pillar and brought
him back to Gary. He *is* his brother after all – he
might talk some sense into him. 'Of course she
doesn't think you meant it! She's probably telling
Tanya what a prat you are!'

'Or she might be asking Tanya to be her bridesmaid!'

'I don't *think* so, Gary,' I tell him. 'Get real.
You're so pissed, she probably couldn't even understand what you said.'

'Especially if you had your tongue in her mouth at
the time,' adds Phil with a grin.

'But you know what some girls are like about
getting married. What if she phones her parents and
tells them? They might take it seriously!'

'No chance. What kind of parents would want their
daughter marrying some drunken git she's just
snogged at a wedding?'

Gary sighs and shakes his head, not looking particularly reassured. 'It's not like I really even know her.
It was only because I was upset about Chloe.'

'Chloe?' Phil's eyes narrow with interest. 'What

about Chloe? You *do* know she's a lesbo, don't you?'

'Yes, all right, all right, don't go on about it. It's not Chloe that's the problem now – it's fucking *Siobhan*. I wish I'd never set eyes on her.'

'Setting eyes on her was all right, bruv. Dancing with her, kissing her, that was all good. Where you started to go wrong, just *possibly*, like, was where you took it into your head to propose to her.'

'OK, go ahead, laugh. I didn't *mean* it, for Christ's sake. I was pissed. She was nice. She was saying how lovely the wedding was. I just kind of said it, like a joke, and next thing I know she was whooping with excitement and rushing off saying she just had to tell her mate! She's probably picked the date and done everything except bought the fucking *dress*.'

'Probably do that tomorrow,' says Phil without missing a beat.

I hit him. 'Stop it. It's not funny. Gary's really worried.'

'Well, then, I guess there's only one thing to do.'

'Hide?' says Gary hopefully, peering around him for suitable places.

'No. That's the *coward's* way, boy. That's *not* the way a real man handles this sort of thing, is it?'

'So how does a real man handle it?' says Gary sarcastically, not looking particularly keen on being a real man.

'You'll just have to go through with it,' says Phil with a shrug.

'With what?'

'The wedding, you jerk. You'll just have to bloody well marry her, won't you?'

For a minute Gary does a double take. He might be

drunk but he'd have had to be paralytic not to realise Phil's taking the piss.

'Fuck off,' he says. 'Bastard.'

'Is that her coming over now?' asks Phil. 'Tall, blonde, green dress?'

'Yes!' says Gary. 'Shit, has she seen me? Does she look ... serious?'

'What – like a serious bride-to-be?' Even I'm laughing now. He's being so ridiculous. Poor Siobhan probably wouldn't marry him if he was the last man in the universe.

'You were saying, in your speech,' Phil reminds him unkindly, 'how you'd like to find a lovely girl like Sam to marry.'

'But not yet! Not *yet*, for fuck's sake – not tonight!'

'Well, here she comes, Gary. I hope you're going to introduce us. Your blushing bride ...'

'Phil,' I say, 'Leave off! Gary – calm down and don't be so stupid. Of *course* she doesn't believe ...'

'Believe what?' says Siobhan, smiling round at us all.

Gary shrinks and looks at us pleadingly, but Phil and I both turn away, nudging each other and trying not to laugh.

'Look, Siobhan, I hope you didn't think ... you know, I didn't really mean ...'

'What?' Her face crumples. 'Oh! But Gary! I've just phoned my mum, and she's so excited!'

Gary looks like he's going to faint. 'Fuck off,' he says in almost a whisper. 'You *are* joking, aren't you?'

'*Joking*!' she exclaims. 'What do you mean?'

For a split second, there's a horrible silence. I'm thinking – *Surely* not? Surely she didn't really think

341

this idiot boy was capable of any rational thought while he was indulging in his drunken antics with her, much less making a decision about anything as important as marriage?

And then, suddenly, there's a screech of laughter. The laughter is high-pitched and almost maniacal and it's coming from Siobhan, who's doubled up, holding her hands over her mouth to try to stop herself from screeching again. She looks like she's almost wetting herself. Her eyes are bulging with the effort of containing herself.

'Oh my God!' she cries, grabbing hold of Gary's arm. 'I'm sorry, but it was *so funny*!'

'What was?' asks Gary, looking somewhat offended now the heat seems to be off him.

'You! Mouthing off about getting married! "We could be the next happy couple. We could be like Sam and Phil!"' she mimics mockingly. 'It was hysterical! Tanya and I have never laughed so much.' She starts giggling again.

'You rushed off to tell Tanya so that you could *laugh* at me?' he retorts, wounded.

Siobhan can't seem to answer. She's had to sit down now. I seriously think she should get herself to the toilet before it's too late.

'Oh dear, *sorry*!' she laughs, struggling to get herself together. 'But you must admit, you were talking shite.'

'You didn't phone your mum, then?'

'Of course I didn't! What do you take me for? A bloody idiot?'

'Well, thanks! You seemed happy enough with me . . . out there . . .'

'Gary, come on, I'm not saying we weren't having

342

a nice time, you know.'

Right – I think Phil and I need to clear off now, if these two are going to start talking about the nice time they had outside.

'. . . but the wedding stuff – well, it was ridiculous, wasn't it?'

'I was only joking,' he says, looking at her hopefully. 'You're not pissed off with me?'

''Course not. It's the best laugh I've had for years! Tanya's almost wet herself!'

'Great! Glad I'm a source of amusement for everyone.'

To say nothing of causing urinary incontinence all round, by the sound of it.

'You great plonker,' says Phil mildly, thumping his brother on the back as he heads off in the direction of the bar. 'You need to learn to laugh at yourself.'

'Huh. What's he know about it?' grumbles Gary.

But I've caught Siobhan's eye and we're both starting to snigger again.

'OK, OK,' he says, holding up his hands in defeat. 'I've made a twat of myself. I'll just go and drown my sorrows, now, if you don't mind. Or maybe I should go and drown myself instead – then everyone can have a *real* laugh.'

'Don't be like that, Gary,' says Siobhan, suddenly quietening down and looking at him almost coyly. 'Don't go. Let's have another dance. I promise I won't laugh at you any more.'

She tucks her arm through his and raises her eyebrows invitingly.

Unbelievable. By the time I head back to the dance floor to join in the last half-hour of the celebrations, he's got his arms round her and she's kissing him.

343

I hope he doesn't get carried away and mention weddings again.

But he could do worse. She's a nice girl. Good sense of humour.

'Come on and dance!' calls Sam, catching sight of me. I hesitate. She's with Julia, who still seems pretty energetic despite the bump she's carrying in front of her. 'It'll all be over soon!'

'OK.'

That's true. We must be onto the last few numbers now. You can always tell it's near the end of a party when "Hi Ho Silver Lining" comes on for the second time and everyone's nearly knocking each other out with their arm-waving.

'It's been fantastic!' shouts Julia above the music.

How would she know? She's only been here for the last hour or so.

'So glad you came!' Sam shouts back.

'So sorry you missed *my* wedding.'

'Never mind. I'll be there for the christening.'

They both smile at me, encouraging me to be happy for them. *See?* – their smiles are saying – *We're friends again. No harm done. All's well that ends well.*

But what about *me*?

'Abbie,' says Julia as the music finishes and I'm turning away again, 'don't walk away.'

'I'm only going to get my drink.'

'I mean – don't walk away from *this*.'

'What? I'm fine. I just . . .'

'You're not fine. Please, can't we talk?'

'What about?' Shit. I don't want a row with her. Sam's within earshot – I'm not going to let this spoil her day.

344

'Look, a lot's happened since we last saw each other.'

'Obviously!' I nod at her swollen tummy. 'When's it due? Who's the father?'

This is a spiteful thing to say to someone wearing a wedding ring. It's tantamount to asking her if she *knows* whose it is.

'My husband's called Mike,' she answers evenly. 'We've been married for over a year.'

'Congratulations.'

'He's working tonight. He's a doctor.'

'Good for him.'

'But he persuaded me to come. He said it's never good to let things fester.'

He would do, wouldn't he. Being a doctor.

'He could have just prescribed you some antibiotics. Saved you the journey.'

Her mouth twitches and I see, in surprise, a smile dancing in her eyes. 'You always were funny, Abbie.'

'Thanks,' I respond, sourly.

'Funny and clever.'

'Yeah, right. I was the one who left school at sixteen, remember? The one who *didn't* get a clutch of A levels and a top-notch job in London.'

'That was your choice. You always knew your own mind, too.'

I'm sighing with exasperation. What exactly is the point of all this old flannel? Buttering me up with a load of stupid compliments isn't exactly going to change anything at this stage.

'So, when's the baby due?' I ask bluntly to change the subject.

'The end of September. It's a girl. We're going to call her Daisy.'

'Lovely.'

'Abbie . . .'

'Well, I hope you'll be very happy . . . with Mike, and Daisy.'

'Abbie, I'm sorry.'

The music's started again. "Come On Eileen". Everyone's joining in, shouting along with the words, but it's just making me feel sad. I wish she'd go away.

'Can't hear you.'

'Come outside, then. *Please*. I can't go home without telling you . . .'

Shouldn't have come, then.

But she's pulling at my arm, leading me away from the dance floor, away from the music and the shouting and cheering and clapping. If I shake her off, it'll cause a scene. Sam'll notice and be upset. For the sake of five minutes, listening to Julia droning on with some pathetic excuses, trying to make herself feel better so that she can poodle off home to Mike and say how glad she is that she's made her peace with everyone, I might as well go along with it and just nod and smile.

'I've wanted to say sorry to you,' she says as soon as the double doors shut behind us, cutting off the sound of the party, 'since . . . well, since eight years ago.'

'So why didn't you?'

'You wouldn't have let me.'

That's true enough, I suppose. I wouldn't be letting her now, if I had any choice in it.

'I can't expect you to forgive me.'

'So what's the point of all this, then?'

'I just wanted the chance to explain. That's fair

enough, isn't it?' She smiles. 'Even the condemned man gets to say a few words.'

I look at my watch but don't say anything. What am I supposed to say?

She sighs. 'All right, Abbie. I'll make it as short as I can. I had a breakdown after the Venice trip.'

I look at her sharply. Is this a ploy to get my sympathy?

'I'm not expecting you to feel sorry for me. You probably think I deserved it. Maybe I did, but not on account of anything that happened in Venice. You *know* that. You know nothing went on between me and Phil, don't you?'

'I suppose so,' I admit grudgingly.

'But you chose to let Sam think it. Because of what happened with Jamie.'

So what? It's my fault she had a breakdown?

'I don't blame you,' she goes on, giving me a quick look. 'But I suddenly found myself with no one. You and Sam both hated me. And, well, my family . . .'

She stops, and swallows, several times. I'm intrigued. What about her family? Come to think of it, who *were* her family? Why did we never meet them? Why did we never go to Julia's house, always Sam's, or mine, or one of the other girls'? What was wrong with her family?

'My dad,' she says very quickly, and I notice her hand is trembling slightly, 'used to hit us. Me and my mum. He put my mum in hospital once. And one time when I was off school for two weeks with the flu – it wasn't really. He'd punched me and broken my nose.'

'Oh! I . . .' Shit. I can't pretend to be glad about this. It's horrible. I don't know what to say. 'I had no idea.'

347

'Nobody did. Mum kept it quiet, and made *me* keep it quiet. We acted like it was *our* fault – our guilty secret. I was so ashamed.'

'You didn't tell Sam?'

'No. If anything, Abbie, I wanted to tell *you*.'

'Me?'

'Yes. You were always so sweet and understanding with everyone. And with your lovely patient mum and dad, and your lovely calm, peaceful house – I was so jealous of you.'

'Of *me*?' I repeat, parrot-fashion.

'Of course I was. I was desperate to have somebody for myself. My poor mum was too busy trying to stay out of Dad's way to pay much attention to me.'

'That's *terrible*!' I've almost forgotten, for a minute, who I'm talking to. 'She should have been protecting you! She should have taken you away from him!'

'I know she should have, but life isn't always the way it *ought* to be. She was scared, and downtrodden, and, well, eventually he was arrested for beating up his mistress, so . . .'

'His *mistress*!'

'Yes, and he wound up in prison, thank God. And Mum went to live with my auntie in Bournemouth. This was all after I left home, of course, so it didn't make a lot of difference to me,' she adds quickly with a shake of her head that tells me how much she's lying.

'I kept trying to get a boyfriend,' she goes on, 'but I just . . . couldn't seem to get it right. I sabotaged any half-decent relationships; I preferred going out with married men. Stealing other people's boyfriends. I was a mess.'

She hangs her head, looking up at me from under her fringe. Her eyes are full of tears. If this wasn't Julia, I'd be hugging her. If this wasn't Julia, I'd have forgiven her the moment she started talking.

'I'm sorry, Abbie. I'm so sorry I hurt you so much. I should have said so at the time. I don't know why I did it; I didn't even like Jamie. He was a total shit.'

'I know,' I whisper.

'I think . . . in some kind of warped way . . . I was trying to be like you.' She stops, takes a deep breath, and adds, 'No. That won't do, will it? I can't make excuses. I did that for too long – made excuses to myself; and in the end, my psychiatrist told me I had to stop doing that, and face up to how I'd behaved.'

'How . . . bad was your breakdown?' I ask carefully.

'Bad enough. I was an inpatient for nearly a month.'

'We didn't know . . .' Fuck. *I'm* feeling guilty now.

'When I started to have problems, after Venice, when Sam wasn't talking to me either, I was staying in bed, crying all day, not eating . . .'

'Shit, Julia. I'm sorry.' At last – I've got something to apologise for. It's such a relief, I want to cry. 'That was my fault. If I'd told her . . .'

'No. It would have happened anyway. Like I say – I was a mess. In the end, I gave in and phoned my mum. If I hadn't, I don't know how I would have ended up. She came and fetched me, took me down to Bournemouth to stay with her. Got me seen by the mental health service.'

'You never came back.'

'No,' she says quietly. 'It seemed for the best. After I came out of hospital I got my own flat down there, retrained, got a new job . . .'

'And met Mike.'

'Yes.' She smiles, at last. 'Turned things around, Abbie, I think. I hope.'

'I'm pleased.' I can't believe I'm saying this. Can't believe I'm now actually hugging Julia. Actually crying. We're both crying.

'I'm not telling you all this because I think it makes everything all right,' she says, wiping her eyes. 'I know it doesn't. I don't expect you to suddenly like me again. I just wanted to set the record straight, really.'

'So did I,' I admit. 'But I didn't have the guts to try.'

'Well, I needed to get it off my chest. I'm sorry I've upset you. This is supposed to be a happy occasion!'

'Yes. And it is!' I say, firmly, sniffing back my tears. 'We'd better go back – the bride and groom will be leaving and we're missing the end of the party.' I stop and look at her for a moment. 'Thank you, Julia.'

'What for? I hardly thought you'd ever be *thanking* me!'

'For making me listen. Not before time.'

'Is it too late?' she asks me quietly as we make our way back into the hall.

'No – look, they're still dancing.'

'I mean, Abbie, is it too late for us to be friends again? Do you think?'

'Let's give it a go, shall we?' I smile at her, after only a tiny moment of hesitation. 'Maybe I could come down and see Daisy when she's born.'

'I hoped you would. I thought I might ask you and

Sam to be her godmothers,' she says shyly, patting her stomach. 'Is that OK?'

Bloody hell. Back to church again.

'Why not?' I joke. 'I know the christening service practically off by heart.'

She squeezes my arm as we make our way to the dance floor.

If I'm totally honest, I'm still not altogether sure about this. It's all a bit too sudden. It's hard to think of someone you've hated for years as a friend again, just because of a fifteen-minute conversation. But I'm feeling somehow lighter inside, so that must be a start, mustn't it?

And Sam's looking at us, smiling, with a brightness in her eyes which makes me feel a bit wobbly with happiness. And it's her wedding day, after all. So I guess I'm doing the right thing.

OK, Dad? Are you proud of me?

I'm trying, all right? I'm doing my best.

Quarter to twelve

'We're going to be godmothers,' I tell Sam as she envelopes me in a tight hug, 'you and me, apparently.'

'I know! How cool is that! We can go down to Bournemouth together, and take her out in her pram, and ... well, you know, do whatever godmothers do. Teach her Bible stories and stuff. Almost as good as having a kid of our own!'

I freeze and hold her out at arm's length, staring at her.

'But ... I thought ...'

'I know, I know. It's not that I don't *like* children.'

'You do, don't you? And you're so good with them. I never understood. And then ... Phil said something in his speech today about *if* you ever had kids ... I don't get it! Doesn't he think you're serious about it?'

She shrugs. 'He's not keen either. But he says if I ever change my mind ... like some girls do when they turn thirty, you know, and start hearing their body clocks ticking ... then we'll discuss it again if it happens. Maybe one day I will. But I don't think so. Not after ...' She stops and shakes her head.

'What? After what?'

'It's just ... things that have happened, in the family.'

'What things?' She's lost me now. 'Troy? I know he's a pain, but you love him really, don't you?'

'I know. That's it. That's the point.'

'What is?' I'm feeling breathless with anxiety. *What* is she keeping from me?

But she just smiles and says, 'Oh, look, it doesn't matter now, anyway – sorry – I'll tell you another time. OK? After the honeymoon. I promise.'

How can I argue? She must be all right, anyway, whatever it is. She's positively glowing with happiness.

'OK. As long as you promise.'

'You've been such a great bridesmaid, Abbie, such a great friend.'

'Stop it! You'll have me crying again!'

'Me too! Come on, one more dance!'

'I'm worn out!' I protest. But the DJ has obviously decided everyone is probably now worn out anyway, and is slowing things down again. Phil claims his bride for a slow dance to "Just The Way You Are", so I stand on the sidelines, watching, feeling happy for them, trying to squash the uncharitable little question in the back of my mind about whether anyone's ever going to hold *me* in their arms and look at me that way ...

'Come on,' says David gruffly, grabbing me round the waist so that I jump and squeal with surprise. 'This one's for us.'

'What do you mean?' I manage to ask him finally after I've been whirled into the centre of the dance floor and swung around a couple of times.

'Listen to the words.'

I don't have to. I know what they are – all about not changing, not trying too hard, being yourself. Being loved just the way you are. They're lovely words, but they have as much to do with me as "Nellie the Elephant" does.

'It's what I've been trying to tell you,' David mutters against my ear. 'But you won't listen.'

I feel myself coming over hot. I wish he wouldn't keep on like this, but he's probably much too drunk to know what he's saying. It's probably best to just make a joke of it.

'Shut up, you fool,' I tell him, trying to laugh. 'It's a good thing I know you're pissed.'

'I've never felt more sober. I've never been more serious, Abbie. I'm trying to tell you – I *do* love you just the way ...'

'David!' I can't treat it as a joke any more. I'm flushed and trembling and I'm going to go and sit down in a minute if he doesn't stop looking at me like that. 'Stop it. I don't like you talking like this. It isn't fair.'

'Fair to who? To *whom*?' he corrects himself before I can do it for him.

To me. To *me*! I realise, with a jolt like an electric shock, that it's not Heather I'm upset about. How terrible is that? What a terrible, awful person I must be. Here I am, dancing with someone else's boyfriend, partner, the father of her child – and he's holding me much closer than he should, and looking at me in a way that's all wrong, and saying stuff to me that he really, really, shouldn't – and I'm nowhere near as bothered about Heather being hurt as I am about myself. This isn't fair to *me*. Because right down deep inside my soul, the truth is that I love this man. I've always loved him! I've loved him since we were both eleven-year-old kids arguing in his back garden. I've had to hide my feelings away, bury them so deep I've managed to pretend I didn't even know they were there. I can never, ever, allow those feelings out into the daylight. He belongs to someone else; he has a girlfriend and a child, and to acknowledge how I feel would be to cause a rift in the family I love like my own. He's taking the piss. He's teasing me, winding me up, and it isn't *fair*!

'Why am I being unfair?' he repeats softly, leaning closer to me so that our faces are touching.

This is unbearable. My whole body is screaming things at me that my mind can't accept.

'You *know* why!' My voice comes out choked and wobbly. 'You know we can't ... we can't be like this with each other. Don't tease me! Please.'

'I'm not teasing. How many times do I have to tell you? I've always loved you, Abbie.'

'Yes! As a friend! As brother and sister! Don't ...'

His lips just brushed my cheek. I feel like I'm having a heart attack. David's kissed me on the cheek, over the years, more times than I can count, but this is different, and he knows it. He touches my face now, gently, with his fingertips, and my cheek's burning and tingling like a million nerves have come alive there. We've stopped dancing. The music's going on, everyone's going on dancing around us, and we're standing here, dead still in the middle of the dance floor, staring at each other. I'm terrified out of my life – but I want this moment to go on forever. I'm upset, and confused, and horrified ... and

355

ecstatic, all at the same time.

'I need to ... to ...'

To run away. To hide. To leave the country.

To kiss you. To tell you I love you. To be with you for ever.

'... to finish my drink.'

I don't know how I walk back to the table. He's watching me walk away, but he doesn't follow me. Thank God. I make it to the table, sit down and pick up the pint glass of lemonade I ordered after the confrontation with Julia. I can't turn and look back at David. I can't ... but I do, and he's still watching me. This is terrible. I feel lost, and exposed, like I've walked naked into a strange house.

'Are you OK?' Sam's beside me, looking at me anxiously.

'I don't know.' I can't tell her – not this, not tonight. 'I feel a bit ...' I take a gulp of lemonade and feel it fizzing down my throat, mixing with the bubbles of excitement and fear. *I'm in love with David.* 'I don't know – a bit strange.'

'Shattered, I should think!' she laughs.

No. I'm in love with your brother.

'Have you ever felt like ... something's been bugging you, and you suddenly know what it is?'

'Mm?' She smiles at me, her head on one side. 'I don't know ... Why, what is it, then?'

I've been in love with David all my life.

'I ... I ... think I'm over Jamie,' I offer lamely.

'Of course you are!' She laughs at me affectionately. 'You've been over him for years – since even before you finished with him! You just seemed to want to hang on to the hurt.'

'What an idiot I've been.'

356

'Not an idiot. Just a nice, gentle, person. Nobody should ever hurt you. You don't deserve it. You deserve so much better.'

'Don't cry, you daft thing!'

'Sorry. I just feel a bit emotional. I'm so happy, Babbs – I want you to be happy too.'

'I will be. I promise. Don't worry about me!'

I'm in love with your brother, and I think he's in love with me.

But it's out of the question. And I think I'm going to have to emigrate.

But apart from that, I'm fine. Absolutely fine!

Five to twelve

The DJ's announcing the Last Waltz.

'Oh!' cries Sam in disappointment. 'I don't want it to end!'

The party's supposed to be finishing at twelve-thirty, but the bar's closed now and the bride and groom are supposed to be leaving after this last dance. They were torn between the tradition of leaving before the rest of the guests, and not wanting to miss a minute of their own wedding reception, so we agreed a compromise – by the time they've gone round and said all their goodbyes it'll be nearly half past, anyway.

We all clear the dance floor and Phil takes Sam by the hand and leads her out into the centre, where he takes her in his arms as the music starts. Everyone claps and a few aunties, and Christine, of course, wipe their eyes all over again.

'They're so perfect for each other.'

It's Julia, standing next to me, smiling as the happy couple glides past us, entwined in each other's arms.

'I know.'

'Thank God he came to his senses and realised he wanted to commit.'

'Yes.'

I seem to have lost the power of speech. Too many shocks for one day. Only a few hours ago I was never going to see or speak to Julia again, and I was certainly never going to be in love with David.

'Sometimes people don't seem to see what's right in front of their eyes.'

'No.'

'The right person for them can be there all along, part of their life, and they just don't seem to realise.'

'Mm.'

She catches my eye and in an instant, I think: She knows.

She saw David and me dancing together just now. Probably everyone in the room did. Probably Heather did. Shit! She must know. She must hate me . . .

'Don't worry,' says Julia quietly. 'Heather's outside, talking to Chloe and Eva. And everyone else is far too busy watching the bride and groom tonight.'

'It's no good,' I whisper, looking at the floor, feeling my face burning again. 'It's impossible. He's with Heather . . . He's got Troy . . .'

She takes my hand and holds it. For a minute we stand like this, holding hands, watching Sam and Phil dancing.

'You need to talk to him,' says Julia. 'Talk to him about the situation . . . about the possibilities . . .'

'There is no situation. There are no possibilities. I'm not breaking up a family. It's *out of the question*.'

'I understand.' There's sympathy in her eyes. 'But you and David were always meant to be together. What took you so long?'

She's moved on before David arrives to take her place.

'I'm sorry,' I tell him quietly, my heart bashing against my ribs so that I have to breathe in shallow gasps, 'about rushing off.'

'That's OK. You needed a drink.'

'Not really. I needed to get away from you. I couldn't bear you touching me.'

'I didn't think I was *that* bad,' he jokes softly.

'You know what I mean.'

He doesn't argue. We listen to the song lyrics: about two lonely people having the last dance together. He gestures to the dance floor but I shake my head. I can't risk having his arms around me again; I might spontaneously combust. I imagine myself as a pile of hot ashes in the middle of the floor, with everyone standing in a circle around me, staring, and saying they didn't realise I'd been burning up . . . if only they'd known . . . and David saying it was all his fault . . .

'What are you thinking about?'

'Being a pile of ashes in the middle of the dance floor.'

He laughs. 'Not ashes, Abbie. Ashes are dead, and grey, and dry. You'll never be like that. You're like the sparks.'

'I'm *what*?' It doesn't sound complimentary.

'They take on the heat of the fire . . . and they *glow*. They fly up, shimmering in the air. And they never look back.'

'Unless they land on something and set the whole bloody town on fire.'

'You have no soul,' he says, smiling into my eyes.

Oh, but I have. I so have.

'Bye, Mum! Don't cry . . . we'll be back in a fortnight!

Bye, Dad. Thanks for everything. Chloe, Eva – lovely to meet you. Look after my little sister, won't you? She can be quite a handful . . . Yes, I bet you *do* know that already! Julia – I'm *so* glad you came tonight, let's stay in touch now, and you take care of yourself and my goddaughter! We'll come down to Bournemouth to visit you soon, won't we, Abbie? Abbs . . . what can I say? Thank you for everything, darling; give my love to your mum and our thanks to your dad. David – see you soon, Dave . . . try not to worry – it's all going to work out fine, I promise.'

What was that?

I stand stock-still, staring after Sam as she moves on around the circle of well-wishers. Sam doesn't know about this! She can't do! Has David been talking to her? He surely hasn't *told* her? There's nothing to tell!

'What's going on?' I whisper to David as Sam and Phil continue to the other side of the room to say goodbye to Phil's family.

'It's what I need to tell you about. I've been trying to tell you all evening—'

'*Daddy*!' screams Troy suddenly, sitting up, bleary-eyed, and shrugging himself out of his nest of coats. He starts to cry pitifully. 'I want Daddy! I want to go home! I want a wee-wee!'

Heather rushes to comfort him but he pushes her away, looking around the room wildly.

'Where's Daddy? Where's *Daddy*?'

'Hang on,' says David, looking from me to Troy anxiously.

'No. It's OK – we can talk later. Go and sort him out. He's just woken up. He doesn't know where he is. He needs his daddy.'

'Yes,' says David in a strange tone I don't recognise. He gives me a last, lingering look before heading towards Troy. 'Abbie, I *will* explain . . . just don't go away. OK? Don't leave without me.'

I might never leave at all. I feel incapable of even finding my way home.

Sam and Phil finally make their exit, looking back and waving until the very last minute. People are sitting around, finishing their drinks while the bar staff collect up the empty glasses. A very drunk middle-aged couple are trying to dance, swaying around the floor despite the lack of music, holding each other up and giggling. Chloe's sitting with her head on Eva's shoulder and her eyes closed while Eva talks to her softly. Gary and Siobhan are laughing together, holding hands very loosely as if they've known each other forever. And Frank . . . Frank's putting his jacket on, staring wildly around the room, shuffling towards the door . . .

'Wait!' I shout, pushing my way through a crowd of Phil's drunken mates – 'Excuse me, sorry, sorry' – 'Got to get to him before he goes again' – and finally catch up with Frank just in time to grab his arm seconds before he opens the outside door. 'Where are you going? You'll get lost again.'

He looks at me as if I'm mad. 'Lost? I'm not lost. Who are you?'

'Abbie,' I say, impatiently. 'Remember? Come on, Frank – come back and wait for the others.'

'I'm going home,' he insists, pushing the door open.

I slam it shut, narrowly missing his fingers. He glares at me.

'Young lady,' he says imperiously, 'whoever you are, you're being very rude. I need to find my car and go home now. Open the door, please.' He hesitates, frowns and starts to rummage in his pockets. 'Where are my car keys? Have you stolen my car keys?'

'Frank, you can't drive. You haven't got a car. You're going home with Christine and Brian in a taxi. OK? Now, why don't you . . .'

'I haven't got a car?' He looks at me in puzzlement for a minute, and then seems to suddenly fold up on himself, all his anger evaporating. 'I lost my car? I don't . . . I don't remember . . . Did I have an accident?' He stares around him, looks back at me again and asks, in a pitiful whisper that wrings my heart, 'Where am I?'

I take his arm and lead him gently back into the room, sitting him down and beckoning to Christine, who's looking around for him with worry etched into her face.

'Dad, where on earth did you think you were going?' she asks him anxiously. 'Did you need the toilet again? Brian will take you out there.'

'No, I don't need the bloody toilet, woman. Stop fussing. I was going home.'

'You're coming home with us, Dad. In a taxi. You can't . . .'

'What's happened to my car?'

'You haven't . . .' She looks at me questioningly. 'You haven't had a car for a long time.'

'He thought he was going to drive home,' I tell her with a shrug. 'He didn't remember where he was.'

'Of course he knows where he is! Dad, we're at the wedding, aren't we? Remember? Sam's wedding.'

'Sam? Little Samantha?' He looks around for her.

'Where is she?'

'She's gone now. We'll be going soon, don't worry, as soon as the taxi comes.'

He sighs and leans his head on his hands as if he's got a terrible headache. I feel a sudden urge to hug him and tell him he's all right, not to worry, but I don't want to frighten him.

'He'll be all right now, bless his heart,' says Christine, patting his arm.

'But he doesn't even know where he is.'

I'm beginning to wonder if he's safe. I mean, what if he wanders off when he's left at home on his own?

'Did he try to walk off again?' asks Brian, coming to join us and pulling up a chair next to Christine.

'He's fine,' she says stoutly. 'You're fine, aren't you, Dad?' He looks up at her with a helpless grunt which she obviously takes as a yes. 'See. He's fine.'

'Chris.' Brian puts his arm round his wife's shoulders. 'You have to stop kidding yourself. He's not fine.'

'Let's not start this again, Brian. Not tonight. Please.'

I don't think I want to be listening to this. It's obviously a regular source of conflict between them. I start to get up and move off, but Brian stops me.

'Abbie: what do you think?'

They both look up at me, hopeful expressions on their faces, wanting me to take their sides. Bugger. I think I'll find a sudden need to go to the toilet.

'I . . . er . . . look, it's none of my business.'

'But as an independent opinion,' says Brian. 'Tell us what you think. Honestly. Don't you think Frank's becoming a danger to himself?'

'He's fine!' retorts Christine before I can answer.

'He walks off when he's at home on his own. He's had strangers bringing him home. He'll hurt himself one day,' says Brian, looking at Christine urgently.

'Don't talk about him ... in front of him ... as if he's not here,' says Christine, stroking her father's arm and beginning to look upset.

'Chris, that's the whole point – half the time he's *not* here. I keep telling you: he needs more care.'

'*I* care for him! He's my father, he doesn't need anyone else!'

'But you have to go to work.' I shouldn't be getting involved, but I can't help it. 'You can't be watching him all the time, Christine. Aren't you worried ...'

'Thank you, Abbie,' says Brian surprisingly quietly. 'That's what I've been trying to tell her.'

'But maybe tonight's not a good time,' I add desperately, seeing the tears starting to well up in Christine's eyes. 'Why don't you talk about it tomorrow?'

'Because there's something I need to tell Chris tonight.'

Oh, God. Please don't let him say he's booked Frank into a nursing home behind her back. Please, no; let's not have a major family drama at this late stage of the proceedings ... I couldn't bear it.

'Why tonight? Go home, Brian, and have a good night's sleep, and talk to Christine tomorrow. Yeah?' I feel like a nurse, like a nanny, trying to take control and send the naughty children home to bed.

'Yes, let's just leave this now, please, Brian,' says Chris. 'Look, Dad's fine now, aren't you, Dad?'

'But I've got a surprise for you,' Brian blurts out. 'A present.'

I look at him suspiciously. He doesn't normally do

surprises. Or presents. What's he playing at?

'A present?' echoes Christine, looking as amazed as me. 'For me?'

Brian shuffles in his chair, looking a bit bashful. 'Yes, well, I wanted to give you a treat. After all the hard work of the wedding and everything. And ... you know ... losing a daughter, kind of thing.'

Bloody hell. Can it be true? Has the man really got a heart, hidden away somewhere under that lazy, miserable exterior?

'What is it?' asks Christine, breathlessly, turning pink with excitement.

He reaches into his jacket pocket. I'm thinking – jewellery. An eternity ring, or a necklace, or bracelet, or ...

'Here you are.' He puts a plain brown envelope on the table in front of her and waits for her to pick it up. 'Have a look,' he adds gruffly. 'Open it up.'

She fingers the envelope cautiously for a moment, as if it's likely to explode in her hands. Then slides her finger under the flap and rips it open. A folded page of paper falls out onto the table. She picks it up, opens it out, studies it slowly and then suddenly gasps and claps her hand to her mouth. She puts the paper back down on the table, looks across the detritus of empty glasses, wine stains and party food at her husband, and leaps up, grabs him round the neck and kisses him so forcefully on the mouth that I don't know who's more shocked, Brian or me.

'Oh my *God*!' she squeals. 'I can't believe it! After all these years! What I've always wanted! What I've always *dreamed* of!'

'Are you pleased?' he says almost shyly. 'It's supposed to be a good one.'

Obviously I can't resist it. I have to take a look.

It's a booking confirmation for a safari holiday in South Africa. Two weeks, all-inclusive, first-class flights included.

Christine's crying again. 'I can't believe it!' she keeps repeating. 'It's what I always dreamed of!' Then she suddenly stops and looks at him worriedly. 'How did you manage to afford it?'

'Don't ask questions.'

'You didn't ... You haven't robbed a bank or anything?'

'Don't be bloody stupid, woman. I've been studying form. Had some good wins. And I've given up smoking, haven't I. Been saving up.'

'You've *really* given up, this time?' squawks Christine. 'In that case, I'd better, too, hadn't I? Then I can save up some spending money.'

Blimey. The Patterson house is going smoke free. Next thing we know, they'll be giving up the drink too. Or maybe not!

By now the rest of the family are crowding around us, alerted by Christine's squeals of delight.

'Two weeks in South Africa!' exclaims Chloe. 'Cool!'

'Excellent! Wouldn't mind that myself!' agrees Eva.

'What about Granddad?' says David.

There's a horrible silence.

'What about me?' says Frank, who's obviously taking more notice than we thought he was.

'Who's going to look after him?' says Christine, suddenly realising the fly in the ointment and sitting down with a thump. 'I mean, don't get me wrong. I know he's fine, but a whole two weeks ... I'd be

367

worried . . . ' She looks back at Brian, disappointment colouring her face. 'I couldn't do it, love. I couldn't leave him for two whole weeks.'

'I could go round,' offers David at once. 'I could stay over!'

'Or I could!' I agree hurriedly.

'I'd be there, wouldn't I?' points out Chloe somewhat aggressively.

'No, love. You'll be back at uni. And I know you mean well, David . . . Abbie . . . but you work all day. I'm only part-time. It's not long enough for him to get into trouble.'

Nobody has the heart to argue the point. I'm thinking frantically. There must be a solution. There must be a way. She can't refuse her dream holiday.

'The thing is, Chris,' says Brian very slowly, very carefully, watching her face, 'I've arranged something.'

'What do you mean? What have you arranged?'

'A holiday for your dad.' He turns to Frank, who looks like he's on the point of falling asleep. 'You'd like that, wouldn't you, Frank? A holiday?'

'What holiday? Not Margate again? I don't like the beach.'

'It's respite care,' Brian tells the whole family. 'At Greenfield Lodge.'

'That's a nursing home,' says Christine indignantly. 'He doesn't need . . .'

'Maybe he does, maybe he doesn't. But for two weeks, it won't hurt him. He'll be looked after. We can enjoy the holiday without worrying. And we can see whether he likes it or not.'

'I don't want him going there permanently. He'll hate it.'

'He might not, Mum,' points out David. 'He might actually like it. You don't know.'

'It's not right for him to be shut up, away from his family. It's not nature.'

'It's sometimes the only solution,' says Brian gently. 'But let's not argue about that yet, eh? Let's just agree he can go for these two weeks?' He taps the booking confirmation and smiles at her broadly. He looks almost nice for a moment, smiling like that. He should do it more often. 'And we can go to South Africa.'

She smiles back at him. 'It does sound wonderful, Brian.'

'It will be. Like a second honeymoon, eh?'

Blimey. Leave off. That thought is slightly too yucky for my liking.

But they're cuddling each other before the rest of us can make our hasty retreats.

'And they think *we* don't behave appropriately!' says Chloe, shaking her head. 'Disgusting, I call it.'

But she's smiling. We all are. It must be the romance of the wedding affecting everyone.

Half past twelve

There's a fleet of taxis waiting outside.

'Are you coming back with us, Abbie?' asks Christine, tucking her arm through mine. 'For a nightcup?'

'Nightcap.' I smile at her. Her eyes are sparkling and she's pink-cheeked with happiness. I almost (*but not quite*) want to kiss Brian for being so unexpectedly, so amazingly, thoughtful in saving the surprise of the holiday for the end of the evening, when Chris was possibly going to feel a bit of an anticlimax.

To be honest I'm so shattered I can hardly stand. I think I'll just get in a taxi and go home. Home to my nice little one-bedroom flat with its view over the park and its tidy kitchen, its lack of clutter and confusion. I can fall into my nice neat single bed, pull the duvet over my head and stay there all night, all day tomorrow, and forget about David and the things he's been saying, the way he's been looking, the way I felt when he touched my cheek . . .

Or can I?

'OK,' I find myself saying. For some reason, my nice tidy flat doesn't feel appealing right now. 'OK, thanks. A nightcup would be great.'

*

David's watching with concern as I head towards the door.

'Abbie!' He catches up with me and lays a hand on my arm. 'You're not going?'

'Well,' I joke, to try to disguise the tremble in my voice, 'you know – the bar's closed, the bride and groom have left, everyone's said their goodbyes, they're waiting to lock up and go home ...'

'But aren't you coming back for a drink at the house?'

'Oh. Yes.' Somehow I didn't think David and Heather would be coming back. I thought they'd need to take Troy home to bed. 'Are you?'

'Don't sound so disappointed,' he laughs gently.

Disappointed? At the thought of perhaps another hour in his company, instead of going home to my single bed? I laugh too, but the confusion in my brain is making me feel almost giddy. To be honest I need another drink like I need a hole in the head. If I was completely sober maybe I wouldn't be having these strange thoughts and feelings about someone I've known almost my entire life.

Or maybe I would.

I'm sharing a taxi with Brian, Christine and Frank. Chloe and Eva are getting into the one behind and, as we pull away, I see David sauntering out of the building and following them. He turns to say something to Heather, who's leading a sleepy, whining Troy by the hand, and he smiles as he ruffles the boy's hair.

The image of that smile is fixed in my mind, imprinted like a digital attachment to the back of my eyelids as the taxi speeds us back through the empty streets to the Pattersons' house. How did this happen?

How has David gone from being boy-next-door to love-of-my-life in the space of a few short hours? Am I drunker than I thought? Am I dreaming? Am I going mad?

Or maybe I'm just beginning to face up to something I've known all along? And that's the most scary possibility of all.

OK. I'll admit it.

We nearly had sex once.

I wasn't going to mention it. It was a long time ago, OK? We agreed, at the time, that it was a mistake, and we've both pretended ever since that it never happened. I don't know why I'm even thinking about it now.

It was a little while after I finished with Jamie. I was upset, I'd had too much to drink, and Sam was being sweet and looking after me. I stayed over at their place. I couldn't sleep so I went downstairs to make myself a hot drink, and took it into the lounge. I was going to put the TV on so I didn't switch on the light, and as I crossed the room a voice came out of the darkness:

'Are you all right?'

It made me jump in fright and splash my hot chocolate down the skimpy T-shirt I'd been wearing in bed.

'Shit!' It was scalding. I dumped the cup on the floor and tried to pull the fabric of the T-shirt away from my body but in an instant David was beside me, his eyes, in the darkness, shining wide with concern. Apparently he'd fallen asleep on the sofa with his Walkman plugged into his ears instead of going to bed. 'Sorry! God, sorry, Abbie – didn't mean to frighten you. Are you OK?'

I couldn't answer. I was still gasping from the shock of the hot liquid on my chest. Before I knew what was happening, David had snatched the hem of the T-shirt out of my hands and with one swift movement, pulled it off over my head. I was naked apart from my knickers.

'Cold water,' he said, ignoring my attempts to cover up my breasts with my hands, and pulled me out to the kitchen, where he wetted a cloth under the cold tap and handed it to me to place over the red area of skin where the drink had splashed me.

'It's OK,' I said as I managed to get my breath back. 'I don't think it's actually burned me . . . it was just the shock.'

'Here.' He passed me a glass of water. I could see that he was trying to avoid looking at my boobs just as desperately as I was trying to hide them. 'Drink that.' He glanced at me quickly and looked away again. 'You look a bit pale. Sit down in the lounge and I'll go and get you something to put on.'

It was still dark in the lounge. I sank gratefully onto the sofa, feeling a bit faint. After a minute David reappeared with a huge shapeless sweatshirt of his own.

'Here, put this on. God, you're freezing!'

His hand had brushed my arm as he passed me the sweatshirt.

'Not really.' But my teeth were chattering. 'I think it's just . . . I feel a bit . . .'

'Put your head down between your knees.'

I obeyed, now beyond caring about my nakedness. Gradually, the spinning of the room slowed down and everything came back into focus. I sat up, slowly, and became suddenly aware that David's arms were around me and his face was very close to mine.

'Are you OK, Abbie? Really?' he whispered.

'Yeah. I had too much to drink earlier.'

'But are you *OK*? That bastard Jamie . . .'

I'd thought I was all cried out, but hearing Jamie's name again, my eyes suddenly filled up and I let out a long, shuddering sob.

'Don't cry. Please don't cry, Abbs. He isn't worth it. He's a stupid, ignorant, git. He didn't deserve you.'

I sniffed and wiped my eyes.

'Come here. Put this on. Let me warm you up.'

It was an innocent enough gesture – pulling me towards him, taking my head in his hands to pull the sweatshirt over my neck. We'd been childhood friends – there wasn't any sexual intent. But something about his concern and compassion, something about my pain and vulnerability, suddenly got to both of us, at the exact same moment, and almost without taking a breath we'd fallen on each other's faces like starving animals, kissing and groaning and crying all at the same time, with such utter desperation that I wondered, afterwards, if I'd actually had a fleeting nervous breakdown. My knickers were on the floor, his trousers were round his ankles and we were both grappling frantically with his underwear when he gasped, sat up, took both my hands firmly in his and said with a shudder: 'God! My God! What the *hell* am I doing? Abbie . . . I'm so sorry.'

'No . . . it wasn't your fault . . . I was just as . . .'

Just as *what*? Horny? Desperate? Drunk? I flopped back against the sofa, picked up the sweatshirt and pulled it on roughly over my tingling nipples.

'I don't know what came over me. Abbie, I'd *never*

mean to take advantage. I'm much too fond of you . . . you know that.'

It was the word 'fond' that snapped me out of it. 'Fond' is something you feel for your grandma, or a friend's child, or a cousin you don't see very often. It's not a word you use to your lover, not a word whispered at the height of passion.

Oh my God! You're wonderful / beautiful / amazing / sexy, and I'm so fond of you!

'Can we pretend this didn't happen?' asked David quietly. His face was flushed with shame. He couldn't look me in the eye.

He obviously didn't really fancy me.

And why should he? Jamie hadn't wanted me, either, at the end of the day.

No change there, then.

I poured myself another vodka before I went back to bed. It helped to numb the pain.

Of all the memories to drag up, this really was the worst one I could have picked tonight, of all nights, with the picture of David smiling as he ruffled his son's hair etched into my brain as if I've been staring too long at the sun.

'Here we all are, then!' sings Christine gaily as the taxi chugs to a halt outside the house.

How the hell is she so bright and breezy when I feel like I could lay down my head and sleep for a year?

Inside, with all the lights on, a CD of 1960s pop classics playing and the smell of coffee brewing in the kitchen, I start to feel slightly more human.

'There are the others, now,' chirps Christine as the doorbell sounds. 'Let them in, Abbie, there's a good girl.'

Obediently I trot to the front door and fling it open.

'Hi Chloe, Eva. Come in. Christine's got the coffee brewing. David ...' I hesitate, staring after the departing taxi. 'Where's Heather? Taking Troy home? Shouldn't you have gone with ...'

I stop, seeing the expression on his face. For a moment I stand, frozen, holding the front door open while he loiters on the step like a nervous salesman. Then he steps forwards and I stand back to let him in.

'*This*,' he says quietly, close to my ear, as he passes me, 'is what I've been trying to talk to you about.'

One o'clock

I wonder what Sam would think. What would she say, if she could see me now, sitting on the sofa in her mum's lounge, balancing a cup of black coffee in one hand and a glass of cheery brandy in the other, listening to the Beatles singing "I Want To Hold Your Hand", and looking furtively at her brother over the rim of my cup as if he's some stunningly fit stranger I've only just met.

But then again, I'm pretty sure she's much too busy having happy just-married sex with her new bridegroom in her hotel room, to worry about what's going on here.

And what exactly *is* going on here?

It's like some kind of elaborate game. I sneak a glance at him, catch him looking at me, look away quickly, wait a couple of minutes for my heartbeat to return to normal, dare myself to look again, catch him still staring at me, look away again quickly . . .

And all the while, Christine is jabbering on, and on, and on, about what Great-auntie Hilda and her daughter (Cousin Vera) were wearing today, and what about Phil's mother's hat! Have we ever seen anything like it? And wasn't it a shame about the rain, but then again if Cousin Vera *would* insist on wearing those shoes ... and did we notice those two girls in identical dresses? Did we think they were twins? And the dinner was lovely, wasn't it, although did we think there were enough potatoes? And is it *really* normal these days to have those little stalks of berries decorating the cheesecake? Are they edible? Did anyone try them, only speaking for herself, she certainly hadn't liked the look of them?

I'm sipping my coffee, and letting it all wash over me, and suddenly there's a loud, theatrical yawn from across the room and Chloe gets up, stretches, sighs and announces: 'Right, OK – I'm off to bed.'

Christine looks slightly uncomfortable for a moment; she clears her throat and echoes: 'Right, OK. Now then, Eva, dear, would you like me to show you where Sam's bedroom is, and get you a nice clean towel, and—'

'It's fine,' interrupts Chloe quickly. 'I'll sort it.'

''Night, Christine. Thanks for everything. 'Night, all,' says Eva as they leave the room together.

We sit in silence for a while, Brian staring slightly aggressively into his whisky glass, Christine gazing into the middle distance as if she's *not* thinking about her youngest daughter possibly tiptoeing into Sam's room during the night, David and I still playing the game: look, look away; look back. Or is it a game? I wish I knew.

'She's a nice enough girl, anyway,' says Christine finally.

'Nothing wrong with her,' mutters Brian, finishing off his whisky, 'as long as she stays in her own room.'

'Who the hell is she, anyway?' asks Frank. 'And where's Julia?'

378

Julia had left just before we did, amongst hugs and kisses and promises of keeping in touch and letting us know as soon as the baby's born, and being sure to introduce us soon to the wonderful Mike.

'Have you two made it up now – you and Julia?' asks Christine now, as if she's talking about a playground punch-up.

'I . . . hope so. She explained a few things to me. And anyway, it was my fault too.'

'I don't know about that, dear. She *did* go in for a bit of boyfriend-stealing, didn't she? Not very nice,' says Christine stoutly.

'I needed to get over it, though.' I'm at the looking-at-David-to-see-if-he's-looking-at-me stage of the game. He is, and this time I hold his gaze. 'I was being stupid. Hanging onto something that didn't even matter any more.'

'Ah, well, dear. She *did* hurt you first.'

'Yeah, but I wallowed in it.'

Look away quickly; calm down; look back again; he's still staring.

'Well, it's lovely that you're all friends again, Abbie. And her married to a doctor – who'd have thought it? And having a baby! Now all we need is for you to meet a nice young man yourself. Eh?'

Look away; count my heartbeats; look back again; keep looking. Keep looking.

'I don't know about that, Christine,' I joke shakily. 'Who'd have me, eh?'

Keep looking; he's still staring. Keep looking. Now I just can't stop.

I thought they were never going to bed. Christine was getting tearful again in the end, after a couple more cheery brandies and joining in drunkenly with Elvis singing "Are You Lonesome Tonight?".

'Oh, it was such a lovely day, wasn't it?' she cried as Brian hustled her out of the room and up to bed. 'Wasn't it a lovely, lovely wedding?'

'It was, Christine. It was wonderful,' I assured her.

'It was great, Mum,' said David, without taking his eyes off me.

'Wedding?' muttered Frank, who'd got into his pyjamas half an hour before and wandered back downstairs again. 'Whose wedding? Who's getting married? That floozy Julia?'

'Goodnight, Granddad,' said David, pushing him gently up the stairs.

And now we're on our own. David's phoned for a taxi to take us both home. Soon. But for now we're alone with just the beating of my heart, and the stomping of the Dave Clark Five singing "Glad All Over".

'You know what's going on here, don't you?' says David, sitting down next to me and taking hold of my hand.

I can't answer. I stare at his hand, holding my hand, and feel the room lurch as if I'm drunk all over again.

'You must know how I feel about you. How I've always ...'

'David!' It comes out as an anguished squeak. 'Stop it! Please, stop it – it isn't right. I'm not ... getting into this. I'm not even going to talk about it. You're with Heather, and you've got Troy, and ...'

'I'm not.'

'Sorry?'

The music stops; the CD's finished. The silence in

the room is sudden and frightening. I can hear David breathing.

'I said, "I'm not." I'm not with Heather.'

'Don't be ... Don't be silly. You can't just ... Look, you can't just suddenly ... because you've had a row, or whatever, after all these years, and with a child to consider ... You'll make it up tomorrow ...'

'Abbie, listen to me. We haven't had a row. This isn't anything sudden.'

He drops his head and sighs – a long, deep sigh that sounds like all the breath's leaving his body.

'What, then?' I whisper.

'We split up six months ago.'

'Six ... ? Six *months*?'

I want to tell him not to be ridiculous. Of course they didn't split up six months ago! They've been round here together almost every week! I've been to their place myself – I've seen them there together, cooking meals, watching TV, doing the housework, playing with Troy ...

It's ridiculous. But I can't say it, because of the way he's looking at me. It might be ridiculous, but I think it's true.

'What happened?' I ask him instead.

He shrugs. 'I've been wanting to tell you for ages, Abbie, but I didn't really know where to start ... '

'So start now. Wherever you like. I've got all night.'

Funny how I ever thought I might be tired.

Quarter to two

DAVID

So here we are: this is the moment I've thought about constantly for bloody *years*. Last night, when Sam insisted I should talk to Abbie, I started to feel quite brave and positive about it. I decided she was right: it was no good moping and pining – I was going to tell Abbie today about me and Heather, and I was going to ask her out. But as soon as I saw her this morning I felt sick with nerves about it. I've been putting it off all day, and now the moment's finally arrived I almost want to backtrack and *not* ask her, in case she says no. In case she doesn't feel the same way that I do.

Sometimes I think she does. Sometimes I'm sure I can see it in her eyes: this evening, I knew I was right. But most of the time she just treats me like a brother, or a friend. OK, so she likes me, but that's not enough for me any more. I'm crazy about her, always have been; she's the only girl I've ever felt like this about. I loved her even when we were kids. When we went out together that time at school, I know she thought I was just being kind, rescuing her from the humiliation of being laughed at by her horrible friends, but I was going home every night almost delirious with excitement. I was only fourteen but I knew what I wanted: for me and Abbie to go on together and be a real boyfriend and girlfriend. I wanted to kiss her, desperately, but I was too shy, awkward, self-conscious and hormonal to attempt it. No wonder she got bored with me.

Then there was the time we nearly had sex – in this room, on this sofa. What an absolute bastard she must have thought me, taking advantage of her when she was so down, so unhappy after that nasty piece of work Jamie cheated on her. I probably should have told her then: that it wasn't just a quick screw I was after; that I loved her and wanted to make her happy again. But she was telling everyone she didn't want another relationship, didn't want to put herself through all that again ... so I kept my mouth shut. For years, I kept my mouth shut and pretended this wasn't eating me up inside.

And then there was Heather.

She was one of many to be honest. They never lasted long; they were never anything serious. But after the first time we had sex, Heather cried her eyes out. I was a bit gutted – I didn't think I was that bad.

'It's not that,' she sobbed. I remember thinking that some girls cried prettily and managed to look vulnerable and desirable all at the same time. Heather didn't. Her face went red and blotchy, her make-up ran all over the place and she made a noise like a strangled duck. 'It's just that I'm in love with someone else.'

Well, that's great, isn't it? Just what you want to hear when you've just used all your very best, tried and tested techniques to make a girl feel good.

'I'm sorry,' she cried, wiping her face with the corner of my duvet cover. 'I'm really sorry. I shouldn't have come back with you. I shouldn't have done this.'

Oh, bloody hell. Surely she wasn't going to come over all Victorian on me and pretend she never did things like this, she was a nice girl really, she only normally had sex with someone after twenty-five dates . . .

'I'm pregnant.'

I tell you what: I nearly fell off the fucking bed; you'd never seen me move so fast.

'What!' I shouted, making her burst into a fresh torrent of tears.

'I'm sorry!' she grizzled, searching on the floor for her knickers. 'I'm sorry, I shouldn't have . . .'

'Hang on, hang on!' I was terrified. At twenty-four, I'd never even *met* anyone who was pregnant before, apart from my own mum when she was having my little sister. I didn't know the first thing about it. 'Are you telling me . . . that we've just . . . and you've got a baby in there . . .'

I stared at her stomach. She didn't *look* pregnant. Where was she hiding it? What if I'd hurt the baby when I was . . . well . . . you know, poking around in there? Suppose I made her lose it, or have it early, or, God, I don't know, have something wrong with it?

'Don't look so worried,' she said with a sniff, suddenly starting to smile through her tears. 'It's all right. I'm only ten weeks.'

That meant absolutely nothing to me. Ten weeks? What was that – about two or three months? How much of a baby would there be inside her after ten weeks? Would it be a proper little ... baby thing, with a head and arms and legs and stuff? Would it be moving around? Would it have ... Jesus, would it have *felt* me?

I was so freaked out, I couldn't even talk. I stood by the bed, rooted to the spot, the erection I'd been brewing in the hope of a repeat performance shrivelling spectacularly, the sweat cooling on my bare skin leaving me shivery and clammy.

'Sorry,' she said, quite calmly now, getting herself dressed and seeming to pull herself together. I watched her putting on her bra. Did her nipples look a bit odd, or was that just because of what I'd been doing? Maybe she always looked like that. Or didn't women's boobs change when they got pregnant? I tried to think back to my sex-education lessons at school, but, let's be honest, all the boys in the class lost interest after the how-to advice about condoms and the diagrams of how to actually get inside a girl, and the various positions for doing so. Who wanted to know about pregnancy, apart from trying to avoid it?

Now, faced with a living, breathing, pregnant girl who'd actually been to bed with me, it suddenly seemed to matter. Somehow I couldn't just ignore it. To watch her walk out of the door and just get back into bed, turn over and go to sleep would be unthinkable. She had a potential new person inside her and, although it was nothing to do with me, I felt like I'd *trespassed* on it.

'Would ... Would it have *hurt* the baby?' I managed to croak eventually when she was almost fully dressed.

'Don't be daft. Do you think I'd have done it if it would?'

385

'Are you ... um ... Are you still seeing the father?'

At this, she immediately started blubbing again. Shit. OK, OK, I get the picture – the bastard's finished with her and she's still in love with him.

'Sorry,' I said awkwardly. 'Here. Wipe your eyes on the duvet again. Be my guest.'

She managed a feeble laugh.

'You're a nice guy, David,' she said as she finally brushed her hair and put on her shoes. 'It's my own fault. I thought I was ready .... you know? I thought it'd make me feel better.' She stroked her stomach sadly. 'It was a bad idea. I think I just need to concentrate on my baby, now.'

She kissed me on the cheek as she left. The whole thing really got to me. I couldn't get back to sleep for ages.

I tried phoning her but she never picked up. I didn't see her again until a couple of weeks later. I went into a hairdresser's that I never normally used – one of these unisex places – and there she was, doing some woman's highlights. I watched her for a few minutes before she glanced in the mirror and saw me. She was still very slim, but did she have a little bit of a bulge now, or was I imagining it? Another hairdresser beckoned me to a chair, but I shook my head. 'Thanks – I'll wait for Heather.'

By the time she'd finished with the highlights I'd read an old copy of *Woman's Own* from cover to cover, learned how to bake the perfect fruit loaf, how to treat vaginal thrush and what to do if your husband likes dressing in women's clothes. And I'd exchanged glances with Heather over the top of the highlight woman's head. And I'd wondered whether it was good for the baby, her being on her feet like that all day, and using bleaches and colourants and stuff.

'So how are you doing?' I asked her when I was finally sitting in her chair, having my normal cut.

'OK.' She looked at me in the mirror, a bit shyly, like we weren't shagging the breath out of each other a few weeks ago. 'Not feeling sick any more. Bit tired, though.'

Sick? Christ, I never thought about *sick*. Pregnant women always felt sick, didn't they? Was she feeling sick when we were having sex? Did she have to hold herself back from vomiting when I was pumping away on top of her? Jesus! It was making me feel queasy now, just thinking about it. I felt like the whole episode had put me off sex for life.

'Should you be working like this? On your feet all day? Shouldn't you be sitting down and taking care of yourself?'

She laughed sarcastically. 'Yeah, right. I'll go home to my palace and lie on my chaise longue, shall I? Look, David, it's nice of you to pretend you're interested, but you don't have to.'

'I'm not pretending.'

And where the fuck did *that* come from? Because, with a shock, I realised it was true. I *was* interested. I'd known this girl for a matter of weeks, had sex with her once, and somehow, here I was feeling *involved* with her and her baby.

'Well, then, if you really want to know, if you're really interested, I'll tell you. I've been dumped by the love of my life. He kicked me out of his flat. He doesn't care that I'm pregnant. I've moved back in with my mum and dad. They haven't really got room

387

for me – never mind the baby when it's born. I've got nothing in the bank. My dad's just been made redundant. And you really want to know why I'm working?' She stopped, holding the scissors in mid-air and looking at me as if she wasn't sure whether I was capable of understanding basic economics. 'This job is all I've got, David. This and my baby.'

I don't know what happened to me at that point. Look, I was no better or worse than any other single young man. I liked girls, but apart from Abbie, I'd never met one I really *liked*. You know? There's a difference. I hardly knew Heather – barely knew the first thing about her except that she was a hairdresser, she had a liking for purple underwear and fast sex, and she was about three months pregnant by some bastard who'd dumped her like a piece of old rubbish. Like I say, I hardly knew her, but I knew she didn't deserve that. Nobody did.

'Come and stay with me,' I said before I could stop myself.

She put down the scissors. I'm glad she did: her hands were shaking. 'Don't be silly. You hardly know me.'

'I know. But you're in a fix and I can help.'

'Why? You're crazy!' She laughed. 'What's the matter with you? Never met a deserted pregnant woman before?'

'No,' I admitted.

She stared at me in the mirror.

'Are you joking?'

'No.'

'But you share with three other guys!'

'I know. They'll be OK You can have my room. I'll sleep on the couch.'

She shook her head. 'I can't. It's ridiculous. I can't let you.'

'But . . .'

'No, honestly. No way. I'm looking for a flat of my own. OK?'

I went with her to look at flats. We weren't going out together: not exactly. Not in the normal sense of it. We were like a couple of friends who just happened to have had sex once. At first she seemed a bit unsure about me. She said later that she'd thought I was weird. What normal bloke wants to spend all his time with a girl who was having someone else's baby – taking an interest in her pregnancy, buying little things for the baby, discussing names for it and even going with her to an antenatal appointment? She said if it hadn't been for the fact that she'd enjoyed the sex, she'd have suspected I was gay.

It didn't take long for us to realise that on her hairdresser's wages she couldn't even afford to rent a room, never mind a flat. She was sleeping on the sofa at her parents' place and they were getting worried about having an extra mouth to feed.

So I told the guys I house-shared with that she was moving in with me. Their silence, their expressions when I brought her round and introduced her, the way they pointedly turned up the TV and stared at the football, ignoring her, told me all I needed to know. Maybe they weren't such great mates as I'd imagined. Maybe it was understandable.

It's strange how life sometimes gives people what they've been asking for, but not until after they've stopped wanting it.

Heather admitted to me later that until she met me,

she'd been wondering whether to have an abortion, but didn't feel strong enough to go through with it. A week after she moved into my place, she came and woke me up in the middle of the night. She was groaning, clutching her stomach, doubled up with pain. And there was blood. A lot of blood. I still wasn't by any means an expert on female physiology but I knew only too well what was happening. I called an ambulance.

She was kept in hospital overnight after the miscarriage. When I went to bring her home, the nurse assumed I was the father, and told me sympathetically that she'd feel very low for a while but physically she was fine, and there should be no problem with trying for another baby after a month or so.

Another baby.

I know the situation was a bit unusual, but I'd been looking forward to Heather's baby. I'd imagined a scenario where she was somehow, magically, going to be installed in a place of her own by the time it was born, and that I'd call round once or twice a week like some sort of kindly uncle, teaching the kid how to kick a football and taking him (I was hoping it was a boy) out to the park. It didn't, obviously, affect me in the same way as Heather, who lay on the sofa day after day, white faced and tearful, blaming herself, blaming her ex-boyfriend for abandoning her, blaming God, and losing weight so fast it frightened me. But I was upset for her, of course, and I was – *disappointed*. The baby had gone before I even met him.

One evening when the other lads were out at the pub, Heather's crying really got to me. I felt so sorry for her, and wanted so much for her to feel better. I suppose, in my way, I was beginning to love her, but it was a love that came from compassion. It didn't even feel like a sexual love, so you might think it was a bit bizarre that I took her in my arms, kissed her very gently and told her: 'We can try for another one.'

'What?' she said, her eyes so wide with shock that I thought for a minute I'd upset her even more. Belittled the grief she was feeling for her lost baby by suggesting he was replaceable. 'A baby? You and me?'

'I don't mean ... I know it won't be the same. I know it can't be ... Well, it won't stop this *hurting* ... but perhaps ... when you're well enough ...'

Next thing I knew, she was kissing me back, passionately, desperately, as if I was the most wonderful thing that had ever happened to her. Look, I was still a young, virile guy and I hadn't had sex since she'd moved in with me. I'd be lying if I said I wasn't starting to respond.

'I've been in love with you ever since you bought me the cot mobile and the nappies,' she said.

Nappies? I've heard of girls being wooed with flowers and chocolates, but ...

There were tears in her eyes. Tears of happiness now.

'I didn't know you loved me too,' she said, nuzzling up to me and smiling contentedly. 'I thought you just felt sorry for me.'

A little voice in the back of my head was telling me to explain to her. To let her down gently before everything got too out of hand. Yes, I loved her – kind of – but I wasn't *in love* with her. I didn't feel the swooping of my heart I felt when I was with

391

Abbie. I couldn't imagine spending my life with her. But how could I tell her that *now* – when the sadness had gone out of her eyes and she was sitting up, brushing her hair, making excited plans for *our future* and *our children* as if we were already an old married couple?

I wasn't sure what I'd gone and done.

But three months later we were expecting Troy, and we were moving in with my parents.

The Pattersons might be slightly mad, but we know how to rally round in a crisis. Heather was accepted as one of the family. Everyone made a fuss of her and, in due course, the baby too, and for a while we were happy enough together. Of course, it was never going to last for long – how could it? By the time Troy was wearing out our welcome in the family home, and I was earning enough to support us all in a place of our own, we were already looking at each other and wondering what the hell we were doing together. We hadn't really loved each other – we didn't even have much in common – but there was a lot of mutual respect between us. Through Heather, I'd changed from a brash and self-centred boy to a man who understood tenderness and caring. Through me, Heather had regained her trust in the male species. And of course, we'd both got a son.

And that, of course, was the sticking point six months ago when we decided to separate.

Quarter past two

To say I'm stunned would be the understatement of the century.

'She was pregnant when you met her? I don't remember you telling us that.'

'Heather still gets upset when she thinks about that first baby. We don't really talk about it now.'

'But ... you must have loved her. To go on and have a child together.'

'I cared about her,' he says cautiously. 'And she thought she loved me because she was grateful, I suppose.'

'But I don't get it. Why are you still together, if you decided to split up six months ago?'

'I couldn't do it, Abbie. I didn't want to be with Heather any more, she didn't want me either, but I couldn't walk out on my child. So we've kind of ... separated but stayed together. For Troy.'

'But that's ... that's ...' I'm struggling here. I can't get my head round it. What sort of life is that – living together when you want to be apart? 'That's *so* not going to work!'

'I know. It's already not working.'

This, of course, is what I've been seeing. It's what

was wrong between them – what I couldn't put my finger on. Not that they'd had a row, or that they were upset with each other, just that they shouldn't have been together. They weren't a couple any more.

'Abbie, Heather's a nice girl, but we were never really right for each other. You must have seen that.'

How can I answer this? How can I say, *Yes, of course I did! She was never right for you – I hated you being with her but I couldn't even think about it, much less admit it to myself!* I've hardly even got as far as stringing those thoughts together consciously, never mind voicing them.

'And now,' he adds, quietly, watching my face, 'Now, she's seeing Steve again.'

'Steve?'

'Her ex. The one who ...'

'Not the one who dumped her when she was having his baby? *Please* tell me she isn't ... '

He nods wearily. 'What can I say? She says she's never stopped loving him; he apparently says he made the biggest mistake of his life.'

'You're *joking*. For God's sake! She's *surely* not going to take Troy and move in with him.'

He just nods again, looking at his feet.

'Are you going to fight her for custody? Because you can, you know, and you'll win! She's not that great a mother. Everyone knows – she's overprotective, she panics, she makes him wear shoes ...'

'But she loves him, Abbie.'

'So do you!' I'm so cross, so frustrated, I'm almost crying. 'He's your son! You can't just ... let him go!'

'I'm not. I'll be having him every other weekend, every Easter, and every other Christmas, and for two whole weeks in the summer ... Don't worry, Abbie, this is all going to be sorted out amicably. There's no question of Troy suffering.'

That's what they all say.

'No wonder he's been such a brat lately,' I say before I can help myself. 'He must have been aware something was going on.'

'Probably.' He sighs. 'Look, I'm not pretending it's an ideal situation, Abbs, but we're doing the best we can. It was always bound to happen, sooner or later.'

'What? She was always bound to go back to that bastard who dumped her?'

'No. But one or other of us was bound to fall in love with someone else. And to be honest, that actually happened a long time ago.'

'Well, good for her.'

'No. I'm not talking about Heather, Abbie.'

I'm cuddling up to him before I even realise what I'm doing. He nuzzles the top of my head and kisses me softly on the cheek. I start to sit up, quickly, guiltily, before it suddenly hits me: it's OK.

It's OK!

I'm actually allowed to feel like this!

I don't have to hide it! I can admit it!

He's free!

'You're not with Heather any more, then,' I say, shakily, as if I still can't quite believe it.

I still *can't* quite believe it.

'No. I'm telling you, Abbie, I haven't been, for six months.'

'Why haven't you told everyone? All the family! They still believe you're together.'

'I know. It probably sounds ridiculous but I suppose until Heather decided to move in with Steve, I've been hoping we could just keep things going – living in the same house, being together for Troy's sake. I was kidding myself that if nobody knew, it would mean that Troy wouldn't be affected. I wanted to tell *you*, but I just felt so bloody miserable and depressed. I felt a failure. I'd failed Heather because I didn't really love her. I'd failed Troy because he wasn't going to have a proper family. And you weren't interested in me anyway.'

'What are you *talking* about? Of course you should have told me! You *should* have had someone to talk to, if you were feeling depressed.'

'Well, I did just tell Sam.'

'Did you?' I look at him in surprise.

'Yes, six months ago when we first decided to split up. I made Sam promise to keep it to herself, though. I didn't want Troy being upset – everyone talking about it . . . making a fuss.'

I rest my head on his shoulder and we sit like this for a while, silently. My mind's all over the place, thinking about Heather, and Troy, and this unknown, unliked Steve. Thinking about how I've been pretending to myself for years, and years, and years, that David was no more than a friend and a brother to me. How long I've been in denial, punishing myself, and making myself miserable, living with a shitload of bitterness about Julia and Jamie, thinking I was doomed to be lonely and alone forever. And all the time, right here under my nose, the loveliest man in the world was sitting out his time in a loveless relationship.

'If you'd ever showed any sign of wanting me,'

he's saying now, lifting my face to his, looking solemnly into my eyes, 'if you'd had any interest in me at all, of course I'd have told you I wasn't staying with Heather. No – I'd never have got together with her in the first place! But you still seemed so hung up on Jamie.'

'I wasn't,' I whisper. 'I was just hung up on my own stupid pride.'

'And now?'

His lips are so close to mine, I can feel the heat of his breath against my mouth.

'I feel like I've been asleep half my life.'

'Sleeping Beauty,' he says with a gentle laugh. 'Shall we have a go at the approved method of waking her up?'

And without waiting for me to answer, he's kissing me, very slowly at first, but almost immediately I'm completely lost. My senses are drowning me. They say some people see stars, or rainbows, or hear beautiful violin music – me, I'm hearing bells in my head.

'Shit,' says David, staggering to his feet. 'It's the doorbell. The taxi's here.'

And it'll wake up the whole bloody family if we're not careful.

We look at each other and laugh as if we've both spoken the same thought aloud.

'Are you coming back to my place?' I ask him brazenly as we follow the taxi driver down the front path.

'Did you need to ask?' he responds softly, squeezing my hand.

I feel like I'm twenty again and about to have sex for the very first time. I can hardly sit still in the back of the taxi, I'm so conscious of David beside me. I

397

can hear him breathing. I can smell his skin. I'm shivering.

'Are you cold, Babbie?' he whispers as the taxi pulls up outside my flat.

I never thought I'd be so enchanted at being called by that silly old nickname.

'No,' I whisper back. 'I just . . . I just feel like I'm dreaming. Like I'm on drugs.'

Actually everything looks startlingly clear, as if I'm seeing it all for the first time. My bright-blue front door. The little entrance hall with its white walls and pot plants. The lounge, dark and cosy behind the closed blinds. The bedroom, neat and cool with its dressing table, its single bed and its plain white duvet.

In the bedroom doorway I turn to look up at David. There's a question in his eyes. In answer, I take him by both hands and pull him, laughing, towards the bed.

I've spent my entire life waiting for this moment, without even realising it. I can't bear to wait another minute. I'm ripping off his clothes as fast as I can move and he's in such a hurry to get me out of my special silky expensive bridesmaid's underwear, he rips the seam of the knickers and neither of us even notice till afterwards. We're going to break all records for the fastest sex from first kiss to post-coital doze. I'm almost afraid we're going to burn ourselves in the heat of it. But I don't care. I'm not stopping for anything. Not this time.

And not ever again.

A note from Sam

3 a.m. Saturday

Hi Abbie!
I must be mad – sitting up in bed in the early hours
of the morning of my wedding day writing this note to
you. I don't know when you'll find it. I'm not even
sure whether you're going to end up coming back to
the house tonight or going straight back to your own
flat, so I'm going to put it in your overnight bag and
hope for the best.
Abbie, I know all about it. You and David! To be
honest I've always suspected you had a bit of a thing
for him, but you got so bogged down with all the
misery and self-pity about bloody Jamie, you couldn't
see what was staring you in the face.
I didn't know all the stuff about my brother and
Heather until he told me, earlier this year. I was
totally shocked: gutted, to be honest. I know Troy's a
pain in the arse but that's not the point. He's my
nephew and I love him. I love David too of course,
and I've hated seeing him so upset, being torn in two,
because however civilised he's trying to be, the fact is
that his child is going to live with another man. I've

399

decided that if having kids can cause this sort of hurt, I don't want any. Well, you've been asking me why: now you know. It's all David's fault!

Don't get me wrong: he's been lovely to Heather – he is a lovely guy, even if he is my own brother – but now I know why he never loved her properly.

I've got to tell you this now, Abbie, 'cos I might not get another chance until I get back from the honeymoon – you know how it'll be tomorrow: everyone will be interrupting us, wanting to talk to me and dance with me and take my photo and everything because ... I'll be the bride!!! At last! Can you believe it? Anyway, after you read this you might never want to talk to me again ... but I hope not. I hope you'll be grateful to me: you bloody well ought to be!

Last night, after we got back from the restaurant, David and I were chatting while you were in the kitchen with Mum. I was saying that I thought he'd coped really well with the situation of Heather and Steve ... most people would have flipped if their girlfriend decided to bugger off with the kid.

'She might be my girlfriend,' he said, 'but it was never like that. It's only Troy I'm going to miss.'

I said surely he must have felt something for her, and he came out with all this stuff about respecting her, liking her as a person, her being Troy's mother and all ... it sounded quite cold.

'I can't help it!' he said. 'I can't feel anything for anybody else, Sam, when I'm being eaten alive by what I feel for *her!*'

Well, I must be so dense ... I must have been such a blind, stupid, friend, and such a blind, idiot of a sister ... that I actually asked him: 'Her? Who?'

He just nodded in your direction – the direction of the kitchen, and gave me this look ... I couldn't believe it!

'How long has this been going on?' I asked him.

'I don't know. Forever.'

'Haven't you ever told her?'

'No, of course not. She's not interested. And anyway, she's never got over Jamie – she doesn't want anyone else – you know that.'

I'm sorry to say that at this point, I called him a stupid fucking idiot. I also told him – and this is where you might decide never to speak to me again – that I thought you really, really liked him and that it was about time you stopped moping about Jamie anyway, and that he (David) was the right person for you if only you could be made to see it, but that nothing was ever going to happen unless he talked to you about it.

'Talk to her tomorrow!' I told him. 'It's the perfect opportunity. I'm sure she likes you, David ... but until you tell her you're not with Heather any more, she's not even going to think about it.'

Now I'm worried. I'm lying awake, thinking I shouldn't have said anything, I should have minded my own business, I shouldn't have told him you liked him when I haven't even asked you. Do you? I think you do. I hope you do, Abbie ...

I'm going to finish now, but I don't know whether I'll be able to go back to sleep – I'm too excited. By the time you read this I suppose it'll all be over ... I'll be old, married Mrs Reynolds and maybe I'll be wearing an apron and stirring stews on the hob with a wooden spoon and cleaning cobwebs with a feather duster! Eeeeek!

And now I'm just going to give Phil a ring – see if he's lying awake too! – and tell him about David, and what I've done – what I've said. I want him to reassure me that you won't be angry with me!

Bye Abbie. See you when I get back from Portugal. I hope you'll have some news for me ... I hope you're going to be happy.

Lots of love

Sam xxxx

One Year Later

Four o'clock already?

I think I've been awake all night. It's starting to get light now, and already there are some sweet little birds awake at this beautiful hour, practising their trills and arpeggios ready for the full-blown chorus. I was too excited to sleep, but I'm much too excited to feel tired. I can't believe it – the most important, wonderful day of my life is looming ahead of me. How amazing is this!

I turn over to try and get back to sleep, but suddenly the bedroom door creaks open a crack and a whisper floats across the room to me: 'Abbie? Are you awake?'

I sit up and put on the bedside lamp. 'Yes. Can't you sleep either?'

'No – too excited.'

Sam creeps across the room in her bare feet and jumps onto my bed, then snuggles down with half of my duvet. We're in my old bedroom at my parents' house. We've both stayed here overnight – Sam was sleeping downstairs on the sofa.

'We haven't done this for ages!' she says. 'It reminds me of all those times at my house, Abbs, when we were teenagers . . .'

'Lying awake all night giggling about what boys we fancied . . .'

'Who we'd kissed, and who we'd like to . . .'

'Ssh!' We're both giggling now as if we were still those fourteen-year-old schoolgirls. 'I don't want to wake Mum and Dad up.'

'No.' She lies quietly for a minute, studying the ceiling. 'It's going to be a big day for them, isn't it? Their only child. Do you think your mum will be OK?'

'Yes,' I say, nodding happily. 'She's been so determined to make it today – all the practice outings she's had with Dad over the last couple of months have given her a lot of confidence. And she's got this lovely gang of ladies from the church who are going to sit with her, hold her hand, talk to her, keep her calm.'

'Blimey. If I'd known the church provided gangs of ladies for keeping calm, I'd have booked a few for myself!'

'You don't need it! You're fantastic. You've got everything under control.' I grab her hand and hold it tight. 'You're the best bridesmaid anyone could wish for, Sammy.'

'And you're the best *bride*,' she says, swallowing hard, 'that I could ever have wanted for my brother.'

The other bridesmaid arrives soon after we've finished breakfast.

'This brings back memories,' she says, kissing me and her sister and throwing her leather jacket on a chair. 'Happy Wedding Day, Abbie. You look radiant.'

'I'm still in my 'jamas!'

'You still look bloody radiant. Be told!'

Chloe looks pretty radiant herself. Against all the odds, she's still seeing Eva. They've had their ups and downs, but I think Chloe's grown up a lot over the last year and Eva's managed to smooth off some of the rough edges so that we can see the real Chloe underneath – clever and funny and passionately loyal.

'Come on, now, girls, time's getting on!' says Mum, who's flushed with excitement.

I squeeze her hand and hope desperately that it's excitement and not nerves.

'It's OK, Mum. I'll run and put some clothes on now, and we're still in plenty of time for the hair-dresser.'

It's a bit different from Sam's wedding day. We've got no Heather turning up with her scissors and bag of tricks to do scary blue stripes in *my* mum's hair. Mum wouldn't want them, anyway. She's not an extrovert like Christine. She's booked us all into the salon just down the road. We had a trial run there a couple of weeks ago and it went really well; we arranged a quiet time when the place wasn't too busy, and now Mum's been there once she's not frightened of going back today.

'Come on, slowcoach,' says Sam, banging on the bathroom door for me ten minutes later. 'You ready?'

I jump. Where was I? Leaning on the sink, gazing at myself in the mirror and wondering who was this person looking back at me. Could it really be Abbie, little mousy lonely Abbie, who's going to be the bride today – the centre of attention, the queen for the day? Marrying her Prince Charming who's been waiting there in the wings all along? How did this happen? Can it be true?

'Yep! Coming now, Sam! Don't go without me!'

I tug on my jeans and T-shirt and give myself one last smile in the mirror. The next clothes I put on will be my wedding finery. It *is* true. And I'm going to enjoy every minute of it.

'Hello, everyone, and welcome to All Saints, on this beautiful summer afternoon – this very *special* afternoon for Abigail and David. This *very* special afternoon for Susan and myself, of course, as well as for David's family.'

Dad beams around at the congregation. There's nobody here in the church who doesn't know that it's the bride's father performing the ceremony. I don't feel nervous at all. I smile back at Dad and, for a split second, it's just me and him, caught in this moment of time in this, the most special place in his world. His own daughter, his own church. I feel a wave of love and respect for him; for the values he's gently instilled in me, for the quiet, dignified way he brought me up, without ever forcing his views on me or on anyone else. I feel a lump come to my throat, and then as Dad announces the first hymn I turn to take another sneaky look at my bridegroom. He's already looking at me.

David.

What can I say?

He moved in with me almost immediately after Sam and Phil's wedding and we began to plan our own straight away. Why wait? We'd known each other almost our whole lives – what more was there to find out?

I hate it when people talk about finding their soul-mate – it sounds so yucky. How do they know there isn't another soulmate round the next corner of their lives? How do they know they're still going to be soul mates this time next year, never mind in twenty or thirty years' time? But I'll just say this: David and I are as happy, right now, as I can ever imagine anyone, anywhere, ever being. And that's more than enough for us.

We're going to have babies, too – we've already decided: at least two, maybe more. I don't want a sad and lonely only child. I want a big happy house full of noise and laughter. Like his parents' house only maybe not quite as weird. We already have Troy, of course: he stays with us on alternate weekends, and we had him with us at the Pattersons' for Christmas, which was fantastic fun. He's growing into a sweet little boy; now things have settled down a bit and he's got used to the arrangements, he seems to have adapted really well. He told me very seriously the other week that it's really quite normal – all his friends at school have at *least* two different daddies and different homes to go to. Apparently Heather is pregnant again now and Troy's been telling us that he hopes it's a girl because he can boss her around and beat her at all the games. I've told David he needs to work on the kid's under-standing of gender differentiation.

Sam and Phil, on the other hand, seem to be more sure than ever about not having children. I found it hard to get my head round this for a while, but one day when I was talking to Christine about it – think-ing she'd be upset about the lack of grandchildren from that source – she put me quite firmly in my place.

'At the end of the day, Abbie, there are enough people having children and deciding afterwards that they don't want them. Poor little sods. It's much more sensible to decide that from the start, isn't it? It's only nature, you know: not everyone is cut out to be a parent.'

She's right, of course, and to be honest I can see why staying child-free suits Sam and Phil's relationship. They're still having such fun together – going for days out at the seaside like two excited teenagers, scuttling off on trips to Paris or New York at a moment's notice without a care in the world . . . They make me smile, but that's not for me and David. We're going to start the new generation of Pattersons, God help us!

I should be singing. The hymn's already started. We've chosen "Amazing Grace".

I once was lost, but now am found;
Was blind, but now I see.

I couldn't have put it better myself.

When it's time to hand my bouquet to Sam, she smiles at me and mouths silently: *Go for it!* – making me want to giggle. My bouquet is entirely of white and yellow roses – my favourite flower – and no cat has been allowed anywhere near it, trust me, and my two lovely bridesmaids are wearing pale-yellow satin, which sets off their golden colouring and auburn hair better than you would believe. Of course, Sam would have looked beautiful in anything, but she'd have a hard job to outshine her twin brother today. In his wedding suit and gold-coloured waistcoat, David

408

looks more gorgeous than ever.

Sam and Chloe go to sit down in the front row, where by now Christine is probably already starting to cry. I hope she doesn't set *my* mum off ... and then I catch myself thinking: Oh, well – I suppose it's only nature! I almost burst out laughing – just as Dad's asking the congregation about any just impediments – at the thought that I'm already turning into my mother-in-law.

We're going to Morocco for our honeymoon. We wanted to try somewhere completely different. We've already had one holiday this year: back at the beginning of April, we went to Italy for a week with Sam and Phil. We stayed at Lake Garda but we did a day trip to Venice. I wasn't sure if Sam or Phil would be up for it, but they said they wanted to 'lay the ghost' – and create some new, happy memories of the place. It was a lovely, romantic time and I have to say, we didn't talk about Julia once. We do see her fairly regularly now – Sam and I go down to Bournemouth for weekends, just as we promised, and take little Daisy out for walks in her pram. Things are OK between us, and she seems very happy with Mike and the baby. But it's hard to turn the clock back *all* the way. She came for the hen weekend, and she's here, today, of course, and I'm glad about that. Mum did ask me if I wanted her to be a bridesmaid but I couldn't go quite that far.

It's time for Dad to ask me and David the thousand-dollar question and, yes, sure enough, I can hear Christine sniffling softly behind us. Why was I so embarrassed by her crying at Sam's wedding? Now, I find it quite endearing. Bless her – a daughter last year, her son this year. I wonder if Brian's organised another surprise holiday for her? Now that Frank's settled down in the nursing home, there's nothing to stop them.

Will you, David, take Abigail to be your wife? Will you live together in marriage; will you love her, comfort her, honour her and support her during good times and bad, and will you remain faithful to her as long as you both shall live?

There's a split second of silence. I can hear my own heart beating. I never actually thought that I, Abbie Vincent, would be standing here, in church, in front of the congregation, anxiously waiting for someone to say ...

I will.

I turn and smile at him. Yes. And I will too.